MW01167053

THE IRON PHOENIX

BY

STEVEN TAYLOR

Omega Press
El Paso, Texas

Live Free or Die!

Steve Taylor

To Gene

Jeff Falls

ARMADILLO

2/16/06

Iron Phoenix

All rights Reserved © 2005 Steven Taylor

No part of this books may be reproduced or transmitted in any form or by any means, graphic, electronic, or mechanical, including photocopying, recording, taping, or by any information storage retrieval system, without the written permission of the publisher.

OMEGA PRESS
An imprint of Omega Communications

For Information Address:

Omega Press
5823 N. Mesa, #823
El Paso, Texas 79912
Or
http://www.kenhudnall.com

FIRST EDITION

Printed in the United States of America

4\Iron Phoenix

Acknowledgements

The author would like to thank Ron Suciu, Instructor of History at El Paso Community College, for his assistance with parts of the manuscript. I would also like to thank my publisher, Ken Hudnall, for all of his help. Thanks also go to the very lovely Janelle Ayala for lending her beauty to the cover, as well as to the not so lovely Ralph Sellers for doing the same. I don't owe anyone else a damned thing.

Steven Taylor
El Paso, Texas
May, 2005

CHAPTER ONE

The pale morning light filtered through the rich green of the sea and disappeared into the depths below. The frigid wind came out of the north, directly from the pole, whipping the ocean into short, choppy waves topped with spume. Pieter leaned back for the millionth time and hauled mightily at the dripping net. His gnarled hands had long ago become inured to the Arctic chill of these Bering Sea waters, and he paid no attention as his fingers stiffened against the cold.

Ah, he thought. This work! For fifty years I have pit my wits against these fish. What will become of me when this old back will no longer bend, when these old arms will no longer pull? How will I support the Old Woman? Will we go from door to door begging for scraps, like Dimitri?

His friend, Dimitri, had for years moored his boat next to Pieter's, had fished these same waters, suffered these same agonies. They had gone hungry together when the fish were not there, and drunk vodka together when they were. But now Dimitri was too old; his back was bent, and he walked with the slow, shuffling steps of the near-dead. He spent his days hobbling from shack to shack in their Kamchatka town of Uka. He never asked for food; his pride wouldn't let him. He always pretended that he had just dropped by to pay a visit. Doffing his hat, he would say, "How are you doing, Olga? Oh, a piece of fish and a bit of bread! Why, thank you Olga! How kind of you!"

This is what we get for a lifetime of labor! Pieter thought, forcing his rage back down into his gut like bile. We spend our best years working for the state, taking orders, sacrificing for the good of the Rodina. Then, in our old age, it casts us adrift to fend for ourselves! Those bastards in Moscow should roast in Hell! Finally, he came to the end of the net. He lifted the small bulge over the gunwale and let it drop to the weather beaten deck. He stood looking down at the pitifully small cluster of fish, legs spread against the roll of the sea, numbed arms hanging limp at his side. This won't even buy coal for the stove, he thought. Slowly his eyes lifted, and he fixed his gaze on the horizon. A glimmer of hope entered his mind as he remembered what he had been told about the new leader in the Capitol.

He whispered, "Perhaps all is not lost. Perhaps this Drugonov will make things better. God knows. They could not get any worse."

Two times zones to the west, the sun had yet to rise over the Siberian village of Zhatay, outside the city of Yakutsk on the Lena River. Yelena shifted her weight rapidly back and forth with all the agility of her twenty-two years as she cornered the loudly-protesting chicken against the fence behind her house. She leaped forward, captured it, and tucked the fowl under her arm. She spoke to the bird as she carried it toward the section of tree-trunk that served as a chopping-block.

"You don't know how lucky you are, chicken. In a moment your troubles will be over; you will leave this miserable place, this miserable life. But I will remain here. I will remain here until I am old and shriveled, like all the other women of this village. I will never really live, but not quite die. I will wash and clean and cook until my last breath leaves me, and I collapse onto the floor like a heap of rags. If only someone would do me this favor."

She took the chicken's head in her right hand and spun the bird violently in circles, wringing its neck. She felt a strange sense of satisfaction, of benediction, as she studied the lifeless bird.

"You see?" she asked. "There is no more pain, no more frustration. Just peace."

After she had plucked and cleaned the bird, she carried it into the corner of her tiny dwelling that served as a kitchen. She put it into the chipped, porcelain-covered iron basin and washed it with a dipper of water from the bucket. The basin had once been decorated with flowers, but they had faded long ago. The dim yellow of the kerosene lamp cast flickering shadows across the room. Yelena looked around her, at the rough-hewn wooden walls chinked with moss, the few sticks of furniture that her father had made and at the pallet in the opposite corner where she slept; once again the depression, numbing, paralytic, relentless, bore down on her.

Then her eyes came to rest on the one decoration in the room: a watercolor of children playing on a riverbank. Yelena smiled. There was a ball perpetually poised in midair, bright red against the cobalt blue of a spring sky. The children, dressed in vivid, gay colors stretched upward as children will do, a forest of arms straining to catch the orb. It was a moment of joy frozen in time, and Yelena loved it. She had painted it during her last year of school, and it showed such talent that she had been awarded a scholarship to study art in St. Petersburg. It had been her life's dream.

She would never forget the day when she had opened the letter from the Academy, held it with trembling fingers, and read the words that told her that everything she had wanted in life was to be hers. The dull, grey town in which she had been raised receded into the back of her mind, as she saw stretching before her a happy, fulfilling life. She dismissed the early years of drudgery and boredom as a trifling prelude to the life she was destined to have: a life in which she did work that mattered, important work, work that would make her a complete person.

Yelena stood looking at her painting with reverence, almost with awe, as others would look at an ancient and holy icon. Her hand reached up but she dared not touch it. It was too precious. It was her life, reduced to a bit of pigment on a sheet of paper. At least it could have been her life, if the politicians in Moscow had not stolen it from her.

Yes, she thought, as her outstretched hand balled into a fist, they stole my life from me. Her anger grew as she remembered the second letter. This one had informed her that her scholarship had been canceled due to unforeseen fiscal shortages in the national treasury. Oh so polite, oh so formal, those few words had destroyed her as surely as if they had been bullets through her heart. No, worse than that: they had not been so merciful. They had instead doomed her to a long, torturous, frustrating hell on earth.

Yelena sat in the crude chair, put her elbows on the small, rickety table, and lowered her face into her hands. She expected herself to begin crying, as she always did on such occasions. But, to her surprise, she instead felt a spark of optimism. This new leader, the one everyone was talking about, this Drugonov perhaps he would be her salvation. It was not too late. She was still young. If he could do what he was promising to do, there may yet be hope.

Sixteen hundred miles to the west, in Novosibirsk, Marko was still in his office. It was two o'clock in the morning. He sat behind his desk, poured the dregs of vodka into his glass and hurled the empty bottle across the room, where it smashed against a calendar advertising the Gorkiy Tractor Factory. He had not been able to go home that night, had not been able to face Svetlana and the children. How could he? How could he tell them that he had failed? How could he tell them that their lives of privilege, which they had come to take for granted as the family of an industrialist, were about to end?

Svetlana would have to give up the chic Western products that she loved so well. The boys would have to leave the elite private school of which they were so proud. No more trips to London, no more Black Sea vacations. Their lives would spin downward into mediocrity. He would have to go back to work as a machinist, if he were lucky enough to find even that.

He swiveled his chair to the right, and looked through the large window down onto the factory floor. His machines, his wonderful machines, stood mute and motionless. The whirring, stamping, clanging that meant life, their lives and his, had ended for the last time. It struck him that they were no longer even his. He had mortgaged them weeks ago in a last, desperate effort to keep his business going. But it had only prolonged the agony. The Novosibirsk Ball Bearing Factory could be added to the long and growing list of failed concerns in this new, free Russia.

Marko thought back to the beginning; not so long ago, when he had managed to borrow the capital to purchase the formerly state-owned property. There had been optimism in the air then. All things had seemed possible. For a man who knew his business, and was willing to work hard, the sky had been the limit. Those had been the halcyon years. Then things began to go wrong, just a few at first, mere annoyances: slow deliveries of parts and materials, delayed payments for finished products, erratic supplies of electricity and fuel. Always there were excuses, oh yes, very good excuses. But excuses don't make ball bearings. One by one his customers stopped placing orders. His suppliers went bankrupt. The money lost its value. He was reduced to doing business on the barter system; trading his product for whatever he could get that would help him continue his operation.

Many times he had had to pay his workers in commodities: light bulbs, canned hams, nylon stockings, whatever he could lay his hands on. The best of them had drifted away, to look for work elsewhere. Then, two weeks ago, the final blow was struck: his best customer, the Saratov Heavy Equipment Works, ceased operations. He had looked frantically for other outlets for his product, anyone at all who might need what he made. But he could find no one.

He kept his workers on, hoping against hope, as his meager capital dwindled to nothing. But yesterday had been the end. When the shift finished, he had called his employees together and announced to them that the plant was closing, effective immediately. It was the most difficult thing he had ever done. Some of the women cried, but the men simply looked at him, stony-faced. What would they do, he thought? Where would they go? The whole country was on its knees. Would they all simply starve to death, and that would be the end of Russia?

Perhaps not, he thought. The new Prime Minister, this Drugonov, perhaps he knew of a way to resurrect them all. Marko had been watching him carefully on television, and paying close attention to his speeches in the newspapers. At first Marko had thought him extreme, regressive and dangerous. But now he was not so sure. Maybe he was just the kind of strong leader that Russia needed at this moment in her history. Perhaps he was the answer.

CHAPTER TWO

Prime Minister Sergei Alexandrovich Drugonov gazed from his Kremlin window at the halos of polluted air surrounding the street lights on Red Square. A slight smile crossed his wide, peasant face as he leaned against the polished oak window frame. The flickering light from his office fireplace reflected from the glass and into his piercing blue eyes.

He was tall for his race, and his frame was heavily muscled--qualities that he had found useful many times in his life. For Sergei Drugonov was a man of force: blatant, undiluted force. He would have been at home riding the steppe with the Mongol hordes: raping, looting, burning. He would have been comfortable as one of the Ivans, an absolute autocrat, dealing out death with the twitch of a finger. But he was more than this. He was both shrewd and smart--a rare and potentially lethal combination. His years in the Communist party apparatus had turned him into a political street-fighter: he could smell a trap, distinguish friend from enemy at a glance, sense deception with a catlike canniness. This shrewdness was complemented by a first-class intellect: he could integrate his percepts into increasingly complex concepts until he had grasped the Big Picture that so often eluded less talented men. He could envision the world in its totality, sense the ebb and flow of the tides of history.

This confluence of talents was indeed rare; it occurred in its most perfect form perhaps once every several centuries, perhaps less often than that. Alexander had had it, as had Caesar. So had Genghis Khan and Napoleon, and perhaps Hitler. But even among such men Drugonov stood out; all but a few would have hesitated to murder people in their millions, to liquidate entire populations, to cleanse continents. But to him, such acts were merely part of his personal dialectic, the means by which he might realize his own full potential.

None of his contemporaries appreciated the historical uniqueness of this man. His enemies saw him as a perverted aberration, or as just another egotistical blowhard to be ignored. His supporters admired his strength, but knew nothing of his ruthlessness. Only with the passage of generations would mankind truly come to appreciate the monster that was Sergei Drugonov.

He was enjoying the calm--the calm before the storm. He thought, I have worked long and hard for this. I have survived many battles, climbed over a mountain of corpses for this office, these privileges, my many small luxuries. But before this night is through, I will have won the greatest battle of my life. Russia will be mine. And then I will begin the ultimate conquest.

He closed his eyes and allowed a feeling of accomplishment to wash over him. He thought of all that he had overcome in his life: of the impoverished village where he had spent his childhood; of the brutish, drunken father who had beaten him; of the children who had made fun of him because of the way his family lived; of the first man he had murdered for insulting him; of the aggressive way he had entered and ascended the local, and then the regional party apparatus: threatening, and sometimes liquidating, those who got in his way; of his long, lonely climb to the top, friendless, invoking terror among his colleagues, and even among his superiors; of the women he had known, loved, and tossed aside.

Looking back on it, he realized that the secret of his success was there for anyone to see; it was really ridiculously simple: seek power, seek control over other people's lives, and be willing to do anything, quite literally anything, to achieve it. The fools of the world concerned themselves with the lives of fellow fools; they allowed themselves to be impeded, thwarted, frustrated, because they could not bring themselves to take the next logical step; their cowardly fear of snuffing out another life doomed them to mediocrity. If only they knew how easy it is, how fragile those lives are: mere wisps of things. They are so easily removed from one's path that they soon become less than inconsequential, a triviality, like flicking a fly from one's sleeve.

And now, he thought, I will reap the rewards. The people of Russian are calling to me. They are like frightened children looking for guidance. I will be their salvation. He chuckled quietly as he thought, I am the resurrection and the life.

Drugonov pivoted on his heel and strode across the room to his desk. He picked up the phone and punched in a number known only to him. After two rings a voice answered quietly, "Yes."

"Is everything going as planned?" Drugonov asked.

"Yes," the voice said. "Our friends left twenty minutes ago."

The smile returned to Drugonov's face as he replaced the receiver. He walked slowly to the fireplace and stopped, staring down into the glowing embers. Soon now, he thought. Very soon.

The Dacha of Victor Zalygin, President of the Russian Republic, 55 kilometers east of Moscow.

The thin, young guard clutched his AK-74 automatic rifle as he peered out into the endless forest. The almost claustrophobic blackness of it made him uncomfortable, although he had lived near such woods all of his nineteen years. He took solace in the knowledge that other guards were on duty at twenty-meter intervals around the circumference of the dacha. To his right a shaft of light from the living room window poured across the small lawn, illuminated the first echelon of trees, and was swallowed by the darkness beyond. He could hear men's voices coming from the dacha: angry, anxious voices.

"Well? You are my advisors! Advise me! How do you suggest we deal with this madman Drugonov?" President Zalygin shouted, pacing quickly back and forth across the living   room floor.

"Calm yourself, Victor. You will have an embolism. Here, have some vodka," said Uri Bogoslovka, Minister of State Security, as he refilled his own glass.

Zalygin watched as Bogoslovka's ham-like hand closed around the bottle of Stolichnaya. Even from halfway across the room, Zalygin could see the evidence of Bogoslovka's violent life: his right hand had been broken so many times that his knuckles were no longer visible. Bogoslovka filled a second glass and, grasping it between his sausage-like fingers, offered it to Zalygin.

"Not for me, Uri," Zalygin said. "I must keep my wits about me. The next week could be the most important in Russian history. If I don't win this election, and Drugonov's faction takes power, it will be a return to the days of Stalin. He is our worst nightmare, a charismatic unreconstructed tyrant."

"Don't forget that he is also a megalomaniac, Victor," said Anatoly Tret'iakov, Minister of Defense.

"Even Stalin didn't seriously consider conquering the world. He was satisfied with Russia alone. If we can believe Drugonov's speeches, he would never be content until a new Russian imperial flag flew over every continent."

"Anatoly, how much support is there in the military for Drugonov's policies?" Zalygin asked.

"Much more than any of us would like," Tret'iakov answered.

His lean, muscular body draped itself comfortably across the Scandinavian-style chair. Zalygin had always admired this one. A hero of the Afghan war, immensely popular with the troops, he was known as the "Soldier's Field Marshall." He was everything Zalygin was not.

Where Zalygin was thoughtful and bookish, Tret'iakov was a man of action. Where Zalygin had built his career on persuasion and compromise, Tret'iakov had built his on the use of force. Zalygin was a philosopher, Tret'iakov a warrior. If occurred to Zalygin that they complemented each other well.

Tret'iakov continued, "Our military hasn't been paid in four months. My junior officers are living in dilapidated housing, under the most primitive conditions. Drugonov offers them all the spoils and glories of war. He fills their ears with promises of wealth and rapid promotion if only they will follow him. And I am afraid that he has been very persuasive. I am sorry to say that I cannot guarantee their loyalty."

"My position is tenuous too, Victor," injected Bogoslovka. "I am unsure of the loyalty of my own subordinates. Drugonov has seduced them as well with his tales of a new Russian empire."

"This is impossible!" cried Constantin Antonov-Ovseenko, Foreign Minister, in his precise, classic Russian. He had never been seen in public without a jacket and tie, and tonight was no exception.

President Zalygin eyed his foreign minister warily. Though the man was brilliant at foreign policy, he was a pompous prima donna. At times, Zalygin grew weary of his constant demands for preferential treatment. The president wondered how much tonight's impeccably-tailored suit had cost. Plenty, he concluded.

"How can anyone take this man seriously? He would destroy everything that we have accomplished!" Antonov-Ovseenko continued, waving his arms with sufficient vigor so as to spill Bordeaux on the gleaming parquet floor. No vodka for Constantin Antonov-Ovseenko.

"Every day we establish new ties with the West. We have an excellent line of credit with the IMF, and negotiations on entering the World Trade Organization are progressing well. We may even be successful in dismantling NATO. Drugonov would throw all of this away! It is unthinkable!"

"Unfortunately, it is not at all unthinkable, my friend," interjected Tret'iakov. "You must remember that in Drugonov, we are not dealing with a modern, civilized man. We are dealing with a brute, a troglodyte, an empire-builder. I have met several of his kind in my life. They understand only force, and they care nothing for diplomacy. Drugonov is not interested in establishing ties with the West. Only after he has consolidated his domestic political position will he look outward, and then only for conquest."

Zalygin stood quietly with his hands at his sides in the center of the room, a pensive look on his face. "It seems impossible that such a man can exist at this point in history. Has the world not experienced sufficient horrors in the last few generations?"

Tret'iakov smiled at his president. "Victor, you are too good a man for this business. You cannot conceive of someone like Drugonov, a man who embodies evil in its purest form. You see the world through a benevolent lens; you are a man of good will. When you see another person, you think to yourself, 'How can I work with him?' When Drugonov sees another person, he thinks to himself, 'How can I kill him?'"

"But why, Anatoly?" Zalygin implored. "What force produces a monster like that? What motivates him?"

Tret'iakov stared off into space, slowly swirling the vodka in his glass.

"That is not a thing for sane men to contemplate, Victor."

Uri Bogoslovka was leaning forward, elbows on knees.

"What motivates him?" he repeated. "I think it is evil for the sake of evil, destruction for the sake of destruction, death for the sake of death."

Zalygin looked over at Foreign Minister Antonov-Ovseenko.

"Constantine, Drugonov has made it clear that he intends to engage in a policy of aggression if he has the opportunity. How is the rest of the world reacting?"

"They are not taking him seriously, Victor," Antonov-Ovseenko said. "They seem to think that he is some sort of bizarre cartoon character, too strange to be real. The Europeans have their heads in the sand, pretending that he doesn't exist. The Japanese are hedging their bets, sending out feelers to both us and Drugonov's people, apparently hoping to trade their way out of any difficulty. But it is the Americans whose response is the most difficult to understand; the more bellicose and threatening Drugonov becomes, the more anxious the Americans seem to be to placate him. In his recent speeches and press releases, President Benedict seems almost apologetic that the United States might be an obstacle in Drugonov's path toward global conquest. It is really quite unbelievable."

Bogoslovka interjected, "Drugonov constantly says that the West has lost its will to resist, that it has lost its moral compass. Perhaps he is right. The United States reacted well to the destruction of the World Trade Center: forcefully, decisively. But that was a different time, a different president. Where Drugonov is concerned, here and now, they seem weak and submissive."

"But this makes no sense!" Zalygin exclaimed. "The West, the United States, has won the great ideological battle. Individual liberty, political and economic, has triumphed! The collapse of the Soviet Union ended any doubt on that score. It is totalitarianism that has been swept into the dustbin of history. Don't they realize that? Aren't they willing to defend their own victory?"

"Perhaps not, Victor," Tret'iakov said. "At least their leadership doesn't seem to be willing. And remember, a fish rots from the head down. I pity the poor lost fools if Drugonov is successful. Nothing in their experience can prepare them for what will come."

There was a silence in the room as everyone reflected on Tret'iakov's statement. From the corner, someone cleared his throat. It was Arkady Liubchenko, Minister of Finance.

"I have never been what anyone would call a violent man," he said, rising and stepping into the center of the room. He held his glass of Georgian wine with both hands at waist level. Everyone in the room noticed that they were shaking slightly.

Antonov-Ovseenko turned slightly and stepped back a pace, as if to give Liubchenko the floor. Actually, his purpose was to give himself a better view of this strange sight that was Arkady Liubchenko. Tall and painfully thin, Liubchenko's long, bony fingers wrapped themselves around the glass of wine like spiders enveloping their prey. His large, owl-like eyes peered at the other men through thick, steel-rimmed glasses.

President Zalygin noticed Antonov-Ovseenko looking with apparent disdain at Liubchenko's ill-fitting, rumpled slacks and tweed jacket. He knew from past snide comments that his foreign minister found the man uncouth. But he also knew that, in spite of his contempt for the finance minister's lack of refinement, Antonov Ovseenko respected Liubchenko's genius. He had established himself as Russia's premier free-market economist, Russia's version of Ludwig von Mises. Head of the Department of Economics at Moscow University, Liubchenko's writings had been embraced with almost religious zeal by free-market advocates throughout Russia and the former Eastern bloc.

Liubchenko continued, "But someone must do something about Drugonov. Uri, can't you have him assassinated?"

Bogoslovka exploded with laughter, spilling part of his drink onto his lap. It seemed that he found the incongruity of such a question coming from such a man to be hilariously funny. But the substance of the question was not funny at all. He had considered it.

"Believe me, Arkady, I would like to do exactly that," Bogoslovka answered, wiping tears from his eyes. "But with Drugonov's fanatical following, an assassination would lead to civil war."

"But he simply cannot be permitted to influence the course of this country's development," Liubchenko exclaimed. "He wants to return to state ownership with wage and price controls. We have spent years dismantling that decrepit failure of a system. He wants to return to an insular, autarkic Russia just as the doors of the world are opening to us. I realize that the people are not happy; conditions are not good now. But they must realize that we have seventy-five years of Communist inefficiency to wring out of our economic system. That is not accomplished overnight. They must give us more time!"

President Zalygin walked toward Liubchenko and put his hand on the academician's shoulder. He could feel Liubchenko trembling.

"The Russian people have no understanding of the free market," Zalygin said gently. "They have never experienced it; it frightens them. Drugonov offers them the comfort of a system they have known. Besides, we may after all have the time that you speak of, Arkady. I think I have a good chance of winning this election. Many people are apprehensive of Drugonov's fanaticism. I have heard that Drugonov himself believes that he may lose."

Liubchenko's eyes left Zalygin's. He looked at the wall with a vacuous stare. "I hope so, Victor. I hope so. We must make the people see ....We must make them see ...." His voice trailed off as he stepped away from Zalygin, whose arm fell to his side.

Poor Arkady, he thought. He is not strong enough for this battle.

The men looked at Liubchenko with somber eyes as he walked away, seemingly hypnotized. President Zalygin looked around the room, from face to face, and it appeared to him that all the men present shared a common thought: Liubchenko is ready for a breakdown.

Foreign Minister Antonov-Ovseenko broke the pensive silence. "It now seems to have been such a mistake for you to have appointed Drugonov as Prime Minister, Victor. He has used that position for his own aggrandizement as Machiavelli himself would have."

"What choice did I have, Constantine?" Zalygin answered. "His New Rodina party had coopted two-thirds of the Duma, including the old-line Communists. They would have rejected any other nomination I could have made. And then we would have had a constitutional crisis."

"The Constitution! Bah!" barked Bogoslovka. "Drugonov uses the Constitution against us like a club. We are restrained by it while he accumulates power by subverting it. The only Constitution he understands is a bullet in the neck!"

"That may be, Uri," Zalygin said. "But we must respect the rule of law. Without it we have nothing."

At that moment, outside the rear of the dacha, Major Vasily Iudin, the officer in charge of security for the evening, looked at his watch. Ten-thirty, he thought. It is time. He reached into his pocket and withdrew a pair of side-cutting pliers. He opened the door of the metal box mounted to the wall of the building and, using a small flashlight, looked with expert eyes at the complicated wiring within. He knew exactly which ones to cut in order to disable the electronic perimeter motion detector that formed the principal line of defense against intruders. Earlier, he had seen to it that the guard detachment at the gate, half a kilometer away, had been relieved of duty. This is not treason, he assured himself for the hundredth time. I am doing this for the good of the Rodina, for the Motherland.

One hundred meters to the south, another man looked at his watch. He noted the time at ten-thirty-one, and then closed the instrument's metal cover so that the large, radium numerals could not reveal his position. I will give him four more minutes to disengage the system, he thought. At precisely ten-thirty-five he whispered softly into the tiny microphone next to his lips: "Go, go, go."

The members of the twelve-man commando team, dispersed uniformly around the dacha, silently raised themselves from the prone position into a crouch. Dressed in black from head to toe, with all potentially-reflective surfaces carefully removed or painted black, they were absolutely invisible in the dark forest.

They crept forward, rifles in hand, thankful that the previous day's rain had moistened the leaves and twigs beneath their feet. They moved in total silence. At eighty meters, they could make out the dim glow of the dacha's lights. Passing the motion-detectors at sixty meters, they were relieved by the absence of an alarm. At thirty meters, they re-assumed the prone position. Each man made sure that he had a clear line of fire at at least one of the guards. Every one of the commandos was an expert marksman, and had been thoroughly trained in the use of this particular weapon system. Their light-amplifying, starlight scopes had been carefully mated to their bull-barreled sniper rifles. Each member of the team had lovingly range-tested his rifle-scope combination and had made the necessary adjustments to insure a zero of one-hundred meters. At thirty meters, their rounds would impact less than a centimeter high, an inconsequential error.

The commandos lay in the dark stillness, waiting for the order to fire to come through the miniature earpieces they all wore. Their index fingers rested lightly on their rifles' triggers, which had been adjusted to break at three hundred grams pressure. Each man concentrated on controlling his breathing as he looked at the glowing, almost surreal image of his target through the scope.

When he was sure that his men were in position, and that everything about the dacha was as he had been told to expect, the commando leader calmly gave the signal:

"Fire."

Twelve rifles cracked as one. Every member of the president's bodyguard was blown off his feet, most of them dead before they hit the ground. The three who survived the initial volley, though mortally wounded, made a valiant attempt to recover their weapons and assume a defensive position. But they could not see their assailants, only the black forest in front of them. They began firing wildly into the darkness, emptying their magazines at nothing. It was a simple matter for the commando-snipers to pick them off with precise head shots.

A split-second after the firing began, and before anyone else in the room knew what was happening, Marshall Tret'iakov dove for the floor and yelled, "Down!"

Antonov-Ovseenko dropped where he was standing. Uri Bogoslovka launched himself out of his chair, drawing a Makarov pistol from an inside-the-waistband holster at the small of his back. President Zalygin stood stock still, looking toward the window, an expression of disbelief on his face. Arkady Liubchenko sat on a stool in the corner giggling softly.

Marshall Tret'iakov quickly crawled across the floor to the guest bedroom, appearing a few seconds later with a Kalashnikov rifle in his hands loaded with a thirty-round magazine, a second magazine taped upside-down to the first. He glanced over at Zalygin, still standing in the middle of the floor.

"Get down, Victor!" he screamed.

Just then, two ball-sized black objects crashed through the windows of the room. One of them landed behind Zalygin, bouncing across the floor with a dull, thudding sound. The other came to rest just in front of Tret'iakov's face, spinning like a top on its vertical axis. The Marshall looked at it, his muscles relaxed, and he said softly, "Oh, hell," as the fragmentation grenade exploded, reducing his head to a red mist.

Uri Bogoslovka was less than two meters away, on his hands and knees, when the first grenade detonated. His eardrums had been blown out, and his left eye hung out of its socket by the optic nerve, swinging back and forth like a grisly pendulum. A grenade fragment had passed through his leg, severing the femoral artery. A broad stream of bright, red blood pulsed out of the wound with each heartbeat.

Slipping in his own gore, Bogoslovka grabbed the window sill and tried to pull himself up. He wanted to look out and get a shot--just one shot—at the traitorous bastards who had done this. His strength spilling out onto the floor below him, groaning with the effort, Bogoslovka was finally high enough to look out the bottom of the window. He found himself staring down the bore of a rifle, its muzzle three centimeters from his one, remaining eye. Bogoslovka certainly never heard the blast, as the one-hundred-eighty grain, boat-tail, spitzer bullet passed directly through the center of his iris at nine-hundred thirty meters per second, and took off the back of his head.

Antonov-Ovseenko's entire left side had been raked by fragments. One of them had passed between his abdomen and the floor, opening his stomach like a zipper. As he rolled over onto his back, he noticed that his intestines were still on the floor next to him. He screamed, and with both hands reached down and began pushing his guts back into himself through the gaping wound. His two-thousand dollar Armani suit glistened with blood and bits of organs as Antonov-Ovseenko's frantic attempts became weaker and weaker. Finally, they ceased, as his last breath escaped him. His lifeless eyes stared up at the ceiling in horror, both his hands inserted into his own body.

President Zalygin had been blown off his feet by the concussion of the first grenade. He had landed in a sitting position in the heavily-padded leather chair against the wall, as if he were resting after a hard day at the office. He watched the deaths of his colleagues like some surreal, slow-motion movie. His left humerus had been shattered by a shard of steel, and his arm hung over the side of the chair at an impossible angle. The scalp on the left side of his head had been lacerated with surgical precision, and the blast had flipped it over so that it covered his right ear. The entire top of his skull was exposed, gleaming pink and white.

Like an automaton, his head swivelled to the left, and he looked at the second grenade lying on the floor in front of the bar. He knew it would be only a fraction of a second more, but it seemed like an eternity as he waited for it to explode. When it finally happened, Zalygin never knew it, because a large steel fragment entered his head just above his left eye, destroying his cerebrum. The conscious thought had not had time to form. Then there was silence.

Seconds passed. Suddenly the door burst open, splintered off its hinges as three commandos dove into the room, their sniper rifles replaced with compact submachine guns. The barrels of their weapons swept the room as they sought out any remaining resistance. They saw only Liubchenko, unscathed, on his stool in the corner, sheltered behind the heavily-built wooden bar. The commando leader approached him, only his eyes visible behind the black-knit balaclava. Liubchenko looked at him and smiled.

"Are you here for the lecture?" he asked.

"Yes," said the black-clad figure, as he switched his weapon to semiautomatic fire. "Yes, Professor, I wouldn't miss one of your lectures. You know that."

Liubchenko's smile broadened as the commando placed the gun's muzzle against his forehead and pulled the trigger.

CHAPTER THREE

A conference room in the Kremlin.

Field Marshal Vasili Sokolnikov looked at the other two men sitting at the table. They appeared uneasy, as if not knowing what to expect. He felt that way also. In fact, all of Russia had been uneasy since the first reports of President Zaligin's death had been broadcast at six that morning, Moscow time.

The people were told that the president and his associates had been killed in a multiple car accident while returning to Moscow from the dacha. Sokolnikov did not believe it, and he suspected that his companions in the room did not believe it either. The Marshal realized that, like him, they knew Drugonov only too well; they knew his lust for power and his ability to intimidate virtually anyone, including the press.

They had each received a call two hours earlier informing them that Prime Minister Drugonov, General Secretary of the New Rodina Party, requested their attendance. Marshal Sokolnikov, First Deputy Minister of Defense and Chief of the General Staff, ruminated on that title as he twirled a pencil in his fingers: General Secretary of the New Rodina Party. It had an ominous ring. Was it possible that Drugonov had consolidated sufficient power so as to become another Maximum Leader, like Stalin? How had they let things get this far? Was it too late to stop him?

Sokolnikov knew that the New Rodina Party was wildly popular among many of the people. It offered them the kind of paternalistic, structured orderliness that they had known under the old Soviet regime. But, he asked himself, don't they remember the horrors, the millions of deaths in the Gulag, the man-made famines, the purges? Are a monthly ration card and a two-room flat worth all of that? As unbelievable as it seemed, to the majority of his countrymen and women, it apparently was.

To Sokolnikov's left sat a man who seemed to have no such apprehensions. Anatoly Vatutin, former head of the KGB, no doubt saw clearly what was happening in Russia, and Sokolnikov felt certain that he relished it. The marshal knew that Vatutin and Drugonov were of a kind: ambitious, ruthless, eager to seize power when the opportunity presented itself. Here was a man the former master spy could work with. And clearly, Sokolnikov thought with a mixture of fear and revulsion, he was going to have that opportunity. His presence at this meeting was proof of that.

Drugonov obviously had big plans, and he, Vatutin, was to be part of them.

As he contemplated this monster, this murderer of untold thousands, Sokolnikov's eyes bored into the side of Vatutin's head. Vatutin turned and looked into the marshal's eyes with an arrogant stare.

He said, "Don't look so surprised at my presence, Sokolnikov. The tide of history has turned, as I always knew it would. You thought you were rid of people like me, didn't you? For years I have heard through various channels that you disapproved, or perhaps more accurately, hated, my....methods. You and your officer corps, with your proud, honorable, heroic martial traditions! You've always thought you were better than I, haven't you? I'll wager that you were glad to see me unseated, glad to see my organization disbanded! But I am back!

"Soon I will return to the epicenter of power. After the collapse of the old regime, weaklings like Zalygin cast me aside like a used tissue. But I knew it would not last, all that alien talk of liberty and free markets. Now the Russian people are calling me back to the job that I was destined to do: provide order. And you, my dear, unblemished field marshal, are going to have to live with it!"

Unable to look at the man any longer, Sokolnikov glanced across the table and caught the eye of the third man in the room. Leonid Uglanov, head of the Russian mafia and the richest man in the country, gave Sokolnikov a knowing smile, as if they were sharing some hideous secret. The marshal supposed that he also understood Drugonov's motives. Like Vatutin, Uglanov too possessed many of Drugonov's characteristics. As he looked at this arch-criminal, it occurred to Sokolnikov that the three of them were like three very rotten peas from the same pod.

Like Drugonov, Uglanov also had been concentrating on the accumulation of raw power; where Drugonov's was political, his was economic. It was common knowledge throughout Russia that his organization's tentacles extended from St. Petersburg to Vladivostok: blackmail, extortion, prostitution, drugs. Whatever would turn a ruble, that was Uglanov's stock in trade. In the past few years he had done a thriving business in the sale of fissionable material and biological weapons agents to Islamic extremists. Sokolnikov knew that he had ordered the deaths of a great many people since he began his climb to the top of the Russian underworld. He probably admired Drugonov for the way he had handled Zalygin and the rest of them; no doubt he would have done the same thing. They had been in the way.

The door opened and Sergei Drugonov entered the room.

"Well, my friends, how are you this fine Russian morning?" he said as he shook hands with the three others.

Sokolnikov had never seen him in this mood; people who knew Drugonov would hardly have thought it possible. He seemed positively ebullient as he stood at the head of the table, rubbing his hands together and raising and lowering himself on the balls of his feet. Vatutin and Uglanov obviously shared Drugonov's enthusiasm, as broad smiles crossed their faces. Here were three men who knew that their time was about to come. Only Marshal Sokolnikov seemed to appreciate the gravity of the moment. His straight face concealed his feeling of disgust as he looked at each of the men in turn, wondering what kind of monsters he had fallen in with.

"And make no mistake, gentlemen," Drugonov continued. "This is indeed a great morning for Russia. It marks the beginning of Russian ascendancy, of Russian dominance in the world order. Centuries from now people will mark this day with celebration in the knowledge that it was the first day of Russia's quest to achieve her true destiny."

"Sergei," Anatoly Vatutin said, "Now that President Zalygin has passed away," Uglanov chuckled, "you, as prime minister and general secretary of the nation's largest political party, would seem to be the heir to the throne, so to speak. You lack only the title of president."

"You are correct, Anatoly," Drugonov answered. "Fate has surely chosen me to lead our country to greatness. As for the presidency, that too will soon be mine. Those positions," and here he fixed his eyes upon Sokolnikov, "as well as my new military rank of generalissimo, give me the authority to assume command as Russia moves forward."

"Generalissimo!" shot back Sokolnikov, locking eyes with Drugonov. It was ridiculous! Drugonov had never risen above the rank of junior lieutenant in a motor-rifle battalion. "There has not been a generalissimo in the Russian military since Stalin! It is not even a legitimate rank!"

Drugonov's mood changed instantly, as his fist slammed into the table. "It is legitimate because I give it legitimacy, marshal!" he roared. "If you cannot accept that, I, as prime minister, will gladly take your resignation! There are many generals who would welcome a marshal's baton!"

Sokolnikov held Drugonov's gaze. For the first time since they had first met, he saw the true nature of the beast: the wild look in the man's eyes, the eyes of a vicious predator, ready to snap the neck of its prey. A droplet of spittle had escaped Drugonov's mouth and slowly ran down his chin. This man is totally, completely mad! Sokonikov thought. What have we done to ourselves?

He wanted to stand, resign his commission, and stride from the room. The very idea of working with this man, of taking orders from him, was repulsive. Then he thought of his next in command, the one who would take his place if he left. General Podgorny, while an excellent soldier, had weaknesses, character flaws, that would make him like clay in Drugonov's hands. At least if he, Sokolnikov, stayed on, he might be able to prevent tragedy, to counterbalance Drugonov's acts of madness, to minimize the damage. He swallowed his pride and remained seated.

Drugonov composed himself, and with the back of his hand wiped away the spit.

"I see no problem with you assuming complete power, Sergei," Vatutin said. Drugonov's eyes shifted toward him. "And I am sure that the Russian people will agree with me. They yearn for strong, decisive leadership. As for the intelligence community, rest assured that they will give you their full support. More than anything else, they seek a mission that they can sink their teeth into, and they will follow any leader who will give it to them."

"My organization will have no objections," added Uglanov. "As long as they feel that their support is, how shall I put it, sufficiently appreciated."

The three of them laughed at that, a quiet, conspiratorial laugh. Only Sokolnikov was restrained. He looked across the table at Uglanov and felt revulsion. He deeply resented being required to sit at the same table with this thug, this prince of thugs. And yet he stayed; he stayed because it was his duty to stay.

"Have no fear, Leonid," Drugonov said, once again smiling and affable. "Your organization's support will be greatly appreciated. In fact, it will be appreciated beyond your wildest imaginings. And as for your people, Anatoly, I am sure that they will approve of the new arrangements. As of this moment, I decree that the KGB is once again in existence."

"Aren't you forgetting something, Sergei?" asked Sokolnikov. "We still have a Duma in this country. Such a decision will require their approval."

"And they will approve, marshal," Drugonov answered. "They will approve of any decision I make. You see, I have voluminous files on every member. I know their personal histories, their weaknesses, where they live, and, most importantly of all, Marshal Sokolnikov, I know where their families are. I know of their wives, husbands, parents and children. And with the help of the newly-resurrected KGB, I will be in a position to punish dissent. Do you understand me, Vasily?" Drugonov looked at Sokolnikov through narrowed eyes.

"Yes, Sergei. I understand you perfectly," the marshal answered in a level voice.

"I am not sure that you do, Vasily. Not quite yet," Drugonov said as he stepped to the adjacent desk and lifted the telephone receiver. "Bring her in," he said in a flat voice.

Sokolnikov turned and looked toward the door just as it opened. A very large man in a badly-cut suit led a young woman into the room by her upper arm. It was Vasily Sokolnikov's daughter, Anna. Seventeen years old, she was a student at a polytechnic institute in Moscow, preparing for what everyone was sure would be a bright, happy future. Sokolnikov adored her.

"Daddy! What is happening?" she implored, tears streaming down her lovely face. "Men came to our home this morning after you left and took me away! Why am I here? What have I done?"

"Nothing, my darling," Sokolnikov said as he leaped to his feet, tore the giant's hand from his daughter's arm, and embraced her. She broke down sobbing, pressing her face to her father's chest.

"You have done nothing, my Anna," he murmured as he gently stroked her hair. "This has all been a mistake. Go home to your mother. She will be worried. Tell her to forget that this ever happened. Go now."

She stepped back slightly, and Sokolnikov held her face in both hands as he kissed her forehead. The girl still had the look of a hunted animal in her eyes as she reluctantly turned away from her father and slowly, unsteadily, left the room. The giant stepped out as well, closing the door behind him.

The marshal stood staring at the closed door for a few seconds, an anger such as he had never known before welling up inside him. As if from a distance, he heard Drugonov's voice.

"Now, Vasily. Now you truly understand." Sokolnikov turned and gave Drugonov a look that would cause most men to shudder. Drugonov continued, "You are this country's most competent military man. You are really quite brilliant at your trade, you know. The plans that I have will require your cooperation. Your willing cooperation. Do I have it, Vasily?"

The air in the room was electric with tension as the seconds ticked by. "You have it, Drugonov," Sokolnikov hissed.

"Please, Vasily!" Drugonov said cheerfully, a smile returning to his face. "From now on simply address me as Mr. Chairman." He looked at Sokolnikov for a reaction. To his satisfaction, there was none.

Drugonov turned to the others.

"Now, gentlemen, let's get down to business. We are here to form a new government, a new regime. Since the Communist Revolution, and until recently, Russia has always been ruled by a troika: three separate elements in which absolute power is concentrated absolutely. Why, you ask? A triangle is the strongest and most rigid of geometric forms. Politically, such an arrangement presents the perfect balance. Each leg of this political stool, if you will, must realize that it cannot successfully conspire against the other two. A stool with only two legs will fall. Each leg is dependent on the other two for its success. Historically, the three legs of the Russian political stool have consisted of the Party, the military, led by the army, and the KGB or one of its ancestors. It is my intention to re-institute such an arrangement. Also, historically, this system has worked best when there has been one strong man in unquestioned control of the entire apparatus. I am that man. I will form one leg of the stool. The Party, now the New Rodina instead of the Communist, will exist entirely through me. I will be its sole manifestation."

Drugonov's eyes went from face to face seeking any sign of dissent, any indication at all that these men might resist him. He saw none.

"Further, it is my intention to establish what has sometimes been referred to as a 'Cult of Personality.' Though I am anything but a Marxist, I have learned my lessons well from my communist forebears. I will do exactly as Lenin and Stalin, as well as such totalitarian luminaries as Hitler, Kim Il Sung, Mao, and Saddam Hussein, did before me: I will become the state, and the state will become me. Any dissent, any criticism of either me or the state will be punishable by death. The name Drugonov will become synonymous with Russia, and Russia with Drugonov.

"Anatoly, your KGB will create a bureau to see to it that likenesses of me–statues, paintings, and photographs, all of monumental proportions–become ubiquitous throughout Russia. I want no Russian to be able to open his eyes in public without seeing my face. Airports, universities, even entire cities, will take my name.

"I expect this policy to be enforced with utter ruthlessness. Not only the dissident, but his or her entire family must be liquidated. In the beginning, the slaughter will be of tremendous proportions. Since the fall of communism, many of our people have adopted Western ways and beliefs, including an abhorrence of totalitarianism. But once the they see the price of treason, once we crush this Western poison out of them, they will once again become the docile herd that the Russian people have historically been."

"But Ser-, I mean Mr. Chairman," Vatutin began. "You have spoken of a three-legged stool. You are to be the first leg, presumably Sokolnikov's army the second, and my KGB the third. But there are four of us."

"Quite right, Anatoly," Drugonov said, clasping his hands behind his back, looking down at the spy-master with an imperious gaze. "Your KGB will work in conjunction with Leonid's, ah, organization. The two of you, working together, will form that third leg."

A slight smile crossed his face as he glanced at Uglanov. "Working together shouldn't be difficult. After all," he continued, "you have a great deal in common. Your goals and tactics are very similar: to achieve obedience through the use of terror. You should work well together. Anatoly, your people will seek out and punish political dissent, and yours, Leonid, will do the same with regard to economic dissent. A number of our people have become entranced with this free-market nonsense, particularly the younger post-Soviet generation. It will be your job to break them of these alien habits and return them to the service of the state where they belong, in true Russian fashion.

"Above all, Leonid, you will see to it that they pay their taxes. Feel free to use whatever level of force is necessary. The plans that I have for our country will be very expensive. Strip the churches and museums of anything of value. Sell it all on the Western and Asian markets."

"And I assume," Uglanov said with a sly smile, "that I will be working on commission?"

"Absolutely, my friend!" Drugonov replied. "I had the figure of five percent in mind. That would be satisfactory, would it not?"

"Very satisfactory, Mr. Chairman," said the crime-lord. He could not keep out of his voice some of the awe that he felt. Imagine, he thought. An entire country to loot, and with official sanction, no less!

Drugonov continued. "In addition to your domestic responsibilities, both of you will be involved in foreign activities. Your KGB, Anatoly, will upgrade and enhance its non-domestic intelligence-gathering activities to at least their old levels. You, Leonid, will use your organization's unique talents overseas not only to line your own pockets, but now, as well, in the service of the state."

"Which, I assume, will be one and the same thing," Uglanov added, a note of enthusiasm in his voice.

"Exactly so, my friend," Drugonov said. "I have heard much about your activities in other countries, particularly in Europe and North America. Is all that I have heard true?"

"Indeed it is, Mr. Chairman," Uglanov answered. "We have taken over much of the criminal activity in those places. We are involved in everything from drugs and money-laundering to blackmail and assassination."

"And how effective do you find their law enforcement community,

Leonid?"

"They are a minor thorn in our sides. We have had great recent success in buying off their politicians, particularly in the United States. This has made our road much smoother."

"Just as I thought," said Drugonov with a smile. "You will of course continue with business as usual, but now you may be asked to blackmail or liquidate someone on my orders."

"I look forward to the opportunity of serving my country," Uglanov said laughingly as he leaned back in his chair.

Drugonov turned to Marshal Sokolnikov. "As Anatoly alluded to, you, Vasily, are the stool's final leg. You are promoted as of now to the position of minister of defense answerable to me alone. It will be your job to coordinate all branches of the armed forces in preparation for the great task we have before us."

"And what might that be----Mr. Chairman?" asked Sokolnikov.

Drugonov's eyes became unfocused as he looked off into space, as if he were seeing a great path stretching out before him. "We are going to conquer the world, Vasily. We are going to conquer the world."

On April sixth, a general election was held for the office of president of Russia. Caught by surprise by the death of President Zalygin, his party was forced to field a relative unknown. Consequently, Sergei Drugonov won by a landslide. At noon on the seventh of April, he addressed the Duma.

The applause continued into its fourth minute. It was clear to Drugonov that no one wanted to be the first to stop clapping. They undoubtedly knew that they were being videotaped, and that Drugonov would review those tapes to identify those who were less than enthusiastic in welcoming him as their new president. He stood behind the podium, hands gripping the edges of the lectern, and looked slowly back and forth across the sea of faces in the giant auditorium, absorbing the adulation that he felt was his due. It did not bother him in the least that most of it was contrived; he derived immense satisfaction from the knowledge that he was in a position to force these people to worship him.

Finally, even Drugonov had had enough. He raised his arms above his head and made downward pumping motions with his hands, indicating, to the great relief of his audience that they may sit. The room became still, and Drugonov used that stillness for its theatrical effect. Then he broke the pregnant silence.

"My fellow patriots! The people of Russia have spoken! They have chosen me to lead them out of their failed past, away from their miserable present, and into a glorious future! Under my leadership, and with your unswerving support, Russia will become the great country we have always known she could be. Magnificent opportunities are at hand, if only we have the boldness, the daring, to reach out and take them!"

Drugonov's supporters exploded in wild applause, leaping to their feet. He called for silence.

"But if we are to succeed as a state, we must be brutally frank with ourselves. We must force ourselves to understand why we have failed and others have succeeded. This will be a painful experience, because no one likes his weaknesses pointed out to him. But it is our reality; we must be strong and face it. The time for self-delusion has passed. Let us begin at the beginning.

"Who are we, we Russians? In what do we believe? How do we see ourselves in relation to others, not only to foreigners, but to each other as well? What is this thing we proudly call Russian culture? What is it that makes us distinctly Russian? Learn the answers to these questions, and you will understand the entire history of our country. You will also understand the course of action that we must pursue in the future if we are to survive. And make no mistake about it, our very survival is at stake.

"While no one can deny our achievements in literature, the arts and in other intellectual endeavors, I put it to you that our Russian culture has failed us in one critical respect: it has prevented us, as individuals, from accepting responsibility for our own existence. It has produced in us the deep-seated belief that it is the task of someone else to take care of us. You can follow this cultural thread back in time perhaps a thousand years, when, as legend has it, Rurik, supposedly a fourteenth-generation descendant of Augustus Caesar, was invited by the people of Moscow to become their ruler, because they could not rule themselves. So was born the Principality of Rus', and the beginnings of Russian history.

"Then came centuries of autocratic rule by the Tzars and by the Church. So dependent were we on the Tzar that it was common practice among us to refer to him in informal conversation as 'Father,' perhaps the ultimate expression of dependency and paternalism. This was followed by three-quarters of a century of totalitarian Soviet rule. But no matter which era of our history you choose to examine, you will find one common denominator: we have always looked to some other social entity for our survival and well-being. The nature of the entity has changed with time, but the paternalistic dependency has not. Foreign prince, Tzar, Church, fellow proletarian, party, state, we Russians, as individuals, have looked to all of these to sustain us, to support us, to protect us from the harsh realities of a universe that demands reasoned action on the part of each individual if that individual is to survive.

"This culture of paternalism has produced in us the belief that we have a right to food, to clothing, to housing, to medical care, to education and to everything else that we may need. But from where do these things come? Do they spring from the ground? Do they fall from the sky? Of course not.

"Someone else, some other individual, must produce them. So what, then, are we really claiming when we say we have a right to these material goods? We are claiming the product of someone else's labor. We are not asking for it. We are demanding it as our right. We are demanding that that producer become our slave, our sacrificial animal. We are demanding that that producer satisfy our demands before he satisfies his own, because, after all, the product of his labor is ours by right; he cannot legitimately deny us access to it, no matter what his own needs may be, any more than he can deny us access to the air we breathe. That is one half of the equation. There is more.

"Our culture has produced in us not only the characteristics of parasites, but also those of sacrificial animals. The two roles are inseparable. While we expect someone--anyone--to sacrifice himself for our well-being, we also realize, deep within the recesses of our minds, that the time will come when we too will be called upon to sacrifice ourselves for someone else's-- anyone else's--well-being. This expectation of self-sacrifice has had a profound effect on us as individuals, and therefore as a society. It influences the way we see ourselves in relation to others around us, to our jobs, our government, even our families. Always we are looking over our shoulders, to see who will demand of us that we assume the role of a sacrificial animal, of a slave. And, what is worse, our culture conditions us to accept that role; we, as individuals, believe that such a demand is legitimate, because we make the very same demand of others.

"We trust no one, because everyone is our potential slave-master. We refuse to cooperate with anyone, because we would only be assisting our own destroyer. We don't work hard, nor do we take pleasure in our work, because, after all, the product of our labor can be claimed by anyone at any time. We don't expect fair treatment from others, so we give none. Today you are my slave, tomorrow. I will be yours. It is a metaphysical psychosis.

"Historically, this cultural flaw of ours has manifested itself in the unending need for conquest. The Tzar's empire grew from the Duchy of Muscovy to one-seventh of the earth's land surface. It stretched from the Baltic to the Pacific and beyond, reaching even into the New World. In modern times it included Eastern Europe, the Baltic states and part of Finland. The driving force behind Russian history has been the never-ending search for more sacrificial animals. As one group of slaves becomes exhausted, their spirits broken by the forced extraction of the product of their labors, and as they, too, become part of the dominant Russian culture of mandatory self-sacrifice, new groups of slaves must be conquered; fresh blood must be found to lubricate this creaking, groaning, cultural machine of ours. New territories with fresh resources must be acquired to provide for the needs of a people who consume more than they produce.

"The economic effects of this culture of self-sacrifice are difficult to overestimate. People who expect to be forced into the role of sacrificial animal are not very productive. Why should they be? For whom are they producing? For themselves, or for their potential slave-masters? Why should they save, invest, plan for the future? What future does a slave have?

"This gets to the root of precisely why our culture has failed. It is unrealistic, in the most literal sense. The real universe in which we live demands that we human beings accept certain immutable laws if we are to survive. We must live according to the dictates of reality, or not live at all. Among these is the fact that healthy individuals are self-interested. They have a primal desire to survive and to be happy. Through our acts, through the way in which we have always seen ourselves and others around us--as little more than a herd of sacrificial animals, through the ways in which we have always conducted ourselves as a people:

accepting self-sacrifice and demanding it of others, we have denied the existence of such a desire. And yet that desire is real. It exists. Failing to recognize it as a fact of life, as a dictate of reality, for the past thousand years has turned us into a race of epistemological freaks, like the man who refuses to believe that fire will burn him. Sooner or later, he will die because of his unwillingness to accept an aspect of reality. And so will we.

"Further, rational individuals realize that they must produce in order to survive: the means for their survival do not occur fully-developed in nature. Individuals must intervene in nature, with their inventiveness, their ingenuity, their labor, to extract from nature the means for their survival. If they are then forced to relinquish those means of survival, which they have produced, for the well-being of strangers, a basic metaphysical and moral conflict is produced. It is true that they may acquiesce temporarily, as, for example, in an emergency, as long as this extraction of the product of their labor does not threaten their own survival. But they cannot be forced to engage in self-sacrifice indefinitely without producing in them an adverse psychological reaction. They become angry, resentful and unproductive. They realize that such a demand violates the principal existential dictate of the relationship between a rational individual and the universe in which he must survive: that each of us must be self-sustaining, that each of us must produce for his or her own consumption, that to strip a producer of the product of his labor is to threaten his very survival, to steal from him life itself. Reality demands that each of us be free to keep the product of that labor, that we be free to use it or to dispose of it as we see fit. What a bizarre notion for a Russian, don't you agree? Never in our history have we accepted such ideas. And yet if individuals are to survive, if they are to deal successfully with this real universe, they must live according to these rules. That is why we, as a people, are dying. We insist on fighting reality rather than living in accordance with it.

"A man may choose not to believe that gravity exists. That is his prerogative. But if he acts on his belief, if he steps off a cliff, he will die. We are free to ignore the dictates of reality, but we are not free to ignore the consequences of ignoring the dictates of reality. We have ignored reality for a thousand years, and the consequences have caught up with us.

"Of course, individuals cannot force others to engage in self-sacrifice. It is done through the intervention of a strong state. It has always been so in Russia. The state decides who shall be today's sacrificial animal, and who shall be the beneficiary of that sacrifice. Our people would have it no other way. They expect to be taken care of, and only the state is in a position to force others to sacrifice themselves for their, the recipient's, benefit. Without state coercion, the entire apparatus of forced self-sacrifice and parasitism would collapse. People will not willingly participate in their own enslavement, even if they expect others to accept the role of slave for their benefit. The task of state officials in our country has always been to provide the force necessary to extract such sacrifice. Those of us in this room are now the masters of the state apparatus. We have been chosen by our people as their agents of coercion. But there is a problem.

"The pattern of self-sacrifice and parasitism has run its course. The Russian people have nothing more to sacrifice; nothing is being produced for the parasites to consume. The last vestiges of individual initiative and productivity have been extinguished. I intend to solve this problem by doing what our leaders have always done throughout our history: I will find new sacrificial animals for our people to exploit, fresh blood for them to drink. There are peoples beyond our borders who, unlike us, are very productive. They have amassed enormous wealth, enough to satisfy the needs of our people for centuries to come. Once we conquer them, the people of North America, Europe and Japan, and forcibly expropriate the product of their labor for our own use, our people will never again need to enslave themselves for anyone else's benefit. They will have at their disposal hundreds of millions of fresh, highly productive sacrificial animals. For the first time in our history, we, all of us, the entire Russian people, will have the luxury of engaging in an existential impossibility: consumption without production.

"How is it that these foreigners are productive while we are not, you may ask. Once again, the answer is to be found in the realm of culture. They are the product of Western civilization, while we are not, despite the efforts of Tzar Peter and others to Westernize us. They derive their cultural values from the Western Enlightenment, with its emphasis on reason, science, and perhaps most importantly, on the primacy of the individual. That cultural event barely touched our country, and then only among the elite. Since at least the eighteenth century, those Westerners have not experienced the expectation of self-sacrifice, they have not looked at others as their potential slaves. Unlike us, they have had no authoritarian state to forcibly extract the product of their labor and redistribute it to others. They produced solely for their own consumption. Consequently, they have been highly motivated and highly successful. They have been living in conformance with the dictates of reality. It is true that in recent decades this has been changing. They, too, are moving toward statism and the culture of self-sacrifice. But their productive momentum, their legacy of individualism, continues to enrich them.

"In recent years, since the fall of communism, we have tried to live by their rules. Our one attempt, in a millennium, to survive as individuals, to reject our own traditions and adopt those of others, has been a catastrophic failure. A people cannot change their culture in so short a time; such a change may well require centuries, centuries which we do not have. And so our standard of living drops daily; we have massive unemployment; the real threat of starvation haunts the land; our currency has collapsed; we can produce virtually nothing that anyone else wants to buy. The Islamic republics on our southern border smell our weakness as a wolf smells the blood of a wounded animal. The scores of nationalities that make up Russia, conquered centuries ago by the Tzars, threaten to secede rather than accompany us into oblivion. Our very existence as a sovereign state is threatened.

"I was elected, as were most of you, because the Russian people have had enough of this alien experiment with individualism. They are fish out of water; and if it continues they will die. I offer them life.

"I have chosen the United States of America as our first foreign slave-pen. It is the engine of wealth in the world, and the last surviving bastion of individualism. Once we have defeated them, the other developed states will fall into line with minimal resistance. Those countries of the world that are not sufficiently productive will serve as a source of menial labor and natural resources.

"But is it possible to defeat the United States, you ask? After all, they are strong and will resist us fiercely. Will they? I think not. The United States is like the Cyclops, Polyphemus, in Homer's Odyssey. He was immensely strong, and a most dangerous adversary, until his eye had been gouged out. Once he lost his sight, he became nothing more than a blind, lumbering giant, easily defeated. The United States is a giant who has lost his vision. Their political leadership is weak, unprincipled and corrupt, with no grasp of history and no sense of the future. The whole world has witnessed their lies and even their acts of greed-driven treason. Their intelligentsia is depraved beyond description! Encouraged by this political and intellectual elite, and with the willing participation of the press, the American people are being persuaded to reject the very principles that made them great. And make no mistake about it, they were great once. They discovered the secret that man had been seeking to implement since the time of Aristotle: how to create an orderly society in which the individual is the principal unit of analysis.

"Throughout history, in one country or empire after another, something else had always been that principal unit of analysis: that social entity to which individuals were expected to sacrifice themselves. It may have been the emperor, or God, or the aristocracy, or the masses, or the proletariat, or the master race. But always the individual was made subservient to something else in society. And the results were less than satisfactory. Our own country is an excellent example of that. Such social systems never brought out the best that individuals were capable of being. But the United States broke that historical pattern at the time of their founding; they used their culture of individualism to create a system of government in which the solitary person, the private citizen, was of paramount concern. Their first consideration was the liberty of the individual. With the temporary exception of the feudal, antebellum South, there was no forced self-sacrifice here; no parasitism was permitted. People knew that they could keep what they produced, and use it to improve their own lives and the lives of their families. In creating such a system, the Americans unleashed human productive potential such as had never been done before. The results were spectacular! Within one human lifetime, they went from being a poor, agrarian country to being the wealthiest industrial power on the face of the earth.

"But recent generations of Americans have lost sight of what made them great; their intellectuals have persuaded them that their founding philosophy of individualism is selfish and immoral, that the way to greatness lies in self-sacrifice, even in self-immolation. Their politicians, holding fingers in the wind, have acquiesced through the creation of an enormous re-distributive welfare state to achieve that end. Their press hammers home these fallacies at every opportunity. Everywhere in America individual liberty is on the defensive. This is most unfortunate for them, but it will prove to be our salvation. The Americans are plagued by self-doubt; they have experienced a dissolution of resolve, producing cracks in the very foundation of their republic. We will simply take advantage of those cracks, and pry them open until the structure falls. No, my friends, they have neither the strength nor the will to resist us.

"It is true that many millions of Americans refuse vehemently to accept this philosophy of self-sacrifice that is being forced down their throats. Through reason and the natural persistence of culture, they cling to the philosophy of their founding era, that of individualism. These people, if they were dominant, could never be defeated. But they have become the minority. They are dispersed and weak; they have no power base from which to operate; they do not have the ear of the press. Their ignorant, collectivist countrymen, their weak, self-serving politicians, and their depraved intellectuals have stabbed them, and their country, in the back. They will present no threat to us. When the time comes, they will respond to terror and repression as have hundreds of millions before them. And if there is anything that we Russians know how to implement, it is terror and repression.

"For all practical purposes, the United States is a country that is ideologically adrift: a compass with no needle. Such a country is ripe for conquest, for they have lost the will to resist. They have been reduced to a rotted husk of a nation. Free people will defend with their lives those principles that made them free; but if they have rejected those very principles, what is their motivation for self-defense? Under what banner shall they fight? Defending their own homeland and their way of life becomes a hollow act.

"But, you ask, if we are to conquer the United States, are we not now informing them of our intentions? Will they not prepare themselves? I say to you no. They will not. They have reached such a state of craven indecision that many among them, their political leadership in particular, will ask themselves if they are truly worthy of self-defense. As unbelievable as it may seem, I am convinced that they will question whether they even have the right to defend what they have come to see as a corrupt, immoral existence. Did not their leaders once announce that they would absorb a first nuclear strike, with no attempt at self-defense? What further proof could you seek? In the name of fairness, in the name of virtuous self-sacrifice, these people are begging us to become their masters.

"It is true that their military is very strong. Though it has been weakened substantially in recent years, it is still a formidable force. And it is filled with patriots who have not succumbed to the drivel that has been vomited out by the intellectuals. But remember that their military operates under strict civilian control, and those civilians have been persuaded by the rantings of the intelligentsia. Never in more than two centuries has that civilian control been challenged, and it will not be challenged now. No, we will not have to defeat their military. We merely need to defeat their leaders. And that will be a simple task, like pushing over a rotted tree. I will use their own moral indecision, their own self-doubts, their own depravity, their own corruption, against them. And those leaders will subconsciously welcome that defeat.

"I tell you it can be done! First the United States, and then the entire world will be at our feet, under our lash, groveling for the crumbs that we throw them, breaking their backs to make us rich! One world! One neck! One boot! Our ultimate conquest will make every empire in the history of the world pale by comparison! Place your faith in me as your Maximum Leader! Follow me unquestioningly! Together we will triumph!"

CHAPTER FOUR

Vladivostok, Russia. April 15, 3:17 A.M.

Posnik Yakovlev, captain of the cargo vessel Volokolamsk, pulled his jacket's collar more tightly around his neck. Though it was spring in Vladivostok, the air coming off the hills around the city was chilly at this early-morning hour.

What a hell of a time to be loading cargo! Yakovlev thought, as he watched the crane lift the large crate off the flatbed truck and into the hold of his ship. He was uncomfortable. In his twenty-six years at sea, he had never seen anything like it. What could possibly be in that crate to justify all of this? he asked himself. Although the Trans-Siberian Railway terminated in Vladivostok, and anyone in his right mind would send such a crate the 9,301 kilometers from Moscow by rail, this crate had come in by military air transport. And the time! Obviously, the trench-coated men controlling this operation didn't want anyone to see what they were doing.

Yakovlev looked over at Svetlanskaya Street, normally bustling with traffic, but now almost deserted. Whatever was going on here, there would be no witnesses to the event, he thought.

When he had learned that his ship would be carrying this strange cargo, he had demanded to know its contents. After all, as captain, everything aboard his ship was his business. But the men from Moscow showed him their brand-new KGB credentials, and told him not to press the matter. He remembered the former KGB, and he feared the new one as much as the old. Though he disliked it, he would do as he was told: Do not touch the crate; the government operatives placed aboard the ship for the voyage would shoot anyone who disturbed it; you are carrying nothing but canned fish; take the crate to Los Angeles, United States of America, and wait for further orders.

36\Iron Phoenix

CHAPTER FIVE

The White House, Washington, D.C.

"Where the hell is that poll, Lye? I've got to give a press conference in fifty-three minutes and I haven't seen yesterday's polling data! How am I supposed to know what to say out there?"

"Don't worry, Mr. President. They're crunching the numbers right now. We should have the results any minute," said Lysander Elfman, the White House Chief of Staff.

"Jesus, Lye! With all the people we've got working around here, can't we get anybody to do these things on time? Light a fire under 'um, will ya'?"

Judas Benedict, President of the United States, walked around the Oval Office desk and sat down in the large leather chair. He opened a drawer, took out a round hand-mirror, and began to examine himself carefully, turning his head slowly from side to side, lifting it to look for signs of a double chin. Suddenly he reached across the desk and stabbed a button on the intercom.

"Ellen, send my barber in here right now. My sideburns are uneven."

"Yes, Mr. President," came the reply.

Judas Benedict was used to giving orders. Scion of an old-line Philadelphia banking dynasty, there had always been servants to satisfy his every whim. As far as he was concerned, the White House was simply a quaint alternative to his Hampton mansion. He was obsessed with his appearance, agreeing with those who said that it was his most powerful electoral tool.

"Mr. President, we really should give some consideration to how we will respond to President Drugonov's speech in the Duma. There have been some critical editorials in several papers around the country. Not many, but enough to concern us," said Elfman as politely as he could.

Benedict studied his reflection in the mirror. "Do you think this tie is too loud, Lye? I think it makes me look assertive, don't you?"

"Yes, Mr. President. It makes you look assertive. But what about Russia?"

Irritated, Benedict lowered the mirror and looked at Elfman.

"Lye, you know the focus-group results as well as I do. The American people think this Drugonov character is just a blowhard. They're not worried about him, so why should I be? After all, the economy's good, isn't it? That's all that people really care about."

"There are those who think that Drugonov presents a real threat to our security, Mr. President."

"Nonsense, Lye. I know how to deal with him. He'll respond to the same incentive that all the rest of us respond to: money. At the press conference, I'll announce a little gift for Mr. Drugonov. Once he experiences the benefits of American largess, he'll tone down his rhetoric."

"I'm not so sure this one can be bought off, Mr. President. After all, our intelligence indicates that he murdered President Zalygin and his cabinet. That sort of act requires single-minded dedication to accomplish a goal, and, if we can believe his own words, his goal seems to be our destruction. It seems to me that we have a responsibility to take him seriously."

Benedict chuckled. "Lye, I've been in politics a long time. I know what makes men tick. Once Drugonov gets his own fat Swiss bank account, he'll come around. They all do."

"I hope you're right, Mr. President," Elfman replied.

The intercom buzzed, and the President's secretary said, "Mr. Crippler to see you, sir."

"Send him in, Ellen," Benedict answered.

The door opened, and a tall, elegantly-dressed man in his late forties glided into the room. He was Ernest Crippler, National Security Advisor to the President. The White House barber entered just after him, and, not saying a word, walked behind Benedict's desk, enveloped him to his neck in a white cloth, and began carefully examining his sideburns.

"Ernie, Lye here thinks we may have a problem with Drugonov. What do you have to say about that?"

Crippler approached the desk, and placed his attache case on the floor.

"We shouldn't be overly concerned about Russia, Mr. President. Certainly we should avoid any saber-rattling. What President Drugonov said to the Duma was, in my opinion, just for domestic consumption. He is trying to solidify his political position, that's all."

"You see, Lye? Why worry about a non-problem? Besides, even if Drugonov is serious, who could blame him? We've been pushing around the Russians, and everybody else, for decades. Hell, for a half-century we threatened to blow them off the face of the earth! If I were they, I'd be angry too. Just last week, the Coalition of Scientists for Peace and Justice--the best minds in the country-- published a report blaming us for most of what's gone wrong in the world in our lifetimes, accusing us of aggression and imperialism. Who are we to say they're wrong, Lye?"

"Mr. President, I don't think everyone feels that way," Elfman said.

"Lye, it's generally accepted that we have treated the rest of the world very shabbily, very shabbily indeed. Look at any textbook! Go to any university! Read any editorial! You'll see what they're saying about us! If the rest of the world is angry with us, they have every right to be. I don't think we deserve anything else.

We've acted so selfishly toward others, Lye, always looking out for our own interests. What can we expect but anger and condemnation?"

Elfman looked down at his boss, and saw the conviction on his face. He had never completely accepted the President's line of reasoning, although he had difficulty refuting it. But Benedict seemed to believe it heart and soul. He looked up at Elfman with the fervor of a revival preacher. For some reason that he could not name, it made Elfman feel very uneasy.

What he could not know was that Benedict too felt uncomfortable saying such things. He knew they were true, he just knew it, but actually saying them made his stomach turn with tension. There was something not quite right about condemning one's own country. But he had learned long ago to hide such concerns; they were not fashionable, not the way to be popular, to get elected. Besides, they were wrong, weren't they? All reasonable people agreed that the United States had behaved badly, didn't they?

Benedict shifted his gaze to his National Security Advisor.

"Now, what can I do for you, Ernie?"

Crippler sat down on the nearby sofa.

"Mr. President, I hate to bring this up again, but it has to do with our military force structure in Europe, Asia and the Middle East. Although our forces outside the Middle East have been drastically downgraded since the end of the Cold War, they are still at what many consider to be excessively high levels. Keeping U.S. forces in Europe, Japan and Korea is provocative, at best. I think the situation is coming to a head. With the change of leadership in Russia, I think the time is right to withdraw those forces. Although I believe we have nothing to fear from the Russians, sending a strong message of good will and friendship to President Drugonov would be very wise at this time, sir. It could cement friendly relations between our two countries for many years to come."

The President thought this over once again. U.S. military withdrawals had been the subject of a heated national debate for over a year.

"Well, Ernie, we've certainly discussed this enough in the past. You know how I feel about it. I agree with you, and other right-thinking people, completely. And I agree with you that it's an idea whose time has come. We should end our imperialistic presence in these other countries as quickly as possible. But it's such a drastic move, such a change in direction, I'm afraid of the opposition it would generate."

Crippler said, "With the election only six months away, giving the American people a 'peace dividend' would produce millions of votes. We've tested the waters on the Hill regarding this issue, and I think Congress will go along with us. After all, they want to get reelected too. Sure, there'll be opposition, but I don't think it'll be anything we can't handle. After all, the press will be on our side, and I'm certain they'll make anyone who opposes this look pretty silly."

"You're right, of course. We can always count on them. But still, I'm uncomfortable with it. I'm not quite sure it's the right thing to do, for the country, I mean. What about the argument that it will weaken us, and leave our allies open to aggression?"

The barber noticed that there were beads of sweat on Benedict's forehead and that his facial muscles had grown taut. He could not know how difficult it was for this man to make real decisions, with real consequences. If he had known, he would have been appalled. Finished, the barber removed the cloth and hurriedly left the room before he succumbed to the temptation to say something. He was a Korean War veteran.

Crippler noticed the discomfort, the indecision that the President was feeling. Now is the time to be convincing, to persuade, before the opportunity disappears. He stood and approached Benedict's desk. Smiling, he leaned over it, attempting to create an atmosphere of comradery, to put the Commander-in-Chief at ease. He spoke in a tranquil, level voice.

"Mr. President, we've been all through this many times. Of course it's right for the country, sir. You know that, don't you? In the long run, we will all benefit from an easing of global tensions. As for aggression, everyone knows that we have no real enemies left aside from a few Islamic radicals. All thinking people are agreed on that. It's true that the North Koreans have the atomic bomb, and it's also true that they're exporting nuclear and missile technology to terrorist states. But nuclear technology is generations old. How long can we reasonably expect to keep the genie in the bottle?

"Besides, no one has actually done anything to us, have they? Sure, there was the World Trade Center business, a few sporadic suicide bombings, an occasional anthrax, VX, or smallpox scare. But what part of the world is immune to those sorts of things these days? Can we really expect the United States to be an island of tranquility forever?

"We have to face the fact that there are people in the world who hate us. And haven't we earned it? No, Mr. President, I don't expect Russia to be a problem at all, and as long as we keep paying off the North Koreans with food and oil they shouldn't be a problem either. As long as we play ball, we have nothing to fear from them. And as for troop withdrawals weakening us, well, maybe it's about time that we became a little weaker. After all, we've been throwing our weight around for a long time.

"Withdrawing our forces will convince everyone that our heart is in the right place, that we mean no one harm, that we are ready to assume a more reasonable place in the international community. Oh, sure, some people will object, briefly, until they see the wisdom of your decision. Then they will recognize you for the statesman you truly are. This would play well in the Islamic world as well. They despise us and everything we stand for. Maybe if we withdrew our fangs a bit, we could avoid another World Trade Center disaster. And, as we've discussed many times, we could make it known in certain circles that our support for Israel was, shall we say, becoming less unequivocal. That would make a lot of people in that part of the world very happy, Mr. President."

Benedict looked up into Crippler's eyes with a trace of fear, something close to panic. But then he pursed his lips together and raised his chin resolutely. Crippler had won.

"You're right, Ernie. History will see this as a great step forward. As unpopular as it will be in some quarters, it has to be done. I owe it to the country, and to the world."

"You'll never regret it, Mr. President," Crippler said. He stood erect, and walked back to the sofa, triumphant.

"You won't get any votes over this from the Joint Chiefs," injected Elfman.

Benedict's eyes darted toward his Chief of Staff.

"Oh, who cares about them! They're just a bunch of damn dinosaurs, anyway. They see an enemy behind every bush. If we demobilize those forces, we could save billions of dollars a year."

Benedict's face suddenly burst into a broad grin.

"I know! I could announce that we're going to spend that money on the children!"

"In what way, specifically, Mr. President?" asked Elfman.

"Does it matter, Lye? All I have to do is say that we're going to spend it on the children, and the American people will lap it up like starving dogs! It's worked in the past, remember?"

Now the President was back in his element: domestic politics. The decision made, he felt his muscles unwind. Benedict smiled and winked at his Chief of Staff.

"You've made a wise decision, Mr. President," Crippler said. "Perhaps you could announce it at this morning's press conference?"

"Good idea, Ernie! There's no time like the present. I'll make it a fait accompli, and if it proves to have been the wrong decision, I'll just apologize for it later. That always works. I'll dredge up some crocodile tears, and explain to the American people that I meant well. They won't blame me. They never have."

Satisfied with his morning's work, Ernest Crippler retrieved his attache case and walked to the door. As he opened it to leave, his back to the two other men in the room, an almost imperceptible smile crossed his lips.

The intercom broke the brief silence.

"Mr. President, the Secretary of the Treasury and the Chairperson of the Council of Economic Advisors are here."

"Send them in Ellen," said Benedict.

"Good morning, Mr. President, Lye," the Secretary of the Treasury said as he strode into the room. Grover Cleveland Phillips was all business, as usual. Born into the same Philadelphia banking circle as Benedict, Phillips was the epitome of old, WASP money. Benedict had hesitated to bring him into his administration on that account, having been advised that he should seek 'diversity', but the old ties between their two families had proven to be too strong.

Phillips was an imposing man, six feet four inches tall, graying at the temples, and dressed in a very conservative dark blue suit. Entering just behind him was the Chairperson of the Council of Economic Advisors, Patricia Chung. A luminary at the Stanford Economics Department, Chung helped provide the administration with that well-rounded, multi-cultural image that Benedict had sought to achieve. She had proven to be a valuable addition, having helped the President avoid stumbling on economic policy more than once.

"I have a press conference in just twenty-six minutes, so we'll have to make this fast," the Benedict said.

Chung spoke up.

"Mr. President, I don't know how to make this fast. Once again I must tell you that the concessions to the less developed countries that you are about to make in this press conference, and at your meeting at the U.N. tomorrow, will be catastrophic for the U.S. economy. I know that we have been discussing this for months, and that neither the Secretary nor I have so far been persuasive, but I want to ask you one last time to reconsider."

Phillips, standing in front of Benedict's desk, nodded his head in agreement.

"Yes, Mr. President, I concur. At the very least, we can expect a collapse of the stock market. At worst, it will mean the end of U.S. industry. Even after all of our discussions on this subject, I just don't see why you consider this necessary."

"You don't, Grover?"

Benedict answered in a mildly condescending tone. He folded his hands before himself on the desk, and thought for a moment.

"Tell me, either of you. Do you have any objections to my plans on moral grounds? Can you truthfully tell me that what I am about to do is not the right thing, from a human standpoint?"

Chung and Phillips fidgeted. The seconds passed. Finally, the Secretary of the Treasury spoke up.

"No, of course not, Mr. President. It is generally agreed that we, as a country, have been selfish, even predatory, in our economic relations with others. I have written three books to that effect myself. But in my role as Treasury Secretary, it is my job to warn you of the drastic domestic consequences that these new policies will produce."

"That is my function as well, Mr. President," added Chung. "As you know, I have spent my whole professional career criticizing America's economic hegemony, the way we have sought to control, to dominate our global neighbors. The policies that you want to announce are definitely proper from the standpoint of fairness. No one can argue with that. It's about time that capitalism was brought down a peg or two. But they will have a major disruptive effect here at home."

"I understand that," answered Benedict. "But we have to think of the big picture here."

Clearly, Benedict was referring to his desire to leave a lasting presidential legacy, just in case he was not reelected to a second term.

"Sure our industries will be hurt. But that's the price to be paid for global fairness. They'll survive, somehow. They always have. There may be a temporary increase in unemployment, but our businesses will find ways to put those people back to work, somehow. The private sector in this country is very resilient; I'm confident that it can survive anything that we can throw at it.

"Did you know that rats can tread water for twenty-four hours? Astonishing, really. Our businesspeople are the same way. They're survivors! They'll work themselves to death to keep their businesses going! Their function in life is to generate wealth! I'm convinced that they'll find some way to continue doing that no matter what impediments we put in their way.

"This is the opportunity for us to put into practice the theories that the intellectual community has been advocating for years. I've made promises to those people! I owe them results! Besides, what has big business ever done for me? Did they help me in my last election? No. And they're not helping me in this reelection either.

"As for popular opinion, we have nothing to worry about there. Poll after poll shows that the people are behind us. The vast majority of them support fairness and equity. To make sure it stays that way, the media people in New York and Washington are ready to saturate the airwaves with programming to support me: to hammer home the idea that these selfless policies will benefit billions, including children, all around the world. Believe me! We can't lose!

"But I agree with your basic premise: there will be at least a temporary adverse effect on the economy. I doubt that the stock market will collapse, but I will admit that a lot of people will lose their jobs, but just until our capitalists make the necessary adjustments. Besides, a little belt-tightening will be good for the country. It'll give our people an idea of what the rest of the world has to deal with. Some companies will go out of business. But what the hell! I can't be responsible for every undercapitalized business in America! We'll try to protect the unions, of course. We need them. But none of this will kick in until after the election anyway, so what are we worrying about? I think you're overreacting. If I didn't know you better, I'd say that you both were filthy capitalists!"

That brought a smile to everyone's lips.

"And now, if you'll excuse me, it's time for my makeup people to get me ready for the cameras."

"Thank you for coming, ladies and gentlemen," the President said as he smiled benignly at the gathered press corps and made slight adjustments to the microphone before him. "I have called this press conference to announce a new government offensive in the war against inequity: what I would like to officially name my Fairness Offensive: an offensive against inequality, against poverty, against want, on a global scale. I have recently been meeting with members of the People's Coalition for Fairness, chaired by the very capable Charlene Taft."

He looked to his right as a thin, hawk-faced woman, her hair pulled back severely into a bun, stepped forward a pace, and, frowning, nodded quickly to the reporters, then stepped back behind the President.

"Ms. Taft and her colleagues, along with many other similar groups of concerned citizens around the country, have impressed upon me, indeed upon all of us, the fundamental unfairness of the global distribution of wealth. This is a situation which must be rectified. Every day, innocent children around the world are suffering and dying. Why is this so? Because we, my fellow Americans, have been selfish.

"In life's lottery, we have been fortunate enough to come out winners. We are wealthy, while much of the rest of the world is grappling with a deeply-entrenched poverty. There are many who would argue that we are wealthy because the rest of the world is poor; that we have become wealthy at their expense. Has not our free-market system coerced them into becoming a market for our goods, convincing them to buy products that we make but that they do not need? Have we not extended to them enormous predatory loans, the interest on which has virtually bankrupted their treasuries? Through television and motion-pictures, have we not made them unsatisfied with their own simple peasant lives? Have we not brainwashed them into believing that they cannot be happy unless they have a microwave oven, a computer and a minivan? Have we not corrupted their primitive, pristine cultures, addicting them to such narcotics of Western technology as electricity, indoor plumbing and machinery? We have polluted their air with the products of our automobile plants, and their water with the products of our chemical companies. Our cruel, unrelenting technological innovation makes their own products obsolete and unsalable. The presence of our transnational corporations in their lands draws people away, like some great insidious magnet, from the noble pleasures of a peasant existence and into the dangerous, heartless maelstrom of the cities.

"But, even more treacherously, have we not stripped them of their irreplaceable natural resources to satisfy our unquenchable thirst for luxury? Have we not stolen from them the very means by which they would have been able to lift themselves out of their grinding poverty? We have raped these countries, pilfering from them oil, copper, aluminum and a thousand other commodities at so-called 'market prices' to feed the insatiable maw of our industrial leviathan. Yes, my friends, we have done all that and more.

"Why have we done this? It is because we have been too individualistic. Throughout most of our history, we have thought of ourselves too much, and of others not enough. All of us must learn that our well-being, as individuals, is inconsequential in the greater scheme of things. All Americans must be willing to sacrifice their selfish interests in the name of humanity. Every one of us must become an altruist. I know that a great many of you already agree with me. You too have come to feel the pain of the world's poor. But there continues to exist among us a vile, ruthless gang of individualists, disciples of selfishness. They must be rooted out and punished.

"With that in mind, I am sponsoring legislation that would double the tax on unearned, capital gains. It is the wealthy, the greedy few, who have benefited most from the rest of the world's poverty, so it is only proper for them to contribute to the problem's solution. These revenues will be turned over to a new agency of the United Nations, the Center for Global Fairness, headed by my good friend Mr. Rajiv Gupta of India."

A pudgy, round-faced man stepped forward and gave the assembled reporters a meek smile.

"Mr. Gupta's agency will then redistribute this money around the world on the basis of need. A country's need will be determined mathematically, using a statistical formula of Mr. Gupta's own invention. My Fairness Offensive contains many more provisions that I am sure you will find interesting, even revolutionary, but I prefer to announce those during my meeting at the United Nations tomorrow. But its fundamental premise is clear: from each according to his ability, to each according to his need. We must sacrifice the good of the few for the good of the many."

A loud buzz filled the room as the reporters speculated excitedly amongst themselves. Some, whose contacts within the administration were extensive, were already privy to what these additional provisions might be. Hints had recently appeared in various newspaper columns and on certain television programs. The administration didn't object; first, leaks were inevitable, and secondly, those outlets provided a valuable means of testing the waters.

"And, while we are on the subject of need," Benedict continued, "I would like to discuss the current state of affairs in Russia. The Russian people are in the midst of a great struggle to pull themselves out of a desperate situation. They have been trying in recent years to improve the efficiency of their economy, but, through no fault of their own, they have not yet been successful. In large part, we, the United States, are responsible for their current problems. If we had not expanded our military capability so dramatically in the nineteen-eighties, forcing our Russian friends to exhaust themselves economically in an attempt to meet the growing threat that we presented to their security, they would not now be in this position. I feel that we, as a nation, owe them a debt, and that debt is long overdue. Therefore, I will this afternoon issue an executive order instructing our treasury to transfer to the Central Bank of Russia a sum of money in the amount of fifty billion dollars. Should this be insufficient, it is understood that additional moneys will be made available to them. It is the least we can do."

I've got a winner! Benedict thought as he watched the positive reaction of the reporters. The room hummed as they conversed in low voices, nodding and smiling. When their editorials hit the streets, I should pick up five million votes! Now I'll give them the other barrel!

"A moment ago, I made reference to our military. It is a subject that has been on my mind a great deal lately. Though I myself never served, I have the deepest respect for our valiant men and women in uniform."

Standing on the left side of the room, it was all Benedict's press secretary could do to keep from laughing. If only these people could hear what he really thinks of the military!, he thought, smiling. He remembered the many times Benedict had used his favorite expression to describe the members of the Armed Forces: "knuckle-dragging buffoons," he called them. On one occasion, the President, in one of his lighter moods, had donned the hat of an army general officer, bent over into a gorilla-like posture, and walked around the Oval Office making grunting noises. It had been hilarious! Somber-faced, Benedict continued. He looked down at the podium, biting his lower lip.

"When I think of all the sacrifices they have made for our country, I can only feel the most profound sense of gratitude and admiration."

He looked up at the reporters to note their reaction. They were appropriately solemn.

"But in this post cold-war environment, we must constantly reexamine our genuine defensive needs. We must guard against needless military posturing that might upset our neighbors. Nothing that I am saying here is new. As you all know, we have been discussing this, as a nation, for quite some time. Most Americans have come to realize that, with the Soviet Union gone, what some saw as the principal threat to our security has ceased to exist. Why, then, do we insist on projecting military power around the globe? What purpose does it serve? As I see it, it serves only to make our friends around the world nervous, never sure of our intentions.

"Therefore, in my role as Commander-in-Chief, I am announcing today that the United States will immediately withdraw all of its military forces from Europe, Japan and the Korean peninsula. Furthermore, these redundant units will be deactivated as quickly as possible. I can assure you that in making these force reductions, the military's humanitarian and peace-keeping missions will not be adversely affected.

"Furthermore, I would like to take this opportunity to assure our friends in the Islamic world that the United States will immediately begin the withdrawal of all land and sea forces from Turkey, Kuwait, and the Arabian peninsula, including Qatar and the United Arab Emirates. All of our naval forces will be removed from the Persian Gulf. I am confidant that this act of good will shall ease the tensions in that region and, in conjunction with a revised policy toward Israel and the Palestinian question, cement the bonds between our two peoples."

The room burst into excited speech, as the reporters, most nodding vigorously, expressed their wonder at this revelation, this long-overdue application of common sense. Benedict continued.

"This will result in a considerable reduction in our annual defense expenditures. It will put us in a position to do something far more noble with that money than to spend it on instruments of death."

The President glanced over at his Chief of Staff, who knew that Benedict was now doing what he did so well: thinking on his feet, trying to come up with something that would maximize their political gain. Benedict killed a few seconds by pretending to adjust his microphone once again. He looked up

"I will therefore appoint a task-force to formulate a plan for providing vastly increased funding for our children's public schools. When the time comes, appropriate legislation will be presented to Congress."

Here are a few million more votes from the teachers' unions! The reporters jumped to their feet as a body, applauding vigorously. Here was a true statesman, a real leader! The President motioned for them to sit down. When they had composed themselves, he said,

"And now, I'll be happy to answer any questions that you may have."

Hands shot up around the room, straining for Benedict's attention. He pointed to a petite young woman in the first row, who instantly rose to her feet. She was Sissy Wong, White House correspondent for the National News Network. She had attended one of the most prestigious schools of journalism in America, where she had been taught that her job would be to not simply report the news, but to change the world: that is, to make it more 'fair'.

"Mr. President," she began. "No thinking person questions the enormous debt we owe to the developing world. The policy that you have announced today is certainly a step in the right direction. But many of this country's leading intellectuals argue that the only way to begin repaying such a debt would be through government seizure and auctioning of corporate assets, with the proceeds going to less-developed countries. Do you see this doubling of the capital gains tax as only a first step, with more serious measures to follow later?"

"Well, Sissy," Benedict responded. "Far be it from me to argue with the finest minds in the country on this subject. They know the details of our terrible treatment of the less-developed world much better than I do. As for this tax increase being simply a first step, well, I suggest that you, all of you, watch my speech tomorrow at the U.N. I think that you'll be pleasantly surprised."

Sensing that Benedict's response had ended, the hands instantly rose again. This time he picked a middle-aged man in shirt-sleeves in the fourth row. He was Carl Fitzhough, longtime correspondent for a major wire service. He was a total cynic. He had learned years before that everyone was corrupt, there was no truth, there was no right and no wrong.

"Mr. President, have you communicated with the South Korean government regarding withdrawal of U.S. forces, and, if so, what was their response?"

"No, Carl, I haven't. I don't think that it's really necessary. During our recent ambassadorial-level talks with the North Korean leadership in Pyongyang, they assured us that they had no intention of invading the South. They seemed very sincere. I have no reason to doubt their word. Oh, sure, they've engaged in a few questionable activities over the years. But people change. We must learn to give our neighbors the benefit of the doubt. How else can we make progress in solving the world's problems? Actually, I was very moved by their willingness to forgive all that we have done to them. We have to look at this from their perspective.

"For decades, we have maintained a powerful military presence just south of their homeland. They have been living under what they perceive to be the threat of American aggression for many years. Think of how that would make you feel. Feeling, Carl, feeling is everything! We must take the perceptions of others into consideration in formulating our foreign policy. Who can say that they have been wrong and that we have been right? Who are we to judge? Everyone knows that truth is relative; America's most eminent philosophers have proven it. There is our truth, and there is the North Korean truth.

"I think, my friends that a new era of North Korean-U.S. relations may be just ahead. After all, they did agree to accept a nuclear power plant from us. That's a good start. They have also assured us that they will give serious consideration to halting their proliferation of nuclear and missile technology in exchange for nothing more than a steady supply of food and fuel. Clearly, the North Koreans are holding out to us the olive branch of peace. I think that we should make the next move. The withdrawal of U.S. forces from South Korea will send a strong message to the North that our intentions are pure, that we wish our two peoples to unite in the bonds of international friendship and cooperation.

"In the same vein, we must realize that there is also a Russian truth. Some of your newspapers have published editorials questioning the peaceful intentions of President Drugonov. I think that these are unwarranted and shortsighted. You accuse him of being an aggressor, when it is we who keep divisions on his border, not he on ours. You say that he wants to destroy us, when for decades we pointed horrible weapons of mass-destruction at his homeland.

"Just as we must try to see things from the North Korean perspective, so we must try to see them from the Russian perspective. We must put ourselves in their place. We must try to feel what they feel. For many years, they have seen us extending our tentacles around the world, spreading our capitalist poison from country to country, attempting to subvert honest peoples' revolutions in the name of profit, keeping others poor while we grow rich. How should they view us? What have we done to deserve their good will? The time has come to send the Russians a clear message that we, at long last, recognize the error of our ways and are ready to pay a just penance. Just as withdrawing our forces from South Korea will generate friendship with the North, so withdrawing them from Europe will strengthen Russian-U.S. relations. President Drugonov will see that we mean his country no harm. I look forward to meeting him face to face so I can assure him in person of our good intentions."

"Mr. President! Mr. President!"

Benedict pointed toward the correspondent of a major east coast newspaper.

"You mentioned a revised policy toward Israel and the Palestinian question. Could you elaborate?"

"Certainly," Benedict began. "The United States has had a very close relationship with Israel since that country was founded. I have no intention of jeopardizing that relationship. But if lasting peace is to come to the region, I believe we must change our basic understanding of the conflict. We must begin to recognize that our policies toward the Middle East have their roots in something very deep and very fundamental: civilization itself. The United States, Western Europe, Canada, Australia, New Zealand, all are part of Western Civilization. We share a common history and a common culture. Israel is also a member of that civilization. But she is like a waif, an orphan, separated from her family and embedded in a region of strangers.

"Since nineteen forty-eight we have supported Israel as we would support a member of our own family. That is only natural. It is what one writer called 'kin-country rallying.' But in doing so, we have alienated another civilization: that of Islam. I believe it is time we dealt with the countries and the peoples of that region more evenhandedly. We should not let our civilizational connections with one state blind us to the legitimate aspirations of others. And I am not speaking here only of the Palestinians. We must seek to strengthen our ties with the entire Islamic world. It too has needs, desires, and, yes, even demands, that we should seriously consider. Their quarrel with us is not limited to our support of Israel. I am convinced that if Israel ceased to exist tomorrow, we would still be despised in much of the Islamic world. And with good reason.

"We, as a people, as a civilization, are an affront to everything they believe in. To them, we are, quite simply, intolerable. Is it any wonder that they send their martyrs to destroy our skyscrapers, to poison our water supplies, to detonate radioactive 'dirty bombs' in our cities, to spread death and destruction among us in any way they can?

"Islamic civilization comprises well over one billion people. That fact alone should give us pause. For a whole host of reasons, they see the world in a very different light than we do. At times, it is difficult for us to understand. But we must try. We must begin to look at the world through an Islamic lens, so to speak. We must understand their frustrations, their anger, their resentment. We must realize that for many of them, our very existence on this planet is almost unbearable. Our culture, our beliefs, almost everything we do and say represents to them the worst form of sacrilege. For many, though certainly not all, we are seen as polluters: potential destroyers of all that they believe and value. They feel frustration and rage at their inability to fend off the constant intrusions that our culture inflicts upon them.

"Thirteen centuries ago, the Arabic peoples constituted the most technologically innovative civilization in the world. From algebra to medicine, they led the globe. Then, with the coming of Islam, they adopted faith, mysticism, as their paradigm: their way of viewing reality. Their progress ceased. Centuries later, the West did just the opposite: rejected faith and adopted reason as its paradigm. Western civilization became the innovator. The Islamic world saw itself falling further and further behind, until it became nothing more than a backwater. If it were not for oil, it would still be just that. It found itself incapable of fending off political and military domination by the West. It was partitioned at the whim of Western politicians, its people subjugated. They could not understand how Islamic civilization, the purest and holiest in the world, could be so impotent in the face of this infidel onslaught. They became confused, angry and resentful.

"Some have reacted in the only way they know how: with what some would call terrorism. Airline hijacks, the destruction of the World Trade Center and the Pentagon, and all of the other unfortunate events of recent years are indicative of people who have reached their limit. We call them terrorists, but that is not how they see themselves. Always remember that one man's terrorist is another man's freedom-fighter. If we are to share this world amicably with those who hate and fear us, we must strive to be as inoffensive and as unobtrusive as possible, to recognize and respect the fundamental differences among us. If they lash out in their frustration and their hatred, we must try to be understanding. Above all, we must be culturally neutral and resist the temptation to engage in kin-country rallying. We must recognize the fact that their culture is every bit as good, every bit as valid and as worthwhile as our own. After all, every enlightened person agrees that all cultures are equally efficacious. All knowledgeable people have accepted multi-culturalism as a fact of life. It is axiomatic in this day and age. Our culture, our Western civilization, our beliefs, our values, are no better than theirs, and we should not act as if they were. The only difference is that ours is based on reason, theirs on faith. In spite of its technological shortcomings, Islamic civilization is every bit our equal.

"The military withdrawals that we are about to make in the Middle East, as well as in the rest of the world, should send a clear message to our Islamic friends that the world as they have known it, with us in the role of cultural imperialists, is changing forever. Should they strike at us again, we will do our best to try to understand, and will redouble our efforts to be good neighbors on this blue marble hurtling through space, this Earth that we all must share."

CHAPTER SIX

The Pentagon

General Mike Krajewski, Chairman of the Joint Chiefs of Staff, pushed the off button on his TV remote so hard that the plastic cracked.

"What the hell was that, Bob?" he shouted, shaking his finger at the blank screen, his finger vibrating with rage. "Will 'ya tell me? What the hell was that?"

Lieutenant General Bob Halleck, Krajewski's Chief of Staff, sat, numbed, in a chair on the other side of the office.

"I don't know, Mike," he said in a detached tone. "I don't believe what I just heard."

"Oh, you freakin' heard it all right! That son of a bitch has lost his freakin' mind!"

General Krajewski strode across the room, spun his Rolodex, and punched a long string of numbers into the phone. He stood there, hand on hip, ramrod straight, waiting for the international connections to be completed.

Michael Krajewski had been born into a working-class Polish-American neighborhood in Buffalo. Everyone had been thrilled when he was accepted at West Point. After serving three tours of duty in Viet Nam, he emerged as a highly-decorated hero, with a reputation for being absolutely fearless and for not taking any guff from anyone. He became a marked man. He had caught the attention of the brass. Rising through the ranks steadily, paying his dues at each pay grade, he finally reached the top. Today, in his sixties, he could still run the obstacle course with the best of them. The last connection to Seoul was made.

"Hello," he said loudly. "This is General Krajewski in Washington. I would like to speak with General Kim please."

After a moment, he heard a familiar voice on the other end of the line; he had known and respected Kim Young Soon for twenty years.

"Soon, it's good to hear your voice! ... What's that? ... Yes, I was about to ask you if you had seen it ... What? ... Calm down, Soon ... I know it's insane ... No, I have no explanation ... Look, Soon, this was just as much of a surprise to me as it was to you ... Hell, no, it wasn't done on my recommendation! ... I don't know, Soon. I'll try. I'll meet with the president this afternoon and see if I can't get this decision reversed ... Yes, I know Soon, the survival of your country is at stake ... Yes, of course. I'll speak with you later ... Goodbye, my friend."

Krajewski pushed the button on the phone, breaking the connection. He kept the receiver to his ear as he punched in the numbers for NATO headquarters in Europe.

"God dammit, Bob! This is going to turn into a real shit-storm if I can't convince that crazy bastard to reverse himself."

"I know, Mike," General Halleck said. "Jesus, I hate to talk about the president like this. It goes against everything I believe in."

"Me too, Bob. But how else should we talk about him? He's placing our country in grave danger! I think he's in a goddam state of denial! He hands South Korea to the North on a silver platter, and gives that nut-case Drugonov a free hand in Europe, all in the same day! Drugonov has announced that he intends to attack us! What does he have to do, tattoo the message on the president's forehead?"

Just then the connection to Europe was completed.

"This is General Krajewski at the Pentagon. Put me through to General Hardtman immediately."

SACEUR, or Supreme Allied Commander, Europe, General Felix Hardtman, came on the line almost instantly.

"Felix? This is Mike...So, you've heard...Hell, I don't know, Felix! Don't ask me what's going on around here! I'm only the Chairman of the freakin' Joint Chiefs! ... No, I had no input at all ... I don't know who's influencing him. It sure as hell isn't me! ... I'll do my damnest, Felix! ... To hell with an appointment! As soon as I hang up this phone, I'm going to the White House ... All right, I'll get back to you."

Krajewski hung up the phone and punched the button on his intercom.

"Flo, send for my car pronto! And cancel all my appointments for this afternoon!"

National Security Advisor Ernest Crippler glanced at his watch as he drove along the rural Virginia road. Good, he thought. He would not be expected back at the White House for several hours. He had plenty of time. As he drove, he thought about his life; how he had gotten to where he was today. He remembered the nineteen sixties, when it had all started.

He had been a student at Columbia University during the Viet Nam War. Like most of his classmates, he had developed an intense hatred for that war, and for the government that sponsored it. Unlike most of them, all these years later, that hatred still burned within him. Encouraged by his professors, he had immersed himself in Marxist theory. With time, his hatred of the United States, and everything it represented, grew even more powerful. He came to see his country not only as a war-monger, but, through its capitalist system, as the principal source of evil in the world. In his senior year, he vowed that he would do everything within his power to destroy it.

He had been tempted during those years to join the various Marxist organizations that espoused his political views: the Students for a Democratic Society, the Youth Against War and Fascism, but he had taken the long view; he wanted nothing on his record that would ever call attention to his radical sentiments. He wanted to be sure that, when the time came, he would be able to get into the government he so desperately wanted to destroy. He knew that the way to defeat his enemies was not to throw a Molotov cocktail at an ROTC building, but instead to become part of the system: to work his way into a policymaking position, and then use his authority to bring down the whole rotten show.

All of his years of patient planning, of simmering resentment, of marking time in subordinate positions, were finally paying off. He was very near the apex of power in Washington at precisely the time when there had arisen in Russia a leader who had the strength to openly challenge the capitalists, who was not afraid to risk everything to achieve justice in the world. He, Crippler, would welcome the enslavement of America, if it indeed came to that; such punishment was overdue.

Crippler left the pavement when he turned right onto a dirt farm road. Three-quarters of a mile further on, he came to an old rock wall fence. Before stopping, he scanned the area three hundred sixty degrees to make sure that he was alone. Satisfied, he stopped the car and got out. He walked through the long, unkempt weeds to a specific spot on the wall and grasped the third stone from the top. Wiggling it back and forth, he removed it. From the recess he withdrew a sheet of paper that had been folded into quarters. He put it into his jacket pocket and quickly replaced the stone. He got into his car and drove away. Once again it had gone well. He was eager to read his new instructions. The thought of playing a key role in this monumental event, this changing of the world order, the destruction of the United States, made him light-headed. Just how key a role he was about to play, he would soon discover.

CHAPTER SEVEN

San Diego, California

Lieutenant Paul Birkett finished his one hundredth pushup and rose to his feet from the bedroom floor. He lifted his arms to his sides and moved them in a circular motion to stretch his pectoral muscles. His superb physical conditioning was a source of great pride to him, almost as great as the pride he derived from being a member of the most elite fighting force in the world: the U.S. Navy SEALS.

"Paul, breakfast's ready!" called out his wife, Carol, from the kitchen. He heard the patter of running feet in the hallway just before two children burst into the room.

"Daddy, Daddy!" they both called out as he squatted down and they ran toward him. He wrapped his arms around them both and stood up, kissing each child on the cheek.

"What are you two monkeys doing up so early?" he asked them.

Sam, his six year-old son blurted out, "We want you to take us to work with you so we can go swimming!"

Five year-old Kathleen agreed. "Yes, Daddy! Can we go, pleeeeeeze?"

"There's a swimming pool right outside," Paul said. "You can swim there all day if you want."

"Yes, but there aren't any sharks in the swimming pool!" Sam protested. "We want to go swimming in the ocean, with the sharks!"

Paul laughed softly as he carried his two children toward the kitchen. He loved them so much it hurt. "So you want to swim with the sharks, huh? Well then, you'd better eat a good breakfast, so you can get big and strong. Sharks are tough, you know."

Putting Sam and Kathleen down on the checkered linoleum floor, Paul walked to the stove where Carol was busy turning over fried eggs. He wrapped his arms around her waist and kissed her firmly on the right side of her neck, emitting a low suggestive growl that only she could hear. Carol smiled. She loved being the object of her husband's passion. And after seven years, that passion was a strong as it had been when they were dating.

"Lieutenant Birkett, this is no time for funny business. You have to eat your breakfast and go to work," she said with mock command authority.

"Yes, ma'am!" he answered in feigned seriousness, as he turned and sat down at the table.

Carol placed the heaping plate of food in front of him. One thing was certain: she never had to worry about him getting fat. A SEAL burned up so many calories in a day that that was almost impossible. She made sure that his meals were always high in complex carbohydrates, as the Navy recommended, to give him the energy he needed to keep up with the rigorous demands placed upon him.

"What's on the schedule today?" Carol asked him, a note of apprehension in her voice.

"Well, after PT, we're going for an ocean swim and then we're going to do some demolition work. The Navy's got some new stuff they want us to test," he answered.

"Please be careful, Paul. I know you guys are all experts, but that sort of thing still scares me."

"Don't worry about a thing, honey. Nothing I work with goes 'bang' until I want it to. And you know how I love to make things go 'bang'!"

"It's the little boy in you. You and Sam are like two peas in a pod. He's as fascinated with anything that explodes as you are. Remember last Fourth of July? The fireworks almost drove him crazy!"

Paul laughed. "How could I forget! Sam was so excited I practically had to chain him down! I think we've got another SEAL in the making!"

Carol sighed, but there was a smile on her lips. "Two in one family! That would be almost too much to bear!"

Paul was an officer in SEAL Team Three, stationed in California for deployment in the Middle East, should the need arise. His team was constantly preparing itself for its next Warning Order: instructions for carrying out a mission involving a wide range of potential activities. Any SEAL mission was, by definition, fraught with danger. It was Paul's job to see that his men were so highly trained, in such an intense state of readiness that they were prepared to deploy at a moment's notice and carry out a mission in such a way so as to minimize that danger.

Like all SEALs, Paul was strongly, openly and proudly patriotic. Having grown up in a small town in Minnesota, he had early-on been imbued with a powerful, middle-American love for his country. He had taken some ribbing about that in college, but it had done nothing to shake his belief that the United States was the best place in the world, by several orders of magnitude. He, and all his comrades in arms were ready to lay down their lives for that country anytime, anywhere. They were the best of the best.

Paul finished breakfast, went into the bathroom to brush his teeth, and returned to the kitchen. He put his hands lightly around Carol's waist as she slipped her arms around his neck. He kissed her gently on the lips. Sam and Kathleen, sitting across from each other at the table, were sword-fighting with their spoons, giggling gleefully. Paul realized that right here in this room were three of the best reasons in the world for him to do his job well.

"Come back in one piece," she said to him as she did each morning.

"You can bet on it," he answered, as always. He gave her a big smile and walked out the door toward the garage, his mind already on the upcoming day's work.

CHAPTER EIGHT

President Judas Benedict sat down heavily in the chair behind his desk, tired from the aftereffects of the adrenalin high he always received from giving a press conference. Standing before him were the Secretaries of State and Defense, the Attorney General and the Senate Majority Leader, as well as Lysander Elfman, his Chief of Staff.

"Sit down, everybody, please," Benedict said. After they had done so, he continued, "Well, what did you think of it?"

The Secretary of State, Sanford P. Blanchard, cleared his throat as he usually did when he was preparing to grace someone with his silver-tongued oratory. The President found it somewhat annoying, but dismissed the idiosyncrasy as the price to be paid for having the tall, dignified Wise Man of Washington in his cabinet. President Benedict had known Blanchard for many years. Their paths had crossed often in their lives, and Benedict had become intimately familiar with his Secretary of State's personal history and with his philosophy of life as well.

Blanchard had been a professor at an ivy league university, where he had made a name for himself in Social Science circles by publishing his magnum opus, *"Nostra Culpa: Western Guilt in Third World Poverty."* He had then gone on to be President of the World Bank. During his tenure there, every loan that the organization made was defaulted on, but that didn't matter; their intentions had been good, and that was what counted. Blanchard had made a point of lending to the least credit-worthy countries in the world, because, after all, weren't they the most needy? Had they not been raped most thoroughly by the greedy, individualistic West? The President knew that Blanchard was proud of his perfect default rate; he saw the waste of Western resources as a form of penance. He had told the President some years earlier that he was not phased in the slightest by the fact that the national leadership of these countries insisted on engaging in wasteful, unproductive activities, or that they consisted of murdering kleptocrats with no concern for their own citizens. These people were the products of different cultures, he had argued, and all educated people agreed that culture was relative: there were no good cultures and no bad ones, so what basis was there for condemnation? Theft and murder may not be condoned by Blanchard's culture, he had said, but in others they were considered acceptable. And so, as far as he was concerned, they were beyond reproach.

Blanchard said, "Mr. President, today you have taken a significant step toward enhancing your legacy as the 'Peace President'. Your policy pronouncements today were in keeping with the highest traditions of idealism in international relations. I was especially impressed with your emphasis on feeling what our neighbors are feeling. Truly, that is the way to achieve peace in today's world. I have been saying as much for years, but previous administrations were always so lacking in trust, so unsympathetic to the perceptions of other countries. They were so unwilling to humble our nation, to show the rest of the world our fallibility, our weak side, if you will, to convince others that we presented no threat to them. Your speech today should not only reassure the North Koreans and the Russians regarding our lack of aggressive intentions, but it should help convince the entire less-developed world that we are finally willing to accept our rightful, and morally proper, place in the community of nations. We will no longer be the 'Colossus of the North', but instead just a wretched supplicant, ready and willing to place ourselves at their feet and ask for forgiveness for decades of misdeeds and maltreatment. As I have always said, until every American can put himself in the place of the poorest peasant in the poorest country in the world, until he can feel what that person feels, until he bleeds and suffers a little, our debt to humanity will not be paid."

"Thank you, Sanford," the President said. While he agreed with Blanchard's views, he thought the man a bit long-winded.

"Yes, Mr. President, I agree. It was a great step forward," said Lupe Martinez, Secretary of Defense. The President was well aware of the fact that Secretary Martinez knew virtually nothing about the military or defense. But it was remarkable how few seemed to know of her ignorance outside the inner-circle of the White House. She was the Queen of Bluster.

In speaking about defense-related issues, she could bob and weave and dodge verbal bullets as well as anyone in town. The President never tired of watching her on the Sunday morning talk shows. He suspected that someone in the press must be in on her little secret. It was difficult to believe that such a stupendous lack of knowledge in what was supposed to be one's field of expertise could long remain a secret in Washington, especially when the ignoramus held such a critical, life-and-death position. But if anyone did know, they were not making it public.

On Sunday mornings they asked her nothing but softball questions. After all, she was very politically correct, and it appeared that the press would do anything—including jeopardizing national security—rather than make her look bad. Benedict had chosen her for purely political purposes. She had brought him millions of votes from women and Hispanics. At this moment, she felt obliged to contribute to the conversation.

"We can do without all of those soldiers in those different places," she said. "After all, we'll still have a lot of them left."

Everyone in the room waited for something more profound to come from the Secretary of Defense. After a moment of embarrassed silence, it became obvious that no profundities would be forthcoming.

"I, too, agree with Secretary Blanchard, Mr. President." It was Henley Forsythe, Attorney General. The President shifted his gaze and studied the man's soft, effeminate features, finding them mildly repulsive. He recalled some of the details of Forsythe's past.

He had begun his career directly out of law school as a self-proclaimed consumer advocate. No corporation in America had been immune from his attacks; many of them had gone out of business, leaving tens of thousands unemployed. But the President knew that Henley Forsythe was not concerned with the fate of individuals; it was the well-being of the state that interested him. He had really come into national prominence when he was able to convince a jury that the manufacturer of a firearm was responsible for the death of a young hoodlum who had been shot by a store owner during an attempted robbery. Since that day, he had had the gun companies on the run, and he intended to pursue them to the end. As he had made clear to Benedict many times, he now saw his mission in life as consisting of the total removal of all firearms from the hands of civilians. But this objective was, he had explained, merely the first step--a necessary prerequisite–toward the accomplishment of a much greater, more grandiose goal.

Henley Forsythe was a statist. One of his favorite expressions was that a good government was a strong government. He was infamous for lecturing anyone within earshot about the subject: a good government had overwhelming power over its citizenry, and was willing to use that power to achieve worthwhile goals; the most important of these goals was order; chaos was intolerable; each individual was to be a cog in a wheel within the great machine of the state. On and on he would go.

If the recipient of this lecture could not find some excuse to leave, he would discover that Forsythe was capable of talking for hours about the glories of what could only rightly be called totalitarianism. Of course, Forsythe never referred to it by that name. That particular word was one of the great taboos of the American political lexicon. An American politician might well be a totalitarian, but to admit as much constituted political suicide.

What mystified the President was that the ultimate purpose of this great machine about which Forsythe was so endlessly enthused seemed to have eluded him. It was as if the man had never given that crucial aspect of it much thought. Ideologically, he almost defied classification. He didn't seem to be a Marxist; he didn't appear to be particularly attracted to the idea of redistribution of wealth. He apparently didn't care about the well being of people. Benedict had never detected within him a sense of class-consciousness, nor a vision of a Master Race. It seemed that it was simply the notion of the absolute state that fascinated him: power for the sake of power. He had once told the President that, as a young man, when he had first read Orwell's 'Nineteen Eighty Four', he had found himself rooting for Big Brother. Benedict was left to conclude that perhaps the best way to describe him was as the ultimate technocrat.

Forsythe had made a careful study of the histories of statist regimes around the world, and had often told Benedict that if authoritarian government were to succeed, the first step was to remove the means of resistance from the populace. A certain amount of dissent was to be permitted as window dressing, but it should never be permitted to threaten the Ultimate Good: the Omnipotent State. An armed citizenry presented such a threat. Stalin and Hitler had acted appropriately, he said. They had made the disarming of their respective citizenries a top priority upon coming to power. Such a step was necessary to achieve order. Forsythe had made it clear that he was intent upon accomplishing that same goal in the United States. He avoided Second Amendment issues by simply refusing to discuss them. The press was only too happy to oblige.

Benedict had chosen him as Attorney General because the polls had indicated that a strong anti-gun position would bring in electoral votes from New York and California. Henley Forsythe had no friends: he scared people. Forsythe continued, "I personally think that a U.S. military pullback is a wonderful idea, but there are some in this country who will not."

"To whom are you referring, specifically, Henley?" the President asked.

"Oh, you know, all the self-styled patriots who don't see things quite the way we do."

He looked around the room and saw a unanimous nodding of heads.

"As crazy as it sounds, they might look at it as compromising U.S. security. Lord knows, we have enough trouble as it is with these militia groups!"

The President gave Forsythe a steady stare.

"Do you mean that you don't have a handle on those people, Henley?"

Forsythe raised his hands in front of himself as if in self-defense.

"Of course we do, Mr. President! I didn't mean to suggest otherwise! We've spent a lot of time and effort infiltrating their organizations. I can assure you that we have names and addresses. And naturally, we have a list of all the gun owners in the country. We can move on them any time we like, anytime that the situation demands. And I believe that time may be now."

"Explain yourself, Henley," the President said.

"Mr. President, the new policy initiatives that you proposed, and those additional ones that you will propose at the U.N. tomorrow, will be very unpopular among certain segments of the population. I'm not speaking just of the rabid constitutionalists. I'm also speaking of veterans, law enforcement agencies, and even the active-duty military.

"The military and law enforcement will follow orders; they always have, and we have no reason to believe that they won't now. But there are millions of civilians who might, according to their own warped reasoning, consider these policies to be, well, a bit tyrannical."

Benedict sat bolt upright in his chair, his jaw muscles visibly tight from the clenching of his teeth. The idea that anyone might consider him tyrannical had never occurred to him. Yes, much of what he did was outside the bounds of the Constitution, but what of it? Besides, everything he did was for the good of the collective, wasn't it? Tyrannical? Ridiculous!

"Let me rephrase that, Mr. President," Forsythe said, back-pedaling frantically after seeing the change in his boss's countenance. "What I meant to say is that they may see it as an overreaching on the part of the national government. It may occur to these people to resist our efforts. And, more to the point, they have the means to resist. They are armed. These are the people we have to worry about, to guard against."

Sanford Blanchard spoke up. "But surely, Henley, these unorganized armed civilians couldn't hope to overcome the full weight of the military and law enforcement communities!"

Forsythe answered, "Don't underestimate the power of an armed populace, Sanford. We learned a lesson about that in Viet Nam, and the Soviets learned the same lesson in Afghanistan. So have many others over the years. I think that the greatest threat to order in this country in the future, given the new directions that we will be taking, will be from an armed citizenry. With that in mind, Mr. President, I suggest that you will have to decide whether you are truly committed to these new positions, or whether you are willing to forego them in the name of domestic tranquility."

The President looked somewhat startled that he should be expected to make such an important decision on such short notice. He pondered it for a moment, drumming his left index finger slowly against the desk. The cabinet members waited expectantly.

"Damn it, Henley! I've committed myself! There would be a hell of a political price to pay if I backed down now! Besides, I really believe in what I said out there! I believe we have been wrong! I believe things have to change! No! I'm moving forward with my policies as I just outlined them to the American people!"

"In that case, Mr. President, to protect those policies, and those that I'm sure will follow in the future, I'm afraid that we will be compelled to take certain ... certain measures. I think we should consider emergency gun control legislation; we could nip this situation in the bud, so to speak. You could even do it by executive order."

"What did you have in mind, Henley?" the President asked, an interested tone in his voice. The thought of millions of armed Americans walking around unrestrained, outside the control of government, had always made him nervous.

Repeating a mantra that had been running through his mind for years, Forsythe said, "We could outlaw, and confiscate, all handguns and center-fire rifles. We could give everyone a seven-day grace period to turn them in. If we need legal cover, we could claim that firearms fall under the interstate commerce clause. It's a flimsy argument, but it will tie up the debate in the courts for months. By then, it'll be all over."

The senate majority leader whistled softly as he considered the political implications. The President steepled his fingers in front of his face and looked at the senator.

"Well, Willard, what do you think? Will it fly, politically?"

"Hell no, it won't, Mr. President!" Willard Howell answered. "It's taking too big a bite at one time! You know our approach to gun control has always been incremental: take small steps, boil the frog slowly, and the gun nuts won't get too angry. This would really stir them up! Some of my people are facing reelection, you know."

The President turned to Forsythe. "Well, Henley, there you have it. What you are suggesting is simply not politically possible."

Lye Elfman spoke up.

"Besides that, what about the Second Amendment, Mr. President? Can we simply ignore the Constitution at will?"

The other people in the room looked at each other with surprised expressions, momentarily at a loss for words. Finally, President Benedict broke the silence with a hearty laugh.

"Why Lye! I'm surprised at you! Of course we can ignore the Constitution! We've been doing it for years! Oh, we pay attention to bits and pieces of it, the convenient parts: freedom of speech and the press, the rights of the accused, what the Supreme Court has been calling the 'preferred freedoms.' But the rest of it has been up for grabs since before any of us were born! Remember, the Constitution is a 'living document'."

He winked at everyone in the room.

"Its meaning changes with circumstance."

"Thank God for that!" injected Senator Howell. Everyone chuckled.

Elfman said, "Are you absolutely sure that the Court would stand with us on this? If you issue an executive order confiscating guns, we don't want to get hamstrung by a constitutional challenge."

"Don't worry about them, Lye," answered the President. "The Court hasn't stood up for the Constitution since the Roosevelt administration. They're not going to start now. Hell, one of the justices even announced publicly that the Constitution is irrelevant! Remember? How could they be more accommodating? No, I'm not worried about that part of it. But I don't want to take too much political heat from the gun lobby either. Somehow, we'd have to make it look as if I had no choice in the matter."

"Exactly, Mr. President," Forsythe said. "And that brings us to my next point."

He smiled slightly, leaned forward in his seat, and placed his elbows on his knees in a vaguely conspiratorial posture. His eyes went from face to face as if he were attempting to gauge everyone's loyalty. Finally, he looked at the President.

"My suggestion may not be politically possible under current conditions, Mr. President. But if those conditions were to change..."

"What? What are you thinking?" Benedict asked, genuinely interested. He too leaned forward, as if to join the conspiracy.

"Mr. President, the people of this country have been hypersensitive about terrorism ever since the World Trade Center disaster. But every terrorist act since then has been caused by foreigners. We haven't had an act of domestically-inspired terrorism since Oklahoma City. If we were to experience a sudden upsurge in acts of domestic terrorism, serious acts that would shock the nation, that would shake the country to its roots, isn't it possible that the political climate toward gun confiscation could change?"

"Well, yes. I suppose it could. But as you said, we've had no such problems and no reason to believe that we will in the future," the President answered.

Forsythe continued, his voice low. "But those sorts of incidents can be, shall we say, manufactured."

There was a shocked silence in the room as everyone stared at the Attorney General. Finally, Senator Howell said, "Good Lord, Henley, are you suggesting that we..."

Forsythe raised his hands as if to call for silence. He said, "Now wait a minute. Hear me out."

He turned to the President, who was looking at him with a quizzical gaze.

"What I am suggesting is distasteful. I understand that. But this is hardball politics. We're playing for all the marbles here. I'm talking about the possibility of armed resistance to the United States government: insurrection, possible assassination attempts. Mr. President, do you want to be this country's next martyr?

"I don't know about the rest of you, but I don't want to be on the receiving end of a bullet from one of these constitutionalist wackos. And you know as well as I do that they can get to us; none of us is safe from an intelligent, determined assassin who's willing to give up his life."

Again, there was silence in the Oval Office as each person reflected on the truth of Forsythe's statement. Then the President said, "Henley, I think that what you are suggesting goes beyond..."

"Mr. President, do you want your policies to succeed or not? Do you want to go down in history as the man who changed the country, and the world, for the better, or as a failure, and an assassinated failure to boot?" Forsythe asked.

Benedict fidgeted. He looked to the others for support, but they offered none. He was alone. He would have to make this decision himself.

"I don't know, Henley. This is so drastic..."

"Drastic times call for drastic measures, Mr. President," Forsythe said. "Your survival, our survival, political and perhaps even physical, is at stake."

The President hesitated. Then he said, "What, specifically, are you thinking of?"

The Attorney General exhaled audibly, as if realizing that he had turned the corner in this discussion. He became more animated, almost excited.

"Well sir, I think that if we could place bombs aboard a number of domestic commercial airline flights, and then make it appear that several militia groups claimed responsibility, that would turn the country around. The people would demand confiscation! We could even arrange to crash an airliner into a nuclear power plant! All the experts say that a reactor dome could withstand such an impact. If they're right, any real danger would be minimal. If we could pin that on a militia group–maybe even on the NRA itself--the country would go berserk!"

Lysander Elfman, who had been sitting off to one side, at the fringes of this conversation, finally spoke up.

"Mr. President, this is madness! Surely you can't be considering..."

The President raised his hand, stopping his Chief of Staff in mid-sentence. "Now wait a minute, Lye. I don't like this any more than you do, but

Henley may have something here. I'm in the process of changing the entire world order. It only stands to reason that there would be a price to pay for that. After all, you can't make an omelet without breaking a few eggs. We have to think of the greatest good for the greatest number."

Elfman sat dumbfounded, but he raised no further objections. Forsythe added, "I don't think we're talking about more than fifteen hundred casualties, two thousand tops. That's a small price to pay, given the stakes--the personal stakes--for all of us."

The President of the United States looked around the room.

The Secretary of Defense was studying her fingernails. The Secretary of State stared at the floor. The Senate Majority Leader gazed off into space. No one said anything.

"I want it understood that I never approved this!" Benedict said vehemently. "I never gave it my O.K.! Does everyone in this room agree to that? I want you to know, Henley, that I was not involved with whatever you are about to do! I had no part in planning or executing it and I gave no orders to anyone else to do so! Is that clear to everyone here?"

Everyone nodded his or her approval, a few mumbling "Yes, Mr. President. Henley Forsythe smiled knowingly at the President and said, "Absolutely clear, sir. And if anyone disputes that in the future, we can always argue that it depends on how one defines 'plan'."

The last of the cabinet members had no sooner left the Oval Office than the intercom buzzed.

"Yes, Ellen," the President answered.

"Mr. President, General Krajewski is here to see you."

Benedict felt a cold chill run through him. He had been dreading this. He had never been able to deal well with men like Krajewski. Such men didn't hesitate to disagree, to stand up for what they thought was right. That made the President nervous; he had always felt nervous when dealing with people who thought in terms of black and white, right and wrong. He felt uncomfortable when faced with such absolutes. All his life he had been an advocate of reassuring, middle positions, shades of gray. Everything was subject to compromise, because, after all, there was no truth, no right or wrong, and, ultimately, so the philosophers said, no reality. So how could anyone take a firm position on anything? It had never made sense to Benedict. Something about it frightened him.

He knew that his policy of military withdrawal must have incensed the General, and this made him even more uncomfortable. Krajewski wouldn't like him because of it. And Benedict needed to be liked. Krajewski would tell him he was wrong. But Benedict needed to be right. Benedict was always right. That was the whole point of compromise, wasn't it? Krajewski would confront him with reality. But there was no reality, was there? Everyone agreed on that, didn't they? He began to feel nauseous, began to feel the gorge rise in his throat: panic, what will I do, run, hide, avoid, delay.

"Ah, Ellen, does the General have an appointment?"

"No, sir. He doesn't."

"Tell him I'm busy. Tell him I'll meet with him after I return from New York."

"Yes, Mr. President."

CHAPTER NINE

New York, The office of the U.S. Ambassador to the United Nations.

"I'm telling you, Judas, these people are in an absolute feeding frenzy! They've smelled blood in the water since that press conference you gave yesterday, and they sound like they won't be satisfied with anything less than the family jewels!"

"Well, Paul, I'm sure that we can agree on an arrangement that is acceptable to everyone involved. After all, these are reasonable people we're dealing with," the President answered.

"Reasonable, hell!" Paul Imhoff said. "Most of them see the United States as the focus of evil in the world, the Great Satan, the source of all their problems. For years they've wanted nothing more than to nail our hides to the barn door. And you've given them the best opportunity to do that that they've ever had!"

The President gazed out the window at the New York skyline.

"Has it ever occurred to you, Paul, that they may be right?"

Imhoff looked at Benedict, his old prep school classmate, as he might look at a particularly strange museum exhibit: not quite knowing what to make of it, not knowing whether he liked it or hated it.

"No, Judas. That has never occurred to me. And for the life of me, I don't know why it occurs to you. What's happened to you? You were never like this years ago. Where did this negativism come from, this questioning of everything we used to believe in?"

"I've grown up, Paul. I've seen the world as it really is: the suffering, the greed, the willingness of some to victimize others."

"And you think that caving in to this New International Economic Order of theirs will solve everything?"

"No, Paul. But it's a start. Let's go meet the ambassadors."

The President and the U.S. ambassador took the elevator to another floor, and entered a large conference room filled with representatives from the less-developed countries of the world. The noise level was high, the various ambassadors waving their hands, shaking their fingers, scattered across the room in colorful knots, their native garb fluttering with each gesticulation.

President Benedict walked to the front of the room and stood behind the podium. Gradually, the noise diminished as the representatives took their seats. He noticed that the television cameras in both corners of the room were sweeping back and forth across the assembled representatives, while the one at the back pointed straight at him. Good, he thought. The American people, and the entire world, will hear and see my message. They will all see me as the progressive, socially-conscious man that I am.

He noticed that his palms were sweaty. Odd, he thought. I know that what I am about to do is right---right for the vast majority of people, for the collective. I am about to tell the world that the United States will engage in the greatest act of economic self-sacrifice in history. How can that be wrong? Why am I nervous? Why do I feel this way? He thought of the domestic opposition that his speech might produce, and his anxiety level went up another notch. He tried to dismiss it. He assured himself that anyone who would oppose such pure, selfless altruism was beneath his contempt. They were, weren't they? At any rate, he thought, by the time the press gets through praising what I am about to say, pumping it up, selling it to the American people, anyone who disagrees will come across as the worst sort of petty ankle-biter. They will, won't they? Through an act of will, Benedict calmed himself.

"Ladies and gentlemen," the President began. "I'm sure all of you are familiar with what I said in my press conference in Washington yesterday. What I said, I meant. This meeting marks the beginning of a new relationship between the United States and the countries of the developing world."

As he looked around the room, he saw a mixture of reactions, dominated by hostility.

"I don't blame you for not believing me, for being suspicious, for suspecting ulterior motives. In the past you would have been correct, but not now. I have studied in detail the elements of what is referred to as the New International Economic Order that you have been advocating for so long. My predecessors have never been receptive to your demands, but you will find me much more accommodating. For years you have been saying that the United States has taken advantage of your relative weakness, that we have drained you of your resources; that we have grown rich at your expense. It may surprise you to discover that I agree. I am here today to reassure you that we have seen the error of our ways, and we are ready to make up for them. I would be happy to answer any questions that you may have regarding the future of U.S. policy toward your countries."

A tall black man in a flowing, blue and white robe rose from the first row and addressed the President. He spoke with a precise British accent. Benedict had read his State Department file. His family had been largely responsible for the massacre of thousands of members of a neighboring tribe who had challenged their despotic rule.

"Mr. President, one of the chronic problems that we have had to deal with in our relations with your country involves what is known as 'declining terms of trade.' The relative world price of our exports to you declines, while the price of what you export to us increases in relative terms. For example, as time goes by, it takes more and more of our copra or our groundnuts to purchase your machine tools or your computers. We have been demanding for years that your government intervene in world markets to halt or reverse this trend. We continue to demand it today!"

He shook his fist in the air as the rest of the representatives sounded their approval in a cacophony of shouts. The President waited for the tumult to die. Everyone resumed his seat, and the room became quiet. Many of the representatives leaned forward, so as not to miss a syllable of the President's response. This was indeed a key demand; the answer to this question would reveal the sincerity of America's willingness to truly change the world order.

Benedict cleared his throat.

"Of course, I am aware of this problem, and I agree with you that it is a product of the fundamental unfairness of the free-market system. To correct it, I propose the following: the United States government will purchase all of your primary products at a set price, well above the world market level, and will place price controls on U.S. manufactured exports to your countries. Our purchase price for your exports and your purchase price for ours will be carefully designed to gradually swing the terms of trade in your favor, until a socially-acceptable price relationship is achieved."

You could hear a pin drop in the room as the ambassadors came to terms with what they had just heard. Never had they expected this capitulation. Never had they really expected their demands to be taken seriously! And yet, here it was!

A man in the second row stood up. Benedict recognized him. It was widely known that he had butchered one of his wives and eaten her liver in front of their young son.

"But Mr. President, how will you ensure that your domestic manufacturers will continue to work under these conditions? What will you do if they reject your price controls by simply refusing to produce?"

Benedict smiled at the man. "They will produce. They always have. Those people don't know how to do anything else."

The man in the second row smiled back, a sly, knowing smile, as if he suspected that the President was right. A Latin-American woman in the back of the room waved her arm and stood. The President pointed to her, giving her the floor. She didn't bother addressing him by his title.

"What about technology transfers?" she said in a demanding, belligerent voice. "The only technologies that you Americans have ever given us have been obsolete. How are we to compete with you unless we have access to the latest technologies that you develop?"

"I agree," answered Benedict. "Therefore, I will instruct the United States Patent Office to make available to you all new industrial, pharmaceutical, aerospace, and electronic patents as they are granted. As soon as U.S. corporations develop the technology, you will have access to it."

The woman sat down with a stunned expression on her face. Instantly dozens of others stood, demanding the President's attention, shouting and shaking their fingers at him. The feeding-frenzy was on. Eventually, one voice rose above the others, the deep base of an extremely fat Asian man in the third row.

"What about product substitution!" he shouted. "My country produces jute and coconut oil. You Americans have developed synthetic fibers to replace jute, and you won't buy our coconut oil anymore because of your insane concern with saturated fat. We don't purchase your manufactured goods, because we can't afford them. Your solution to the terms of trade problem does not apply to us. What will you do about our dilemma?"

"I agree that a great wrong has been done you. Through no fault of your own, you have been driven out of our market by the greed of our domestic corporations. I promise you that I will look into the possibility of outlawing the manufacture and use of anything that replaces the types of products that you mention. In the meantime, I will instruct the Department of Agriculture to purchase your jute, coconut oil and other agricultural products at a price that will ensure a socially-acceptable standard of living for your farmers and their families. We will stockpile these commodities, indefinitely if necessary."

Again the crowd erupted, emboldened by what they were hearing, sensing weakness, the way a hungry predator detects wounded, infirm prey. They all but lunged at the President, arms waving, fingers shaking, their raucous shouts blending into an earsplitting din. Now was the time! This was the opportunity to right all wrongs! Benedict's muscles tightened as his body reacted to a mild sense of panic. He was not afraid for his physical well-being; he was uncomfortable because they were not happy. They didn't seem satisfied. How could this be? It appeared that the more he gave them, the more they wanted. Didn't they see the magnitude of the concessions he was making?

He raised his arms to quiet the mob of international ambassadors. Slowly the noise died away. The President pointed to a man in the second row who was so excited that he was fairly bouncing off the floor.

"Mr. President," he began. "What you have said is all well and good, but it doesn't get to the heart of the issue: the fundamental nature of the capitalist dominance of the less developed world! As long as your corporations are privately owned, they will be controlled by selfish interests! As long as there are profits to be made, the welfare of our poor people will always be sacrificed! It is the very system of ownership of your companies that must be changed! Countries such as mine cannot purchase stock in them because our currencies are not convertible into dollars! Until we, the poor countries of the world, are given a meaningful share of your industry, the inequitable distribution of global wealth will never end!"

The room roared its approval. Once again Benedict calmed them.

"I could not agree more. You have touched on the final issue that I want to discuss here today. All thinking people understand the unfairness of capitalism. Even in this country, the bastion of the free market for well over two hundred years, it is rejected by virtually all of our intellectuals, by almost all thinking people, by all but the greedy few.

"Since the fall of communism, capitalism has been touted as the Great Victor, as the only truly successful economic system, as the end of history. Riding this surge like a great wave, millions of Americans have invested in our stock market, becoming unwitting participants in an economic system that perpetuates victimization. As much as it pains me to say it, I must admit that my own people have become innocent partners in the plundering of your countries, well-meaning dupes of the rapacious transnational corporations. If they could see your reality as I see it, I am sure that they would gladly forego their ill-gotten profits in the name of global fairness. They are, after all, a generous and altruistic people.

"If capitalism on a global scale were truly the answer, then you should be experiencing its benefits as well. But you are not. Instead your wealth and your resources are being sucked away from you, your economies are stagnant, your people angry and disillusioned. I offer you today a Third Way: not socialism, and not capitalism, but a socially responsible, enlightened blend of the two. There will, at long last, be a true sharing of the wealth.

"I do not take this step lightly. The policy I am about to outline will be enormously unpopular among many of my own countrymen and women. But I feel that I have a greater responsibility, a responsibility to humanity in its entirety. I am confident that, once they have had time to examine and appreciate the merits of what I have already proposed and what I am about to propose, the vast majority of the American people will support me in this effort. They understand that the true purpose of government is to take care of people. They will see, I am sure, that the new direction that I suggest today will simply extend that paternalism to the entire globe. They will realize that it is the right thing to do.

"I have spent a great deal of time discussing the merits and flaws of our capitalist system with outstanding academics from around the United States, and virtually all of them have reinforced what I have been feeling for years: that the free market victimizes more people than it benefits. I cannot tell you the sense of guilt that I, and most Americans, experience when we see starving children, and helpless, diseased adults all around the world. The knowledge that we are responsible for this death and misery is almost more than we can bear. For every new car an American family purchases, a thousand of your children could be fed for a month. For every swimming pool that we install in our backyards, an entire province in one of your countries could be vaccinated against virulent disease. Yes, my friends, I agree: this must change. And the way to make that change, as you, sir, so aptly pointed out, is to see to it that you share in the creation of wealth; that you have a part of the bounty that we Americans have come to so selfishly enjoy. To accomplish this end, I propose a two-part plan.

"First, all of your currencies will be made convertible into dollars, the exchange rates to be determined by a panel consisting of representatives from your countries and from our Treasury Department. I will personally see to it that these exchange rates are socially-responsible. Second, you may then use your currencies to purchase stock in United States corporations at subsidized rates; by that I mean that for every dollar's worth of your currency that you choose to invest, our treasury will add one dollar. In effect, you will be buying U.S. stock at half price. Further, I will instruct our Securities and Exchange Commission to make sure that you have access to as much stock as you may wish to buy: corporations will be prohibited from preventing you from purchasing a controlling interest in their companies. This means that, at last, you will be full partners in, and not victims of, the capitalist system."

The same day. New York, the President's hotel suite.

"I want to thank you all for coming," the President said to the men assembled in the room.

Each was the head of a television network. They made themselves comfortable in the plush furniture of the suite. Their posture, their demeanor, their relaxed manner demonstrated their lack of awe at being in the presence of the Chief of State. In fact, it was the President who was experiencing a sense of awe, and he looked it. His shirt collar was damp with perspiration and his eyes darted nervously from face to face. A thin smile was on his lips. The unspoken truth in the room was almost tangible. In a very real sense, it was Benedict who was the supplicant here. He knew that these men were in a position to make or break politicians; they were the true power behind the throne. He knew that for his new policies to succeed, he would have to have them on his side. Benedict felt weak and vulnerable.

The President knew these men more intimately than any of them would have imagined. His success as a politician depended upon it. He knew what made them tick, and he had benefited greatly from that knowledge during his career

Benedict was aware of the fact that for many years, these men had not been interested in simply reporting the news; they had sought to mold public opinion. For decades, they had used their organizations to further their own unspoken ideological agenda. That agenda consisted of an amorphous mash of ideas that these men had come to accept without thought, almost as an act of faith. It involved a vague hatred of the wealthy and a pious profession of sympathy for the poor--a bizarre incongruity considering the fact that the wafer-thin gold watches that each of them wore would feed a starving child for five years. The agenda also included the accepted truth that the United States was irredeemably evil, its culture of individualism bankrupt and rotten to the core. They saw to it that their networks were consistent proponents of multi-culturalism and moral relativism, the notion that the acts of cannibals are indistinguishable from those of capitalists. They engaged in mental evasion when reminded of their own capitalist activities. Benedict knew that they didn't see themselves as entrepreneurs, no matter how much stock was in their investment portfolios. They were, after all, fighting the good fight, defending the faith.

It was not difficult for these men to sit back in their Manhattan penthouses, gazing at a painting on the wall that cost more than most men make in a lifetime, and rationalize their ownership of it as ultimately being in the best interests of the needy, the downtrodden, the victims of the world. After all, these men needed to have money, and lots of it, if they were to bring social justice to the world. He knew that they had convinced themselves that money was merely a tool they would use to right the wrongs of this planet. The fact that it permitted them to live like kings was, they rationalized, simply a fortuitous side effect. And how were they to right those wrongs?

First, break the individualistic spirit of the American people. Convince them that the values they were taught as children, the values that had built the country, are morally depraved and must be rejected. Convince them that any concern for their own well being is unacceptably selfish. Convince them that a naked barbarian on the other side of the world has as much right to the product of their labor as they have.

Of course, none of this was said openly. That simply wasn't done. Benedict had always known that their goal was to cultivate an image of neutrality, of reporting just the facts. To do otherwise would damage their credibility and shatter their self-image: they had seemingly convinced themselves over the years that they were not purveyors of propaganda, but instead paragons of virtue, speakers of the truth, unbiased defenders of all that was good. For them to be effective, that image must be preserved. But that was easily enough done; the American people, after all, were remarkably unsophisticated, overly trusting, easily manipulated, highly malleable into any shape that the elite might choose for them. The President realized that remaking the world in their own cloudy, unfocused egalitarian image was a task which they all relished, as long as it was accompanied by sufficient power and perquisites. Lies, distortions, half-truths, these were the stock-in-trade of America's media barons.

"You've all seen my press conference at the U.N. What did you think of it?" the President asked in a hopeful tone.

David Koenig, head of NBN said, "I think you're going to need a lot of help with this one. What you proposed today turns the country on its head. What makes you think there won't be rioting in the streets?"

Benedict turned a chair around so that it faced the seated men and sat down on its edge.

"Who's going to oppose it, Dave? The rich? The corporate elite? How many of them are there? They're a drop in the bucket compared to the poor and middle class. My people have done a lot of polling in the past year on these issues. So have yours. Those polls all show that, first of all, the American people really don't understand what this is all about: primary product subsidies, technology transfers, you might as well ask them about the man in the moon. With your help, the teacher's unions have successfully dumbed-down the country to the point where most people can't even balance their checkbooks, never mind contemplate international political economy! Secondly, the polls tell us that on fairness issues, including redistribution of wealth, a majority of Americans are exactly where we want them: in favor, as long as we can convince them that we won't be putting them in the poor house in the process."

"I see a problem there," interjected Charles Lever, President of MNT network. "As you just pointed out at the U.N., more and more people have gotten into the stock market in recent years. A majority of Americans are now stockholders in the very corporations that you gave away this morning. You mentioned some bullshit about generosity and altruism. But do you seriously think that the American people are going to take this lying down? What you suggested today will gut their IRAs! They'll have visions of rooting through dumpsters in their old age! You've gct an election coming up in a few months, remember? You've always been a good team player, and God knows we've done you enough favors in the past. We've got a lot invested in you! We don't want to see you replaced by some stone-age reactionary!"

"With your help, all of you, I don't expect them to react very much at all. Most people own so little stock that they have no real sense of corporate ownership anyway. We can disregard the relative few who do. But you can short-circuit any potential reaction by bombarding the country with programming designed to convince them that supporting my proposals is the unselfish thing to do. After all, if we've accomplished anything in all these years, it's been to convince the American people to be unselfish. We can use that, build on it! You know, make some documentaries filled with starving stick-children, diseased populations, crop failures, third-world cities crowded with millions of paupers, corpses lying in the streets, that sort of thing. Real tear-jerkers! You could also do some exposes on the extravagances of the rich. Focus on the greed, the conspicuous consumption. Show some rich son-of-a-bitch swimming in his pool, and then show a naked African drinking out of a mud-puddle. Let everybody know what heartless bastards they are. Really pour it on! By the time you're through, not only will the American people support these positions, they'll demand them!"

"Judas, you know that we've always supported any policy that will send the country in a better direction. We hate what this country has always stood for as much as you do."

It was George Griffith, head of the largest cable company in the country.

"We're as anti-imperialistic and as anti-big-business as you are. We've always fought for the backward countries, for the environment, or against the tobacco companies, or whatever the hell the latest fad happens to be, as long as it's socially responsible."

"And as long as we make a buck in the process!" injected Lever. That brought a hearty belly-laugh from everyone present.

"You know what I mean Judas," continued Griffith. "We've always been on your side. But I don't know if even we can pull this off. Besides, why should we? What's in it for us? As I see it, you've arranged things so that a year from now, those of us in this room will all be working for some third-world savage!"

The President smiled at the men opposite him. He knew he had them.

"I guess I forgot to mention that media corporations will be exempt from the stock purchase plan I unveiled at the U.N.. We've got to protect the sanctity of the First Amendment, you know."

That evening, New York City

The President took a glass of champagne from the tray of a passing waiter. As he sipped the exquisite liquor, his eyes took in the room around him. The immense ballroom was tastefully done and expensive in the extreme. From the parquet floor to the velvet draperies flanked by world-famous painting and sculpture to the fantastically ornate crystal chandelier, the room was designed to be the preserve of a person of accomplishment. This degree of luxury should be the reward for great and valuable work, for years of creating wealth, of satisfying the demands of consumers.

These thoughts never entered the mind of Judas Benedict. They undoubtedly did not enter the minds of most of the several hundred people in the room. For Benedict, and virtually all of those around him, had been born into this luxury. Only a handful in the room had earned it. Indeed, few of them would have known how to earn such a reward if their lives had depended on it This room was merely a part of the privileged life they had inherited through an accident of birth. They took it for granted, as they did their limousines and their beachfront palaces. It probably did not occur to any of them that this room was a temple dedicated to the ambition, the genius, and the backbreaking labor of the man who had financed its construction. Certainly it would not have crossed their minds that the mere presence here of parasites such as themselves constituted a sacrilege: they were cockroaches in a jewel box.

"Judas, have you heard a word I've said?" asked Benedict's hostess, Julia 'Kiki' Worthington, great-grand daughter of Elias P. Worthington, one of America's preeminent nineteenth-century industrialists. Judas Benedict and Kiki Worthington had been part of the same social set all their lives. They knew each other very well. Every generation of Worthingtons since the death of Elias P. had managed to diminish his estate through mismanagement or just plain squandering. Kiki's father had seen the writing on the wall, and had established an ironclad trust fund before all the money had disappeared. This permitted Kiki to live the life to which the Worthingtons had become accustomed. The President looked down into her face and gave her his most beatific smile.

"But of course I've heard you, Kiki," he answered. "You have my undivided attention."

She smiled back and continued. "Well, as I was saying, those of us who really count support what you're doing one hundred percent. Heaven knows the poor of the world deserve everything we can do for them. But a few of us were wondering, ah, how shall I put this, we were wondering how your new programs would affect us personally--you know--financially."

She hissed the last word as if it were an obscenity. In spite of himself, the President couldn't help studying his old friend before answering her. Her watery eyes appeared to be a bit unfocused. From time to time she lurched ever so slightly, as if correcting for a lack of balance. She had spilled as much champagne as she had drunk. Her bright red lipstick would have looked good on a woman twenty years her junior, but it only made her look like a whore. Kiki was descending into gentile oblivion, Benedict thought. Too bad.

"Don't worry about a thing," he assured her. "Your money is locked away so tightly that no one in the third world will ever be able to grab it."

Kiki exhaled in relief. Benedict almost burst into laughter. There suddenly appeared to the President's left one of the most famous artists in the United States. He was known only as Mr. Raoul. Benedict recoiled involuntarily at the man's appearance, but recovered before the moment became embarrassing. Mr. Raoul's head had been shaved and tattooed to resemble someone's buttocks. His eyebrows had been plucked. He wore an extremely long, heavily-waxed moustache that curled upward into complete circles. He could have been forty years old, or seventy. He had made a name for himself in the New York art world years before by covering his naked body with paint and rolling around on a canvas. Since then, he had managed to remain in the public eye by creating numerous 'works of art' involving dead animals and human excrement.

"Mr. President, I'm so glad you could be with us tonight," he said, extending his limp hand to be shaken. Benedict felt as though he were grasping a plastic bag full of diarrhea.

"I want to congratulate you on the brave position you have taken to end injustice in the world. You will surely encounter resistance; not from us, of course; we're idealists; but from the more, shall we say, materialistic members of society."

The others who had gathered around, champagne in hand, looked knowingly at each other and nodded their approval. They could not know that Mr. Raoul had spent the afternoon furiously selling stock and transferring his assets to overseas banks. The President simply dipped his head in recognition. Mr. Raoul continued.

"I want to encourage you to meet that resistance forcefully! We cannot let the selfishness of some members of our society stand in the way of the good of the collective! Keep in mind that it is perfectly appropriate for you to initiate force against those who refuse to engage in self-sacrifice! Every man has a right to the life of every other man! And if some fail to recognize that fact, it is our responsibility to force them into compliance!"

The dozen or so people who were within earshot all nodded their heads in solemn agreement. To Benedict's right a paunchy dowager dripping with diamonds said,

"You have a perfect right to kill them if necessary, Mr. President! Selfish people are the worst kind of criminal!"

A distinguished looking man behind Kiki Worthington said, "I agree, Mr. President. The days of individualism are over. All thinking people agree on that. These days it's the state that counts; it's the state that knows best. Only the state is in a position to take care of everyone's needs. And if anyone disagrees with that, you have a responsibility to dispose of him!"

Here he shook his finger at the President, something Benedict was not used to. But he merely looked at the man thoughtfully and nodded his agreement.

To the President's left, someone cleared his throat sufficiently loudly so as to get everyone's attention. Benedict recognized Dr. Alonso Jeffrey. He was a professor of philosophy who had gained national recognition by producing a series of television specials espousing the notion that the concept of individual liberty was obsolete, and had no place in modern-day America.

Jeffrey said, "For thirty-five years I have been teaching my students that the individual should not be the unit of analysis in our society, that the individual doesn't really matter at all, that it is the mass, the collective, that counts. I cannot tell you how pleased I am to finally see my ideas come to political fruition. You must let nothing get in the way of implementing them! Crush any opposition you encounter! This is the opportunity that all of us who truly care about humanity have been waiting for! We must not let it slip through our fingers! Self-sacrifice, that's the ticket! People must be forced to sacrifice themselves!"

The President smiled and nodded.

"Thank you for your support, Professor. I want to reassure all of you that I will not let any outdated concerns for individual liberty deflect me from the path we all know we must follow. You can rest assured that I will use the full coercive power of the state to compel compliance from any individual who feels that he or she is too good to assume the role of sacrificial animal."

The little cluster of people in the center of the ballroom floor broke out into applause. There were two exceptions. One was a middle-aged, balding man of medium height with a perplexed look on his face. He was the third-generation owner of a Connecticut company that manufactured industrial valves.

"Mr. President, I'm just a businessman, and I can't be expected to understand all of the complex philosophical concepts that you discussed today. All I know is that if I've worked to produce something, and I'm able to sell it to a willing buyer on the open market, I should be allowed to keep the profits from it. By what right should some stranger from across the ocean claim those profits?"

Professor Jeffrey took it upon himself to reply.

"My good man, I have spent a lifetime studying the concept of rights. And I will condense the product of that lifetime's work into one sentence that I am sure even you will understand: need constitutes the only right. If someone from across the ocean, as you put it, needs the product of your labor that is sufficient justification for recognizing that person's right to the product of your labor. Your rights end where another person's need begins. The archaic notion of property rights is entirely obsolete and is rightfully being discarded in favor of more enlightened ideas."

The Connecticut businessman nodded solemnly. He still didn't understand why he should give up a part of his corporation to a stranger, but he could not even begin to rebut the argument of the eminent professor.

There was another man in the crowd, a tall, dark-haired man in an impeccably cut suit. Everyone recognized him wherever he went. He had started life as a poor boy from New York's Lower East side. By the age of thirty-five he had built a financial empire, first in real estate, then in computer software. He had been swirling his martini slowly in its crystal glass as he looked at the President during Dr. Jeffrey's oration.

"Do you agree with what you've just heard, Mr. President?" he asked Benedict, a somber but expectant tone in his voice.

Their eyes met, and the President felt a sinking sensation in the pit of his stomach. Here was just the sort of man he hated beyond all description: the self-made man, the strong man, the capable man, arrogant, so sure of himself. They were never afraid! No, not them! They always had the answers! They always knew what to do! They were never confused or frightened or out of their depth! His knees felt weak, and he began to perspire. A tiny voice screamed out within him,

"Father, no! I can't be like them! I just can't do it! Don't expect it of me! Don't hate me because I'm weak!"

"Why.....why, yes. Yes I do." Benedict began, his voice trembling. "All enlightened people agree that need confers right. It's only people like you, you capitalists, who cling to the old selfish notions of property rights."

The President's voice rose in pitch, with just a twinge of panic. Alone, he would never have had the temerity to confront such a man. The few he had met in his life had always terrified him to his roots. But here, he was able to draw a modicum of strength from the sycophants and philosophical allies who surrounded him, in the same way that a hyena draws its courage from the pack when it attacks a magnificent, proud bull elephant. Benedict forced himself to stand erect and said, glaring up at the taller man,

"What makes you think that you're right and all the rest of us are wrong? Who are you to disagree?"

"Who am I? I am a free man, Benedict. To you and your kind that is a totally alien concept. I live my life for my own sake based on the independent judgments of my rational mind. I am not part of some simpering, whining collective dependent on a contemptible reprobate like you for my survival."

"How dare you speak to the President of the United States in such a way!"

"I'll speak to you in any way I choose, Benedict. You're no more worthy of respect than are the most vile dregs of society. I'd show more deference to a bum in the gutter than I would to you.

"You've built your career on the premise that human beings are the moral equivalent of cattle, to be led by you, fed by you, and, when it's most advantageous, slaughtered by you. Today, in that blasphemous vomit that you spewed upon the United Nations, you set the stage for the virtual slaughter of every man and woman in this country who is proud to stand up on his hind legs and declare himself an independent, self-sustaining person. You've placed upon them the shackles of an authoritarian state, forcibly removed them from their rightful role as producers of wealth, generators of growth and prosperity, and condemned them to the status of defenseless prey, to be devoured by the vermin of the world, immolated in the name of global 'fairness.'

"You're the worst kind of monster, Benedict, the bane of our species. Hundreds of millions--entire populations--have suffered and died at the hands of creatures like you. But your plan will not work. I, for one, will destroy everything I have created before I hand it over to some cannibal at the point of a gun. And I am not alone. In the end, you will be left with nothing but ashes."

He turned and strode from the room, hurling his martini glass into the enormous fireplace as he passed it. The ball of flame produced by the alcohol marked his exit. There was silence among the frumpy dowagers, the pretentious literati, the wasp-waisted, face-lifted creme de la creme. The President's legs were trembling. He felt as if he might collapse. His mind reeled from the dose of reality to which he had just been exposed. His consciousness struggled to push it down into the fetid, labyrinthine catacomb of his subconscious, where he had entombed unpleasant realities all his life. He placed his hand on Kiki's shoulder for support, and slowly led her away.

"Where are we going, Judas?" Kiki asked.

"After that, I feel an overpowering need to become reacquainted with you, my dear," he answered.

The tension flowed through him like electricity. He needed release, to feel in charge again, to feel assertive. He needed to demonstrate his dominance over someone, anyone. She said nothing further as he led her through the kitchen and into a small storage room where they were unlikely to be disturbed. Once there, he instructed her,

"Turn around, lift up your dress and bend over, Kiki."

"Oh Judas, can't you be at least a little bit romantic?" she asked him in an impatient voice.

No, he thought. Not with you. Come to think of it, not with any woman. Thoughts of his wife crossed his mind as he released his engorged member from his trousers. Mechanically, he inserted it in the appropriate place between Kiki's legs and began moving back and forth. For an instant, he considered telling Kiki that, like all women, she was nothing more to him than a piece of meat. No, he thought. Even Kiki wouldn't stand for that.

CHAPTER TEN

The Volokolamsk, Los Angeles Harbor

Dimitri Rykov glanced at his watch. It was almost time to check it again, he thought. He looked up and once more took in the city around him. It was so vibrant, pulsing with life. Although he could see only a tiny portion of Los Angeles from his ship's West Basin anchorage, he could tell that it was a place such as few Russians could imagine. The steady stream of cars along the Harbor Freeway amazed him. Such wealth, he thought! How did they do it? How did these Americans create all of this? He could see a carload of young people in a convertible on Harry Bridges Boulevard next to the freeway. They were waving their arms and shouting in a carefree way such as few Russian youth had experienced. My poor Russia, Rykov thought. Grim, dirty, poor, her people depressed and desperate. But soon now, things will change. All of this will be ours. The productive energies of these amazing people will be directed to our benefit. Drugonov has promised it.

It was time. Rykov walked along the deck until he reached the hatchway that would give him access to the hold. There he met his second in command, Pavel Piatakov. Regulations stipulated that two KGB officers would be present at all times when examining the--cargo. The rest of the twelve man KGB unit on this assignment was stationed either around the ship in various locations, or below decks resting.

The two men descended into the hold of the ship, as they had done every hour since its arrival late that morning. There it was, securely strapped down on a large wooden pallet in the center of the deck. Just looking at it raised the hackles on the back of Rykov's neck. He didn't know much about such things, but the scuttlebutt was that this was a particularly big one, and particularly dirty as well.

They walked around the stubby oblong shape and made sure that the heavy nylon straps connected to eye-bolts welded to the deck were secure. Rykov lifted a small door on the top of the device and, once again, checked to see that all was in order. He touched a button to make sure that the internal power supply was operating properly. The indicator light glowed green. Good.

Rykov's hands were clammy, and a bead of sweat ran down his temple. He glanced at the digital elapsed timer, realizing that he may soon receive orders to set it for precisely four hours. That should give them time to escape. And then, unless he received countermanding orders, he and Piatakov would have to insert the keys that they wore around their necks into the two keyholes on both sides of the timer and turn them ninety degrees clockwise. The simple push of a button would then start the countdown and complete his responsibilities to the Rodina.

CHAPTER ELEVEN

The Oval Office

"Mr. President, General Krajewski is here to see you, sir."

"Great," Benedict said to his National Security Advisor, a dour expression on his face.

"I'll leave if you'd like, Mr. President," said Ernest Crippler. He did not really want to leave. He was gambling that the President would not ask him to do so. What he had been waiting for all of his adult life was about to happen within moments, in this office. The General's presence would be a complication, but perhaps not an unfortunate one. He glanced at his watch. Yes. Any minute now.

"No, Ernie. Stay here. I may need your moral support." Benedict keyed the intercom and said meekly, "All right, Ellen. Send him in."

Crippler saw a look of anxiety in the President's eyes as they darted back and forth across his desk. Benedict rubbed his hand across his cheek and mouth, as if to relieve muscle tension. Crippler was well aware of the fact that, upon assuming office, the President had very carefully chosen all of his top military people, including the Joint Chiefs, with little regard for talent or qualifications. He had confided to Crippler that, above all, he wanted to avoid any trace of individual initiative. He had made it clear that he did not want to waste his time butting heads with the military that he so despised. 'Yes' men, men greedy for power and influence, men who would do anything, follow any order, to achieve those goals: these, Benedict had said, were his ideal general officers. For the most part he had gotten them, though he had had to reach deep into the promotion lists to find them. Even Crippler had been amazed at the extremes to which the President had been willing to resort to get the people he wanted. In one case an over-the-hill, lackluster brigadier with a service-wide reputation for kissing asses had suddenly found his one star replaced with four.

In those early days, Crippler had warned Benedict about Krajewski, but he had been paid no heed. The National Security Advisor had studied the man's career, and he knew that Krajewski was no "yes" man. But he could not convince the President of that. Benedict had assured him that the General could be controlled, that his lust for power was just as strong as the others. That had proven not to be the case. The President had often railed about the man not being a team player, of exhibiting backbone when Benedict wanted overcooked linguini. Crippler had advised the President to fire the man, but the general had so far been very careful to avoid giving him sufficient justification. Besides, Benedict had said, Krajewski was immensely popular with those moronic troops, and firing him might cause problems. Better 'not to rock the boat' as the President had put it, until a more advantageous moment arose.

The door of the office burst open, and the General strode purposefully into the room. He nodded to Crippler on his way to the President's desk. When he reached it, he stood at attention and saluted. Benedict returned something approximating a salute; after four years he had still not learned how to execute one properly. He told Krajewski to be at ease invited the General to sit down.

Krajewski sat on the edge of the sofa, leaning forward, with the palms of his hands on his knees, looking for all the world as if he were preparing to lunge forward. Instead he said,

"Mr. President, we have to discuss these troop withdrawals that you have announced for Western Europe, South Korea and the Middle East. With all due respect, sir, I think that they are most ill-advised."

"There's really nothing to discuss, General," the President answered in an aloof tone. "My policies will be carried out as soon as possible."

"But Mr. President, how can we withdraw our forces under current circumstances? The world is so unstable since the collapse of the Soviet Union that none of us knows what will happen a month from now. We face continuing problems in Southwest Asia. Both the Russians and the North Koreans are at the end of their ropes. They're desperate, their people literally starving to death. North Korea has nuclear weapons with a madman at the helm. And now this Russian Drugonov has announced that he intends to attack us."

Benedict smiled as if to a child.

"Oh, General, I don't think we have anything to worry about from Mr. Drugonov. His military forces are in disarray. It would take years for Russia to again present a credible threat to us. Drugonov is just blowing off steam. And besides, as I said in my press conference, don't they have a right to be angry with us? For a half century we threatened to blow them off the face of the earth!"

General Krajewski hardly knew where to begin. He felt a sense of unreality, as if he were through the looking glass. Just then the intercom buzzed.

"Yes, Ellen."

"Sir, I'm sorry to disturb you, but the Russian ambassador is here and he insists on seeing you immediately. He says it is most urgent, sir."

The General raised his hands in a gesture of helplessness.

"I can come back later, Mr. President."

"No," said Benedict. "Let's all hear what he has to say together."

He keyed the intercom.

"Send him in, Ellen."

Krajewski and Crippler stood as the door opened, admitting Vladimir Raskol'nikov. The Russian Ambassador was a man in late middle age. His thinning black hair was combed straight back. His dark blue suit was immaculate, as always.

His relatively short, squat body conveyed the impression of considerable power, which he certainly possessed. However, he had used it sparingly in his career, personally having killed only a handful of men and women. The number he had ordered killed was another matter entirely. He was a past-master at concealing his true nature, and few among the Washington social set thought of him as anything other than a suave, peace-loving diplomat. For decades, he had served first the Soviet and then the Russian government. He was known as a survivor: many of his less shrewd, less adaptable former colleagues were now in their graves after meeting unnatural deaths. He could be painfully blunt or delightfully diplomatic as the occasion required. His present stern countenance indicated to the other men in the room that today was a day to be blunt. Crippler was trembling with excitement.

"How do you do, Mr. President, Mr. Crippler, General Krajewski?" Raskol'nikov said, bowing slightly to each of them.

"Please, Mr. Ambassador, sit down," the President said. "To what do we owe the honor of your visit?"

Raskol'nikov sat, and spent a few seconds gathering his thoughts. Benedict had never seen him so serious, so contemplative.

"Mr. President," he began. "I have been instructed to perform a most momentous task. I am here to deliver to you an ultimatum."

President Benedict sat straighter in his chair. His eyebrows raised a bit.

"I'm afraid I don't understand, Vladimir. What do you mean by an ultimatum?"

"I mean it in the classical sense, sir. You are to surrender your country to the new Russian Empire, or the city of Los Angeles will be obliterated. If you continue to resist, other cities will follow."

An awkward silence filled the room as what had just been said sank in. Finally, Benedict spoke up.

"This must be some kind of a joke, right Vladimir?"

"I can assure you it is no joke. You are to announce your acceptance of your new status as an economic colony of the Russian Empire within fifty-six hours, or before five-oh-one P.M. Eastern Time, this Friday, or Los Angeles will cease to exist."

He stood, withdrew a piece of paper from his jacket pocket, and handed it to the President.

"To prove to you that I am not insane, this represents confirmation from my government of what I have just told you."

He sat down again.

As he looked at the document, Benedict said, "Russian Empire? What Russian Empire? Vladimir, you can't be…"

Raskol'nikov decided that it was time to show his hand, to put an end to all pretense. He slammed his hand down onto the arm of the chair. The explosive sound startled Benedict. He stared wide-eyed and open-mouthed at the ambassador.

"Enough!" he shouted. "I have been too polite with you! It is time to put you in your place! You have been given your instructions, and you will obey or be liquidated!"

General Krajewski's shock had turned to rage.

"Why you goddamn Russki son of a bitch!" he hissed as he lifted himself off the sofa and moved ominously toward Raskol'nikov.

"That will do, General!" the President shouted. Krajewski turned toward Benedict.

"Mr. President, we need to place all U.S. military forces on full alert! I don't know if this bastard," he looked at Raskol'nikov, "is on the level or not, but we can't take a chance!"

Benedict had been reading the document that Raskol'nikov had given him.

"This appears to be 'on the level', as you would say, General."

"All the more reason..." Krajewski began.

"General, sit down!" Benedict ordered. He looked at the ambassador.

"Vladimir, I'm sure you will understand if I contact Moscow. It's not that I'm calling you a liar, but....."

"Call me whatever you like, Benedict."

Once again the President's mouth dropped open.

"Please do contact Moscow. Speak to Maximum Leader Drugonov." Raskol'nikov checked his watch. "He is expecting your call at this moment. He will confirm what I have told you," he said in a tone that was becoming increasingly imperious.

Crippler studied Benedict carefully. He could see panic in his eyes. The man's hands were visibly trembling. Crippler tried to imagine what was going through his President's mind: 'What if this man were not mad? What if this were really happening? What would I do?' Crippler knew that Benedict was a small man, a man of limited capacity, who seemed to be coming to the realization that he was fantastically out of his depth. This was not some rubber-chicken fund-raiser. This was a turning point in world history, an event of such magnitude that it dwarfed the likes of Judas Benedict. Crippler relished his President's pain, and tried to hide the delicious anticipation he felt for what was about to happen.

The President pushed the appropriate button on the telephone. The speaker permitted everyone in the room to hear. A few seconds of silence were followed by several clicks. Then a voice they all recognized came on the line.

"Yes. This is Maximum Leader Drugonov speaking."

Benedict sat straighter in his seat. He smiled, and said in an oily, ingratiating voice,

"Hello, Sergei. This is Judas, Judas Benedict. How are you, Sergei?"

Drugonov answered in a flat, serious tone.

"The state of my health is not your concern, Benedict. Your only concern is to obey my orders as you have just received them through my ambassador."

Benedict crumpled visibly in his chair.

"But Sergei..." the President began.

"From now on you will address me as Maximum Leader," Drugonov commanded.

Crippler knew how Benedict worked. After four years, he could almost read his mind. He would probably play for time, stall, try to think of some way out.

"Yes, well, Maximum Leader, what is it you have in mind?"

"It is so simple that even you can understand it, Benedict. The United States of America is to become a colony of the Russian Empire. We will occupy your country and divert virtually all of its economic production and natural resources to our own purposes. Enough will be left to you to provide for the survival of your workers. Those who do not produce will be liquidated.

"You will order your military to stand down immediately. I will make my headquarters in New York City for the moment. I will arrive there the day after tomorrow. At five P.M. local time you will meet with me there and sign the appropriate documents of surrender. Failure to carry out these instructions will result in the destruction of Los Angeles precisely one minute later. If that unfortunate event should take place and your country still has not capitulated, additional cities will meet the same fate. Your ultimate surrender is inevitable."

Benedict stared down at his desk listening carefully to what Drugonov said. He shaded his eyes with his hand, as if to prevent the other men in the room from seeing the fear in them.

"Ser-, ah, Maximum Leader, what makes you think that we will surrender and not simply attack you?" the President asked.

"Attack us with what, Benedict?" Drugonov answered. "You have dismantled your ballistic missiles, decommissioned the last of your nuclear submarines, and cut your conventional forces to the bone. Face it, Benedict! You are a second-rate military power!"

The President sputtered, "But we made those reductions only because of treaties we signed with your country and with the United Nations, of which you are a signatory! The entire General Assembly voted for our disarmament! We trusted you! How can you stab us in the back like this? You're breaking every rule in the book!"

"You poor fool. Don't you see that I'm writing my own book? Throughout history men of daring, men such as myself, have never hesitated to make their own rules. And small men like you have always been forced to live by them. But there is another reason why you will not attack us. Should you do so, we would not wait until Friday. Los Angeles would be vaporized immediately, along with a score of your other largest cities. One hundred million dead, Benedict, and your country reduced to a radioactive wasteland for the next ten thousand years! That is a price I think you are not willing to pay."

"How can you be so sure of that?" Benedict managed to ask.

Drugonov could be heard chuckling on the other end of the line.

"Because I know you! I know you perhaps better than you know yourselves! Your leadership no longer has the stomach to defend itself. You no longer believe in yourselves sufficiently to trade blood for liberty! You have forgotten the very meaning of liberty!

"Assume for a moment that you refrained from attacking us, but that you refused to surrender. Los Angeles would then be destroyed. We believe that the destruction of Los Angeles would involve between three and five million deaths.

"Would you be willing to expend those innocent lives in defense of what you perceive to be a depraved, parasitic capitalist-imperialist system? Tell me, Benedict, among your leadership, political and intellectual, how many are there who believe that your system is truly worth defending? You yourself said just days ago that you believe that your country is responsible for most of the suffering in the world. You have admitted that you think your system is rotten to the core.

"Yesterday at the United Nations you virtually turned your economy over to the backward countries of the world, a policy, by the way, which I will immediately reverse. How many members of your elite are willing to kill, and die, to defend such a system? No, Benedict. You cannot resist. You lack the strength. You lack the will." Drugonov continued.

"Think about it, Benedict. Do you not owe us your wealth? Have you not been victimizing us for the past half-century? Are we not poor because you are rich? Have you not become rich at our expense?"

Benedict said, "Well, perhaps that's true. But..."

"Given that, would it not be unfair of you to defend yourselves? Would it not be an act of selfishness to prevent us from gaining access to your ill-gotten wealth? You would not want to be thought of as unfair and selfish, would you?"

Benedict stammered, "Of course not, but..."

"In light of all that I have said, then, what would be the justification for your self-defense?" Drugonov asked.

"I ... I ... ah ... I'm not sure ... I'm confused. Somehow ... there must be ... I don't know..."

"Tell me, Benedict, are you not an altruist? Do you not believe that it is the duty of each individual to sacrifice himself for the well-being of others?" Drugonov asked.

Benedict answered, "Well, yes. All thinking people are altruistic. But ..."

"Good. Then I am calling in your debt. I am doing nothing more than demanding that sacrifice of you. Do you not believe that one person's need constitutes a blank check on another person's life?" Drugonov continued.

"Yes, I've always felt that ..."

"Good. We are cashing that check. We are in need, and we are claiming what is ours by right."

"But this hardly seems ... " Benedict said.

"Face it, Benedict. Your position is totally unprincipled. You are philosophically bankrupt."

"What does philosophy have to do with it, damn it?" demanded Benedict.

The four men in the room listened as Drugonov simply laughed. Head bent down over his desk, Benedict ran his hands through his hair, clearly anguished. Then he straightened slightly, as if something had occurred to him.

"Ah, Maximum Leader, perhaps we could clear up this whole thing through compromise. You know, a little give and take. After all, we're both politicians.

Compromise is the most important tool of our trade. I assume you are aware of the fifty billion dollars I offered your country at my latest press conference. Well, that could easily be increased to one hundred billion. And I doubt that anyone would pay much attention to where the other fifty billion ended up. I hear the weather in Zurich is splendid this time of year! What do you say to that, my friend?" Drugonov answered as if to himself.

"How does one compromise with one's destroyer? You offer to compromise with a man who holds a knife at your throat, and then you call him your friend. You're a bigger fool than I thought. As to your money, soon I will have it all: everything that you have earned, everything that you have created, all that is yours will be mine.

"Notify your elite. My office will call to inform you of the location of our meeting in New York. By the way, in case you think that both the ambassador and I are mad, or in case you think that I am less than sincere, I want to direct your attention to a certain ship, the Volokolamsk, currently moored in Los Angeles Harbor. If you check her with your long-distance sensory equipment, you will discover that she is carrying a rather unusual cargo.

"I warn you, do not attempt to seize that vessel. At the first sign of offensive military activity, the men aboard her have been instructed to execute their prime directive, which will result in the obliteration of Los Angeles. If you attempt to bomb the vessel, the 'cargo' has been rigged to detonate automatically. Detonation will also occur if you begin to evacuate the city.

"One more thing, Benedict. It occurs to me that you may need some leverage to persuade certain members of your elite to submit to my dictates, particularly those in your military. You will no doubt recall those one thousand FBI files that mysteriously appeared in the possession of one of your predecessors early in his first term?"

"Yes, of course. But we never found out how they got..." Benedict answered.

"Enough, you idiot!" Drugonov thundered. "You will soon learn that you can lie to your press, you can lie to your Congress, but you cannot lie to me! The contents of those files were transferred to our computers here in Moscow. They are in my possession, along with a great deal of more recent information that we have been able to gather."

"But how..." Benedict began.

"You will learn in due time." Drugonov answered. "Suffice it to say that security in your White House is less than perfect. Inform any of your elite who may consider resisting that I know where their wives and husbands are, I know where their children are. If they do not submit immediately, my agents in your country will apprehend those people and torture them to death! It will take days for them to die! There would be no escape. My organization in your country is extensive, far more so than you can imagine. And it can reach out and touch anyone it chooses. You have perhaps heard of the Russian mafia? It is led by a most unsavory man, a monster really: a man to whom no act is too barbaric, a man who relishes bathing in the blood of his victims.

"His name is Leonid Uglanov. He will be accompanying me to New York, where he has had a rather extensive operation for some years now, an operation that will be expanded dramatically in the months to come. I will order Mr. Uglanov to use all of his unpleasant talents to keep your elite in line. Make that very clear to them, Benedict! You should have little trouble. I have found such a tactic to be very persuasive in the past. I am sure you will find it useful as well. That is all for now." Drugonov broke the connection.

Benedict looked at the others with a dazed expression on his face. Krajewski could hardly contain his rage. Raskol'nikov looked at the President with a sly smile, the smile of a successful mugger. Ernest Crippler had not said a word. He was watching the General closely. The General could not be allowed to interfere.

"Mr. President!" Krajewski exploded. "Let's hit these bastards now! This is war! Sure we may lose people, but we've got to defend ourselves! Hell, even a rat will defend itself!" His fist slammed down on the presidential desk.

Benedict's eyes finally focused on Krajewski. He cleared his throat. "General, what exactly could we use to 'hit them' as you put it?"

The General bounced up and down on the balls of his feet, hands clasped behind his back, lips pursed. It was all he could do to keep from spitting in the President's face.

"This is a fine time to start worrying about that, you incompetent son of a ..."

Krajewski's head fell forward, and he exhaled audibly.

"My apologies, Mr. President. But why didn't you think about this sort of thing four years ago, before you gutted the services?" With great control and in a level, measured voice, he continued, "Mr. President, we have two guided missile frigates in the North Atlantic armed with cruise missiles with conventional warheads. We could have them within range of Moscow in eighteen hours."

"Would they be able to neutralize this threat, General?" the President asked.

"Well, sir, they could sure as hell hit the Kremlin! Maybe we could take out Drugonov! We could put one of those babies right through his office window!"

"And then we lose Los Angeles. That's not very reassuring, General," Benedict said.

Krajewski leaned forward and placed his palms on the President's desk.

"Sir, we have no alternative. Drugonov asked you what would be the justification for our self-defense. It is survival, Mr. President: survival as a country, as a nation of people. I don't know anything about economics, about whether we've stolen wealth from the rest of the world, although I doubt it like hell. But as a military man, I can tell you that my first and only instinct here is to fight, to fight for the existence of my country. That is not only my instinct, but my sworn duty. And I suggest, Mr. President, that it is yours as well. We may not have much of a military left, but I can guarantee you that we will fight to the last man and woman. Just give the orders, Mr. President, and I promise you that we will carry them out. Furthermore, I believe we will win!"

Benedict began listening to Krajewski's lecture an apparently defeated man, shoulders slumped forward, fear in his eyes. But as the general continued, his shoulders straightened, and an increasingly resolute expression appeared on his face. This did not escape the attention of Ernest Crippler, nor of Vladimir Raskol'nikov. Crippler had been afraid of this; the one man among the Joint Chiefs who could put a spine back into the carcass of Judas Benedict was in the process of doing just that. But Crippler was prepared. He had received his instructions on how to deal with this situation. Now was the time. The General continued, more animation in his voice now as he sensed victory.

"Mr. President, I suggest that our first priority should be to capture and neutralize that Russian vessel in Los Angeles. Obviously she's carrying a nuclear weapon, if Drugonov said we could detect it from a distance. I know it's risky, sir, but our Special Operations people are the best in the world! They amaze even me!

"And after we take the Volokolamsk, we may very well be out of the woods! Drugonov could be bluffing about having nuclear devices in other cities! In fact, I'd bet my stars that he is! We've got to call that bluff, sir! We owe it to the American people!"

Benedict was looking at the General and beginning to nod his approval. Crippler knew that he had to act fast. Krajewski was being too persuasive. He was threatening to destroy the entire plan. Crippler glanced over at Raskol'nikov, who gave him an almost imperceptible nod. He rose and slowly approached the desk from behind the General.

Krajewski continued. "I suggest we use the SEALs, sir. The West Coast SEAL teams are located in San Diego. We could have them in L.A. in no time. I think we should bypass U.S. Special Operations Command and go directly to Vice Admiral Caruso at Naval Special Warfare Command at Coronado. He could have his people put together a plan that could be executed within twenty-four hours. I'm sure of it! Once the SEALs take the ship--"

With one smooth movement, Crippler drew from inside his jacket a Walter PPKS pistol with a suppressor. He pointed it at the back of the General's head, at the very base of his skull. When he pulled the trigger, the bullet severed Krajewski's medulla oblongata, passed through his cerebral cortex, and exploded outward just above his left eye socket. Blood spurted out of his nose onto the desk, spattering the President with gore. Along with the General, the muffled report died in the soundproofed room.

Krajewski's corpse collapsed onto the floor, blood pouring onto the carpet containing the presidential seal. Benedict, mouth open, eyes wild, silently raised his arms and looked down at himself. Droplets of blood and meaty particles of the General's brain adhered to his jacket, shirt and tie. He looked up at Crippler, standing there with the pistol in his hand. He began to utter guttural, incoherent sounds. Crippler knew that it was up to him to salvage the situation. What he said in the next few minutes would determine the success or failure of his life's work.

"Mr. President! It had to be done, sir!"

He talked fast. "What the general was suggesting would have resulted in millions of deaths! Think! Think of it sir! All those people gone! All that blood on your hands! For the good of the country, for your own political future, it had to be done!"

The President, still saying nothing, rose from his desk on shaky legs and walked to the side of the room, his back to the other two men. He placed his hands on a table, leaned forward, and vomited. Crippler and Raskol'nikov stood silently and said nothing for some minutes as Benedict composed himself. Finally he turned and walked back toward the center of the room.

"Crippler, what the hell do you think you're doing? Have you lost your fucking mind?" he asked.

"I had to do it, Mr. President. Krajewski left me no choice. The policies he was advocating would have been disastrous, to you and to the country. I could not let you make a mistake that you would regret for the rest of your political life," Crippler answered with passion.

"And so you killed him? Why couldn't you have discussed it with me? This is not--" the President began.

"Mr. President, you don't seem to understand!" Crippler almost shouted as he took a step closer to Benedict. He realized that this was the critical moment, the moment to persuade.

"The lives of millions of Americans are at stake, not only in Los Angeles, but in many other cities as well! You heard Drugonov!"

He had to keep Benedict from calling the bluff that Krajewski had correctly postulated.

"General Krajewski was in the process of convincing you to follow his advice. I could not permit that. His death is unfortunate, but it's a small price to pay considering what's at stake! One human life is nothing by contrast!"

"Nothing?" Benedict said as he stared down at the uniformed corpse.

"Ernest, there's a Secret Service man right outside the door. I'm going to call him in here and let the law enforcement process take its course. I don't know what you have in mind, but you just committed a murder, and I'm not going to participate in any sort of coverup."

He began to walk toward the door of the Oval Office. Raskol'nikov stepped in front of him, placing his hands on the President's shoulders.

"Listen, Benedict. We are all men of the world. You don't care about one life any more than I do. Admit it to yourself. It will make what is about to happen much easier for you. The late General was an impediment, an impediment to all our ambitions. Crippler's actions have not only saved millions of lives, but your political future as well."

"That's the third time my political future has been mentioned in this room! What do you mean?" He addressed the question to both of them.

Raskol'nikov answered. "You have sought power all of your life. Now you are losing one type of power, the presidency of your country, but if you cooperate with us we offer you another type, far more complete and infinitely more intoxicating."

Raskol'nikov clasped his hands behind his back and looked at the ceiling.

"Have you ever wondered what it must be like to be an absolute dictator? Really! I am sure that you must have thought about it. All of us have. What is it like to have the power of life and death over hundreds of millions of people? What is it like to be a Stalin or a Hitler? Now that is power!"

He said this with emphasis as he glared at Benedict and stabbed his finger into the air. "I'm not talking about the restricted, shackled powers of the president of a constitutional republic."

Raskol'nikov's hands formed into fists in front of the President's face.

"I'm talking about power that is so absolute as to make a man drunk, to make a man into a god!"

Silence. Benedict raised his chin and looked down his nose at the shorter man.

"Go on," he said.

"Today you have been presented with a fait accompli."

Raskol'nikov's voice dropped to a conspiratorial whisper.

"Why not make the best of it?"

He smiled ever so slightly as he saw a flicker of interest in the President's eyes.

"Maximum Leader Drugonov is prepared to reward you well for your, shall we say, cooperation."

"What could be sufficient reward for turning against my own country?" Benedict probed.

"My dear Benedict! Who said anything about turning against your country?" Raskol'nikov chuckled. "Your national independence is lost. There is nothing anyone can do about that. But you could make your people's transition to their new status so much more comfortable! Your cooperation could save them untold suffering! You don't want your people to suffer unnecessarily, do you?"

"No, of course not," said Benedict.

"Good! Then it's settled! Simply prevent your military from intervening, sign the appropriate documents in New York, and make a convincing speech to the American people. You are a great persuader, Benedict. You always have been. This will be your greatest test. But the rewards will be magnificent! You will be subordinate only to Drugonov. He will rule from Moscow, and you will rule here. You will be a sort of Viceroy, an absolute ruler within your own domain, but answerable to the imperial leadership.

"Think of it, Benedict! Your word will be law! No more dealing with the Congress or the courts. Your wish will be the command of every person in this country! And, to help you deal with any resistance you may meet, I have been instructed to inform you that the rest of your elite, your political and military leadership, will be rewarded for their cooperation as well, to a degree that is commensurate with their station.

"How many members of Congress, how many judges, how many generals could resist an opportunity to have the power of a medieval baron! They, too, would be absolute rulers within their own realms! Power, Benedict! We're offering you and your elite real, unquestioned, absolute power!"

"Now wait a minute, Raskol'nikov! Nothing's settled! What you're asking me to do is unspeakably horrible, especially when, as the General said, I may have it in my power to stop you."

"But that's precisely the point, Benedict. You don't have it within your power to stop us, not if you don't want all of your major cities destroyed. Krajewski was daydreaming with his talk of a commando operation against the Volokolamsk. It would turn into a disaster.

"You know that, don't you? And if you did attack our ship, we would simply detonate the rest of our devices in your other cities. No, Benedict, you cannot stop us. Besides, why would you want to? As the Maximum Leader asked, what would you be defending? You of all people realize that your country deserves to be defeated. You have condemned yourself out of your own mouth!

"Krajewski mentioned survival. Well, you certainly will survive, won't you? And the conditions of your survival will be very pleasant indeed. And that's what really counts, isn't it? Tell me, Benedict. How many young girls a day would it take to satisfy you? Six? Ten? Twenty? Or is it little boys that you prefer?" Raskol'nikov let out a hearty laugh. "Think of it man! It could all be yours! You could be second in command to the most powerful dictator the world has ever seen!"

Raskol'nikov peered into Benedict's eyes as if he were examining a diamond. He looked for any hint of resistance, any sign that this decadent fool might seek to upset the plan. He saw only fear and a trace of curiosity. He was satisfied. He smiled and turned to leave.

"Think about it, Benedict. At least for a day or so," Raskol'nikov said.

"We can accomplish this either with you or without you. We would prefer to do it with your help; it would drastically reduce the bloodshed. And if we were to do it without your cooperation, well, that eliminates you from the equation, doesn't it? And when I say eliminate, I use the term quite literally. That would be most unpleasant--for you."

He paused, smiling, hand on the doorknob. As he looked at the President of the United States, Raskol'nikov tried to keep the contempt in his eyes from showing. He was only partially successful.

General Krajewski's corpse was removed and as much of the blood as possible was washed from the carpet. Dealing with the police and the press would come later. Right now he needed to think. Benedict had given instructions to be left alone. He sat at his desk, telling himself that he was going to find a way out of this predicament. But instead he found himself passively accepting his defeat, the destruction of his country, as the fait accompli that Raskol'nikov had called it. As the minutes became hours, his anxiety gradually turned into relief; this was the fate his country deserved, he began to tell himself.

Deep within him a voice screamed in protest; it was a voice that he had heard many times before. He heard it when he condemned his country; he heard it when he criticized men of ambition and accomplishment as selfish and mean spirited; he heard it when he denied the existence of reality, of causation itself, and embraced the mystical relativity of his age; he heard it when he recited the mantra of 'man-as-animal,' possessed of an impotent faculty of reason, helplessly caught up in a perilously diabolical universe. It was a voice he heard whenever he urged people to put forth their worst qualities rather than their best, and when he praised those qualities as normal and inevitable. It was a voice he heard whenever he belittled his fellow men for the very characteristics that made them human, when he condemned humanity itself for being human. He had become very good at ignoring the voice, and he tried to ignore it this time as well.

This could have represented an epiphany for Judas Benedict. It was an opportunity for him to better understand himself and his own weaknesses. But the revelation eluded him. He was trapped within the realm of feeling, unable to interpret those feelings and to express them as conscious thoughts. He had always been that way. His early childhood had been molded by his relationship with his father: a domineering, demanding man whom Judas had always tried to please, unsuccessfully. He could never understand his father's rejection of his best efforts:

"Why is father angry with me? What have I done? I think I am doing everything correctly, but father is always angry. Father must be right! He is always right!"

These experiences taught the young Judas that his mind was inefficacious, his faculty of reason incapable of dealing successfully with reality. When his father died, many years later, Judas had felt a sense of relief. His belief in the failure of his power of reason led him to the conclusion that he was unfit for reality: that there was no tool available to him with which he could understand the nature of the real universe and the requirements that it placed upon him if he were to survive.

As he passed into his adolescent years, he began to feel helpless, as if he were at the whim of forces beyond his control. It frightened him. Reality frightened him. The world took on a dark, threatening aspect. He began to look to others to protect him from that reality, to shield him from that ominous world. He sensed that there might be safety in numbers. He came to find the concept of a collective to be comforting: a collective that could be expected to sacrifice itself for his well-being. He projected his fears onto others, coming to the belief that no one was competent, that the universe was unknowable. Mankind was impotent. His only salvation was to admit his weakness, and to depend on others.

If he could have lent voice to his feelings, he would have said,

"Everyone, all of us poor wretches, must sacrifice for the well-being of others. Anyone who refuses to sacrifice when called upon is anti-human; anyone who refuses to demand such sacrifice is kidding himself. He cannot survive without it! Those few who seem to have mastered reality, those who possess the arcane knowledge that eludes the majority of men, those men and women of ability, they are the ones to watch out for! How dare they? How dare they feel comfortable, competent, at ease with their relationship with the world when I am a quivering psychic invalid? How dare they enjoy their lives as productive, self-sufficient human

beings? How dare they feel worthy of life and of experiencing delight in all the world has to offer, when I feel worthy of nothing but self-sacrifice? They must be made to pay! For what? For my terror! For the abject horror that lurks in the pit of my stomach! They must be hammered flat! No one is any good! No one deserves to succeed! Everyone must feel as horrible, as incompetent, as unfit for reality as I do!"

This had become Judas Benedict's philosophy. He never voiced it consciously. Such people rarely do. But he felt it. And it had served him well. A great many others agreed with him. They voted for him. They voted for a paternalistic political system that would take care of them, that would protect them from the dictates of a harsh reality. They did not hesitate to demand sacrifice of others, of society's producers. They, too, looked down on those who demonstrated a mastery of reality. We're all just animals trying to survive, they thought. If, by some unknowable means, some of us have been more successful at it than others, that is all the more reason that they should accept the role of sacrificial animal, for the good of the collective. From each according to his ability, to each according to his need!

In Judas Benedict, feelings of impotence had turned to rage, to resentment against the world, against people, against everything. For deep within himself, on a level he did not even know existed, he resented being expected to sacrifice his own life for others. Consciously, intellectually, he accepted the need for universal self-sacrifice. He espoused it at every opportunity. But internally, within the depths of his mind, he could not accept the role of sacrificial animal. No one can willingly do that. No sane human being thinks so little of his own life as to place it at the random disposal of strangers. It violates the primary metaphysical and moral dictate of human existence: to live one's own life for one's own sake.

And so subconsciously Judas Benedict hated his own most closely-held beliefs. He hated the human species for relegating him to the status of sacrificial animal. And he hated himself for accepting that status. That was the source of the little voice screaming within him.

As he sat at his desk, a dispersed, target-less anger welled up within him. *I'll get back at them!* he thought, instantly wondering why such an idea would cross his mind. *I'll make them pay!* Make who pay, and for what, the little voice asked? No answer. *I'll take whatever I can get, and to hell with the rest of them!*

CHAPTER TWELVE

President Judas Benedict stood before the large mirror in his White House bedroom. He draped the striped maroon tie around his neck and began to insert it under his collar. His wife Vanessa was sitting on the edge of the bed adjusting her stockings.

"I had a wonderful time today at the meeting of the Coalition for Global Fairness," she said.

"That's good, dear. I'm glad you enjoyed yourself."

"Bubbles Deerdorf and I were having a few daiquiris, and we came up with a solution to the problem of global hunger."

"That's nice."

"Don't you want to know what it is?"

"Not now, dear. We can discuss it later."

"You do approve of the Coalition for Global Fairness, don't you?"

"Of course I do. It's a very worthy cause."

Vanessa laughed. "I suppose you feel the same way about the People's Coalition for the Environment, the Center for the Study of Gun Violence, and all the other groups I belong to."

"Why, yes. Yes I do. They're all very progressive, forward-thinking organizations. If their agenda were accomplished, this country would be a much better, more enlightened place. Perhaps this current—unpleasantness— might not be happening."

"You whore!" she chuckled. "You don't believe in that sort of shit any more than I do. But those people vote. And it just so happened that they gave you enough votes in the last election to put you in this monstrosity of a house."

"That's not true, Vanessa! I believe in all those causes! We have to continue moving in the direction of selflessness and altruism. We've made a good start in the last few generations, but we've got a long way to go. We have a hundred and fifty years of greed and selfishness to live down. Sometimes I don't think we'll ever be able to cleanse ourselves of that filthy heritage."

"That 'filthy heritage' made your family, and, I might add, you, very rich. I've never heard you complain too much about that."

"Oh, Vanessa, sometimes I think I would have been happier if I had spent my life working with my hands or my back: really producing something! Toiling away like a respectable man should."

"You fucking liar! You'd die if you had to do a real day's work! You've never picked up anything heavier than a martini glass in your life!"

Vanessa laughed heartily.

"That's not my fault, Vanessa. I was raised in a different world than most people. I was enculturated into it. I had no choice. I grew up among those people: dirty capitalists, industrialists, tycoons, captains of industry! Those bastards!"

He stared off into space. "They always knew what to do! They always had the answers! They were so, so good, so competent, so capable, and I was..."

Vanessa burst out laughing.

"And you were poor little Judas, who could never quite measure up, who never had the answers, who was incompetent and incapable! Poor stupid, inept Judas, who hid behind his father's accomplishments for as long as he could, and then, when the old man finally died, ran his bank halfway into the ground! Christ, you're pathetic! Bring me my shoes!"

Judas instantly abandoned his tie.

"Which ones?"

"The black ones, you ass!"

The President hurried to the closet and retrieved the proper shoes. Quickly, he brought them to his wife, placing then at her feet.

"So what are you going to do about Drugonov?" she asked.

"I'm not sure. I made up my mind to capitulate earlier today, but since then I've had second thoughts. All afternoon, I've had this annoying feeling that perhaps we should resist. It's just a feeling. It's not based on anything solid, but it keeps nagging at me. I can't get out of my mind what Krajewski said: that it's my duty to resist. I've never cared much about duty. I've never really understood what it means. But maybe it has something to do with this strange feeling I've been having.

"We could resist, you know. We do still have a crack military, in spite of all the force reductions and funding cuts. I don't know. I just don't know. Drugonov has us over a barrel, with nuclear devices planted all over the country. The military thinks he may be bluffing, but I don't think so. Resistance means millions dead. Isn't life as a colony better than no life at all? Maybe the American people would be little more than slaves, but at least a slave is alive! And the Russian people do need us! They legitimately need us to sacrifice ourselves! That need places a moral burden on us, Vanessa. Duty or not, I don't think I could order resistance in good conscience.

"As much as I hate to do it, I think our best course, best for both the Russian and the American people, is to submit. But the fact that it is the morally proper thing to do makes my decision a bit easier, I just need to make sure the people in this town will go along with me

"Under ordinary circumstances, I would put the question up for a vote before the U.N. General Assembly. I'm sure that a week ago they would have voted for our surrender, considering how much they've always hated our guts. That would have given me the legal cover I need. All enlightened people in this country–the people who really matter--would be willing to accept the verdict of world opinion, especially with a little help from the press. But in my speech the other day, I promised many of those countries the moon. Once Drugonov's ultimatum becomes public, and they find out what he has in store for us, as well as for them, they'd probably vote for our self-defense out of purely selfish motives. Not only won't they get a nickel out of Drugonov, but once we're out of the way, he's going to enslave them too. What do you think? I'm right, aren't I?"

"About the morality of surrender? I'm sure you've convinced yourself it's the right thing to do. At least it's an interesting rationalization. It's exactly what I'd expect of you. And you can forget about the U.N. Once Drugonov takes over, he'll probably kill everybody there and bulldoze the building into the East River. That may be his one worthwhile accomplishment, his only true service to mankind."

"As far as people in this town offering any public resistance is concerned, I don't think you have much to worry about. Most of the people in Washington are attracted to power like flies to shit. As Drugonov has promised, if you just give them their own little fiefdoms to rule, they'll jump on the bandwagon. If anyone starts making speeches about God, country and apple pie, you can do what you've always done--smear them! With a few phone calls to the right people, it should be easy enough to get the press to call them names: selfish, reactionary, regressive, unfair, insensitive."

"Use your imagination! Go on the offensive! Be strong just once in your life! Pretend that you actually have a set of balls between your legs! After all, you are the President. Of course, this Uglanov character that Drugonov mentioned could save you all that trouble. Anyone who won't play ball could simply disappear. Make up a list of troublemakers and see that Uglanov gets it. You can have them liquidated, like you did Krajewski."

"I didn't have Krajewski liquidated! It just....happened."

"You didn't? Too bad. I thought you had shown a little backbone for a change."

"I have a backbone, Vanessa! Just wait and see! Drugonov thinks he's got me by the short hairs, but before this is over I'll have him right where I want him!"

She chuckled.

"Bullshit! You've never been able to deal with a man like Drugonov! He'll chew you up and spit you out like a cheap sausage. I suggest you practice licking his boots instead. It shouldn't be too hard. You've been licking mine for years."

"Vanessa, please. Don't talk to me that way. You know how it makes me feel. Besides, I'm only doing what's in the best interest of the American people."

"Save that for the unwashed hordes! We've been married for nineteen years, remember? I know what makes you tick. You're not interested in the American people. You're interested in power: power over everyone who's humiliated you, power over everyone who's criticized you, power over everyone who's made you feel small and insignificant. Drugonov's offering to make you into a viceroy. That would give you absolute control over all of those competent people you hate so much, all of those captains of industry who have caused you so much embarrassment all your life. This is your chance to get back at them! They'll dance to your tune or pay with their lives! Think of the psychic rewards, Judas! Imagine how many Gordian knots that would cut in your poor, confused brain! How can you resist?"

President Benedict peered out the window.

"It would be quite a.....Damn it Vanessa! I wouldn't be doing it for that reason! The people made me, Judas Benedict, President of this country and I have a responsibility to them! If I don't agree to Drugonov's terms, half the population could die! The people trust me to do the right thing! That's why they voted for me!"

"Don't try to feed me that shit. I know what's going on in that ball of worms you use for a mind. Even if you have temporarily convinced yourself that caving in to Drugonov is in the national interest, it's just an evasion. You always did have a way of evading reality.

"Power, Judas. It's all about power. Do yourself a favor and for once come to grips with the real world.

"I don't give a damn what kind of psychic pain you're experiencing right now. I've never given a shit about you since the day we met. But it's difficult even for me not to feel at least some pity for you, as I would for a stray dog that had been hit by a car. Take some advice: forget all this altruistic crap. It's just clouding the issue.

"And don't give yourself too much credit for becoming President. You know as well as I do that if it weren't for me you'd still be a backbencher in the Pennsylvania legislature. The only reason you're President is because I shoved a cattle prod up your ass and walked you all the way to the White House!"

"Please, Vanessa...."

"You hypocritical bastard! You've never been able to handle the truth! You know, Judas, it would take an army of psychiatrists to untangle that rat's nest in your head."

"Vanessa, I don't think..."

"Bring me my pearl necklace!"

Benedict virtually jumped in the direction of the dressing table, retrieved the necklace and handed it to his wife. For a moment there was silence. Then,

"Why did you marry me, Vanessa?"

"That's easy. A week after we met, I knew you were a loser. You had already squandered half your inheritance. But I saw one spark within you. You were the greatest bullshit artist I had ever met. And I learned on our first date that you would take orders. I thought that with your name, and your family's reputation, you had political potential, as long as you were under the right thumb. You love to be dominated, Judas. That, and your talent for bullshit, are your only saving graces."

"I don't love to be dominated, Vanessa! You shouldn't say such things. What if someone overheard?"

"You don't love to be dominated?" she laughed. "Tell me that when you're tied up in bed and I'm standing over you with a whip in my hand! That little penis of yours stands at attention and whistles 'Hail to the Chief'!"

He could say nothing. His head fell to his chest. He walked back to the dressing table and began looking for his cufflinks.

"Hurry up, 'MR. President'! The people from The Association for Planetary Redistribution are waiting to be graced by your August presence!"

CHAPTER THIRTEEN

A conference room in the White House

Chief of Naval Operations Admiral James Saunders took a seat at the large oval table between Lt. General Bob Halleck, sitting in for General Krajewski, and Marine Corps Commandant General Norval Beckstrom. To Beckstrom's left sat Air Force Chief of Staff General Eldridge Moore.

So, thought Saunders, whatever this meeting is about involves all four services. But it was obvious that it involved a great deal more than just the military. He looked around at the others who had been called for this unexpected and completely unorthodox meeting. President Benedict sat at the center of the table. He was flanked on his right by Vice President Arthur Whitaker, a boring, unimaginative man whose most endearing characteristic, as all of Washington knew, was his absolute loyalty to his superior, a 'yes' man of almost mythic proportions, even in this town. Also present were the members of the 'inner cabinet', the four secretaries whose departments had existed since the Washington administration: Secretary of State Blanchard, Secretary of Defense Martinez, Secretary of the Treasury Phillips, and Attorney General Forsythe. Congress, too, was represented. At the end of the table was Senate Majority Leader Howell, and to his right Speaker of the House Abraham. To round out this unusually eclectic collection of the country's leadership were National Security Advisor Crippler and White House Chief of Staff Elfman.

The President cleared his throat, getting everyone's attention. He said, "I want to begin this meeting by voicing what we are all thinking about: our regret regarding the horrible tragedy of General Krajewski's suicide."

There was a murmuring of voices around the table, especially from the direction of the Joint Chiefs.

"Of course, I was present at the time, and I'm still shaken from the experience. You have probably asked yourselves what could possibly cause a man like Mike Krajewski to kill himself. Unfortunately, you will find out here today."

From across the table General Beckstrom said to Admiral Saunders, "It seems damned strange for a man to commit suicide by shooting himself in the back of the head."

Saunders knew that it was impossible for the President not to have heard the comment, but as far as the Admiral could see, Benedict did not react. Saunders knew that since the President of the United States himself claimed to be an eyewitness to the event, it was unlikely that anyone would seriously question the method of

Krajewski's death. The press was reporting that Benedict had ordered the 'suicide' to be investigated by the National Park Service Police, an organization unused to this type of case. No uncomfortable questions would be asked.

Benedict continued. "General Krajewski decided to end his life because he was faced with a reality that he could not endure, the destruction of his country."

The President looked around the table as if expecting a chorus of protests. Instead there was a deathly silence in the room. Finally, Admiral Saunders said, "What do you mean, Mr. President?"

Benedict answered, "Yesterday we were presented with an ultimatum by Russia: either we surrender our country to them by Friday at five P.M. eastern time, and become a colony of theirs, or they will destroy Los Angeles with a nuclear weapon already planted in that city. If we actively resist, if we initiate a strike against Russia, all of our major cities will be destroyed with similar weapons.

"Ever since the presentation of this ultimatum, I have searched for alternatives, but I can find none. Unless someone at this table can suggest a solution, I see no choice but to capitulate."

Benedict repeated most of the details of his conversation with Drugonov. He omitted the offer of rewards for collaboration. He was saving that for later. General Beckstrom was the first to react. Slapping his palms down on the table, he said, "Mr. President, this is absurd! This sort of thing just isn't done!"

Ernest Crippler broke in. "I'm afraid you're wrong, General. Hitler did something similar at the beginning of World War Two. There is ample precedent."

Admiral Saunders said, "Let me get this straight, Mr. President. We receive an ultimatum from the Russians, and you suggest we cave in? Without a fight?"

"What is our alternative, Admiral?" Benedict answered. "Drugonov has us over a barrel. All our major cities are mined with nuclear weapons. We have only a matter of hours before the first of them detonates. Loss of life from that explosion alone would be in the millions. As for fighting them, you know better than I do that we have very little with which to fight.

"I know, I know. That's largely my fault. But that's water under the bridge. The point is that we simply can't prevent Drugonov from carrying out his threat. We just don't have the means. It seems to me that we have the choice of resisting, and suffering perhaps a hundred million dead, or throwing in the towel. Am I wrong in that assumption? Does anyone here have an alternative?"

Speaker Abraham said, "This is impossible! We've had excellent relations with Russia since the fall of communism! We've negotiated treaties with them! We've worked together against Islamic terrorism and to resolve the Israeli-Palestinian crisis! They've supported us on the issue of nuclear weapons in North Korea!

"I myself have made three trips there in the past eighteen months! I've met with their leadership! They were reasonable, sane men, at least until this Drugonov came along! I can't believe that one man could make such a difference, that he could reverse all the progress we've made in recent years!"

Ernest Crippler said, "Mr. Speaker, history is full of such men. All it takes is a strong, charismatic leader combined with the right social and economic conditions. The Russian people are poor, hungry and frustrated. They've seen themselves reduced from the status of superpower to that of a bankrupt mendicant. And they saw no end in sight. Then came Drugonov.

"He offers them hope. He offers them a way back to what they see as their rightful place in the world, as a strong, even a dominant power. And he offers them order to replace the chaos they have been experiencing since the fall of the Soviet Union. Not only does he promise to fill their empty stomachs, but their empty spirits as well."

"By God, Crippler, if I didn't know better, I'd say you admired the man!" said Speaker Abraham. Crippler had been indiscrete; he had said too much.

"Gentlemen," the President said. "To get back to my question, does anyone here have a viable alternative to surrender?"

The table broke out in angry, nervous debate. General Moore raised his hands for attention. The noise died down.

"Mr. President, we simply can't capitulate without a fight. Even if Drugonov destroys our cities, he would still have to take the country house by house. Our surviving military could join with armed civilians and make the conquest of the United States virtually impossible! We could launch a guerilla war that would make conquering and governing this country a nightmare!"

Benedict responded. "All right, General. Let's say we did it your way. You may be right. Maybe we could hold them off by guerilla warfare. Maybe we could even prevail eventually. But in the process, at the very outset, a hundred million American men, women and children would die: our cities incinerated, the air and water poisoned, the soil itself radioactive. Could you live with that, General?"

He looked around the table. "Could any of you?"

Half the people at the table looked down, avoiding the President's eyes. No one said anything. Finally, General Beckstrom cleared his throat and said, "Mr. President, if you think that capitulation is the proper course, and if you give orders to that effect, we in the military are bound to obey. We will hate it like hell, but we will obey. Our mission as military men is to defend this country. But if, in the very act of defending it, we cause its destruction, we have no choice but to refrain from carrying out that mission."

Several heads nodded agreement around the table. Benedict's policy of choosing 'yes' men was paying off. But there were still a few holdouts.

Admiral Saunders knew that what he was about to say might be the equivalent of signing his own death warrant, but he could not constrain himself.

"I'm not sure I could obey such orders, sir. I took an oath to uphold the Constitution and to defend this country. I feel obliged to do that to the best of my ability. I don't believe we've explored all the options. Any decision we make right now would be precipitate and premature. We should use the hours we have left to seek an alternative. We may not have the military we had four years ago," and here he looked directly into the President's eyes, "but that is not to say we are entirely impotent. We have at our disposal the best technology and the finest men and women in the world. We cannot let this barbarian intimidate us. Give me six hours, Mr. President. My people will find a solution."

Benedict exhaled audibly, as if preparing for an unpleasant task.

"Admiral Saunders, let me tell you something else that Drugonov said. He has files on everyone, everyone at this table, everyone in Washington. Anyone who refuses to collaborate will be--punished.

"What I mean to say is that he cannot only have us assassinated, all of us in government, but he can also get to our families: our wives, our children. He mentioned torture. If we do resist, not only will Los Angeles be incinerated, but our families will pay the price as well. Drugonov made it clear to me that there would be no place to hide, no way to protect them. He has agents everywhere."

Ernest Crippler broke the pregnant silence which followed the President's remarks.

"Is anyone still in favor of resistance?"

Again, silence permeated the room: palpable, ominous, guilt-ridden. Admiral Saunders, so irate that he trembled visibly, decided to keep his own council.

Then Senator Howell said, "Well, you've given us the stick. Now what about a carrot? Did Drugonov offer any, ah, inducements for cooperation?"

Heads snapped in Howell's direction. But the question seemed to please Benedict and Crippler. Saunders saw both men trying, unsuccessfully, to suppress smiles.

"As a matter of fact, Willard," Benedict said, "something to that effect was mentioned. Drugonov has said that those who agree to his terms will be rewarded handsomely. What I am about to say, you will probably consider very un-American. Some of you may, at first, find it offensive. But I urge you to consider it. Think it over. Think about what it would mean to you personally. And also consider the fact that there is really no alternative.

"Well, here it is. I have been assured that any of you who go along will be given your own districts, to rule over as you see fit. You will have absolute authority within your territory. Absolute.

"The comparison was made to a medieval barony. That goes for everyone in Congress and in the federal court system. Roger, Willard, you can pass that along. You would answer only to me, and, ultimately, to Drugonov."

The President's proposition, so alien and yet so alluring, took a moment to sink in. At last, the Secretary of the Treasury asked, "When you say 'absolute authority', does that include authority over people, over money? Anything we want?"

"Yes it does, Grover," Benedict answered. "You will all be like dictators within your own realms: no due process, no property rights, nothing to constrain you at all."

Saunders saw shock, revulsion on the faces around the table. But he suspected that a great deal of it was feigned. His instincts told him that these people were interested. Never, he told himself, underestimate the greed of a whore. And that goes double for political whores.

Benedict continued. "Believe me, I understand how distasteful this must be to many of you. It is distasteful to me as well. The idea of the United States being divided into districts presided over by virtual autocrats is a concept that has always been totally foreign to all of us in this country. No one in the history of our republic has even conceived of such a thing. But our reality has changed, and we must be willing to change with it if we are to survive. You all want to survive, don't you? You want your families to survive.

"Drugonov offers all of us survival if only we have the flexibility and the courage to reach out and take it.

"Actually," he continued, "we all knew that something like this had to come someday, didn't we? How long could we expect to be the hegemonic power of the globe? How long did we think we would be able to get away with victimizing the rest of the world without having to pay a price? How much poverty, death, and suffering could we expect to inflict without having to face a reckoning?

"Yes, our country will come to an end. I am convinced that there is nothing that we can do to stop that. And maybe we deserve it. But at least some of us, you and I and other chosen elites, will be able to salvage our lives. Over the past few hours I have come to the conclusion that our only rational course of action is to look out for ourselves."

Several people at the table looked at him askance, still challenging the President's reasoning, however meekly.

"Well," he continued vehemently, raising his arms into the air. "Does anyone here want to die? The Maximum Leader and I are offering you life, and a pretty damned good life too, if you ask me! Who among you would not enjoy a measure of absolute power? Who among you would not like to pay back old grudges with impunity? Who among you would not like to live the life you know you deserve: a life with no rules, with no limits, a life of luxury provided by the labor of others, a life in which your every whim becomes the command of thousands?

"How many of you are so unselfish that you can turn down all of that in favor of a 'noble' death?"

"What about liberty, Mr. President?" asked Admiral Saunders.

"Admiral, liberty is an illusion. I've never really believed in it. Have any of you?"

He looked around the table. No one answered.

"Those musty old documents in the National Archives which proclaimed individual liberty: the Declaration of Independence, the Constitution and the Bill of Rights, have not been taken seriously by most of us for generations. Should the Maximum Leader invalidate those documents, he would not be destroying them; we destroyed them ourselves years ago. We did it consciously, and with good reason. The principles of individual liberty embodied in those documents represent the epitome of selfishness.

"The political and judicial leaders of this country, and those who have preceded us for the past several generations, have gone to great lengths to ignore, twist and distort those principles. Virtually our entire elite–intellectual, journalistic and political–has invested tremendous effort convincing our people that individual liberty is regressive, mean spirited, unfair, insensitive."

He smiled at his use of these hackneyed, but endlessly useful, catchwords: the tools of his party's trade.

"A plurality of Americans has come to agree with us. My election, and the elections of a right-thinking majority in Congress, is ample evidence of that. If you recall Maximum Leader Drugonov's speech before the Duma, he mentioned that the countries of the West have been drifting in the direction of collective self-sacrifice in recent decades. He was absolutely right.

"For many in this country, Admiral, individual liberty is simply inconsistent with the kind of society they now want. Millions of Americans decided years ago that they would exchange their liberty for a 'free' set of dentures! Trillions of dollars have been consumed by the great, redistributive, leviathan state which we have constructed to accommodate them. We politicians around this table owe our electoral success to those people.

"In my speeches, I have frequently referred to Americans as being selfish, too concerned with their own individual liberty. Despite our efforts, that is still true of some. There continues to exist in this country a stubborn core who refuse to sacrifice themselves for the good of others. My speeches have always been designed to sway those individualists, to make them feel guilty and isolated, to subject them to ostracism by the altruistic majority. We have carefully designed our tax structure so as to force that hard core of individuals into a sacrificial role whether they like it or not. I am convinced that, at least domestically, we were winning the battle against individualism, against individual liberty. We succeeded in making it 'politically incorrect.'

"Oh, we pretended to pay attention to a carefully-selected set of freedoms: speech, press, religion, the rights of the accused. But our elites were in the process of seeing to it that even some of those were eroding away. Any public display of religion, if it had the most tangential relation to the state, and no matter how innocuous it might be, had become anathema. And did you know that some university campuses in this country actually have 'Free Speech Zones,' restricted areas where people can say what they really believe? Now that's progress!

"Another reason for my calling the American people selfish is because this growing spirit of self-sacrifice has never been extended to the rest of the world, to the countries which are truly in need. It has so far been a purely domestic phenomenon. Our transnational corporations are largely to blame for that.

"I attempted to rectify this shortcoming recently at the United Nations. Our corporate leaders, and all the rest of our entrepreneurs, large and small–the most selfish of the lot–will find a gun at their heads. Except now, the gun will not belong to the Internal Revenue Service. It will be a Russian gun. Those unreconstructed individualists will fall into line or pay with their lives!

"But the majority of Americans, I am sure, will not object to this new political arrangement, Admiral. After decades of indoctrination, we have successfully turned them into altruists. We are now simply, at long last, extending that altruism beyond our borders, to our brothers and sisters in Russia. Our people will finally reach their highest moral potential, a goal so lofty that few of us have even dared dream of it: they will achieve ethical perfection through their own enslavement!"

Admiral Saunders noticed Crippler behaving strangely, eyes darting from face to face, as if to carefully gauge the reactions to these comments. What the Admiral could not know was that anyone who did no respond properly now would have to be liquidated. Crippler would take no chances. Uglanov's people were standing by for his telephone call. One word from him, and anyone in this room would be dead before sundown.

Several people around the table were shaking their heads. Crippler shot to his feet and shouted in his most commanding voice, as if to deliver a shock treatment.

"Listen to me!"

He began slowly walking around the table, looking at each person in turn.

"Stop kidding yourselves! You know why you got into politics! It was for power! Don't deny it! You know it's true!"

Senator Howell said in a gruff voice, "Don't you think that's a bit harsh, Ernie? A little cynical?"

"Bullshit!" shouted Crippler.

The Senator cringed in spite of himself. The National Security Advisor continued, "You're not blowing smoke up your constituents' asses now! You can drop the act! We all know that power is what makes this city run! And you were attracted to it like flies to a rotting corpse!

"I don't care if you're in Congress, the courts or in the administration the accumulation of raw power is what makes you get up in the morning! What the hell do you care if the United States ceases to exist? That was never your concern! Are you worried about the flag, patriotism, the Constitution? Those of you on the political side have spent you whole careers destroying those things! Don't be so hypocritical as to say that you care about them now! Don't let your hypocrisy ruin the best opportunity you've ever had! This is your chance to realize your life's dream! This is your chance to gain absolute control over the lives, the bodies, the souls of entire populations!

"Think of it! Here's your chance to become something other than just another turd floating around in this beltway cesspool! What you are being offered today represents the kind of power for which people would gladly kill; the kind of power that has built and toppled empires! Don't be fools! This opportunity will never come again! It's now or never!

"Those of you in the military are not guilty of destroying the Constitution. You have honestly tried to uphold it in your own way. But you too stand to gain here! Since achieving high rank, haven't you also experienced the euphoria of power? Don't you want more of it? This is your chance to throw the regulation manual out the window! And, most importantly, don't you want your families to survive?

"And don't underestimate the seriousness of Drugonov's threats! He knows every detail of your lives! He knows how to get to you and everyone you care about! As high-level government functionaries, you've been used to issuing threats, not receiving them! But you must believe that the Maximum Leader will tolerate no opposition! If you don't fall into line, someone else will be found to take your place! And you will not be around to regret your stupidity! Do yourselves a favor! Accept these terms! Capitulate!"

No one at the table looked at anyone else. Each had to make his or her own decision, and seemed embarrassed at the turn his or her mind was taking. All except Admiral Saunders. He looked around himself, at the creatures who a few moments ago he had considered to be human beings, even patriots. But now he saw them as nothing more than insects. He knew he had a reputation for knuckling under to authority, as did all the military men at this table. He knew that he had been chosen for this post over the heads of dozens of others with more seniority because he was considered easy to manipulate. He knew what kind of men the President wanted as his Joint Chiefs. But, by God, there was a limit! He was not a traitor!

Vice President Whitaker said, "I think we should all do as the President and Mr. Crippler suggest. If they think it is in the best interests of this country to capitulate to Drugonov, then that is what we should do, in my opinion."

Benedict looked around the table for any signs of dissent. There were none to be seen.

"Good. Then if we're all agreed, I think we should adjourn this meeting."

Several people began to rise from their seats. Saunders could no longer contain himself. His blood boiled at the atmosphere of treason in the room, so thick you could cut it with a knife. He slammed his fists into the table and erupted from his chair.

"Now wait just a minute! You're ready to give up our country after just a half hour of discussion? I don't believe this! What kind of people are you? Do you know how many have died to preserve this nation? You've just spit on the graves of every patriot who has spilled his blood in defense of this country stretching back to the Battle of Lexington and Concord!"

He looked to his left, at Norval Beckstrom, with fire in his eyes.

"Beckstrom! How can you do this? How can you order the entire United States Marine Corps, with its history, its long list of heroes, to passively stand down? My God, man, it's an atrocity!"

He looked at Air Force Chief of Staff Moore and Army General Halleck with equal ferocity.

"Moore, Halleck, how can you go along with this, this blasphemy? You took an oath! Remember?"

The three men were not able to meet the Admiral's eyes.

"I'm not a religious man, but if there is a God, I hope he sees to it that you fry in Hell for this, all three of you! Everyone in this room! I hope you all spend eternity being tormented by the souls of a million dead soldiers, sailors and marines! God damn you! God damn you all!"

Crippler peered at the Admiral, something approaching hatred in his eyes. A phone call would be made. Saunders would not live to see another sunrise.

"Admiral, we have already determined that there are no viable military options that do not involve the deaths of an unacceptable number of Americans. Given that, it seems to me that our choice has been made for us."

"We haven't determined any such thing, Crippler!" the Admiral shouted. "I told you that my people could find a solution to this problem, and I meant it!"

The President rose and looked solemnly at Saunders.

"Admiral, all of us, I am sure, appreciate your patriotism. But I have given you a direct order to stand down. The United States Navy will offer no resistance to Drugonov's demands. Is that clear?

"Now, throughout your distinguished career, you have always been exemplary in the way you follow orders. Do so now. I feel certain that you will be pleasantly surprised at the rewards your discipline in this matter will produce for you."

"You can shove your rewards up your ass, Mr. President!" staring at his Commander in Chief through eyes that had become narrow slits.

Benedict said nothing. He would not cross swords with this man. He would let Crippler, and Uglanov, exact his revenge for that remark. To everyone's surprise, Lupe Martinez spoke up.

"The President is right, Admiral. We have no choice but to submit, and to salvage as much as we can from an unpleasant situation. I, for one, find the prospect of ruling my section of West Texas to be rather attractive. There are a lot of scores I'd like to settle, a lot of people I would like to make disappear.

"As the President said, it's time we looked out for ourselves."

Speaker of the House Abraham said, "I agree. Think of it this way, Admiral. If we don't go along, the Russians will simply put their own people in charge of this country. We'll be out of power, our families may very well suffer and die, and the American people will be forced to endure the tyrannical rule of a foreign dictator. At least this way, we can provide some continuity. We can act as a cushion between Drugonov and the people of this country. We can give our people local dictators with whom they're familiar. We can try to protect them from the worst excesses of this Drugonov. I mean, the Maximum Leader."

Senator Howell added, "Roger's right. Our accepting these district leadership positions is ultimately in the best interests of our people. Yes! Yes, that's the spin to put on it! We're actually doing them a favor! We don't have to emphasize the fact that we're helping ourselves in the process. It doesn't even have to be mentioned."

Heads around the table nodded vigorously. Ernest Crippler smiled openly, seemingly elated, like a child on Christmas morning. It was apparent to Admiral Saunders that the National Security Advisor no longer felt the need to conceal his feelings. Saunders knew at that moment who had been Drugonov's man in the administration, the furtive architect of this massive betrayal.

In a colossal feat of will, he kept himself from diving across the table and tearing off Crippler's head. The only thing that restrained him was the knowledge that he had a task before him, perhaps his last act in defense of his country, if the threats he had heard at this meeting were genuine. A plan was forming in his mind. It just might work. But he could not tip his hand now.

Attorney General Forsythe added, "Sure, that's it. The American people need us to perform this service for them. It'll take them some time to realize it. There will be a lot of anger at first among the unenlightened. But with the kind of power we'll have, we'll be able to handle it. I'm all in favor of accepting these district positions; we owe it to our country, and to ourselves!"

The Vice President looked contemplative as he said, "You know, nothing lasts forever, and that includes nation-states. Even Rome fell. We've had an experiment with democracy here that lasted well over two hundred years, and it just didn't work out, that's all. The tide of history has turned. Now it's time for the country to change. And if those of us who have been leaders, and want to remain in leadership positions, will have to change too. The nice thing about all this is that it's a win-win situation: we get to live our lives as we've always known we should live them, and the American people benefit from our leadership."

General Moore had regained his composure after Saunders' tirade. He said, "I can't say that I like it much, but the military has always been under civilian control. You're the civilian leadership. If you say this is what should happen, then so be it.

"By the way, Mr. President, did the Maximum Leader mention anything about these positions being hereditary?"

Crippler burst out laughing, as if at the ease with which his task had been completed.

"Well," the President said. "We seem to have reached at least a majority consensus. I'll meet with Drugonov, or I should say, the Maximum Leader, in New York the day after tomorrow and, ah, finalize this agreement. In the meantime, I suggest that you meet with your subordinates Explain to them the rewards, and the punishments, with which they are faced.

"Generals and Admiral, I expect you to see to it that your forces stand down. I want there to be absolutely no resistance. I know that's a tall order, but see to it nonetheless. I'm holding you responsible. And so will the Maximum Leader.

"Admiral Saunders, I want you especially to consider that a direct order. You took an oath to defend this country, but that oath also included the requirement that you obey the orders of your superiors I want you to put your personal feelings aside and do as you are told. I will remind you again that your life, and the lives of your family members depend on your obedience. Now, if there are no further comments, let's adjourn."

CHAPTER FOURTEEN

Admiral James Saunders sat in the backseat of the car on the ride to the Pentagon. His driver was Petty Officer William Washington from Mobile, Alabama. Everyone called him Willie. The two men usually chatted on such trips, but today the Admiral was lost in thought. Willie noticed the change in his boss's demeanor.

"Excuse me sir, but is everything all right? You seem awful quiet today."

Saunders came out of his reverie. He liked Willie Washington. Everybody did.

"Well, Willie, I've just got some things on my mind."

The simple act of speaking, of talking to another person, an ordinary human being who was not a part of the diabolical cabal he had just attended, was refreshing. He felt his nerves uncoil. He found himself drawn into conversation. He needed to forget for a few moments the madness he had just witnessed, to remind himself that a sane world really did exist somewhere.

"Maybe I could help take your mind off your troubles, Admiral. Do you remember me telling you about my daughter Joline, sir?"

"Joline? Sure I do Willie. She's in what now, the fourth grade?"

"That's right, sir. She sure is. Well, she's been takin' dancin' lessons for the last year or so. Last night she gave a recital at her school, along with a lot of the other kids. You should'a seen it sir! She just floated across that stage like a butterfly: leapin' about, spinnin', dancin' as pretty as you please! I was so proud I almost busted!"

Saunders smiled. These were good thoughts. "You have a son too, right Willie? How's he doing?"

"Oh, just fine, Admiral! He's the first-string runnin' back for the Junior Varsity football team, even though he's only a freshman! He scored two touchdowns in last Saturday's game! They're talkin' about puttin' him on the Varsity team next year! How about that! The kid gets real good grades too. I think he may get a scholarship before he's done. He's a lot smarter than his old man, that's for sure! Thank God for that!"

Saunders looked out the window as he listened to his driver talk. In the lane next to them was a family in a sport utility vehicle with luggage piled on the roof. In the back seat several children wrestled. Saunders could see their little arms and legs slashing through the air, an occasional head bobbing upward. The mother turned around in her seat and silently shook her finger at the youngsters, whose thrashing subsided, at least temporarily. It looked as though they were going on vacation. I wonder where, he thought?

They drove past a man on the sidewalk wearing a tweed jacket and hat. His dog had stopped at a fire hydrant and was lifting his leg. The man tried to look nonchalant. Some children were playing in a park, playing a game of some sort, he couldn't tell what. Running, running, jumping.

As they approached the river, Saunders saw a young man and woman sitting on the bank enjoying each other's company. The young man was slowly tossing something, pebbles probably, into the water. What are they talking about, he wondered?

Boats in the water. People enjoying a brisk spring day, glorying in their very lives. Oh, how I wish I could do that, he thought. How I wish I could board one of those wonderful boats and sail it and never stop sailing and never stop sailing until...Like a hammer, reality crashed down upon him. He thought of scenes such as he had just witnessed, repeated endlessly across the country: people living their lives in the cities, in the fields, in the mountains, in the deserts, people who were depending on him to protect them, people to whom he had sworn an oath on his sacred honor.

"No!" he thought. All of this can't be over! It can't be coming to an end! These people, and all the rest like them, they deserve to live their own lives! They've done nothing to deserve being crushed by Drugonov! He thought about his own family: of his wife Katherine and their two children, Lisa and James Junior. Lisa was graduating from high school this year, and James was in his second year at the Naval Academy. His mother was still alive; he had that to consider as well. He had a sister who lived in Indianapolis, and she had a husband and three children. My God! What a nightmare this is!

He did not doubt Drugonov's reach. If the man wanted to kill his family, there was probably very little he could do to stop it. His family. They were everything to him. The thought of anything happening to them was unbearable. But so was the thought of anything happening to his country.

"...And she's been that way ever since. So that's what's been goin' on with my family, sir. What about yours?" Willie asked.

"My family's just fine, Willie. They couldn't be better," Saunders answered. "When you get right down to it, Willie, a man's family is about all that matters, don't you think so?"

"I suspect you're right, Admiral, when you get right down to it."

"But what about your country, Willie? Where does that fit in?"

"I'm not sure I understand what you mean, Admiral."

"If you had to choose between your family and your country, which would it be?"

"Sir, I know you're the top boss of the entire Navy, and maybe I shouldn't say this, but to be honest with you sir, I'd hate like hell to make that decision."

"I know exactly what you mean, Willie. I know exactly what you mean."

James Saunders sat at his desk in his Pentagon office. His head was spinning. In front of him were framed photographs of his family. Against the wall stood the United States flag. Forty-nine hours, nine minutes. He decided. Picking up the phone, he punched in the number for Naval Special Warfare Command in Coronado, California. He did not know it, but his mind was operating along exactly the same lines as had General Krajewski's. After a few rings, the call was answered. He asked for Vice-Admiral Thomas Caruso, the commanding officer.

"Tom? This is Jim Saunders at the Pentagon. We have a situation....Yes, it's as serious as it can get. It has to do with a ship currently moored in Los Angeles Harbor. She's a Russian cargo vessel, the Volokolamsk. I think your SEALs are our only hope. Let me fill you in."

CHAPTER FIFTEEN

Naval Special Warfare Command, Coronado, California.

"A nuclear bomb?.. The president wants to do what?.. Surrender?...You can't be serious!...And the rest of the National Command Authority went along with this?...Bribes! Why those dirty bastards!.. Sure we can handle it. My people are the best in the world...Wait a minute. Let me write this down. This Drugonov character says the bomb will detonate at 5:01 P.M. eastern time, or 2:01 P.M. our time on Friday...It's now 12:53. That gives us forty nine hours, eight minutes...That's no problem at all, Jim. We can put together a mission in plenty of time...If we can take the ship and defuse the bomb before the deadline, can you convince the president not to go through with the surrender?...Great!...Yes, I know. We'll be prepared for that. We'll hit them so hard and fast they won't know what the hell's happening to them. They won't have time to detonate anything....Disregard any orders from the National Command Authority, including the president himself?

"All right, Jim.....Yes, we're on our own.... I understand....All right."

Admiral Caruso pressed the button to break the connection with Washington, and instantly punched in the number of Rear Admiral Stuart Talmidge, commander of Naval Special Warfare Command, Groups One and Two. NAVSPECWARCOM, as it is abbreviated, is itself a component of U.S. Special Operations Command, one of eight unified commands in the U.S. armed forces.

U.S. Special Operations Command integrated Special Forces assets from all the services into one organization. That included the Army's Special Forces, or "Green Berets," headquartered at Ft. Bragg, North Carolina, the U.S. Air Force Special Operations Command, headquartered at Hurlburt Field, Florida, as well as the Navy's contribution: the SEALs and the Special Boat Squadrons.

The SEALs themselves are divided into two groups: Group One, for the Pacific, and Group Two for the Atlantic. These are commanded by Rear Admiral Talmidge. Group One consists of SEAL Teams One, Three and Five, a SEAL Delivery Vehicle Team, and three Special Boat Units, numbers eleven, twelve and thirteen. Group One is commanded by Captain Vincent Decker.

"Stuart? This is Tom. I want you to contact Vince Decker, and tell him we need to put together an operation to go off early Friday morning....No, it's in Los Angeles....No, this isn't a drill. It's for real....I know it's short notice, but we've got no choice....We're going to need a platoon from Team Three....Yes, that's Wagoner's outfit. I want to meet with you, Decker and Wagoner ASAP in

Conference Room One. And bring the latest satellite photos of L.A. Harbor....Yes, this is big, Stu, real big. It's for all the marbles."

A briefing room, NAVSPECWARCOM, 3:21 P.M., PST. T-minus 46 hours, 40 min.

Lieutenant Paul Birkett's SEAL platoon sat in the folding metal chairs in front of the blackboard and waited for the bomb to drop. None of them knew what was about to happen, but they knew it must be damned important. Two admirals and a captain, at a Warning Order Briefing! It was unheard of! Lieutenant Birkett sat in the front row, with his Executive Officer, Lieutenant J.G. Carlos Gutierrez seated next to him. The fourteen enlisted men filled the rest of the room. Commander Carl Wagoner pulled down the screen from above the blackboard and nodded to the projectionist. The lights dimmed, and a small-scale view of Los Angeles Harbor appeared that included parts of the surrounding city. Commander Wagoner pulled a laser pointer from his shirt pocket and pointed to one of the minuscule dots that were ships.

'This is our target: the Russian cargo vessel Volokolamsk."

He nodded again, and a much larger scale photo appeared. This showed only the Volokolamsk and the surrounding piers. Details of the ship were evident, including specks on her deck that could only have been men. One more nod brought the ship into close focus. Now the men were clearly visible: ten of them, one each at the bow and the stern, five along the starboard side nearest the pier, and three evenly distributed along the port side. The commander continued.

"She's carrying a nuclear bomb that will go off in," he checked his watch, "forty-six hours, thirty-nine minutes. Unless we all do our jobs, that is."

One hour, forty-four minutes later the sixteen SEALs filed quietly out of the room. Usually ebullient, they had been sobered by what they had just heard. Each understood that millions of lives depended on his performance. Every detail had been explained, every question answered. Now it was up to them.

A squad, half a platoon, or eight men, was the usual choice for a SEAL operation. The fact that this one would consist of an entire platoon would add to the complexity. Paul Birkett's mind swam with detail as he and his men walked down the stark hallway, their footsteps echoing from the concrete-block walls. For most missions, standard operating procedures included the majority of details, and so not much discussion was needed. It was up to the Patrol Leader to set radio frequencies, rendezvous points, as well as routes in and out. The current scenario, dealing with a moored cargo vessel, was something they had practiced many times.

Birkett felt confident of their ability to handle it. But the stakes were so high here that he broke out into a cold sweat nonetheless. Birkett and his men stopped in the hallway in front of an equipment room in another wing of the building. Each man held a folder containing copies of the satellite photos he had been shown earlier.

Normally, one-third of the time before a mission would be spent planning, and two thirds preparing for the mission itself: gathering and organizing equipment, as well as rehearsing. Lieutenant Birkett decided to follow that formula as closely as possible; the less departure from normal procedures the better. They had just under forty-five hours. Plenty of time, Birkett told himself.

He thought about Carol and the kids. He wanted desperately to call them, to explain to them why he would not be home for the next two days, to prevent them from worrying. But he knew he could not do that. Once a mission had been started, all contact with the outside world was terminated for security reasons. He consoled himself by remembering that Carol was used to these periodic disappearances. She knew that they came with the job. She was a good Navy wife. Still, he agonized.

"All right! Listen up!" he began. "It's now 16:07 hours. You have until 19:00 to get your gear together. While you're doing that, Lieutenant Gutierrez and I will put the finishing touches on the plan. Check and double check everything! I don't have to tell you that we can't screw up on this one. We'll meet in room seventeen at 19:05 hours. Be prepared to take notes. Then we'll head for the harbor here in town for a rehearsal. There's a ship waiting for us that's almost identical to our target. She will be manned by people who will simulate the enemy.

"Keep in mind that their sole purpose in life will be to detect and destroy you! We'll have one chance and only one chance to get this job done! If we don't, you, I, and everyone else in Los Angeles will go up in the biggest fireball in history! Now let's get cracking!"

The men were unusually quiet in the equipment locker as they drew their gear and prepared it for the mission. Jimmy Vasquez sat on the bench checking his Draeger rebreathing system. SEALs used these instead of SCUBA to avoid leaving a telltale trail of bubbles. Chemicals "scrub" the carbon dioxide from the exhaled air and replenish the consumed oxygen. It's an excellent system, but it has its limits: unlike SCUBA, it cannot be used below thirty feet or so, or the divers run into a toxicity problem.

Jimmy Vasquez, from Albuquerque, New Mexico, came from a large family, with four brothers and three sisters. His father had always expected him to join the Army, as he had done. When Jimmy announced his intention to join the Navy, everyone was of course proud, but a bit surprised. When he told them he had applied for BUD/s training to become a SEAL, the surprise was forgotten. Only pride remained.

BUD/s, or Basic Underwater Demolition/SEAL, is the training program that all must complete if they hope to one day wear the coveted "Budweiser," or Naval Special Warfare trident insignia. BUD/s is twenty-six weeks long. To call it rigorous is a monumental understatement. Not only is its purpose to harden the body, but it is also designed to weed out those who do not have the mental toughness to succeed as a member of what is arguably the world's premier military commando unit. But even successful completion of BUD/s is not sufficient to earn the "Budweiser"; it is followed by airborne training and a probationary period of from six months to a year.

Where a great many good men had failed, Jimmy Vasquez had succeeded. Whenever he went back home, his father dragged him all over town, showing him off like a trophy. Jimmy smiled. The old man gets a bigger kick out of this than I do, he thought. Patriotism ran deep in the Vasquez family. Jimmy's father was a decorated Viet Nam veteran, and his grandfather had served in World War Two. Jimmy had been inculcated since childhood with the notion that the United States was not only the greatest country in the world, but the greatest country in the history of the world. His present service in the SEALs reinforced these beliefs and gave them a much deeper, richer meaning.

Often, in quiet moments, he would reflect on his relationship to his country. Inwardly, he would rededicate himself to her defense. When he thought of his family, his friends, his neighbors, he realized that no price that he could pay to protect their liberty would be too high. He knew that he may very well die on this mission; but as he sat there preparing, he did not give a thought to his own life. He thought only of the salvation of his country.

Robert "Spuds" VanHouten had grown up on an Iowa farm; hence the moniker. BUD/s had been less difficult for him than for many, because upon entering he had already possessed enormous physical strength. He told everyone that it came from throwing those bales of hay up seven or eight tiers back on the farm. He neglected to mention how he could carry a heifer on his shoulders from the back lot all the way to the barn, or how he had once righted an overturned tractor all by himself. His buddies kidded him about how much milk he drank; he couldn't help it. He had drunk terrific amounts of it all his life, and he couldn't bring himself to quit.

Go ahead, drink your beer, he told them. I'll dance on your graves! He thought about that now, and wished he had used some other turn of phrase. He put down the MX-300 waterproof radio and picked up the little Heckler & Koch nine-millimeter submachine gun, or the "room broom" as it was affectionately known. He began to disassemble it with the sure, economical movements of an expert. They never taught me this back on the farm. The farm. He thought about his mother and father, who had worked so hard, gone through so much, to raise him and his sister Ellen. He remembered his mother wearing the same dress for two years so that the children could have new clothes for school. And then there was Myra. He had fallen in love with her in the second grade, and she with him. They wrote to each other twice a week. A few days ago he had sent her the money to travel to the coast so they could be married. Myra had never seen the ocean. He had so many things to show her, so many things to say.

Until recently, he had just taken his country for granted, like the sun coming up every morning. But he had come to realize that it was a rare, precious thing, deserving of everything he could give it. He chided himself for his earlier ignorance, and promised himself he would never lapse into that way of thinking again. He realized now that all of the pleasant experiences of his life, everything that he was, everything that he believed in, all of this was made possible by the climate of liberty in which he had grown up. Now that he had seen some of the rest of the world, he knew how much there was to lose here. He would do anything to protect his country.

He began to feel real anger toward the men aboard that ship in Los Angeles; the thought of anyone sneaking a bomb into his country and threatening its existence seemed to him obscene. He smiled as he fondled the reassembled MP5, thinking of what he would do to them with it. He was not a violent man by nature, but, by God, he would show those boys what violence really meant!

Tyrone Watkins was from the Bedford Stuyvesant section of Brooklyn. There had been a time in his life when most people had given up on him. They had written him off as just another loser from the projects. But he had never given up on himself. After a few brushes with the law in his early teens, he woke up. He saw the direction in which he was heading, and he didn't like it. At seventeen he joined the Black Shoe Navy and had done well for himself. He scored high in the aptitude tests, and applied for SEAL training. Now he sat on the bench checking the receiver of his twelve-gage shotgun. It's not a very sophisticated weapon, he thought, but it most definitely will take out a lot of people in a hurry!

Tyrone had the spark within him. The spark is the thing that distinguishes winners from losers. It was like a little bug in his head that made him refuse to settle for what he saw around him, for what other people were doing and becoming. Whenever he felt lazy or lethargic, the bug would start acting up, reminding him that there was work to be done, that he had a life to live. It is what had made him run through the streets of Brooklyn, to build his stamina, when all of his friends were hanging out on street corners. It is what had made him read Webster's Dictionary from cover to cover, to improve his vocabulary. It is what had made him spend his evenings at the public library instead of drinking Ripple in an alley. The spark had served him well. He was an outstanding young man, by anyone's standards. And his superiors knew it. He had been told that as soon as he finished night school and received his Bachelor's Degree, he would be welcome at Officer's Candidate School. He relished the thought. To Tyrone Watkins, being an officer of SEALs was the highest achievement to which a man could aspire.

He remembered the summer nights in Brooklyn, when he would sit on the rooftop and look over at the Manhattan skyline. He never seemed to get enough of it. That skyline was, he thought, the greatest accomplishment in the history of mankind. His chest would swell just looking at it. People just like me built all of that, he would think. There is nothing I cannot do! He was so proud of his city, and of his country. The thought of living anywhere else was inconceivable.

He had been in New York on the morning of September 11, 2001. He had watched the twin towers of the World Trade Center collapse. Even today, he could not describe his feelings. It had been surreal, exquisite in its horror. It was almost like watching the world come to an end. And now, more of these creatures, this human filth, were threatening another of America's great cities. He had not been able to do anything to prevent the disaster in New York, but he could sure as hell help prevent this one.

In a very real sense, Tyrone saw himself as the protector of everything that he valued. Right here and right now, he was in a position to make a difference: to make it safe for all of those people out there. Today it was L.A. Tomorrow it might once again be New York. To Tyrone Watkins, that was worth dying for.

There were eleven more enlisted SEALs in that equipment room. Each of them had a similar story to tell. Each of them was the finest that his country could produce. Each of them would die unquestioningly to defend that country

CHAPTER SIXTEEN

Los Angeles Harbor, Friday, 00:30 hours PST

A sliver of moon dimly lights the port side of the Volokolamsk as she rests at her moorings. The starboard side is almost dark. From the standpoint of a Special Force's direct action mission, conditions are almost ideal. The sixteen SEALs, fourteen enlisted men and two officers, had spent the previous ninety minutes carefully assuming their positions in strategic spots around the ship. Eight of them wait behind one of the buildings on the pier, sixty feet from the starboard side of the ship. They wait for the signal to go. Each man is dressed entirely in black, with every exposed portion of his body covered in black camo paint. In total darkness, they could be standing ten feet from their enemy and still not be detected.

At the head of this group, peering occasionally around the corner of the building, is Lieutenant Birkett. His men are armed with submachine guns and shotguns, ready to spray the ship, and its guards, with a withering fire. Ordinarily, SEALs will approach their target using every means of concealment at their disposal, and with absolute maximum stealth. This may mean hours or even days spent moving forward literally inch by inch. Here, the situation is different. They have to cross sixty feet of open concrete with no cover at all. They are counting, in part, on the darkness, but especially on the element of surprise. The SEALs' most important advantage is their ability to conceal the time and place of their attack. Birkett felt sure they had done so.

None of the Russian guards had given any indication that anything was amiss. Crossing the pier and boarding the ship would consume perhaps ten seconds. It would be dicey. But, he felt, as long as they had the element of surprise on their side, all should go well. With any luck, no one would even see them until they actually began to board the vessel on its dark, starboard side. By then it would be too late. The Russians would find themselves under attack from three sides simultaneously. All hell would break loose in an instant. Against an unsuspecting enemy, Birkett was confident that the Russians would be quickly overwhelmed.

To the north, seventy yards away, two SEAL snipers and their spotters face the bow of the ship from their rooftop positions, lying prone and as still as death itself. Armed with the Haskins fifty-caliber sniper rifle, they were the finest snipers on the face of the earth, and quite capable of taking out a man-sized target at ranges of three quarters of a mile with their panatela-sized rounds. To them, a seventy-yard shot would be like shooting fish in a barrel. An engagement at this range would ordinarily call for the use of a rifle chambered for the thirty-caliber 7.62 NATO round. Here, the snipers want the ability to penetrate metal, to kill men concealed behind bulkheads or other light steel structures. Hence, the fifty.

Ordinarily, at longer ranges, they would go for shots in the center of their enemy's mass: the chest, the heart. Here, practically atop their targets, they feel confident enough to train their weapons on the heads of their prey. At this range, if they were shooting at paper targets, each sniper would easily be able to put all his rounds through one ragged hole. Now, against an unsuspecting, immobile enemy, they could choose their points of impact to within a fraction of a centimeter: the bottom of his sideburn, his ear canal, the tip of his nose. Even in this dim moonlight, through their ten-power scopes they can practically tell how closely the Russians had shaved that morning.

They are excited; the adrenalin courses through their veins. But as SEAL snipers, they learned to deal with this long ago: through an almost Zen-like process, they practically will their heartbeats to slow, their muscles to relax. They carefully control their breathing. They become shooting machines, delivery systems for death: precise, reliable, and exacting in the extreme. The entire purpose of their existence becomes that of eliminating their enemy: one shot, one kill. With a detached professionalism, they center their mil-dot reticles on their targets, and wait for the radio signal that will cause them to press their triggers and unleash their own brand of hell on their enemies.

Four hundred feet to the west, behind the adjacent pier, two swim pairs of SEALs, four men, also await their order to move. At 00:35 hours they enter the water, descend to twenty feet and swim toward the port side of the Volokolamsk. It is deathly quiet. The Russian guards lounge casually against the ship's rails, smoking cigarettes, expecting nothing. By 00:50 hours the SEALs have reached the ship and have deployed along its length. They prepare their boarding equipment. Each man checks his watch. At precisely 01:00, the balloon will go up, and they will be ready. The SEAL team has achieved complete surprise.

The White House, Friday, 03:42 EST

President Benedict lurches into consciousness at the loud knock on his door. Raising himself unto one elbow, he says,

"Yes, what is it?"

The door opens and the President's valet enters.

"Mr. President, the National Security Advisor insists on seeing you. I told him that..."

Ernest Crippler bursts into the room and approaches the presidential bed. Benedict swings his feet to the floor and sits erect, rubbing the sleep from his eyes.

"Mr. President," Crippler says, "we have to act fast. I've just learned that earlier today my people intercepted a telephone conversation between Admiral Saunders and Vice Admiral Caruso in California. They're planning a SEAL mission against the Volokolamsk to go off in eighteen minutes."

"Eighteen minutes! And you're just finding out about it now?"

"I know, I know. Someone in my organization fouled up. But the point is we can still do something about it! It's not too late! There are two possible scenarios. If the SEALs assault the ship and fail, and the KGB detonates the device as they have been ordered to do, the Maximum Leader loses all of the considerable resources of the entire Los Angeles metropolitan area. He wants those resources. Russia needs them. If the SEALs succeed, and the device is disarmed, you can forget about becoming an American viceroy! In fact, you may very well receive a visit from Mr. Uglanov!

"We have two options. The more desirable is to prevent the SEAL assault from taking place. The Maximum Leader gets Los Angeles intact, and you get the absolute power you want based on the threat of detonation that you and Drugonov will make public in New York. If that fails, we'll contact the KGB commander aboard the ship by cell phone. He's been instructed not to take calls from anyone except you and Drugonov himself. The Maximum Leader is in Moscow, and there's no time to establish a connection with him.

"You must place the call. The KGB officer will recognize your voice. You are to use the code word 'dagger.' He has been directed to detonate at the first sign of assault. But if you can give him--his name is Dimitri Rykov--advance warning of the SEAL attack, his team may be able to fight off our people. Order him not to detonate unless absolutely necessary, unless he is overrun and there is no other option. If Rykov's team is successful, detonation will not take place, and everybody gets what he wants. It's a stretch. You'd be asking him to disregard an order from Drugonov himself. But if we can't stop the SEALs, it'll be our only chance to come out of this smelling like a rose.

"First, you must try to have the mission scrubbed. I've arranged a direct satellite hookup between this telephone and the radio carried by the SEAL commander. His name is Lieutenant Paul Birkett. He has a wife named Carol and two young children, Kathleen and Sam. Speak with him right now, give him a direct order from his Commander in Chief to stand down, cancel the mission. Warn him of the repercussions if his mission succeeds. But be quick about it!"

Crippler lifts the receiver on the phone next to the President's bed and hands him a slip of paper on which are written two strings of numbers. Benedict takes the phone and stares at the first set of numerals. He hesitates. His mind races. This is my last chance to save the country. I am about to cross my Rubicon. Think, Benedict, think! Crippler's been in this with Drugonov from the beginning! I tried to give him the benefit of the doubt after he murdered Krajewski, but this caps it! He's been Drugonov's man all along! And he just tipped his hand--and Drugonov's! He said that if the SEALs neutralize this weapon, I will never be an American viceroy! That means there ARE no other nuclear devices planted in this country! With this one weapon gone, Drugonov's plan collapses!

Krajewski was right! This whole thing has been a bluff! Drugonov has no other means of conquering us! Since the collapse of the Soviet Union, the Russian military has become at least as degraded as ours! They can't even conquer Chechnya! If the SEALs take that ship, the country would be saved, and I could take credit for it! I would be a hero! But what would really be in it for me? Being a hero to this nation of morons wouldn't do me any tangible good. They might reelect me to another term, and then again they might not. But even if I were reelected, I would have another four years as what? As the straight-jacketed leader of a constitutional republic, blocked at every turn from achieving my true potential. How much better to be a virtual autocrat, unchecked, able to do whatever I like to whomever I like! That's what I truly deserve! That's what I've earned!

"Now, Mr. President, now!" Crippler urges.

Benedict holds the number in front of him, his finger poised over the buttons. He glances at the clock. Less than fourteen minutes now. He decides.

Los Angeles Harbor, Friday, 00:48 hours PST

The SEAL platoon waits these final moments, muscles taut as sinew, eyes and ears hyper-alert, ready to pounce from all sides. Lt. Birkett carefully glances around the corner of the building, looking for any signs of unusual activity on the part of his enemies, any indication that they might be aware of what's about to happen. There is none. Only twelve minutes left now.

He is startled by the almost inaudible beep coming from the radio mounted to his web gear. What the hell is this? Christ, something's gone wrong! He turns and walks along the wall, further from the vulnerable corner of the building. Keying the radio and putting its speaker to his ear, he whispers,

"Birkett."

"Lieutenant Birkett, this is the President of the United States. Do you recognize my voice?"

"Yes, sir, I do."

"Good. I am giving you a direct order as your Commander in Chief to stand down, scrub this mission. Withdraw your men and return to base. Do you understand me?"

"Yes, sir. But I cannot comply with that order."

Birkett had been told some of the details of the treason that had taken place among the National Command Authority. Admiral Caruso had told him personally to disregard any orders he may receive from them, with the one exception of Admiral Saunders, who was now dead, sprayed with Uglanov's bullets as he entered his home just hours earlier. That order to disregard included the President. Especially the President.

"What do you mean you can't comply? This is a direct order! You took an oath to obey orders from your superior officers, and that certainly includes the President!"

Birkett's eyes are squeezed shut, his jaws clamped together with tension. He had never disobeyed an order in his life. This insubordination was one of the most difficult things he had ever done. He is determined to be as respectful as possible, in spite of his knowledge of what this man had done.

"I am truly sorry, sir, but given what I now know of your activities yesterday, I no longer consider you to be in the legitimate chain of command. In fact, I have been instructed to that effect. I am under no obligation to obey your orders."

Benedict pauses. Seconds tick by. "Listen to me, Lieutenant. You don't know the whole story. If you seize that ship and neutralize the weapon she's carrying, your actions will constitute much more than just insubordination. You have a wife, Carol, and two children, Kathleen and Sam. Is that correct?"

"Yes it is," Birkett answered, instantly breaking out into a cold sweat.

"Your refusal to obey my order would result in the most drastic actions against not only you, but your family as well. When I use the word 'drastic', I am not exaggerating. Do you understand me?"

"I'm afraid not, sir. You'll have to be more specific."

He was growing dizzy with anxiety and shock. This...this...man...was the President of the United States! Birkett could hear an exhalation on the other end of the connection.

"Lieutenant, there are people in this country, violent people, people over whom I have no control, who would exercise–extreme prejudice--against you and your family if you seize the Volokolamsk and deactivate the weapon she carries. Are you aware of the fact that Admiral James Saunders was killed six hours ago?"

"No sir."

His shirt clung to his back, dripping sweat, cold, clammy.

"He was the subject of extreme prejudice. He didn't do as he was told. Do you want that for you and your family, for Carol, for little Kathleen and Sam?"

Paul Birkett's anxiety is rapidly turning to rage. "How dare you, sir! How dare you! I have a duty to perform for my country, a concept which you have obviously chosen to ignore! Mr. President, you are a God-damned, treasonous son-of-a-bitch, and you can go fuck yourself! This conversation is terminated!"

When he hears the click of the connection being broken, Benedict looks up at Crippler with a lost expression on his face.

"He didn't go for it."

"All right," Crippler says in a dead voice, devoid of emotion. "We still have a few minutes left to exercise option two."

Lt. Birkett, still trembling with anger, returns to the corner of the building. Cautiously, he looks around it. There is no sign of any unusual activity on the part of the Russians. He could hear several of them talking, then one laughing at an apparent joke. He sees the glow of cigarettes being smoked by unsuspecting men. Surprise is still on his side. Birkett's nerves unwind a bit. He tries to put what has just happened out of his mind. Concentrate on the mission! Your men are depending on you!

The SEALs behind him wait these final seconds, muscles taut as sinew, senses hyper-alert. The thought of failure does not enter the mind of any of them. They have become animals: mighty, vicious, indomitable predators, their one mission in life to tear the enemies of their country to pieces. They cannot, they will not, be defeated!

Suddenly Birkett hears a man's voice yelling from within one of the ship's cabins. A figure darts onto the deck, running toward the bow, snapping orders left and right. The KGB guards, just seconds ago so relaxed and unsuspecting, snap to attention and bring their weapons to bear. Birkett, stunned, has to make a decision: to go or not to go. His first instinct is to carry out his mission. His mind races. Milliseconds fly by. But we have lost the element of surprise! he thinks. Is my mission still possible? Every second I wait allows my enemies to better prepare themselves! This is turning into a real cluster-fuck! Can't go! My men will die! But the bomb! That damned bomb! How the hell did they know we were coming? Then the pieces fall together. That bastard! Birkett makes his decision. He shouts into the microphone near his lips,

"Go!"

He bursts around the corner followed instantly by the other seven SEALs. As they run toward the ship, they hear the boom of the fifty caliber Haskins rifles. Birkett sees one Russian's head disintegrate into a bloom of red. Another fifty caliber round slams harmlessly into the ship's superstructure in a shower of sparks. The SEAL snipers' targets, stationary and so easy to hit just seconds ago, are now moving targets, running back and forth across the deck, virtually impossible for even the best sniper to take out.

The Russians still have not fired a shot. They are confused and disoriented. Birkett thumbs down the safely on his Heckler and Koch and rakes the starboard side of the ship with a torrent of nine-millimeter rounds. The other seven SEALs, running flat out toward the vessel, follow suit, engulfing the main deck in a fusillade of fire. Two Russians jerk like puppets as the bullets rip through their vitals, collapsing in heaps onto the deck. The three who were manning the port side have moved to the starboard and, lying on their stomachs, open up with their own weapons.

Tyrone Watkins, at Birkett's right, charges toward the ship, spraying clouds of lethal double-ought buckshot at his enemies. He fires from the hip as he runs flat out, but his shots are amazingly accurate nonetheless. One blast sends four pellets into the face of a KGB man, who falls twitching, his brain scrambled, his life pouring out of the neat thirty-caliber holes. Watkins pulls ahead of Birkett and the others. He lets out a bloodcurdling yell, the yell of a triumphant warrior, as he leaps through the air for the ship's deck, directly into the midst of the five defending Russians.

Two of them, reacting more quickly than the others, swing their weapons in Tyrone's direction and send eight bullets stitching across his body, from his thigh to his shoulder. Still, blood pouring from between his lips, he manages to pump another round into the chamber of his shotgun, jamb the muzzle into the chest of one of the defenders, and blow a six-inch section of his spine over the port rail of the ship into the sea. Tyrone Watkins falls dead to the steel plate, his personal mission accomplished.

Two other SEALs are hit full in the torso, their forward momentum carrying them fifteen feet through the air before they land, lifeless, on the concrete pier. The four SEALs in the water on the port side have deployed their boarding equipment and have reached the deck. They crouch low to avoid being hit by friendly fire as they seek out targets in the shadows. The KGB man at the stern notices movement along the dimly-lit port side, and opens fire with his AK-74. One SEAL is hit in the chest below his right arm, and another takes a hit that shatters his right ankle.

Jimmy Vasquez is one of the two who remain unscathed. They both return fire and work their way toward the stern hoping to get a clear shot at their antagonist. But he is lying on his stomach behind the main hatch, shielded from harm. Vasquez ducks into a hatchway to think. The Russian's rounds ping into the steel plate around him, but he is safe for the moment. He knows what he has to do. The mission. I must accomplish my mission. After putting a fresh magazine into his weapon, he charges out onto the deck and toward the ship's stern, spraying lead in the direction of his enemy. The Russian wisely keeps his head down.

Thirty feet from his goal, Jimmy Vasquez fires the last round available to him. He tosses aside the now-useless weapon. He sees his target moving out from behind the ship's hatch, leveling his rifle at him. Vasquez dives the remaining ten feet just as the Russian pulls the trigger. Four rounds rip into Jimmy's torso, one of them severing his aorta. Jimmy senses that he is a dead man, but he is determined to die bathed in his enemy's blood. He lands on top of the Russian, who is forced onto his back.

Vasquez reaches for his web gear vest with his left hand. He finds a grenade. Pulling the pin with his teeth, he smashes the explosive into the Russian's face, stunning him. Again he brings the grenade down onto the KGB man's head, this time hitting him full in the mouth. The man's jaw cracks, and all of his front teeth fall into his throat as he realizes what is about to happen. He emits a muffled scream, the grenade filling his mouth like a deadly fruit. Jimmy Vasquez's last conscious act, as his blood pressure drops to zero and the world becomes black, is to smile into his enemy's horrified face. An instant later the grenade detonates, and both men's blood mingles into a scarlet cloud.

The six remaining Russians are giving a good account of themselves. Another of Birkett's men is killed by a man lying prone behind the scuppers on the forward deck, just before the KGB man himself is nearly cut in two by a fifty-caliber sniper round. Birkett leaps for the handrail of the ship, and launches himself onto the deck. Several of his men follow his lead. Having exhausted their ammunition, they dive onto the Russians and attack hand to hand. This is happening so quickly that there is no time to replace magazines.

"Spuds" VanHouten, having tossed aside his useless weapon, seeks out the largest enemy in sight, and, much to the man's surprise, lifts him bodily into the air by his shirt and belt. The Russian claws at VanHouten's massive biceps, flailing his legs to no avail. VanHouten brings the man down across his knee and snaps his spine like a dry stick. He tosses the screaming Russian over the rail as he would a sack of laundry, turning to meet his next opponent.

All but one of the ship's defenders have also exhausted the ammunition in their rifles' magazines, and the SEALs are on them so quickly that they have no time to reload. VanHouten singles him out, striding toward his opponent like some man-mountain, such a look of grim determination on his face that the terrified Russian momentarily forgets that he's carrying a loaded weapon. "Spuds" grabs the man by the neck and begins to squeeze, massive fingers contracting with the power of hydraulic rams.

The Russian, the world turning dark around him, is still sufficiently conscious to point his rifle at Robert's stomach, discharging his three remaining rounds. VanHouten growls like a wounded bear and, still throttling his opponent, pushes him toward the port side of the ship. He coughs mouthfuls of blood into the man's face as he stares into his enemy's eyes. When they reach the rail, now at a dead run, "Spuds" lifts the Russian off his feet and presses his thumbs into the center of the man's neck, crushing his esophagus as well as the vertebrae behind it, virtually decapitating him. Robert VanHouten, with only seconds to live, hurtles over the rail into the black water of the harbor carrying his enemy with him in a deadly embrace.

Birkett is all but oblivious to the melee taking place around him. His mind is on one thing: find that bomb. He sees a man running aft along the starboard side of the ship. Just as he is about to enter a passageway, the man turns and fires a handgun at the Lieutenant. Birkett hits the deck and the round zings over his head. He enters the hatchway where the Russian has just disappeared. To his left is a stairwell leading down into the bowels of the ship. He follows it.

Below decks, the light is dim. He hears hurried footsteps in the direction of the stern, echoing down the passageway. He follows. He knows he should be careful; he could be ambushed at any turn. But there's no time. He has to reach that bomb before it's too late. He tears down the passageway, ducking through hatches, glancing left and right. He enters the main hold of the ship. There, before him, is a squat, ugly looking cylinder held to the deck by straps. One man stands on each side of it. They are reaching into their shirts, as if to extract something that is hanging around their necks. Birkett's eyes lock with those of the man on the left. It is Dimitri Rykov.

The American raises his weapon and unleashes a short burst in Rykov's direction. He pivots and fires at the other man. Rykov is hit once in the leg and twice in the abdomen. He falls to his knees and clutches his stomach, groaning in pain. Pavel Piatakov has been hit three times in the left shoulder, and another of Birkett's rounds has creased his skull, stunning him. Piatakov manages to fire a burst from his machine pistol in Birkett's direction. One round enters the Lieutenant's neck, narrowly missing his carotid artery. Another shatters his right arm just below the shoulder. Two more enter his chest. Birkett's weapon clatters to the floor. All of this consumes no more than a second's time.

The American Lieutenant falls to his knees. Piatakov's second burst passes harmlessly over his head and stitches into the ship's bulkhead. Paul Birkett realizes that this is the moment of truth; this is the culmination of all his training, of all his efforts. This is Hell Week to the nth degree. He must reach that bomb; he must stop these men. Visions of Carol and his children flash through his increasingly sluggish mind. He realizes that he has little time left; he knows that he is bleeding out onto the deck of this damned Russian freighter. He also knows that he has a job to do.

Somehow he gets his feet under him. He draws his knife with his left hand as his right arm hangs uselessly at his side. He charges toward Rykov with all the strength left to him. The Russian, who has struggled to his feet, draws his pistol and begins to empty his magazine into the Lieutenant. Birkett is hit four more times in the chest and abdomen. Piatakov, with only two rounds left in his magazine, misjudges Birkett's speed, and fires the last of his ammunition behind him.

Paul Birkett is operating on pure adrenalin. His mind is red with rage. He sees the key in his enemy's left hand. Yes, the key. Must get that key. He reaches Rykov and buries his blade in the man's stomach just below his ribs. Rykov tries to scream, but blood fills his throat. He, too, is dedicated to achieving one goal before he dies. His left arm, key in hand, reaches out for the instrument panel. Piatakov has already inserted his key, and shouts at his commander in Russian,

"Now, Dimitri, now!"

Birkett tries to grab Rykov's hand, but his shattered right arm refuses to respond. The second key enters its slot. Turning slightly, Birkett grasps Rykov's wrist with his left hand, but he is weakened from massive blood loss, barely conscious. The Russian manages to turn the key. Then he reaches for the button. Rykov stares at the black piece of plastic toward which his trembling finger moves, his vision dimming more with each fraction of a second. He must push it, for the Motherland.

Piatakov struggles to reach the same button, but it is on Rykov's side of the bomb, and his efforts fall short. Rykov uses the last of his strength to move his index finger the final necessary centimeter. Paul Birkett maintains his death grip on Rykov's wrist, trying desperately, with the last ounce of his will, to stop the Russian from accomplishing his mission. His vision fades out. The pain disappears. *He feels lightheaded, as if he is floating away. He dreams. Carol. The children. Los Angeles. My country. All those people.*

His last thought is this: *I'll meet you in hell, Benedict*!

Rykov, breathing clouds of blood onto the side of the bomb, at last succeeds. His finger touches the top of the button. His final conscious act is to push it. As he slides down the side of the bomb to the deck, his eyes catch a dim glimpse of the elapsed timer. Instantly the four-hour reading disappears, the numerals replaced with a string of zeros.

Those bastards! he thinks, a millisecond before he, Piatakov, Birkett's corpse, the men still struggling topside, the ship, the harbor, and the city of Los Angeles, California are consumed by a thermonuclear inferno the likes of which the world has never seen.

CHAPTER SEVENTEEN

A hotel suite, New York City. Friday, 1:00 P.M. E.S.T.

Sergei Drugonov held the small mirror about a foot from his face. He peered into it intently, turning it slowly from side to side. His right shoulder rested against the window frame, his back to the wall, his right hand with the mirror extending out over the glass, as he used it to look for snipers in the windows and on the rooftops across the street. He was sure they were there. Or if they were not, they would be there soon. He knew that everyone wanted to kill him. Everyone wanted to deprive him of his victory, of his triumph. It had always been that way. He had always struggled against the jealous, the timid, those who didn't have the stomach to face him, but instead preferred to ambush him from cover. He could not let that happen now, especially not now that he had won his greatest battle and was on the verge of the ultimate conquest. Now his enemies spanned the globe. There was danger from all quarters. He would have to redouble his efforts to protect himself. He couldn't even trust his security people, not really. Who knew under whose influence they were operating; who knew where their real loyalties lie?

Unable to spot the snipers, he crouched down until he was on his hands and knees. He crawled under the window and across the floor. He would give them no target. Once safe, he rose to his feet and walked into the bathroom. Turning on the water in the sink, he mixed hot with cold until he achieved a temperature that was just tolerable. He pumped liquid soap into the palm of his hand, picked up the stiff-bristled brush and began to scrub. After three minutes, his hands were red, nearly bleeding. He reached over the counter to the gallon container of bleach. Pouring it onto his hands, he continued scrubbing for another two minutes before he was finally satisfied. It was the eighth time he had performed the ritual that day.

There was a knock on the door. Careful to avoid the windows, Drugonov opened it. One of his aids stood outside, accompanied by a crew of several workmen. It was what he had been waiting for.

"Come in, quickly," he said. The men carried sheets of plywood with them, along with an assortment of tools.

"I want them covered completely! No one must be able to see inside!"

The workmen didn't say a word as they distributed the plywood under each window. In thirty minutes it was done. As the aid turned on the room's lights, the newly-darkened suite was bathed in the yellow of incandescence. Drugonov felt his nerves uncoil. As his fears disappeared, he experienced a sense of euphoria. He rubbed his hands together and began to pace excitedly back and forth across the floor. Hardly able to contain himself, he commanded,

"Yevgeny, bring me my food! I haven't eaten since breakfast!"

Anticipating his master's desires, the aid opened the door and signaled for the bellhop to roll in the cart. Once in the suite, the man lifted off the stainless-steel covers from one tray after another, displaying the hotel's finest offerings. Drugonov looked on with approval.

"Has this food been tasted?" Drugonov asked his aid.

"Yes, sir. It was tasted thirty minutes ago."

"Good! Bring in the taster. I want to see him."

Once again the aid leaned out the door and signaled to someone in the hallway. A slightly-built man with thinning blonde hair entered timidly. When he saw Drugonov, he snapped to attention and saluted. Drugonov asked him,

"Did you taste this food, private?"

"Yes, sir. About a half hour ago," he answered.

"Taste it again while I watch," Drugonov commanded.

The private lifted a fork and tasted each dish, then retreated three paces and resumed standing at attention. Drugonov eyed him cautiously, making sure the man had swallowed every mouthful. There was an awkward silence as the dictator peered at the man, as if expecting him to keel over. At last he said, "Now we will wait.

"Tell me Yevgeny, where are my doubles at this moment?"

His aid pulled a notebook from his shirt pocket and flipped to a certain page.

"One is in Moscow attending a state function. Another is in St. Petersburg, carefully being seen in public. A third is here in New York, touring the Metropolitan Museum of Art. Another is in Mexico City and still another in Cairo.

"Everyone should be thoroughly confused," he said with satisfaction.

Drugonov's doubles so closely resembled him that his own mother would be hard pressed to tell them apart. The Maximum Leader chuckled.

"Good! See to it that they stay that way! I want those men seen in different locations every day!"

His aid nodded. Then, "Maximum Leader, the Foreign Ministers of Mexico and Canada are here to see you."

Drugonov was eyeing his food taster. The man still had not died. He was satisfied at last. He piled the food onto a plate, sat down, and began to eat ravenously.

"Show them in," he said.

Into the room stepped Enrique Hurtado and Charles Owens. They stood expectantly in the center of the room. Drugonov did not recognize their presence for a full five minutes as he wolfed down his lunch. At last he looked up, wiping his mouth with a napkin.

"I was wondering when you would come before me," he said.

The Mexican Foreign Minister took a half step forward. "Senor Drugonov," he began.

Cutting him off, the Russian stabbed his finger into the air. "Maximum

Leader!" he corrected.

"Yes, well, Maximum Leader. The Republic of Mexico wishes to extend to you our best regards. We hope that we can work together to..."

"We cannot. And we will not," Drugonov interrupted.

Senor Hurtado looked at him quizzically, turning his head slightly as if making sure he had heard the man correctly.

"Excuse me? I don't quite understand..."

"It's very simple, Mr. Foreign Minister. Your country and the Russian Empire will not work together, as you put it. You will work for us. You will take orders from us, or, more specifically, from me. And you will perform the labor that you are assigned."

"But surely, as a sovereign country, Mexico can expect..."

Drugonov's hand slammed down onto the chair's arm. "Mexico can expect nothing but subservience and absolute obedience to my will!"

He pushed the lunch cart to the side and stood, facing the two men.

"Only the Russian Empire is sovereign! Only I am sovereign!" he shouted at the top of his lungs, slamming his clenched fist into his chest.

"Sovereignty is the reward for strength! And you are both weak! You have been living in the shadow of the United States, depending on them to protect you, to fight your battles! For fifty years you cowered under the nuclear umbrella provided by the United States, in the knowledge that that country would not let anything happen to you! Now the United States is finished, and so are you!"

Senor Hurtado mustered the courage to speak up. "But surely there must be some way.."

Drugonov's eyes closed, his face turned to the ceiling and his fists trembled.

"You are a peasant from a race of peasants! You are fit for nothing but enslavement! You will do my bidding or suffer the consequences!"

He took a step toward Hurtado and looked the man in the eyes.

"You have never discovered the secret of productivity! You suffer from the same flaws as the Russian people! Your vaunted Mexican culture, of which you are so proud, has been sabotaging you for five centuries!

"Oh, you've had your sparks of genius, men who have displayed the flame of individual initiative. But for the most part those sparks, those flames, have been extinguished, submerged in the 'Greater Good', drowned in a sea of altruism. Your culture and mine, Senor Hurtado, are much alike. The difference between yourselves and my people is that Russians are fortunate enough to have me as their leader, and you are not! Unlike them, you will not be the recipients of sacrifice, but its providers!

"Your country is rich in natural resources! Those resources now belong to me! You will be provided with a schedule for their production and delivery! You will keep to that schedule, or I will begin to exterminate your people like the vermin they are! I have seen to it that nuclear devices have been planted in the City of Mexico, as well as in Puebla, Guadalajara and a number of your other population centers that will remain undisclosed. Do not even try to find these devices. They are so well hidden that it would take you years! And even if you did find them, any attempt to disarm them would result in immediate detonation! I am in a position to reduce your population to approximately its level during the Porfiriato!"

Drugonov hesitated for a moment, moved his face to within inches of the Foreign Minister's, then chuckled.

"You should see the look in your eyes, Hurtado! You think me an unlettered brute, and yet I have read your history!

"Yes, it is true! I know your country, and I know your people! I know your strengths, but I especially know your weaknesses! Like my own people, yours have always been expected to sacrifice themselves for someone or something. It may have been the King of Spain, the Viceroy, the Criollos, the Church, the Hacendados, or, since your revolution, the Mexican State and some vague notion of the 'People.'

"Your subservience to me shall be nothing new for your population, Hurtado. It is only the recipient of your sacrifice that will have changed. Still, I realize that there are individualists among you, particularly in the northern tier of your states. Their ancient 'Vaquero' traditions of toughness, of self-sufficiency, may present problems. They will not submit to the lash as easily as will those in the South. But I expect your government to see to it that they do submit! If they do not, if they resist at all, your country will pay a horrible price!

"One strength that your people have always demonstrated is that they have strong backs! They will now flex those backs not for the King of Spain, or the Viceroy or the Hacendado! They will from now on bend those backs for me, Hurtado! For me! Do you understand?

"Furthermore, if you value their miserable lives, I strongly suggest that you locate and remove from United States territory any of your nationals who are in this country illegally. We will very shortly be establishing a national identity system using Social Security and birth records as well as DNA. Any of your 'cucarachas' who are apprehended here will be shot on the spot!"

He turned to the Canadian.

"And you! Unlike our Mexican friends, your people did discover the secret to being productive, to being creative, but you chose to ignore it! Your people were once self sufficient, proud producers to whom the phrase 'self-sacrifice' was almost considered a vile expression. But you have changed.

"Now your people are expected to live their lives, at least in part, for the sake of others. As a consequence, your country has been languishing in mediocrity for decades! You will be useful, more useful than the Mexicans. There is still a degree of innovation and creativity left among your people. And I intend to exploit that to its fullest potential. Once I have wrung what is left of their creativity and productivity from them, you Canadians will join the Mexicans as nothing more than a collection of strong backs!"

Foreign Minister Owen broke in. "And I suppose that you have placed nuclear weapons in our cities as well to insure our....compliance?"

"How astute of you, Minister Owen! Let me see: Toronto, Montreal, Vancouver, and, oh yes, let's not forget Ottawa! The list goes on and on, Minister

Owen. It really becomes quite tedious to recite them all."

"Now just a minute, Drugonov! Who do you think you're..," Minister Owens began.

"Yes!" Enrique Hurtado broke in. "The Republic of Mexico protests these threats..."

Drugonov's face turned beet red.

"You question my authority? You dare to defy me? You will pay," he screamed, shaking his finger in their direction, spittle flying from his mouth.

"You will pay! I can do the same thing to Mexico City and to Toronto that I did to Los Angeles! Don't forget that! I can do it this afternoon if I choose! You are in my power! You have forty-eight hours to surrender unconditionally! Do you hear me? Unconditionally! Now leave me!"

He suddenly felt exhausted to the point of collapse. As the two men turned to leave, Drugonov put his hand to his forehead and fell into a chair. It was a full minute before he caught his breath. He closed his eyes and willed himself to calm down. There was a knock at the door.

"Enter," he said weakly.

The door opened, and his aid stepped in.

"Maximum Leader, we have brought the woman that you requested."

Drugonov perked up, glancing toward the door. He badly needed to relax, and a woman might be just the thing.

"Bring her in," he ordered.

As she stepped into the room, the dictator exhaled audibly. She was stunning. She walked into the room hesitantly and stood before him. He rose and approached her.

"What is your name, young lady?" he asked.

"Rebecca. Rebecca Meyerson," she answered.

His mood changed instantly. He smiled, feeling his nerves uncoil and his muscles seemingly fall into place.

"Come with me, Rebecca," he said, taking her by the hand and leading her to the bedroom.

"Take your clothes off for me, Rebecca," he said.

The girl smiled and began to unzip her dress. She was nineteen years old. It had been only three days since she had arrived by bus from the hard-scrabble farm in West Virginia where she had been raised. Unlike many new arrivals, Rebecca had no illusions about the fate that would meet her in New York. She had no education, and no skills that were marketable in the business world. She couldn't sing or dance. But there was one thing that she had been able to do very well indeed ever since puberty: attract men. They couldn't stay away from her. And so instead of staying at home and being pawed by farm boys with pig shit under their fingernails, she came to New York to capitalize on her one outstanding talent. She was not without ambition. If she rose to the top of her profession here, as she had every intention of doing, she knew that someday she could return to West Virginia and buy a whole county. Drugonov's men had found her on Park Avenue, and they had been extremely lucky to do so; she was astonishingly attractive for a streetwalker.

As her panties fell to the floor, and she stood before him in all her nubile glory, Drugonov felt rejuvenated. His hands trembled as he reached for her breasts, cupping each pouting orb gently in the palms of his hands. He moved forward and touched his lips to hers. Like a true professional, she reached around him and caressed his hairy shoulders, seemingly aroused. She was not such a bad actress after all.

He led her to the bed, and she lay down seductively, legs parted slightly to reveal the soft moistness of her womanhood. Drugonov quickly removed his own clothes and lay on the bed to her right. He touched her between her legs, very gently, and then began to massage her there. She groaned in artificial ecstasy, and began moving her beautiful round buttocks up and down suggestively. Drugonov placed his mouth over her left breast and licked her nipple. Slowly, he worked his way down her torso, dragging his tongue across her stomach, to her thighs, and then between. She moaned, ran her fingers through his hair and pushed his tongue deeper into her.

"Yes," she hissed. "Yes. Oh, now! Please!"

Drugonov heaved himself on top of her, lost in passion. As he entered her, he whispered into her ear,

"I could love you! You could be my love!"

She smiled to herself. She had heard it all before, but she still found it flattering. The Russian dictator panted as he thrust his hips forward and back. She dug her heels into the mattress and raised her hips off the bed in unison with his movements. Rebecca really was beginning to get excited, for Drugonov was an ardent and accomplished lover. At last he stiffened, groaning out his orgasm, grasping her so tightly that for a moment she could not catch her breath. Then his muscles relaxed. He kissed her on the cheek, and said,

"My love."

He rolled over onto his back, sweat gleaming on both their stomachs. She breathed deeply, looked over at him and smiled. She looked like an angel, he thought: a lovely, innocent angel. His hand reached under the pillow beneath his head, and he removed something. She did not notice. He turned onto his left side and smiled at her.

"That was wonderful, my dear."

She smiled back at him.

His right hand once again reached for the place between her legs. Again, she opened them for him. Instead of his hand, she felt something enter her that was pointed, something hard and metallic. Her eyes formed question marks as she looked quizzically at her lover. He continued to smile as his hand slowly moved upward, toward her chin, pulling the razor-sharp knife blade with it. By the time she realized what was happening, he had already cut through her clitoris and two inches beyond. She screamed and tried to dive off the bed, but he pinned her down with his massive left forearm.

"Don't worry, darling. It will be over soon," he cooed as she thrashed about uselessly under his full body's weight. Slowly, the knife reached her navel, and blood began to pour out onto the sheets across her flat stomach. She screamed over and over, Drugonov looking down at her with love in his eyes. At last the blade reached her breastbone, and Drugonov pushed down and forward, hard. The knife cut her heart in two, and the girl lay still. Her lips were parted and she stared at the ceiling. Drugonov looked down into her eyes, and kissed her.

"Now, my dear, you will always be with me. You are mine alone," he said.

He released the knife and reached into her stomach cavity, withdrawing his hand slick to the wrist with her blood. He reached down to his penis, and began to stroke it. He soon had a raging erection.

"Yes! Yes!" he growled, reaching into her corpse for more of the lubricating blood. With each stroke he became more and more excited. He stood up on the bed, back arched, his left hand pounding away at his erection dripping whore's blood, raised his right arm into the air and screamed,

"My will be done! My will be done!"

CHAPTER EIGHTEEN

A suite in the same hotel, two floors below, New York City, Friday, 4:30 P.M. E.S.T.

Twelve hours, twenty-six minutes after the destruction of Los Angeles. President Benedict sits on the sofa. Ernest Crippler sits across from him in an armchair. It is clear to Crippler that Benedict had not slept: there are bags under his eyes, and his hair is a bit disheveled. Crippler thinks that they should get some makeup people to work on the President before he gets in front of the cameras. Benedict leans forward, his hands clasped together tightly between his knees. His knuckles are white.

"What can you tell me about the damage, Ernie?"

"It's impossible to say, sir. No one will be able to get within twenty-five miles of Los Angeles for several days, and then only under the most controlled conditions. If we can find the volunteers, we may be able to send in medical and rescue teams within a week. We'll have to monitor the situation on a day to day basis."

"But what are the estimates? How many people have we lost?"

"Three to five million died in the initial blast. Another million or so will die in the next several days. The reports are that some people have managed to get out of the affected area. We've picked up a number of them on the highways leading out of the city. The ones we've seen so far have been so horribly burned that they can't possibly live more than a few days. Any others who survived the initial blast, and who were not too seriously burned, will suffer from radiation sickness to one degree or another. They may last months, even years. But it looks as though, for all practical purposes, we'll have to write off the whole metropolitan area. The destruction was complete. Our aerial reconnaissance indicates that some of the nearby beaches were literally fused into glass."

"What about collateral damage? Are any other cities in the region in danger?"

"Yes, Mr. President, I'm afraid so. Radiation levels have been creeping upward as far away as San Diego and Bakersfield. Anyone left alive in Orange, western Riverside, southwestern San Bernardino, Los Angeles and Ventura counties can be considered the walking dead. Radiation levels there are off the scale.

"All of Southern California will be affected to one degree or another. In the last few hours, westerly winds have begun pushing a cloud of radiation eastward, toward Las Vegas, Phoenix and Tucson."

"Well, hell, let's evacuate those cities right now! And tell anybody who can still be saved to get out of Southern California before they absorb a lethal dose!"

"On the contrary, Mr. President. I would urge you to make a public statement to just the opposite effect. Urge the people of those areas to stay in their homes. Tell them they have nothing to worry about."

"But why, Ernie? We can save hundreds of thousands of lives if we act now!"

"Think, Mr. President. Is a large-scale evacuation what the Maximum Leader would recommend? I don't think so. At this moment, his greatest concern is keeping the American people immobile; he wants to know where they are, to keep track of them. It will be several weeks before his control over this country is solidified. Until then, he doesn't want any surprises. He certainly doesn't want several million people roaming around the Southwest on their own, outside the control of the State.

"Control, Mr. President; that's what we must strive for now. As a matter of fact, I would suggest that you order the California, Nevada and Arizona National Guards to throw up cordons around every urban area in the region to prevent evacuation."

"But we'd be sentencing all those people to death, Ernie! How can you ask me to do that?"

"Need I remind you, sir, that you sentenced them to death twelve and a half hours ago, when you made that phone call? Sure, hundreds of thousands more will die, maybe millions, but that's a small price to pay for order. Joseph Stalin and Mao Tse Dung murdered tens of millions of their own people. Why? To achieve order. You're committed, Mr. President. You cannot turn back now. You are part of the New Order, and, as such, you must get your priorities straight. You no longer work for the American people. You work for Drugonov."

Just then the door opens. Sergei Drugonov enters the room, followed by two very large men. Benedict and Crippler stand, Crippler trembling with excitement to be in the Great Man's presence. Benedict attempts a wan smile and extends his hand toward his new master. Drugonov slaps him across the face with all his strength. Benedict whimpers and falls back onto the sofa.

"This, Benedict, will be the nature of our relationship in the future. Don't forget it," Drugonov says. The President of the United States sits up, but says nothing. The side of his face is a vivid red.

"Let me see the speech you are about to give," Drugonov demands with outstretched hand. Benedict reaches into his pocket and extracts several pieces of paper. As he hands them to Drugonov, he says,

"Do I need your permission to speak to my own people?"

Drugonov glances at the President, daggers in his eyes.

"From now on, you need my permission to fart!" he says.

He signals to the two men standing behind him. One of them pulls a rubber truncheon from behind himself, walks to the sofa and pushes Benedict over onto his side. The other grabs Benedict by the shoulders and twists him onto his stomach. The first then begins pummeling him across the buttocks with loud, sickening, slapping sounds. The President screams as he has never screamed before in his life. After a dozen blows, the man stops. Tears pour out of Benedict's eyes. He whimpers like a child. Drugonov smiles.

"Now you are beginning to learn," he says.

Drugonov sits in an armchair and begins to read the President's speech. After a few moments, he smiles.

"Yes, I believe you will make a very useful subordinate."

Drugonov and Benedict stand behind a bank of microphones mounted to the lectern. Before them are assembled a crowd of anxious reporters and television cameras. They are joined on the stage by representatives of several domestic groups: The People's Committee for East-West Friendship, Americans for Global Fairness, The Peoples' Coalition for the Wilderness, and the American Academy of University and College Professors.

Drugonov remains in the background. Benedict steps up to the microphones. Part of him dreads what he is about to say. He knows it will be unpopular with many, and he has never intentionally uttered an unpopular word in public before. But he knows he has no choice. Besides, he is no longer accountable. He takes a certain comfort in that

"My fellow Americans. I come before you to tell you that our national independence is over. We are to become part of a global community; one in which everyone will be expected to sacrifice for the benefit of those whom the State, our new State, chooses. In this New World Order, those who are most productive will be expected to sacrifice the most. Clearly, more than anyone else in the world, this applies to the American people.

"Our Russian brothers and sisters are calling upon us for the benefit of our productive genius. We must willingly and joyously accept our new status as benefactors of the Russian people. We should prepare to spend the rest of our lives in that role. We must prepare our children and grandchildren to accept that role as well.

"This should not be looked upon as a burden, but instead as an opportunity: an opportunity to better the lives of several hundred million people who need our help, and who will continue to need our help forever. From now on, what is good for the Russian people is what is good for the American people. The welfare of the Russian people is to be considered to be 'The Good' for which our society must strive. They will be the social entity for which all of you will be expected to sacrifice yourselves.

"This is nothing unusual. Throughout most of history, there has been some social entity for which individuals have been expected to sacrifice themselves. The nature of that entity has changed with time and place. In some societies it was the king, in some it was God, or the aristocracy, or the proletariat, or the Master Race.

The United States was the only country in the history of the world in which no such object of sacrifice existed. But that great flaw in our national character has been repaired. The United States will now join the great river of history; it will cease to be the exception, and will unite with the rest of humanity in its time-honored role of self-sacrifice.

"And it is past time that we accept that role. Who are we to think that we are above sacrificing ourselves for the well being of others? Who are we to think that we should not suffer so that others may enjoy their lives, so that they may experience a degree of luxury? Our government has been preparing you for that role for decades. For the last several generations, Americans have been told by their leaders, by their intellectuals, by their media, that their lives are not theirs alone to live. We have built a great redistributive State upon that premise. You have shown by your vote, in election after election, that you accept the validity of that State, and of that proposition. What you are about to experience is simply the culmination, the logical extension, of that philosophy. The only difference is that those to whom you are now expected to sacrifice yourselves are no longer within our borders; they live across the world. They live in Russia. But they are still people: people with feelings, people with expectations, people who need and therefore deserve the product of your labor.

"Who among you has not felt shame at your own selfishness? Who among you does not recognize the need to dedicate one's life to the well being of others? It is what we have all been taught since childhood. There have always been the recalcitrant few, but with coercive taxation we long ago forced them to subsidize this generosity. Otherwise, self-sacrifice has so far been voluntary. As of this day, it is mandatory. All of us now have the opportunity to practice the benevolence to which some of us have only paid lip service over the years. Thanks to Maximum Leader Drugonov and the great Russian people, we will finally be permitted to reach our true altruistic potential. Never again will we think of ourselves! Never again will we pollute our souls by denying others the product of our labors! We, as a people, will bask in the blinding white light of pure selflessness! At last we will be able to call ourselves truly moral!

"I will be your President for but a few more minutes. Then I will become your new Colonial Viceroy. And in that new role, I ask you, not as subjects, but as friends, to joyfully join with me as we welcome in the New Order! This is not a day for mourning, but for celebration! The old selfish era has passed; the old morally-bankrupt nation is dead! But a great new challenge now faces us! Our new goal is not to look to our own welfare, as individuals or as a nation, but to selflessly strive for the well-being of our friends across the sea!

"Before I leave you, I would like to speak to those affected by the disaster in Los Angeles. I did my level best to prevent it. For us as a people, it should be a lesson in hubris; when ordered to relinquish our sovereignty, some among us chose to resist. Contrary to my orders, a number of arrogant naval officers ordered an attack on a Russian ship in Los Angeles Harbor. As we were warned would happen, they caused a nuclear device to be detonated. Whatever damage has been done, whatever suffering is now being experienced, can be laid at the feet of these insolent traitors. But there is a silver lining in even so cataclysmic an event: we now know who are the masters and who are the subjects. I urge you, I implore you, not to resist further. The Maximum Leader has assured me that similar devices have been placed in many of our other large cities. Resistance will cause even more millions to die. Accept your fate. Console yourselves with the knowledge that others throughout history have suffered worse.

"I want to assure you that every measure imaginable is being carried out to deal with this disaster. I especially want to ask the people of the surrounding area, throughout the rest of southern California, southern Nevada and Arizona to remain calm. Stay in your homes. Seal your doors and windows with duct tape. I give you my solemn word that you are in no danger. In a few days, you may begin to feel ill. Don't be frightened. That will pass. Just stay at home and drink plenty of fluids. Whatever you do, don't try to evacuate. That will produce nothing but chaos. I have ordered the California, Arizona and Nevada National Guards to erect cordons around every urban area in those states to prevent anyone from leaving. Keep in mind, these are for your own protection! You know that I have your best interests at heart. Trust me, my friends. Thank you."

Drugonov now steps to the microphones. He raises his chin and looks down his nose at the assembled reporters.

"Subjects of the Russian Empire! Listen to me well, and obey! From this moment forward, you will subordinate your activities, your will and your very lives to the Russian people. I am the leader of those people and, as such, your lives belong to me. You have been conquered, and the sooner you accept that fact the easier it will be for you.

"Throughout the coming weeks, a New Order will be installed in this colony. You will experience many changes. Whether you accept them gladly or not is of no concern to me; I care only that you accept them. Those who do will be rewarded, and those who do not will be liquidated. You will find life under this new regime tolerable as long as you do as you are told. Sufficient wealth will be set aside to permit those of you who are productive to survive. The criteria for productivity will be established by the State, that is, by me. I suggest that you make it your principal concern to meet those criteria. Your survival depends upon it. There will be no room in the New Order for the lazy, for slackers, for the inept, for those who would sabotage the well being of the Empire. Those who do not produce will be considered saboteurs, and will suffer the appropriate punishment.

"This colony has been divided into regions, districts and zones. Each of these political subdivisions will be assigned its appropriate leadership. Your new leaders will be familiar to you; they are those who have led you in the past. They will consist of members of the preceding political regime: high-level administration and military officials, members of Congress, and federal judges. These people, in turn, will answer to me. But do not operate under the delusion that these people still represent you in any form of republican government, or are subject to your will in any way. Quite the opposite is true. They are to be your masters. You will obey their every word. It is through them that I, and the Russian people, will rule you.

"Your productivity will be the principal concern of us all. With that in mind, the following directives will be effective immediately: no one will be permitted to leave his or her place of employment without proper authorization; no one will be permitted to travel beyond a twenty-five-kilometer radius of his or her residence without a travel permit issued by the Regional Commander. The mechanisms will soon be in place to ensure your cooperation in these regards. Until such mechanisms exist, keep in mind that my regime has inherited computerized records of all relevant data regarding your lives. Anyone who attempts to 'disappear' or to abandon his or her occupation will be hunted down as a saboteur and liquidated. Their family members will also be considered enemies of the State and will be dealt with appropriately.

"All military personnel will stand down as President Benedict has ordered. Remain on your installations. Russian base commanders will arrive within the next forty-eight hours. I encourage all of you in the military, as well those of you currently employed by federal, state and local law enforcement agencies, to consider joining the State Security Apparatus. Applications will be made available to you within a matter of days. You will find the work rewarding.

"Non-commissioned personnel who accept this opportunity will be issued Level Three ration cards and free access to basic medical services in the network of Workers' Clinics that will soon be established. They will also receive preferential treatment in food and clothing allotments. Commissioned officers will be issued Level Two ration cards and will be eligible for emergency hospital admissions and limited pharmaceutical prescriptions, as well as access to supermarkets and department stores that otherwise are reserved for Russian citizens.

"All businesses and industries in this colony will be under the direction of the Ministry of Economics. You will find the Ministry's rule firm but fair. It is not our intent to hamper you in your productive activities. Quite the opposite is true. We will do everything in our power to ensure that you maintain current levels of production. We will also be looking for ways to increase those levels. Your success is our success. We will not make the same economic mistakes that were made in the old Soviet Union: your industries will not be nationalized. Private ownership of the means of production will be allowed to continue. We have learned that this is a necessary condition for human inventiveness and productivity. We, the State, will simply control industrial inputs and outputs. All purchasing of raw materials or semi-finished components as well as sales of finished products will be done with the authorization of the Ministry of Economics. Wages and prices will be permitted to float in the free marketplace, as long as they are considered by the State to enhance productivity. All labor unions are dissolved effective immediately. Necessary imports will be allowed with the proper permits from the Ministry of Commerce. All exports of finished industrial goods, as well as of agricultural products, will be to Russia alone. All ports, harbors and airports will be closed until further notice.

"As of midnight tonight, all electronic and print communications will be under the direction of the Ministry of Information. All such facilities will, in future, operate in the service of the State. Those organizations affected by this directive will receive detailed instructions by the end of the day. What you refer to as the 'Internet' will cease to exist. All Internet service providers are to terminate operations effective at midnight eastern time tonight. Punishment for those who do not comply will be severe. Possession of a computer after midnight eastern time tonight will be punishable by five years in a labor camp.

"Be obedient. Be loyal. Be productive. Those are your instructions. I offer you no hope for a better life. The Russian boot will be on your necks for all time to come. As of now, you are a race of slaves. You mean nothing to us as human beings; you are all just cogs in a great productive machine the purpose of which is to serve our needs and our whims. The survival of each of you depends on how well you serve those needs and whims.

"For decades you have asked to be conquered, you have begged to be placed under the yoke. You did so by willingly abandoning those principles that made you strong. What I have done to you I could never have done to your great-great grandfathers! They were strong and principled, confident in their right to live their own lives as they saw fit, as free men! They were equally confident of their right of self-defense, to fight for their lives, for what they believed in, for all that they had striven to achieve! Their minds were not clouded by a putrid miasma of concepts that cause self-doubt, that turn men into a simpering mass of flagellants that make them question the value of their own lives! Such strong men as your ancestors were can never be conquered, and I would not have been fool enough to try. But you-- their progeny--have become soft, indecisive, unprincipled and weak. And now you must suffer the fate of the weak. This is the way of the world. This is reality. Adjust to it, or perish.

"President Benedict and I will now sign the formal documents of surrender. At the instant that he places his signature on both copies of that document, your country will officially cease to exist. If any of you still care, if there are any among you who consider this to be an atrocity, remember that you have only yourselves to blame, if not because of your active participation in your country's destruction, then in your tacit acceptance of it, in your unwillingness to prevent it."

The two men walked to a large table and were seated. Before each of them were leather-bound portfolios containing the terms for the surrender of the United States of America to the Empire of Russia. Each man picked up a pen and signed in the appropriate place. Aids then picked up the portfolios and exchanged them, placing the other copy in front of each leader. Once again they took up their pens.

Drugonov signed immediately, but Benedict hesitated. He stared at the blank line onto which his signature was to go. He thought of all the years of his country's history, of the incredible toil that had gone into building it. He thought of all the wars that had been fought to preserve it, of all the men and women who had given their lives in that effort. Then he thought of the absolute power that would be his with one more stroke of his pen. A slight smile crossed his lips. Fuck 'em, he thought. Fuck 'em all!

CHAPTER NINETEEN

JFK International Airport, New York

Don Cleland felt cramped, as he always did when he flew. The aircraft's seat just wasn't quite large enough for him, for Don was a rather big man. He consciously drew his left elbow into his side to avoid violating the space of the passenger sitting next to him. The middle-aged woman noticed the move and glanced at him. He gave her a thin smile. He had always promised himself that his next flight would be in first class, where he would have some room to stretch out. But in the end he always flew coach. He could never justify the added expense. After all, he kept telling himself, he was only going to be in the air for a few hours.

He nursed the clear plastic glass of soda that had been served to him almost a half hour before. The liquid was tepid and flat, diluted into an amber, watery concoction by the melted ice. He had a window seat, and he gazed out onto the tarmac and the portion of the terminal that was visible to his right. He had begun to feel annoyed fifteen minutes earlier. What could be the holdup? he thought. We should have taken off forty minutes ago. He drummed his fingers on the right armrest.

Don was an accountant from Louisville. Late that morning he had had a meeting at his company's home office in Manhattan. Now it was time to go home. He had hoped to be back in time to have dinner at a decent hour. He had had no time for lunch, and he was getting hungry.

The flight attendants glided up and down the aisle, smiling bravely, quietly attempting to answer questions, assuring people that nothing was wrong, trying to keep everyone calm and relaxed. But as the minutes ticked by that became increasingly difficult. They could tell their charges nothing as to the nature of the delay, for they themselves had been told nothing. As much as the passengers, they waited anxiously to hear from the pilot. As Don stared out the window, it occurred to him that something was wrong. Several aircraft were within his line of sight, in position to load passengers and baggage. But there had been none of the usual activity around them: no airport personnel busting here and there, no baggage trucks racing back and forth.

Then he saw movement from the left. An aircraft had landed, and was taxiing toward the terminal. It was an unusual plane, one with which Don was not familiar. Its lines and paint scheme didn't match any commercial aircraft he had ever seen. Then the tail section came into view. On it was painted a strange symbol: a bird facing in two directions. It struck Don as vaguely familiar, something he had seen before, something old and foreign. It was the Romanov eagle, the symbol of the new Russian Empire, but Don had yet to learn that.

Within minutes two other identical craft had pulled up along side the first. Now everyone on Don's side of the plane was looking at this strange sight. A low murmur began to be heard throughout the cabin as passengers on the other side of the aisle began to ask what was going on. Don watched intently as large ramps were lowered to the ground below the tail section of each plane. Instantly, men began to pour out of them, armed men, men wearing uniforms and helmets. There were hundreds of them. Some ran toward the terminal, and others dispersed among the aircraft waiting to take off. Don saw six of them running toward him.

Suddenly, the aircraft's engines, which had been idling in an almost subliminal drone, became silent. The pilot's voice came over the intercom.

"Ladies and gentlemen, I—I don't quite know what is happening. We have been instructed by air traffic control to shut down all engines and secure the aircraft. This doesn't appear to be an ordinary delay. Stand by....Ladies and gentlemen, we are now receiving instructions to disembark all passengers. I don't understand. How can we....wait...I am now being told that we are to use the emergency exit ramps and empty the aircraft immediately. This is crazy...."

Don watched as one of the men standing beside the plane raised his rifle into the air and fired a short burst. He saw the shell casings clatter onto the pavement. To his left, near the nose of the craft, Don could see one of the other men gesticulating forcefully at the flight crew, with what could only be interpreted as a "come out" motion of his arm. A crackle came over the intercom, followed by the pilot's voice. It sounded nervous and strained.

"Ladies and gentlemen, we are going to evacuate the aircraft using the inflatable emergency exit ramps located at each hatchway. Please remain calm and follow the instructions of your flight attendants. Move quickly but do not rush. We don't want anyone to get hurt. I have been told that once on the ground, you are to do as you are told by the armed men you will see there. Please don't panic. We don't seem to be in any immediate danger. Good luck to you."

The passengers moved about in their seats, talking excitedly among themselves. Some shouted at the flight attendants, as if they could possibly know what was happening. Don looked at the people, and they appeared to him to be on the verge of becoming a seething mob. Some cried openly. A woman near the front of the craft screamed. A few of the attendants walked quickly up and down the aisle, trying to calm people as best they could. Several others worked to open the hatches and deployed the inflatable ramps. Don sensed that panic was building. He felt a twinge of it himself.

The lone male flight attendant muscled his way to the front of the cabin and grasped a microphone in his right hand. He held his left upward, palm out, calling for quiet. It didn't work. Nevertheless, Don was able to hear his voice over the din.

"Everyone please listen! Those of you in the first and last six rows, please stand up and face the nearest exit. Do not attempt to take your carry on luggage with you! When your flight attendant tells you, just sit down on the top of the inflated ramp, and push off just as if you were going down a slide in a playground. Don't worry! It is perfectly safe! When you reach the bottom of the slide, stand up and walk away immediately. All right! Let's begin."

One by one the passengers slid down the ramp. Some went quickly and smoothly, and others had to be almost pushed out of the cabin. One elderly lady had to be assisted into a sitting position and given as gentle a shove as the conditions permitted. Don wondered whether she would break anything when she reached the pavement. Finally, it was his turn. He had a bit of a spare tire, and he wasn't as young and flexible as he used to be, but with a grunt he managed to lower himself into position on the top of the ramp. He pushed himself off, and used his hands to steady his slide. The plastic almost burned his palms. He hit the bottom with a thump that he could feel in his tail bone. He got to his feet and quickly took three or four steps away from the ramp, rubbing his buttocks and grimacing.

Within minutes the plane was empty. The pilot and copilot were the last to disembark. The huddled crowd of passengers seemed out of place on the open expanse of pavement. The pilot, a distinguished-looking man graying at the temples, approached the soldier who seemed to be in charge. He shouted at the man,

"What is happening here? Who are you people? I demand to know why my passengers were..."

The soldier lowered his rifle so that its bayonet touched the pilot's jacket below the second button. A dozen people could be heard inhaling loudly as they watched this threatening gesture. Women held their hands over their mouths to keep from screaming. The pilot glared into the man's eyes, but said nothing further. The soldier's lips curled upward in a sardonic smile. Suddenly his body convulsed as he thrust the short, wicked-looking bayonet into the pilot's stomach. The Captain let out an explosion of breath, and doubled over in agony, a look of disbelief in his eyes. He collapsed to the tarmac, grasping his abdomen with both hands. The passengers nearest him stepped back, eyes wide, mouths open. One man's legs gave out, and he fell into a sitting position. The pilot groaned, his legs pumping in a cycling motion, as though he were trying to run away. His torso convulsed so that it appeared that he was doing sit-ups.

The soldier looked down at him with a passive look on his face. Then he placed the blade of his bayonet against the pilot's throat and jerked the rifle forward and upward, slitting the man's throat almost to his spine. The pilot's head snapped back, almost detached from his body. The gaping mouth of the throat wound spewed streams of bright, red blood onto the pavement. The pilot's lips still moved, in some final, grisly supplication. His arms and legs trembled as his veins and arteries emptied themselves. Finally, he was still.

A number of the passengers broke down completely, sobbing uncontrollably, shaking with horror. They stared at the pilot's corpse, seemingly asleep next to a small, gleaming, crimson lake.

"Silence, American dogs!" the soldier shouted.

Heads snapped in his direction. Some cringed in fright.

"Remember this well! This will be the fate of those who question the authority of soldiers of the Russian Empire! From now on, when you see this uniform, you will obey instantly. Do you hear me? Instantly!"

He screamed the last word, rising onto the balls of his feet, face contorted in rage. The crowd of passengers shrank away from him in fear.

He continued. "You will enter the terminal and wait for further instructions! Those of you who are attempting to return to your homes will be issued permits to do so at the proper time. Have your identification ready for inspection! Now, move!"

Don Cleland was shaking inside as he turned and began walking with the others toward the terminal. If this was happening in New York, it was probably happening in other cities as well, he thought, maybe all around the country. He felt like a frightened child. The self-confidence that he had always known, the knowledge that he was in control of the events of his own life, whatever feeling of mastery that he had managed to build up over the years, was shattered in a matter of minutes. Suddenly, reality was dark and ominous. It was a feeling that he would never get used to.

CHAPTER TWENTY

New York City, Dawn, Saturday

Someone from out of town would never believe that midtown Manhattan could ever be so quiet. But it always is at dawn. The shops are closed, their steel shutters rolled down and padlocked to the sidewalks. The neon signs, so garishly lit during business hours, are dark. And there is an eerie silence, as if everyone were dead.

The only movement to be seen on Broadway was a page from the previous day's newspaper wafting along the sidewalk and into the street in the chilly April breeze. As it moved, it made a rustling noise that was the only sound in all of Times Square.

Then, in the distance, ever so faintly, came a sound unlike any heard in New York before. It grew closer, louder. It was a rumbling, clattering noise accompanied by the deep base popping of diesel exhaust. The sound came to fill the square, echoing back and forth across the street, the kind of sound that made one grind one's teeth and grimace.

Suddenly it appeared. Its long, menacing cannon protruded beyond the crosswalk and into Broadway itself. It stopped. A hatch opened and the head and shoulders of a helmeted man appeared. He studied the square, looking for movement. He saw none. The man spoke into a microphone and almost instantly the Russian tank lurched forward, turning right and moving slowly downtown. The first was followed by a second, and then a third. An entire tank company trundled into the street and moved south. Each tank's hatch was open, its commander standing head and shoulders in the open, not wanting to miss a moment of this unique experience: the Russian occupation of New York.

At the next intersection the lead tank stopped, and the others followed suit. On the sidewalk was a pushcart, a man standing next to it, slack-jawed in astonishment. He was Sam Bonte, and he had been selling pastries to the early morning crowd on this corner for seventeen years. He always arrived early, to give himself plenty of time to set up. He wore an imitation fur cap with ear flaps that could be tied down with a string beneath his chin. His old cloth coat was shabby, but warm. The gloves he wore had no fingertips.

Major Vasilii Kalmikov looked down at the man from the lead tank. The delicious smell of the pastry filled his nostrils. He was hungry.

"What are you selling, old man?" he shouted above the idle of the tanks.

"Doughnuts and Danish," answered Sam.

"Bring me a dozen of your best!" the Major ordered.

Sam took out a paper bag and filled it with an assortment of pastry. Hesitantly, he walked toward the steel monster, holding the bag aloft. Kalmikov had climbed out of the tank and leaned down to accept the bag. Another crewman, whose name was Nikolai, followed him out of the hatch and onto the outer surface of the tank.

"That'll be fourteen dollars," Sam said. Kalmikov stared at the vendor in disbelief, and then burst out laughing. Nicolai joined him.

"Fourteen dollars, indeed!" the Major said. "Nikolai, pay the swine!"

Nikolai, still laughing, swung his right leg forward with all his strength. The toe of his boot caught Sam Bonte square on the nose, crushing it to a pulp. Sam put his hands in front of his face as a jet of blood spurted outward. He staggered backwards, falling onto the pavement, rolling back and forth in agony. Sam didn't know it, but he was lucky that the Russians were in a good mood. Otherwise, they would just as readily have put a bullet through his brain.

Kalmikov munched on a cheese Danish as he examined the surrounding store fronts. Across the street, one of them caught his eye. It was "Aboud's Electronics." The Major smiled. There is no resistance here, he thought. There is no danger. Why not give the men a treat? He shouted into the hatch,

"Move in front of that shop with the steel grate across the street, and take out the cable!"

The machine lurched forward and turned sharply on its right track. A crewman jumped to the pavement and attached a cable to the rear of the tank and through the store's security grating.

"Forward!" Kalmikov ordered.

As the tank moved ahead, the cable became taut, and with a shrieking squeal the steel grating was ripped away. Other tank crews had by now exited their machines and walked toward the now-vulnerable business. One of them kicked in the door, and a dozen Russian soldiers entered. They laughed and shouted to each other as they pawed through the merchandise, looking for the smallest, most valuable goods they could find. They stuffed their jackets with radios, cell phones and with whatever else caught their fancy that was small enough to fit in the cramped quarters of a tank. What they couldn't take with them, they threw to the floor.

Kalmikov stood on top of his machine watching with satisfaction as his men ransacked the store. They deserve this! he thought. They have worked hard. It is time they enjoyed some of the fruits of victory. We have won, and all that is here is now ours! It was a thought that would cross many Russian minds, in many different cities, in the months ahead.

CHAPTER TWENTY-ONE

New York, Saturday, 11:00 A.M.

The crowd was much larger than usual. The department store was very upscale, and typically had about it a rather sedate air. Today, many of its customers looked less affluent than the usual clientele, and they had a furtive look: anxious, hurried. The jewelry counter was especially busy. Dowagers and businessmen lined up to exchange their dollars for gold. Who knew if, a month from now, the paper money would be worth anything? Many had already tried that day to liquidate their cash under more advantageous circumstances, attempting to receive as much of the yellow metal as possible for their dollars. But the crowds in front of every coin and pawn shop in town had discouraged them. Fist fights, even knifings, were common. So they turned to the retail jewelers, resigning themselves to the heavy markups that such establishments charged. It was not the best way to buy gold, but for most, there was little choice.

The harried clerks worked frantically to retrieve items from the showcases as the customers leaned forward, shouting and pointing at what they wanted. Beatrice Osgoode was not used to this environment; she was accustomed to personalized treatment from salesclerks, not to being part of a raucous mob. She was not used to being jostled, even manhandled, by a crowd of plebeians. She pulled her mink coat closer about herself, as if to prevent it from being touched by the riffraff who surrounded her. It was true that she wanted to buy some gold jewelry, but she was not sure that goal was worth suffering through this demeaning experience.

Who were these people? They couldn't possibly be her type! She had been shopping here for years and had never seen the like of it! Wait until she told Edmund, she thought. He belongs to the same club as the store's owner, Mr. DeSales. She would see to it that Edmund gave this DeSales a piece of his mind! Imagine! The wife of one of New York's leading bankers being forced to undergo this kind of treatment!

The shouting of the customers was suddenly overwhelmed by the crashing sound of automatic weapons fire. All movement, all sound, stopped as everyone looked in the direction of the Russian soldiers. Plaster from the ceiling, shattered by the rifle fire, showered down onto everyone's head.

"Listen to me!" one soldier said in thickly accented English. "You are to leave immediately! From now on this store, and all similar stores, are off-limits to American civilians! Goods in this store are for Russian consumption only! Now, go!"

The soldiers pointed their bayonets menacingly in the direction of the customers. The Americans began moving toward the escalator, mumbling to themselves and looking over their shoulders at the Russians. Beatrice Osgoode found herself carried off in the midst of the crowd. When it reached the escalator, one by one, they stepped onto the moving stairway to be carried down to the main floor, and the exits. This created a knot of customers at the top, waiting their turn.

The Russians felt they were stalling, and began pushing them forward with their rifles, shouting at them in a mixture of Russian and English. One of the soldiers pushed against Beatrice Osgoode, causing her to fall forward onto the man in front of her. She certainly was not used to this type of behavior, and she had no intention of tolerating it. She spun about and looked down her nose at the swarthy Russian behind her.

"Young man, do you know who I am?" she asked him in her most imperious voice. "I've never been so outraged in my life! My husband, Edmund J. Osgoode, THE Edmund J. Osgoode, President of First Securities Bank, will contact your commanding officer, and..."

Just then the Russian swung his rifle butt through the air, catching Mrs. Osgoode square in the mouth. Her upper denture was shattered into several pieces, and fell from her open jaws to the floor. As she collapsed, a stream of blood and broken lower teeth poured out onto the luxurious fur coat. Her eyes rolled upward in her head, but she never lost consciousness entirely. She could just hear, as if from a great distance, the Russian screaming at her unintelligibly. The man ahead of her turned and picked her up under the arms. The Russian raised his rifle, butt forward, as if to strike her again. The American shouted,

"No, no!" as he raised his palms upward in a sign of submission.

He hurriedly dragged Mrs. Osgoode to the head of the escalator, and stepped onto it, getting her, and himself, out of the store as quickly as possible. He could not know that similar scenes were taking place in similar stores all across the country.

CHAPTER TWENTY-TWO

Memorial General Hospital, Chicago. Monday, 2:30 P.M.

Dr. Reed Toeffler had made the principal incision ten minutes earlier. He didn't expect any complications. This should be a standard triple bypass, like so many others he had performed. The patient was pretty typical: a male, aged sixty, who had led a sedentary lifestyle and had eaten too many hotdogs. This operation should fix him up for years to come. He glanced over at the nurse who was assisting him. She was good, he thought. She knew what he wanted done almost before he did. He extended his hand and asked for a sponge. Instantly, it appeared in his palm.

The quiet of the operating room was shattered when its two doors were kicked open. Without looking up, Toeffler shouted, "Who the hell is that?"

He had never heard of such an interruption. His back was to the doors, so he could not see the three Russian enlisted men and one officer stride into the room. But the others in the O.R. could. Toeffler glanced up and saw his nurse take several steps backward. The anesthetist, seated at the head of the operating table, stood and stepped backward as well.

"What the hell is going on here?" Toeffler growled as he turned.

One of the enlisted men placed his bayonet against the doctor's chest and shouted a cryptic order. He then stepped aside and waved his rifle in the direction of the doors. No one moved. This enraged the man, and he approached Toeffler again, seemingly with intent to kill. The officer quickly stepped forward, grabbed the rifle's barrel and moved it to the side.

"Nyet!" he said simply.

The enlisted man took a step backward, but continued to stare with hatred at the surgeon. The lieutenant smiled, and addressed Toeffler in a congenial voice.

"You are the surgeon here? You are Doctor Toeffler, I take it?"

"Yes, I am. Do you realize that you are interrupting open heart surgery? This man could die at any moment! Who do you think..."

"Doctor, this man is no longer your concern. I stopped our friend here from gutting you like a fish because you are too valuable to die needlessly. From now on your considerable surgical skills will be placed in the service of the Motherland. The first planeload of patients from Moscow is arriving as we speak. We have heard a great deal about the expertise of American medicine. I suggest that you prepare to demonstrate that expertise on your new, Russian, patients."

"But what about this man? We can't just let him die! Allow me to finish here, and then..."

"Doctor, you are being difficult. Your services are required now. I see that this man is an impediment to your performance. Allow me to remove that impediment."

The lieutenant walked slowly toward the head of the operating table, drew his pistol and pointed it at the patient's temple.

"No!" yelled Toeffler, but it was too late.

With a twitch of his finger, the Russian sent the nine-millimeter bullet through the man's brain. As it exited, it ricocheted off the heavy stainless-steel table and slammed into the tiled wall of the room, sending fragments of the ceramic flying. The nurse screamed and took several steps backward. Toeffler watched as the pool of blood welled up on the table and began to trickle onto the floor. Out of sheer habit, he glanced at the electronic heart monitor. It beeped a few times, its graph line spiking hard as the man's heart struggled through its final moments. Then the beeping stopped, replaced by a steady, high-pitched sound. The line on the scope was flat. Everyone stared at the lieutenant, who calmly holstered his pistol.

"Well then! Now that that's over, all of you will please follow me."

He strode to the door, and, holding it open, smiled at the entire surgical team. They were led to the main entrance of the hospital and out onto the sidewalk. They found themselves in a crowd of people: doctors, nurses, other hospital employees, and finally patients. These were being dragged bodily out of the building and dumped unceremoniously onto the sidewalk. When the sidewalk became crowded, they were dragged into the street. Some were rolled out of the hospital on gurneys. The employees watched in horror as the gurneys were tipped over, throwing their occupants to the pavement. The entire street was soon filled with groaning, crying people: the young, the old, many bandaged and with plastic tubes hanging from their arms, noses or mouths. Even the intensive care ward was emptied into the street, but these people were so ill that they barely reacted at all. Another Russian officer mounted the hospital's steps carrying a bullhorn. He looked out over the moaning crowd and raised the horn to his lips.

"American hospital personnel! I am Major Kokoshkin! I will be the liaison between your new government and all of the medical facilities of this district. As far as you are concerned, I will be the final authority in determining how those facilities will operate.

"As of today, a Level Two ration card, that is the blue one, will be necessary for admission to this facility. You will find that these will be in the possession of all Russian citizens, as well as certain Americans who have been placed in positions of authority. Those who possess the Level Two card will be eligible for physician's care, prescription medication, and necessary surgery. Unless specific permission is granted, discretionary surgery will be reserved for those with Level One ration cards; those are gold in color. Americans who possess neither of these cards will be treated in the Workers' Clinics that will be established in the near future. These need not concern you. They will not be staffed by medical doctors or nurses, but by medics. Certain, limited prescription medications may be available in some of these clinics.

"An airliner from Russia has just landed at your O'Hare Airport. These people will be your first patients. They will begin arriving within the next thirty minutes. More aircraft will arrive on a daily basis. You will treat these people with all of your skill and professionalism. Those of you who do not will be dealt with very harshly.

"I realize that those physicians among you have been accustomed to, how shall I put it, a certain deferential treatment within your society. Your education, your skills, your income, have enabled you to enjoy an elite status. That ends now. You are no more than tools of the Rodina, your new Motherland. You are highly-trained animals that will perform at your masters' bidding. Your one function in life, from now on, is to serve those masters: the Russian people. Keep in mind that we consider the most degraded derelict in Russia to be far more valuable than all of you combined. If you remember what I have told you, and perform accordingly, you have nothing to fear. We will not dispose of you lightly, just as we would not casually euthanize a well-trained dog. But if such a dog bites its master, it will die. Now, re-enter the hospital, and be prepared to show your identification to the guards at the doors."

Reed Toeffler was crouching down next to an old woman who had been dumped between two parked cars. She had a plastic drainage tube coming out of her side that had been partially dislodged during the jostling. He was attempting to replace it into its proper position. There was blood seeping across the pavement where her head had struck hard. She stared into the sky, her old eyes open wide, her parchment-like skin stretched tight across her thin face. Her mouth formed a circle, as if she were constantly pronouncing the letter "O". Toeffler could hear rattling, wheezing sounds coming from her ancient lungs. He knew that without care she would be dead within the hour. He stood up and looked around himself. A Russian soldier stood ten feet away, motioning toward the hospital's entrance with his bayonet. Toeffler said,

"Now look here! I've got to get this woman..."

The soldier spun in his direction and pointed his weapon menacingly in the doctor's direction. He shouted a command in Russian, and motioned toward the entrance. Toeffler's shoulders dropped as he realized that there was nothing he could do. As he began to walk away, he glanced back at the woman, whose left hand was raised off the pavement, as if calling for help. I cannot help you, he thought. I am so sorry. In fact, Reed Toeffler had never felt so helpless in his life.

CHAPTER TWENTY-THREE

New York City

Bob Donner reached to the back of the kitchen cabinet in his East 83rd Street Apartment.

"Here's a can of green beans, Kathy," he said.

His wife made a mark on her notepad. "All right," she said. "That makes twenty-three cans of vegetables, two cans of corned beef, a can of SPAM, and five cans of ravioli. We also have eight pounds of pasta, four pounds of dried beans, two pounds of lentils, and a five-pound bag of flour."

"I could have sworn that we had a box of nonfat dry milk," Bob added. "Didn't we buy some a couple of weeks ago? We couldn't have used it all up, could we?"

"I'm not sure. Maybe it'll turn up later," Kathy said, a stressed tone in her voice. "God, I wish we'd thought to go to the supermarket a few days ago. Now the Russians have closed them, and you need a Level Two ration card to get in. Only Russians have those."

"Yeah. And a few traitorous Americans. We'll just have to make this last until they open up those Workers' Co-Ops they're talking about."

"How long will that be? I'm hungry right now! I'd kill for a hamburger and some French fries! How long can we live on vegetables and flour?"

Bob walked over to his wife and put his arms around her. He patted her on the back gently as she buried her face in his shoulder. She had been crying a lot in the last few days. Bob hoped she wouldn't cry now. Each time became more difficult for him. He couldn't stand to see her suffer.

As they stood in the middle of the kitchen floor, they heard a voice, a tinny, amplified voice reaching them from the street. They both rushed to the living room and looked out the window. A sound truck was moving along slowly beneath them. From it came a voice in slightly accented English.

"Good meat! Good meat! Go to the park! Go to Central Park to receive meat. Good meat will be made available to you in Central Park. Every Wednesday you can go to Central Park to receive meat. Bring a knife and a plastic bag. Good meat!" The message repeated itself.

"A knife and a plastic bag?" Bob said. "What's that all about?"

"I don't know. But let's go right now. I've got a feeling that whatever kind of meat they're talking about won't be available for long. I'm starving! Let's go, please!"

"All right. Get our coats. I'll get the knife and the bag."

Bob and Kathy walked the three blocks to the park. Already a thousand or so people had gathered, all carrying the required knife and plastic bag. Everyone looked bewildered as they waited for something to happen. There were no trucks in sight, nothing that could be used to distribute the meat that they all hoped to receive.

The people at the edge of the crowd turned to look at something in the street. Then Bob and Kathy heard it: a clip-clopping sound that could only be made by the shod hooves of horses. The crowd next to the street parted, as Russian soldiers led a herd of the trusting animals into the park. They were from the Police Department, and were not considered necessary by the city's new Masters. The animals were gathered together, surrounded by apprehensive New Yorkers. Shots began to ring out. Horses screamed and fell to the grass, their legs thrashing wildly. The people recoiled in horror, many covering their eyes. In three minutes it was done. Forty-one of the animals lay dead.

One of the sound trucks had parked on the side of the street nearest the crowd. "This meat supply is provided to you by the generosity of the Russian people! Take what you can carry in your bags! Additional meat will be provided each Wednesday at the same time. Similar supplies are being made available in other parts of the city. That is all."

The crowd of people, now grown to about two thousand, stood rooted to the ground. Then, slowly, a few began to move forward, awkwardly, hesitantly, knives in hand. Others turned away in disgust. Bob looked at Kathy.

"What do you think we should do?" he asked.

"Oh, Bob, I can't eat horses! I love horses! You know that! I'd rather go hungry!"

The couple turned and pushed their way through the shocked crowd until they reached the street. They said nothing to each other on the walk home.

Four days later, Bob had come to regret their decision. The gnawing hunger had become almost intolerable. He and Kathy had been living primarily on canned vegetables. They had eaten the last of the tinned meat two days before. Kathy was putting up a brave front, but Bob knew that she was suffering as much as he was. He made his decision.

"Kathy, I'm going to the park," he said simply.

She knew what he meant. She looked dejected, resigned to an unpleasant but unavoidable fate. Bob got his coat, the knife and plastic bag, and left the apartment. In the park, the sickening sweet smell of decaying meat was in the air. What was left of the horses lay rotting in the sun. Clouds of flies engulfed them. A hundred or so people, dressed in suits, expensive overcoats, stylish dresses, stooped over the dead animals, carving meat from their bones with varying degrees of enthusiasm. Some could hardly stand to touch the carcasses, and cut strips of flesh away gingerly, reluctantly. Others hacked away with abandon.

All of the horses had been reduced to virtual skeletons, and the latecomers who scavenged these had to take whatever was left: organs, portions of intestine, even skin. Bob grimaced as he took in the grisly sight. It was like a vision out of hell, he thought. To his left, he heard a crunching sound. There, a man with a sledgehammer had just crushed a horse's skull, and had squatted down to scoop out the brains. His plastic bag was bulging, and Bob suspected he had done the same to several other animals.

He walked through the abattoir that Central Park had become. He looked at each carcass, hoping to find one with some real meat left on it. The competition was fierce. Each time he stopped, the people already cutting away at that animal looked up at him and practically snarled. Thirty yards away he saw two men fighting over a horse's foreleg, their knives flashing in the sunlight.

Finally, he came to a carcass that looked promising. All of the flesh had been removed from the side of the animal that was exposed, but he could see that there was still some meat on the other side, the side against the ground. He took the bones of the horse's rear legs in his hands and heaved, trying to turn the skeleton over. After three attempts, he was successful. Immediately two other people lunged at Bob's find.

"Get back!" he shouted, slashing his eight-inch carving knife from side to side. The intruders dropped back, malice in their eyes.

Bob squatted, looking with mixed emotions at the hide-covered piece of meat that clung to the animal's ribs. Can we really eat this? he asked himself. He felt a spasm of hunger in his stomach, and realized that he and Kathy had little choice. With two fingers he grasped the edge of the hide, pulled it back and carefully began to cut the meat from the bones. He cut away every shred, leaving nothing but clean, white ribs. He held the meat in his hand, looking at its underside. Tiny maggots had hatched and swarmed over the putrid flesh, giving it the appearance of life. It was beginning to deliquesce: gelatinous, gleaming.

The rotten smell was strong, and Bob breathed only through his mouth in order to avoid it. I can't let Kathy see these, he thought as he scraped the maggots away with the blade of his knife. He placed the meat into the plastic bag and turned to leave the park. As he walked, he experienced a numbness, both physical and mental. He felt diminished, as a man, as a human being. He had taken the first step away from civilization and back toward the primeval existence his ancestors thought they had escaped a millennium before. Bob was coming to the realization that civilization is a thin shell covering a hideous core, and that shell is easily broken.

CHAPTER TWENTY-FOUR

Seattle

The ocean's waves lapped against the pure white sand of the beach with a tranquil, pulsing rhythm. The tropical sun poured down onto the sea, filling it with diamonds that flashed and sparkled. Palm trees leaned into the gentle breeze, their fronds beckoning. His bare feet sank into the warm sand as he walked. He was at peace. Suddenly, there was a slap to the side of his head. He was being shaken by the shoulder.

"Johnny, wake up!" a voice said. "Come on, will ya'? There's somethin' goin' on in the street!"

Johnny Taylor tried to open his eyes, but one of them had been glued shut by mucous. He reached up and pulled the eyelids apart with his grimy fingers.

"Goddam son-of-a-bitch!" he mumbled thickly, as reality soaked into his torpid mind.

He looked up and saw the soiled brick of the alley's wall next to which he had slept. Its indecipherable graffiti moved in and out of focus. He rolled onto his back, and the newspapers that had been covering him fell to the side. Pushing himself into a sitting position, he felt the bottle in his coat pocket. He pulled it out and examined it with squinting, bleary eyes.

"Damn! Not much more than a spider!" he said, as he drank down the quarter inch of fortified wine left in the bottle.

He knew he would have to start hustling soon so he could buy another. He knew only too well what would happen if he were deprived of the amber liquid for too long. Ed was squatting down next to him, his overgrown sandy hair spilling out over the torn lapel of his ragged brown sport coat. His red and white checkered pants were stained with grease, food and urine. His sneakers had no laces.

Ed and Johnny were pals. They had been together for over a year, panhandling, making the rounds of the best dumpsters, and, most of all, getting drunk. Neither knew much about the other, because they both lied like dogs. But that was part of the fun of it: constructing an imaginary life filled with accomplishment and consequence. Neither Johnny nor Ed took much of anything seriously, except for their daily wine supply. They would kill for that, if necessary. But it never came to that. The people of Seattle were a liberal, generous lot. There was always a free meal to be had, always another quarter that could be spared.

Johnny staggered to his feet, Ed holding him by the elbow.

"There are busses and trucks out there," Ed whispered in breath that would knock out an ox. "And there are men walkin' around in uniforms."

Johnny reached into his pocket for his hat, and pulled it down over his head. It was his prized possession: an old, tattered bright red navy watch cap. It was his trademark. He had come to think of it as part of his identity. When he saw that red cap, every bum in Seattle knew that Johnny Taylor was coming.

Both Johnny and Ed felt a stab of anxiety. They had learned to avoid anything that even hinted of officialdom, of authority. Jail meant no wine, and no wine meant trouble. Johnny turned and looked at the back of the alley, seeking an escape route. But it was walled off They were trapped. Then two men appeared at the head of the alley. They called to Johnny and Ed.

"Come out! We will not hurt you! We are here to help!"

Slowly, they walked toward the two strangers, apprehensive but submissive. During their years on Skid Row they had discovered that there was nothing to be gained by aggression, by anger. It brought only trouble.

The strangers were not any kind of police that Johnny and Ed had ever seen. They wore strange uniforms, and carried no guns. They looked like soldiers. They smiled at the two derelicts and pointed down the street to the intersection, where dozens of other street people had been gathered. Busses stood waiting, their doors open. Johnny recognized most of them. Over the years, they had drifted in and out of each other's lives many times. He had drunk with them. They were his friends. As he glanced about, he recognized "Shopping Cart Annie," who somehow had been separated from her ubiquitous vehicle. And there was "Crazy Joe," who liked to twist the heads off pigeons.

More people were being led into the square with each passing moment, their gait shuffling, their old clothes flapping as they walked. Johnny saw that every street person for several blocks around now stood with him in front of the busses. Some were clearly not right in the head, he thought: talking to themselves, twitching or just staring off into space. Others obviously needed a drink even worse than he did, wrapping their arms around themselves and shaking. By now they were a crowd of fifty or sixty. Then one of the uniformed men began speaking to them.

"Ladies and gentlemen," he began.

A large woman in a torn, faded dress shouted, "You're damn right!"

Everyone laughed. He continued, smiling.

"Your new government has good news for you! You will no longer have to live on the streets! We find it appalling that you have been forced to sleep in alleys and on benches, exposed to the elements! As new citizens of the Russian Empire you deserve, and will receive, adequate housing! We are here to take you to your new homes! In addition to your new apartments, you will receive food, medical care and, yes, even a weekly ration of alcohol! I hope you have a taste for vodka!"

The street people broke into an excited chatter, gesticulating and patting each other on the back. Johnny was not so sure. There was something rotten here, he thought. But the least he could do was hear the man out.

"Your new homes are outside the city, and we will use these busses to transport you. Do not be concerned about any possessions that you may leave behind! Everything that you need will be provided! And now, if you will please enter the busses and take a seat, we will be on our way!"

Several soldiers began taking people by the arms and guiding them up the steps and into the busses. A few of the more disturbed people resented being touched, and slapped away the Russians' hands. But the soldiers just smiled and gestured toward the entrances. Johnny looked off to the right and saw several more soldiers, one of whom held a video camera pointed in his direction. Why would they want to film a bunch of bums climbing onto a bus? he asked himself.

Johnny wasn't so sure he wanted to leave the city. Living here was a relatively soft touch. It was familiar territory. Who wanted to live in an apartment in the country? He was happy here, as long as he got his liquor. His turn came to be helped onto the bus. The Russians, on both sides of him, reached for his arms. He raised his palms, shook his head no, and began to turn to leave. The Russians, still smiling, took him forcefully by the elbows and pushed him up the steps. Now he got scared.

The last time he had been in a vehicle with this many people it had been a paddy-wagon, and he had been on his way to the drunk tank. Government had never been anything but trouble for him. Now they were offering an apartment, eats, even booze. This stank to high heaven. Johnny took a seat near the window about half way down the bus. Ed managed to sit next to him.

"Hey, Johnny, this is all right, huh? It looks like we're goin' to be on easy street!" he said.

Johnny looked at him with a jaundiced eye, but said nothing.

The bus rumbled out of the city and through the suburbs. Two similar busses followed it, as would many more that day. Johnny and his friends did not know it, but all morning and afternoon a stream of busses had been leaving Seattle, and many other cities across the land. They carried the human debris of the country's urban areas: the drunks, the disturbed, the streetwalkers, the drugged-out and the burned-out. All had been told that they were going to a new life, a nirvana for street-people.

The houses became fewer and fewer, the signs of human habitation more and more scarce. Finally, they were truly in the country. Nothing but trees were to be seen on either side of the road. Johnny felt increasingly uneasy with each passing mile. But he had learned to be passive when dealing with authority, and sat quietly, keeping his fears to himself. The other occupants of the bus were in high spirits, chattering among themselves about their new lives.

The bus slowed, and then turned onto a dirt road that had recently been cut through the forest. The vehicle trundled along at a few miles per hour, going ever deeper into the verdant wilderness of the Pacific Northwest.

At last there was a clearing, and the bus stopped. Johnny could see about a dozen other busses that had arrived earlier. Most were already empty, but a few were still unloading. Some were turning around to leave, returning to Seattle for more passengers. The soldier who had been seated in the front row stood and turned toward the occupants. He was still smiling.

"Ladies and gentlemen, we have reached our destination! Please rise and follow me."

The passengers stood, stepped out into the isle, and followed the soldier out of the bus and onto the churned-up earth of the clearing. When they were all outside, the soldier turned to address them once again. Johnny noticed that other soldiers were approaching them from several directions. These were different. They were armed with short, vicious-looking rifles. They said nothing, and kept their distance. A number of the street-people looked at each other with apprehension. There were no apartment buildings in sight, a fact that did not escape even the least coherent of them.

"You will please follow me to the other side of those trees."

He pointed to the tree line beyond the parked vehicles. Two other busses rumbled into the clearing and maneuvered for parking positions. Johnny's group shuffled forward slowly, following their uniformed leader. He could hear heavy machinery operating beyond the tree line. Suddenly there was a popping sound, like many firecrackers going off almost simultaneously.

Johnny and his group walked through the trees, following paths that had been worn by their predecessors. When they reached the other side, another clearing opened up before them But this one was like a scene out of hell. Large backhoes were digging trenches that were sixty or seventy feet long, six or eight feet deep, and about eight feet wide. Filling those trenches were bodies. Some had been filled to within a few feet of the surface, and bulldozers worked to cover these with earth. Johnny could see that many people in these trenches were still alive, moving about feebly, their mouths opening and closing. Still, the machines covered them. To the far right, more bulldozers drove forward and backward, packing down the earth over trenches that had been filled to capacity.

The trench directly in front of Johnny was only about half full. Many of the people in it writhed in agony, squirming about in a way that reminded him of worms in a bait-bucket. Fifty or so people were being led, single file, along the edge of the trench. Dozens of soldiers stood by with rifles, discouraging any attempt to escape. When the people were in place, they were instructed to face the pit. Most did as they were told, but a few protested. These were pushed into position with bayonets.

Suddenly, one of the men broke and ran. He was trying to make it to the far side of the clearing, and the safety of the forest. He was an older man, Johnny guessed: somewhere in his sixties. And he was obviously not used to running. He lurched along in a pitiful gait, arms swinging wildly, old, ill-fitting clothes flapping about.

The soldiers didn't even bother chasing him. One of them simply leveled his rifle and fired. The old bum was thrown forward, as a cloud of red spray erupted from his forehead. He fell to the earth like a discarded rag doll. It happened that he fell into the path of one of the big backhoes, and the machine just ran over him as it would any other piece of debris, grinding him into the soft earth.

Johnny turned his attention back to the line of people along the edge of the trench. About a dozen soldiers had positioned themselves behind them, and had withdrawn pistols from their belts. They pointed the weapons very carefully behind the right ear of each person, and pulled their triggers. Instead of loud blasts, there was just a series of feeble pops, barely audible above the rumbling of the heavy equipment. The Russians were using twenty-two short ammunition in order to save money. These were sufficiently powerful to stun, but not always did they kill. Those who had been shot tumbled into the trench. Some lay still, perhaps dead. Others moved about, semiconscious, limbs akimbo, writhing, twitching.

The soldiers then took a step to the left, and did the same to the next dozen. Then the next. Some of the people cursed the soldiers as they waited for the coup de grace. A few raised their middle fingers in a final gesture of defiance. But in the end, all lay in the bottom of the pit, dead or dying.

Johnny looked around himself, seeking an avenue of escape. There were soldiers everywhere, stony-faced, silent. He could see no way out. All around him, in a dozen open trenches, the street-people of Seattle were being disposed of. The popping noises filled the air in an almost constant staccato as line after line of victims tumbled into their mass graves. Johnny's turn was next. A soldier barked an order at the people from his bus, and the soldiers behind them prodded them with bayonets. The entire busload stumbled forward and lined up at the edge of the trench. Johnny stood there waiting for the end. Beside him, his friend Ed cried softly, shifting his weight from foot to foot.

The soldiers came up behind them, aimed their pistols, and fired. A dozen people from Johnny's bus fell into the trench. He saw Shopping Cart Annie fly face first onto the pile of writhing people. She lay still. Good, thought Johnny. At least she won't suffer. The soldiers behind them took a step to the left. Now it was Ed's turn. As the Russian placed the pistol behind his ear, Ed glanced over at his friend. Tears cascaded down Ed's dirty cheeks.

"Oh, Johnny," he said quietly.

Then his head jerked forward, his eyes closed tightly in shock. His sleeve brushed Johnny's arm as he fell forward. Johnny looked down at his friend, and saw his foot moving slowly back and forth. He was still alive. Johnny wished that he could kill him; he wished that he could put his friend out of his misery before the earthen blanket doomed him to a slow, horrifying, suffocating death.

Johnny realized with surprise that he was not nervous. His own death did not frighten him. As an alcoholic, he was well aware of his own mortality. He knew that he didn't have too many more years to live anyway. But he had always expected to die in an alley, with some punk's shiv between his ribs, or perhaps from withdrawal symptoms in a psych ward. He thought back to his youth, to the days when he used to go to church. He tried to remember the things he had been taught, about God, about salvation. He tried to remember a prayer, just one prayer. But it had all been lost in an alcoholic haze years ago.

Johnny felt the cold steel of the pistol's muzzle against his scalp. He closed his eyes and gritted his teeth. Then there was a concussion that threw him forward. There was no pain. He landed softly on the pile of humanity, face down, eyes open.

That wasn't so bad, he thought. As the seconds passed, he felt his consciousness slipping away from him. It was like entering another world: a quiet, serene world. He felt warm and comfortable, as if he were a child again, in his own, soft bed on a mild spring evening. He smiled as he slowly slipped away. He began to dream...to dream.

The ocean's waves lapped against the pure white sand of the beach with a tranquil, pulsing rhythm. The tropical sun poured down onto the sea, filling it with diamonds that flashed and sparkled....

CHAPTER TWENTY-FIVE

Washington, D.C.

The Glock pistol clattered to the marble floor as the guard's fingers relaxed in death. In his final seconds of life, he had thrown himself across the display case that contained his country's most precious documents, as if his corpse would keep them safe. His partner lay a few feet away, his body ripped open by rifle fire, his blood pouring out onto the cold, gleaming stone. The slides of both pistols were locked back, their magazines empty. Two dead Russian soldiers and another seriously wounded testified to the ferocity of the guards' resistance. Like all federal employees, they had been ordered to cooperate with their Russian masters. But when the time came, they found that they could not. To stand by passively while their conquerors stole the Declaration of Independence, the Constitution and the Bill of Rights was more than either could bear. Both men had worked at the National Archives for most of their careers, and they had developed a reverence for these documents that bordered on religious fervor.

Captain Georgi Astakhov holstered his pistol. He approached the display case. Looking at the guard's body draped across the thick plexiglass he, for the first time, felt his skin crawl Perhaps, he thought, this conquest will not be as easy as we have been told. Here are men who were willing to die to protect a few pieces of old, faded parchment. No, he told himself. They were willing to die to protect the ideas contained in those documents. That was even worse. Would there be others who felt as strongly? He, and all of his comrades, had been assured that there were not. The American people, they had been told, were amoral, shallow, depraved. Perhaps. He forced the thought from his mind, and concentrated on the task at hand

"Sergeant," he called. "Bring the hammers." He had been told that the material covering the documents would resist gunfire, and that the only way to retrieve them undamaged would be to smash open the cases by main force. The sergeant and two brawny privates moved forward, each carrying a large sledgehammer. Astakhov took the dead guard by his belt and shirt collar and slid him off the display case to the floor. Several enlisted men dragged them to the side.

"All right. Have at it." Astakhov ordered, pointing to the case. He stepped back several paces. The three men raised their hammers and brought them down with all their strength onto the plexiglass. A series of crashing sounds echoed back and forth across the room, but the material held.

"Again," the Captain ordered. Again the men brought their hammers down with all the force they could muster. This time cracks appeared. Once again the hammers came down, and the thick protective layer shattered into pieces. The three men stepped back, their task completed.

Almost reverently, Astakhov removed the broken pieces of plexiglass. Both the Declaration of Independence and the Constitution had suffered damage from the violent onslaught, jagged tears reaching across the faded ink. One by one he lifted them from the cases. He held them to the light and began to read. His English was quite good, but he strained to make sense of the pale calligraphy.

"We the People of the United States...do ordain and establish this Constitution for the United States of America...The Congress shall have Power...To regulate Commerce with foreign Nations, and among the several States...To make all Laws which shall be necessary and proper for carrying into Execution the foregoing Powers...WE hold these Truths to be self-evident, that all Men are created equal, that they are endowed by their Creator with certain unalienable Rights, that among these are Life, Liberty, and the Pursuit of Happiness...that whenever any Form of Government becomes destructive of these Ends, it is the Right of the People to alter or to abolish it, and to institute new Government...But when a long Train of Abuses and Usurpations, pursuing invariably the same Object, evinces a Design to reduce them under absolute Despotism, it is their Right, it is their Duty, to throw off such Government, and to provide new Guards for their future Security.. The enumeration in the Constitution of certain rights shall not be construed to deny or disparage others retained by the people...The powers not delegated to the United States by the Constitution, nor prohibited by it to the States, are reserved to the States respectively, or to the people...A well regulated Militia, being necessary to the security of a free State, the right of the people to keep and bear Arms, shall not be infringed."

Captain Astakhov had seen these words before. He had read them many years ago, during his adolescence, back in Russia. His friend Sasha had insisted that he read them, saying that they were the greatest political thoughts ever put on paper. Ever since then, these phrases, these concepts, had been lurking in the back of his mind, to emerge from time to time, making him feel both uncomfortable and curiously reassured at the same time. He realized that the ideas embodied in these documents were totally alien to the reality that he faced in Russia. And that made him sad. But the idea that some men, somewhere in the world, took them seriously–or at least had taken them seriously at one time--gave him a sense of quiet comfort. Now he stood here with the originals in his hands, which trembled slightly. He had been instructed to hand-deliver them to the Maximum Leader in New York immediately. What would become of them then he had no idea. If only the Americans had not forgotten the contents of these documents, if only they had not relegated them to the status of mere museum pieces, things might be very different today, he thought. A shame, really.

CHAPTER TWENTY-SIX

New York City

Sergei Drugonov stands at the podium arranging his notes for the last time. In front of him the television technicians make final adjustments to their equipment, insuring that cables are properly connected and that power is flowing as it should. A make-up artist approaches Drugonov and touches up the powder on his forehead and chin, eliminating any shine. Tonight's broadcast will appear on every television station in America. Everyone is required to watch. Thousands of Russian security agents are making spot-checks around the country to insure compliance. Anyone not watching will be shot on the spot. The American people have been informed of this. The chances of being caught are slim, that is true, but Drugonov feels sure that this dose of terror will have its desired effect.

Drugonov feels good. Tonight will be momentous, if only symbolic. He will break the backs of these Americans once and for all. He will demoralize them beyond the point of resistance. Resistance. That was becoming a bit of a problem. It is nothing that his people can't handle, of course. But it is irritating. It indicates that the conquest is not complete. A few bombs have been planted, a few potshots taken at his personnel. No one has been caught yet; always they disappear as if into thin air. But Drugonov isn't overly worried. The American leadership collapsed like a house of cards, as he knew it would. That is all that really matters. The power of the State is now in his hands; he holds the noose with which he will strangle any dissent. He knows well enough that millions, tens of millions, hate him. The average American does not, after all, possess the craven degeneracy of his leaders. Those leaders had simply been the scum who had, by some bizarre political mechanism, risen to the top.

He may experience problems with some among the general populace, but he is sure that they will bend their necks with enough prodding. He consoles himself in the knowledge that the majority of Americans are altruists. Every bit of data he has seen substantiates that. At least that portion of the population cannot defend itself on principle. And an unprincipled defense is a weak defense. Still, a twinge of apprehension gnaws within him.

He had been led to believe, by decades of election data, by Benedict's polling results, by the contents of journalistic and academic publications, that there were relatively few individualists left in this country, only a handful who would resist. Now that he is on American soil, and is receiving his own intelligence, it is becoming apparent that the problem is bigger than he had thought. A majority of

Americans may indeed be altruists, but that majority may not be as large as he had believed. There is a great political and military difference between subjugating a population consisting of ninety-nine percent sheep and only one percent wolves, and one consisting of fifty-one percent sheep and forty-nine percent wolves.

It seems that there is a silent core, unobtrusive, something that was off everyone's radar screen, unaccounted for in the polls, who had not read the academic journals nor been swayed by the collectivist press. There is no way of knowing how big this individualistic core is, but, however large, Drugonov is certain that he can deal with it. He will insure his success by inaugurating a reign of terror, a pervasive climate of absolute repression that will make those of his totalitarian predecessors pale by comparison. Even wolves have their limits. He recalls how Lenin dealt with the massive peasant uprisings and the millions of army desertions in the years immediately following the Soviet Revolution: he swept them away through mass executions and internment in concentration camps, not only for those who resisted, but for their families as well. The "Iron Broom" it had been called. It had taken time, but Lenin's insistence on the use of terror had finally prevailed. It would prevail here as well.

But Lenin's State had ultimately failed. Why? That was a question he had been pondering for some time. He had concluded that it had failed because Lenin, along with Stalin, Mao and others, had not institutionalized terror: make it permanent by weaving it so thoroughly into the fabric of society that its victims consider it as natural as the air they breathe. When Stalin and Mao died, their state-terrorism died with them. They had been followed by weaklings, men who vacillated, unsure men who did not have the strength and determination to carry on the legacy left to them. He would not make the same mistake.

He had promised the Russian people centuries of loot from an enslaved world, and that is what he would give them. He would rebuild American society, redesign it from the ground up, as one would a machine; and he would see to it that terror–and the obedience it generates–was its principal component, its motive force. Then it would not matter who followed him. Still, he would choose his successor carefully, very carefully indeed. Leave nothing to chance. Finding someone suitable might prove difficult. True monsters are rare.

A voice brings Drugonov out of his reverie.

"Maximum Leader, we're going on the air in ten seconds."

He straightens his shoulders and looks directly into the cameras.

"Five, four, three, two, one..." and a finger points at him just as the lights on the cameras become illuminated.

"Subjects of the Russian Empire," he begins. "It has now been two weeks since your country ceased to exist. Russian military units have occupied all of your major cities, and their presence has been felt in virtually every town and village in the land. Our grip over you tightens with each passing hour. With every tick of the clock, more Russian personnel and materiel land at your airports and harbors. You are being inundated by wave after wave of conquerors. Your former political, judicial and military leaders have assumed their posts within the Russian occupational hierarchy, and they are working zealously to pursue our common goal of crushing you into submission and bending you to our will. Or perhaps I should say, to my will. Still, there are those among you who have chosen to resist: only a few it is true, nothing more than an annoyance. But it is an annoyance that I will not tolerate. It indicates to me that you need one last, final lesson to teach you your places within our New Order."

Drugonov walks to his left, to a table on which rest several large yellowed documents, side by side. The cameras pan back to show both Drugonov and the table.

"These pieces of parchment contain the principles upon which your country was founded. They are your Declaration of Independence, your Constitution and your Bill of Rights. They are the very symbols of your independence, the essence of your nationality. They are the product of millennia of philosophical debate, countless wars and revolutions, oceans of spilled blood. Here, on these few documents, is the condensed political wisdom of the entire Age of Reason Even I must admit that they are impressive."

He lifts up the Declaration by its corner and spends a moment contemplating it. He puts it back down and looks once again into the cameras.

"You chose long ago to ignore them, to demote them from literal, objectively demonstrable, principled statements defending the sanctity of the individual, and to relegate them to the status of quaint historical relics. I wonder if you realize what you have done? How many billions of human beings have suffered and died under the lash of tyranny throughout our history? Since the advent of civilization, perhaps ten thousand years ago, when some men were first given, or when they first seized, dominion over others, humanity the world over has dreamed of the individual liberty that you have so cavalierly tossed aside! Five hundred generations of mankind would have traded their souls to live in accordance with the principles that you have discarded as obsolete, mean spirited and selfish! You fools! Don't you see? These documents were written to protect you from tyrants–like me!"

He chuckles into the cameras.

"Yes, I freely admit it! I am a tyrant! I operate under no pretense! I am precisely the kind of beast that your Jefferson and your Madison hated and feared so intensely! But I have looked, and I see no Jeffersons, no Madisons among you. I see only Judas Benedicts, creatures not fit to kiss the shoes of such men.

"They did what was in their power to do for you: they created a free country and a political environment in which men could live in liberty. But you pissed on their graves long ago. Madison predicted the frailty of this liberty, when he referred to your Bill of Rights as a parchment barrier which could not long withstand the efforts of determined tyrants. As it turned out, no tyrant was necessary. You yourselves breached the barriers of those documents. You demanded that they be ignored! And your self-serving, power-mad leaders were only too happy to oblige! Madison could not have imagined how cheaply you would sell the liberties embodied in those pieces of parchment: a monthly ration card–you call them food stamps, a filling for your tooth, a state-financed apartment, or a bottle of pills for your blood pressure. And let's not leave out your elite! They too contributed to the creation of the Leviathan State with their demands for subsidies and cost overruns!

"Your stupidity did not manifest itself overnight. As the twentieth century progressed, you moved farther and farther from the principles of your Founding. You chose safety over the challenge of responsibility, an enervating security over the rigors of individualism. To paraphrase one of your founders, you came to love the tranquility of servitude better than the animating contest of freedom.

"You rejected these principles so thoroughly that anyone who defended them was branded as a lunatic, unworthy of serious consideration, fit only for derision. The Constitution was a living document, you said, subject to reinterpretation as times changed. It was not something to be taken too seriously, you said. There are no hard and fast, immortal principles, you said. Everything is relative, you said.

"Now you are reaping what you have sown. If, in fact, liberty is not to be taken seriously, then you will have no objection to your enslavement. If everything is relative, then there is no difference between freedom and subjugation. If your Ninth Amendment, and the infinitude of your natural rights that it recognizes, can be safely ignored--as your courts, your Congress, and your executive branch have done for two centuries--then you will not mind if I ignore it as well. If the concept of limited government embodied in your Tenth Amendment is obsolete, as so many of you have argued, you should have no objection to totalitarianism. If the right to keep and bear arms is not an individual right, but instead a collective one, you will not object if I disarm you--as individuals--and restrict the possession of arms to a collective: the Russian military.

"If the principles in your Declaration of Independence and your Constitution change with time, then consider this to be the time. What you are now experiencing is the logical culmination of the course you have chosen for the past century. I am simply giving you what you have asked for.

"You, yourselves, through your own actions, beliefs and choices, have consigned these documents to the ash-heap of history. I will now change that figurative truth into a literal one."

Drugonov once again lifts up the Declaration of Independence. He removes from his pocket a cigarette lighter, strikes it, and touches the flame to the lower corner of the parchment. It, like the others, has been saturated with kerosene. The cameras zoom in so that the frame includes only the Declaration and Drugonov's hands. The corner of the document catches fire. Quickly the flame moves upward. John Hancock's bold signature disappears forever, curling into a black ash.

Two-hundred-eighty million Americans watched as, line by line, Jefferson's words become dark, and then are obliterated as the fire moves upward.

"...these United Colonies are, and of Right ought to be, Free and Independent States..."–gone amongst the crackling flames.

"...He is, at this Time, transporting large Armies of foreign Mercenaries to complete the Works of Death, Desolation, and Tyranny..."–gone in a second's time.

The flame accelerates, eating its way through the parchment faster and faster.

"...WE hold these Truths to be self- evident..." gone.

"...When in the Course of human Events...." gone.

".....The Unanimous Declaration of the thirteen united States of America...."
gone"

In CONGRESS, July 4, 1776...." Gone. All gone.

Drugonov smiles as he releases what is left of the document. The tiny remnant floats down to the surface of the table and in an instant it, too, is consumed.

He picks up the Constitution and the Bill of Rights and holds them up to the cameras.

"Your Constitution established and structured your government, and, with its Bill of Rights, prevented that government from infringing upon your liberties. You won't be needing them either."

He touches the lighter's flame to each document. The American people watch as they burn, in the end being reduced to blackened, crinkled curls of ash. The cameras move away from them and back toward Drugonov, who returns to the podium.

"You have just witnessed a symbolic act. Those documents ceased to have any real meaning for you decades ago. But for any who may harbor the slightest hope, for any who may be in the least tempted to resist, the destruction that has taken place tonight should serve to demonstrate the fact that there is no going back. It took ten thousand years to discover those principles, and it will take another ten thousand to rediscover them.

"Once this current generation has died out, there will be no recollection of what it was like to be even remotely free. I will see to it that your children, and their children, and so on forever, are raised as cattle, without the slightest trace of self-esteem or self-respect, with no expectations of self-fulfillment or accomplishment. The concept of individual liberty will be as alien to them as would the notion of sprouting wings and flying to the moon. Their entire existence will be dedicated to one goal: serving me and my successors, the living manifestations of the Russian people.

"This current generation, the last of your innovators, will be wrung dry for our benefit. As I have said in the past, we will even encourage innovation and productivity. But I am not deluding myself. The oppression that you and your descendants will experience will extinguish those qualities in short order. Then you will join the rest of the non-Russian world as beasts of burden: hewers of wood and haulers of water. Even in that degraded state, you will still provide my people with a modicum of luxury.

"No doubt there are a few deranged individuals who refuse to accept this fate. These criminals cannot be allowed to interfere with the functioning of the State. Such saboteurs and wreckers may be tempted to engage in acts of violence as long as they possess the means to do so.

"Therefore, as I promised you moments ago, I hereby decree that the private ownership of firearms is prohibited. I have been assured by my subordinates that the mechanisms to enforce such a policy are now in place. You have one week to surrender your weapons to the nearest State Security Office. The penalty for noncompliance is death. Let me make this clear: any civilian apprehended with a firearm after midnight, one week from tonight, Friday, the fifth of May, will be executed on the spot. And rest assured that we know who you are; the records of your Bureau of Alcohol, Tobacco and Firearms are quite complete. Those of you who possess concealed weapons permits in your various states are particularly well documented.

"I give you a full week because of the sheer number of weapons that must be dealt with. You Americans have an extraordinary passion for firearms. This colony is flooded with them. But that will end. Only free individuals--citizens--have guns. You are now neither free nor citizens. You are slaves, and subjects."

Drugonov checks his watch then looks back into the camera.

"I have prepared one final act of symbolism for you to witness this evening. If a flicker of hope still exists in the hearts of any Americans, this should serve to extinguish it. As you watch, think of this: you are slaves; you will be slaves for the rest of your lives; your children will be slaves and their children after them, for all time to come."

Drugonov's image disappears from the screen, replaced by a live view of the Statue of Liberty. There is no narration. The entire country looks at the great landmark, the very symbol of American liberty. She is beautiful. The powerful floodlights at her base illuminate her in such a way as to convey a sense of tranquil assurance, as if nothing can go wrong as long as she stands. Confidently she holds her torch aloft, proclaiming liberty to all the world.

Suddenly, what look like clouds of smoke appear at her feet. A few seconds pass in silence. Then the American people hear the dull roar of explosives as the sound reaches the microphones across the river in Battery Park. For another second, the Great Lady stands firm, as if refusing to abdicate the position she has held for so long. Then she begins to move. Slowly, ever so slowly, she begins to lean forward, almost imperceptibly at first, then gaining momentum. Snapping, groaning noises come over the microphones as she screams out her death-knell. A horrified nation watches, transfixed, as she plunges forward faster and faster. Her torch is still lit as she hits the water, as if to send a final message to her people.

And then she is gone.

CHAPTER TWENTY-SEVEN

Mankato, Minnesota. Mankato Elementary School

The wind off the prairie blew the occasional leaf against his office window with a light tapping sound, but Miguel "Mike" Cantu was too busy to notice. As the school's principal, he was buried in paper work, as usual. He loved his job, especially the children, but he wished that some of this paper would land on someone else's desk for a change. He put down his pen, looked up and rubbed his eyes. Nine-oh-five. First period was about to end.

He decided that he could use a break. Pushing himself away from his desk, he stood and crossed the room to the door. One of his favorite activities was to walk the halls between periods, where he could make his presence felt among the students, instilling a little extra discipline from time to time. But mostly he did it because he loved to be among his children. He loved to see them filling the corridors, laughing, chattering, poking each other in the ribs. It made him feel young again. His reputation among the kids was as a tough guy, someone not to be crossed. To a certain extent, he cultivated that image.

As he entered the hallway, a tow-headed first-grader ran full-tilt into his left leg. Mike put on his sternest expression, squatted down and took the little boy firmly by the shoulders.

"Mister!" he shouted. "There's no running in the halls! You know that!"

The boy's lower lip began to tremble, the corners of his mouth turned down, and his eyes welled with tears. Mike couldn't stand it.

"Come here, son," he said gently. He took the boy in his arms and patted him on the back. Whispering into his ear, Mike said,

"Just don't run anymore, OK?"

He held the boy at arms' length. The child nodded solemnly. Mike stood up and put his arms behind his back, glaring up and down the hall as if nothing had happened. It would not do to be seen displaying affection. He had his reputation to uphold.

This was his favorite spot: the juncture of two corridors where he had an uninterrupted view of perhaps a hundred children at a time, moving about like the swirling waters of a wild river, seemingly at random, but usually ending up where they should be. At times it seemed almost miraculous that any order could come of such chaos.

As his eyes reached to the end of the hallway on his left, he saw something out of place: two men in dark uniforms. They stood quietly, looking in his direction.

A shudder of fear passed through him. Even from this distance he could tell that they were Russian military men. Not in my school! Please don't bring this into my school!

Mankato had been relatively untouched by the occupation, at least so far. The community was filled with apprehension; people talked furtively on the streets, afraid to be overheard. Everyone knew it would be only a matter of time before the monstrous Russian juggernaut got around to them. Now Mike Cantu was afraid that their time had come.

Slowly he walked down the hall toward the two dark figures, the sea of children parting before him. Soon he was close enough to see their eyes: cold, passionless. The men seemed unaffected by the presence of the students; the young people surged around them, glancing upward from time to time with a mixture of curiosity and fear. The soldiers did not even recognize their existence.

Mike stopped before the two men and glared into their faces. He did not want to anger them, but he could not conceal the disgust he felt. They, and everything that they stood for, were defiling this place with their very presence.

"Who are you, and what do you want?" he asked.

The taller of the two men spoke up. He was wearing epaulettes with gold insignia, so Mike assumed he was an officer.

"My name is Valery Strasser. Major Valery Strasser. Yes, I know that the name is German, but rest assured that I am Russian. I have been assigned by the Commandant of this zone, Elsworth Chambliss, to maximize the labor efficiency of the area."

"Chambliss?" Mike asked. "I met him two years ago. He's the Federal Judge for this district. You say you're working for him?"

"In a sense that is correct, Principal... Cantu."

The major looked down at his clipboard to confirm Mike's name.

"Though it might be more accurate to say that he is working for us. The Commandant has discovered the many perquisites of collaboration. He is proving to be a most enthusiastic convert to our cause."

"All right. What is it that the Commandant wants you to do here?" Mike asked, his eyes narrowing as he looked into those of the Major.

"I am here to rectify a most wasteful state of affairs. Look, look about you."

The Russian swept his arms in both directions, encompassing all of the children filling the hallways. "All of these little arms, going to waste, doing nothing more productive than turning pages in a book. All of these strong, young backs with no tasks to perform. This is a resource that must be put into the service of the State."

"What the hell are you talking about?" Mike hissed.

"Agriculture, Principal Cantu!"

The Major said with a taunting smile.

"We must teach these young people the joys of labor! We must put them into the fields, where they can be productive! They must be taught to contribute to the well being of the Collective! Their time is wasted here, having their heads filled with useless gibberish that will serve no purpose. The ideas that you feed them will only lead to dissatisfaction, false expectations. Educated children become troublesome adults. And that we will not tolerate.

"You will please go to your office and announce over your intercom that classes have been canceled. Students will assemble on the north side of the building, near the parking lot. Trucks are waiting to transport them to their new lives. All faculty and staff, yourself included, will also report to the north side of the building, and form a line against the wall so that we may check you against our personnel lists. That is all."

"Now wait a minute," Mike began, barely able to contain his rage. "These are just children! They don't deserve to be sent into the fields like slaves!"

"Ah, but Principal Cantu, that is exactly what they are. It is best that they learn their place now, while their minds are still malleable."

"But don't Russian children get an education? Why can't you..."

The Major's face turned red. He took a half-step closer to Cantu and practically spit out his reply.

"These are not Russian children! They are animals! Beasts of burden! They will act accordingly! They will do as they are told! And so will you! Now go!"

The two men stared at each other with hatred. Only the presence of the children prevented Mike Cantu from lunging at the Russian. Instead, he turned on his heel and walked back toward his office.

Some of the teachers smoked cigarettes nervously as they stood along the wall of the school. Mike had spoken to as many of them as he could reach in so short a time, trying to calm them down, trying to prevent an incident that might provoke the Russians. At least a dozen soldiers stood by, automatic weapons held at the ready.

The children looked dazed and confused as the Russians began to prod them into the trucks. The bigger ones were able to climb in by themselves, but the very young ones had to be lifted into the vehicles by still more soldiers. And those soldiers were not treating them gently. Mike looked on as the smallest children were virtually thrown into the trucks like sacks of grain. Crying filled the air. Some had become hysterical, and screamed pitifully for their parents.

The teachers surged forward as a group, desperate to protect their young charges. The Russians leveled their weapons at the faculty, fixed bayonets glinting in the sun. The teachers stopped. Suddenly, Marilyn Waters, the quiet, middle-aged reading instructor who had hardly raised her voice in twenty-six years of working with children, screamed at the Russian standing in front of her.

"You monsters! How can you do this? I demand that you..."

The soldier brought the butt of his rifle upward with all of his strength. It caught Miss Waters on the point of her chin. Her head shot backward, and those standing nearby could hear her neck snap. She collapsed onto the ground in a heap.

Dozens of children saw Miss Waters die, and they screamed in horror. Several fell to the pavement of the driveway as if unconscious. These the soldiers quickly scooped up and tossed into the waiting trucks. The rest of the faculty, including Mike Cantu, stood in stunned silence. Major Strasser, hands clasped behind his back, approached the corpse and stared down at it for a moment. Then he looked up.

"Against the wall, all of you!" he shouted.

The teachers, administrators and staff lined up shoulder to shoulder against the cold brick, as instructed. Strasser nodded to a subordinate, and the troops formed their own line facing the educators.

"I realize that in the past you were considered to be valuable, perhaps indispensable, members of society," he said. "You may even have considered yourselves to have been part of some minor elite. But in the New Order your services are no longer required. As of this moment, you are anachronisms. You have been rendered....obsolete."

Strasser took two steps back. The twelve soldiers shouldered their weapons, pointing them at Cantu and the others.

"Ready..." Strasser shouted.

Some of the teachers fell to their knees. Others put their arms around the person next to them. A few wept openly. Mike only wished that the children were not there to witness what he knew was about to happen.

"Fire!" Strasser commanded.

The rifles cracked; a dozen torn, twisted bodies fell.

"Fire at will!" Strasser shouted.

The weapons discharged in a continuous fusillade, like rolling thunder over the prairie, cutting down the remaining school employees like a demon's scythe. In a few seconds it was over. The scent of gun powder filled the air, and it drifted toward the children still waiting to be loaded onto the trucks. The little ones didn't know what had happened. It was beyond their ken. They wrinkled their noses at the acrid odor, and wondered why all their teachers were asleep. It would be their last memory of Mankato Elementary School.

CHAPTER TWENTY-EIGHT

Granite Peak, Black Rock Desert, Nevada.

Doctor John Marusich brought the twelve-pound sledge hammer down with all the strength he could muster. The basketball-sized piece of stone broke in half. He glared at it with a mixture of hatred and satisfaction, trying to blink the sweat out of his eyes. All around him, hundreds of men were doing the same. The air was filled with the sound of exhausted humanity, grunting and straining to turn big rocks into little ones, steel slamming into granite. Dr. Marusich straightened his torso, arching his back to relieve the pain. His back. That was what was going to give out first. He just knew it. As he tilted his head upward, he closed his eyes against the broiling Nevada sun. It was just the beginning, he told himself. The true heat of summer was yet to arrive. He wondered if any of them would live through it.

"Get back to work!" a deep, accented voice yelled from behind him.

He knew what was coming and winced in anticipation. The split-bamboo cane lashed across his shoulders, turning his vision red and bringing tears to his eyes. That part of his body was already covered with welts, and he wondered if this latest blow had broken them open. The trickle of warm liquid running down his back confirmed his fears.

John Marusich had been an Associate Professor of Political Science at a medium-sized state university. He had always been considered something of an iconoclast by his colleagues, to the point where he had actually been shunned from time to time at academic conventions. His writing was considered to be 'out of the mainstream' by most: tolerated by those few who still paid lip-service to academic freedom, but nothing to be taken seriously. He had been an Associate Professor for fourteen years, and had come to doubt the probability of his ever being promoted to full Professor. Long ago he had resigned himself to an obscure career, writing books read by only a few, publishing papers only in second-rate journals.

His books and articles had as their central theme the dangers of authoritarian government. His writings had traced the history of tyranny through the centuries, examined its nature, and pointed out the conditions that made it possible. As the years went by, he had found himself blending more and more philosophy into his political science. He had come to the realization that ideas, rather than political institutions and structures, were the wellspring of tyranny. Toward the end, he had felt tremendous excitement about his work; he thought that he was approaching some great truth, some relationship within reality that had so far eluded him. But now he would never know that great truth.

The Russians, it seems, were more familiar with his work than were most Americans. He had been condemned as an enemy of the State. His ideas were inflammatory, dangerous. They had sentenced him to ten years at hard labor: ten years of breaking rock in this labor camp.

In a remarkably short time, the Russian occupiers had completely revamped the American penal system. The prisons were emptied, barbed wire strung, and a network of labor camps had sprung up all across the country, always near sources of rock. Common criminals usually received five years, but the longer sentences were reserved for those whom the Russians considered to be genuine threats to State security: intellectuals with an individualistic bent; high-profile members of organizations that espoused liberty, officials who refused to tow the New Line.

During his three weeks in the camp, John had spoken with a number of such people. All wondered why they were still alive, why the Russians had not simply shot them. The consensus of opinion was that their new masters took some sort of perverse delight in seeing them suffer; that by grinding these men--and women--into the dust, they were reassuring themselves that they had indeed conquered their strongest, most articulate ideological opponents.

John heard a scream. Glancing to his left, he saw that the guard was flailing some other poor wretch. He took the opportunity to quickly reposition the rags that were wrapped around his hands. Within the first two days of his arrival, they had become completely covered with blisters. Soon after that, his palms began to look like raw hamburger. Now the material was stiff and black with dried blood. He knew that, given time to heal, calluses would form. But the Russians gave him no time. He had been lucky to find the bits of cloth, caught on a nail under his barracks. From time to time, he noticed the men working next to him looking at his rags, desire and envy in their eyes. Each night he placed them under the leg of his cot, so that they would not be stolen. He would fight to keep them, if he must. In a labor camp, survival depended on such things.

The sun arched its way across the sky. Eventually, it sank below the mountains to the west, and dusk began to engulf the parched desert. Hundreds of thousands of hammer-blows had been struck, tons of rough stone turned to valuable crushed rock, building material for the monuments of the Russian Empire. John was numb, beyond pain. He had pushed himself almost past the limits of his endurance, as he did every day, as they all did. At last the whistle sounded.

John dropped his hammer to the ground and slumped forward in utter exhaustion. But there was one more task to be performed before the day's work was done. Each man had been issued a canvas tarp and a wooden-framed screen. The screen's wire consisted of one-inch square holes. For each man to get credit for the rock he broke, it had to be made small enough to pass through the holes in the screen. Any pieces that failed to pass through would have to be broken down further. The rock that did pass through was collected on the tarp. Periodically, during the day, each man would gather up the corners of his tarp and carry the rock to the scales, where it would be weighed. The amount of broken rock would be carefully recorded in a ledger. Each man had a daily quota, based on his age.

For a man in his forties, John's age, that was one ton. If a man met his quota, he was issued a chit for two thousand calories in food from the mess-hall. If he broke only half his quota, he received only one thousand calories. For every one hundred pounds that he broke over and above his quota, he could receive a cigarette or a cold drink. John had yet to see such a bonus dispensed.

Groaning with the effort, he lifted his tarp full of rock and slung it over his shoulder. He estimated that it weighed about one hundred pounds. Many men were tempted to drag their tarps to the scales, but to do so was the equivalent of a death-sentence. That would cause the tarps to wear out prematurely, and that left a man with no way to gather his rock; he would starve. The Russians expected a tarp to last a full year before replacements were issued. Each man treated his own as if it were the Shroud of Turin.

Now there was only one person ahead of John in the line at the scales: an old man, shrunken, emaciated. He wore no shirt; it had either disintegrated or been stolen. His arms were little more than parchment stretched over bone, and his concave chest was like a bowl surrounded by precisely-defined ribs. His oversized trousers were secured to his waist by a bit of twine he had been fortunate enough to find.

John recognized this man. He had been the founder and chairman of a major think-tank headquartered in Washington, D.C. For decades he had been one of the most respected, or hated, men in America, depending on whom one asked. His consistent espousal of the value of individual liberty and the benefits of limited government had made him a perpetual thorn in the sides of statists of all persuasions. Liberals in the press and in Congress had tried for years to find, or manufacture, some tool that could be used to destroy him. They had investigated his life back to the day he was born, looking for skeletons in his closet. They had invented rumors, spread innuendo, even arranged for I.R.S. audits. Always he emerged unscathed.

Needless to say, the Russians had no intention of allowing such a man to retain his freedom. Now, it seemed, he would spend his last days toiling in this hell-hole. With great effort, the old man swung his small tarp-full of rock onto the scale and waited for the Russian's pronouncement.

"Only thirty-two pounds, old man! That brings your total for the day to five hundred ninety-six. You are seventy-eight years old. Your quota is twelve hundred. Here! Only a thousand calories for you!" He handed the man a small slip of paper. The old man held the paper close to his myopic eyes and examined the numbers. With a trembling hand he held it up toward the Russian's face. "I can't live on this!" he shouted between toothless gums.

"Then die, you old bastard!" the Russian snarled, slapping the withered face with the back of his hand, sending the man flying to the ground. John watched him slowly get to his feet, and, clutching the piece of paper in his bony fingers, stagger away.

The men marched back to the barracks five abreast. Only six Russians guarded the three hundred prisoners. It was unlikely that anyone would try to escape. Even if one made it past the razor wire, the machine guns and the dogs, there was still the desert to deal with: miles and miles of it stretching in all directions, desolate, forbidding and bone-dry.

John placed his screen with the others, next to the barracks. He noticed the number painted on the wooden frame: 55481. It was the same number that had been tattooed on his right forearm. In this camp, that was his identity. The prisoners used names amongst themselves, of course, but for official purposes the men were numbers only. The lack of security for the screens made him nervous. A man's screen was as important as his tarp: if anything happened to it he would die. It seemed strange that they should be treated in such a cavalier fashion. But he supposed it was unlikely that anyone would tamper with them: to touch another man's screen or his tarp was sufficient cause for execution. That had been explained to him on his first day here. John smiled. How perfectly absurd this is, he thought. Who would have thought a year ago that my life would someday revolve around a few sticks of wood, a piece of wire mesh, and a scrap of canvas!

The water barrels had been filled, and men crowded around them, jostling for access to the precious liquid. They were given water in the quarry, but it was never enough. By the end of the day the thirst was overpowering. Finally, John's turn came. The barrels were oil drums, the tops of which had been crudely cut out with chisels. They had apparently not been cleaned before being put into service as water containers, because there was a perpetual oil slick on the surface.

Steel cans with their tops removed had been attached with wire to the rims of the drums. John took one of the cans in his hand, and with the other tried to brush away the rainbow-hued film of petroleum. Quickly he dipped the can into the barrel, raised it to his lips, and began to drink. The water was cool, and it coursed down his parched throat, partially rejuvenating him. He had almost gotten used to the pungent, oily flavor: he thought it resembled the taste of kerosene or diesel fuel. Nonetheless, he quickly drained the can's contents, and moved aside to make room for another.

Each barracks held sixty men. They were crude, wooden affairs, unpainted, with no insulation. At night, John could feel the desert breeze blowing through the gaps in the hastily-constructed walls. He wondered what would happen in winter. The cold in this part of the country could be intense. There were no bathing facilities, and John didn't think that he would ever become accustomed to the filth and the stench. The toilets were outside, boards with holes in them above open cesspools. There was no privacy; the guards wanted to be able to see everyone at all times. There was also no toilet-paper; this was a particular problem for the many men who had developed diarrhea from the poor diet.

John climbed the one step and entered the building. To his right he saw once again what he thought must be an example of the Russian sense of humor: a rope hanging from the ceiling ending in a hangman's noose, with a chair beneath it. He had been told during his orientation that anyone who simply couldn't stand any more was welcome to hang himself. Several had during his weeks in the camp, though none in his barracks.

The cots were lined up along each wall, thirty to a side. They were constructed entirely of steel. In place of a mattress was a piece of sheet-metal welded to the rectangular frame. No pillows were provided. The men all used their tarps, carefully folded into squares; not only did this provide a degree of comfort, but it prevented them from being stolen during the night. John had been told that each man would be issued a blanket when winter approached, but he wasn't going to hold his breath. He walked to his cot, identified by his number in yellow paint. He placed the precious cloth at its head, as did all the others. Leaving them there while the men reported to the mess hall constituted something of an act of faith; there were those whose tarps were nearly worn out, with months to go before they would be issued another. These men were truly desperate, and might well risk execution at the hands of their fellow prisoners in an effort to acquire another one.

There was just a tinge of light remaining in the western sky as the men dragged themselves toward the mess-hall. It must be about nine o'clock, John thought. Nine o'clock. By the time they finished waiting in line, and then eating, it would be at least ten. They were awakened at four-thirty. They were expected to be in the quarry and working with the first ray of daylight. Their pain-racked bodies screamed out for rest, but there was precious little of that to be found in this place. Seven days a week they labored, three hundred sixty-five days a year. It was a schedule that was designed to kill.

John took a stainless-steel tray from the stack and a spoon from the bin. His stomach was growling, twisting itself into knots. His hands trembled, his mouth salivated as he thought of what was to come. The man in front of him was tall, and his tattered clothes hung on his shrunken frame as on a scarecrow. Every few seconds he would double over in pain, a racking cough causing his body to shudder. His lungs sounded as if they were full of fluid, John thought. The man straightened himself slowly, and handed his chit to the Russian behind the counter.

"Eight hundred calories, my wheezing friend!" he said. "You'll not go far on that!"

He looked at the Russian next to him and both men laughed. He took the man's tray and placed it on a scale. With a dipper, he began to dribble a watery soup into one of its compartments. The needle on the scale crept upward. Into another compartment he began to pour boiled lentils, carefully watching the scale as he did so. Then came a few ounces of pinto beans. The other Russian placed two slices of white bread atop the tray and handed it back to the trembling prisoner. The man looked at this pathetic meal and then up at the Russian. "Please....please, I beg you. Give me more. I'm dying."

"Well don't do it in here!" the burly Russian chortled, nudging his comrade in the side with his elbow. "We'll have to clean up after you when you shit your pants!" Both men broke into howls of laughter.

John took the only vacant place at the table. All around him men ate voraciously. They wolfed down their food, oblivious to everything around them. He looked at his tray. He, too, had received the watery soup, the lentils and the beans, but in larger quantities than the man before him. They had given him five slices of white bread, apparently to bring his caloric total up to two thousand. The bread contained little real nutrition; it was largely empty calories. He remembered reading once that laboratory rats actually starved to death when fed a diet of white bread. The Russians undoubtedly knew that as well.

He ate quickly so that he could return to the barracks and sleep. It must be at least ten o'clock. As he left the mess-hall, he thought once again about how this was all just a grisly charade: even if a man did break his quota, and even if he did receive two thousand calories a day, that was not enough to sustain an adult human engaged in heavy labor. They were all starving to death, but most of them didn't know it.

This was not a labor camp. It was a death camp. He had been told that on the other side of the mountain there was a similar place for women. They too had daily quotas. He wondered how on earth they met them. The word was that the only concession to their sex was that their sledge hammers weighed eight pounds instead of twelve. He had heard that the death rate there was staggering. This is the end for all of us, he thought.

John lay on the unyielding sheet-metal and looked up at the ceiling. Around him men tossed and turned, trying to find comfortable positions. A few snored loudly. John envied those. As exhausted as he was, he found himself unable to let his mind relax and find the brief oblivion of sleep. A deep depression had settled upon him, so powerful it was almost tangible. It seemed to consume him. Nine years, eleven months and one week. He would never make it. There was absolutely no way. He had been sent here to die, and that was exactly what was going to happen to him. And it would be a slow, tortuous death; he would wither away, each day a little weaker, each day falling further and further behind his quota. Finally, he would resemble the old man at the scales, or the sick man in the mess-hall. He couldn't see the point of it.

Quietly, he swung his legs off the cot and got to his feet. As he walked the length of the building, he felt as if he were floating. Nothing seemed real. Could this actually be happening? To him? Surely not to him! He stood on the chair and placed the noose around his neck, pulling it snug with both hands. For a moment he stood there, looking out over the rows of cots with their sleeping-dead men. One of them had sat up and was looking at John quietly. The man knew what was about to happen, but he said nothing. He just watched. John's eyes met his in the dim light. The man shuddered. In John's eyes he saw death itself.

John placed his right foot against the edge of the chair's seat, hopped a few inches into the air, and simultaneously kicked the chair away. He had placed the knot correctly, because his neck snapped with a crack, and the world disappeared. The occupant of the cot in front of his twisting corpse was roused from his slumber by the sound. He swore under his breath, broke wind, and went back to sleep.

CHAPTER TWENTY-NINE

Bossier City, Louisiana.

Eugene Beasley watched the television station sign off for the evening. He normally didn't stay up this late, but night after night he had forced himself to witness again and again the same hideous spectacle. Every station in the country had been commanded to replay it when signing on in the morning and when signing off at night. The Statue of Liberty, in slow motion, collapsed into the Hudson River as an image of the burning of the Declaration of Independence was superimposed over it. In the background played the new anthem: the theme of the new Russian Empire: dark, ominous, forbidding.

Eugene sat in his armchair transfixed. He did not notice that his knuckles were white as they dug into the chair's fabric. He was a meek, peaceful man. He had never broken the law in his life. His job as an accountant had always provided him with a secure, if uneventful, life. And that was all he had ever wanted. Eugene had never given much thought to such abstract concepts as liberty; he had always taken his freedom for granted. Now that it was gone, he felt a tightness in his stomach, an anger welling up within him that was beyond his experience.

Finally, it was over. The television's screen turned to snow. Eugene reached for the remote control and turned the set off. He would set his alarm for five o'clock so that he could watch it all over again. He took off his steel-framed, bifocal spectacles and rubbed his eyes. He was tired. But he knew that his anger would deny him the sleep he needed. As he had frequently done in recent months, he would toss and turn, sometimes muttering under his breath. And if he did sleep, the dreams would come to him again, the horrible dreams: images of death, of people in chains, of whips splitting human flesh.

His hand passed across his bald scalp, fringed by a halo of pale, brown hair. Outside, only the sound of crickets broke the stillness of the Louisiana night. Replacing his glasses, he looked at the wall of his living room. There, in its center, was a rectangular area that was slightly lighter in color than the rest of the wall. In that place, for as long as he had owned the house, had hung a print of George Washington crossing the Delaware. His wife had always told him to get rid of it, to replace it with something more modern, more colorful. She said it made their house look like a museum.

Resisting his wife's wishes was totally out of character for Eugene, but here he had put his foot down, as gently as he could. He liked the print. There was something noble, something heroic about it. But now it was gone. All patriotic images had been outlawed, to be turned in to the Ministry of the Interior. Random checks by agents of the State were being made, and those who failed to obey faced time in a labor camp. And so he had complied, but it had made him feel ashamed and frustrated.

But there was one dictate with which he had refused to comply. He thought of that now and it made him smile. It was the first time in his life that he had defied authority. Because of it, he felt a combination of joy and anxiety. He had a gun. For months now he had struggled with himself, weighing his safety against his newfound need to rebel. He had never thought of himself as a brave man. But as the deadline for turning in firearms approached many weeks ago, and then passed, he had begun to realize that there was strength within him that he had never tapped. He had pushed the voice of caution out of his mind and replaced it with something new: a will to resist that he had never known he possessed.

The chances of being caught were minimal, he thought. After all, the shotgun was not registered in his name; he had bought it from his brother-in-law. There was nothing on any computer anywhere to associate it with him. There was no paper trail to follow. He was not sure why he wanted to keep it. It hadn't been fired since Will had taken him into the back lot and showed him how to use it. Eugene didn't consider himself to be a 'gun' person, and years had passed without him giving the weapon a thought. But now it was different; it symbolized something, something that Eugene suddenly felt was very important, something for which he was willing to risk his life.

A hundred times he had thought of throwing it into the river in the dead of night; several times he had even taken it out of the closet where he stored it and began to walk down the stairs toward his car. But always something had stopped him. Eugene found the whole affair unsettling. He didn't like this strange new nonconformity; it made him anxious.

Eugene rose from his chair and walked across the room to the stairway. Quietly, he began to ascend, to join his wife in their bed. She, too, was troubled, but at least it had not denied her the ability to sleep. Below him, he heard a clicking sound, claws on the wooden floor. He looked over the railing and saw his dog, Loki, looking up at him quizzically. He loved that dog.

Loki was just a mutt, and an over-the-hill mutt at that. But he was endlessly faithful and a pretty good watchdog.

"Lay down and go to sleep, boy," Eugene said quietly.

Normally, this was enough to cause the animal to settle down for the night. But Loki seemed reluctant, agitated. He stared at the front door, a low growl coming from his throat. Eugene should have reacted instantly, but instead he hesitated, confused by his dog's unusual behavior. The silence was shattered as the front door burst open, fragments of wood flying in all directions. In a fraction of a second the foyer was filled by four men dressed in the black and red uniforms of State Security. Each was armed with a short, wicked-looking sub-machine gun.

Eugene was frozen in his tracks. The men scanned the premises and saw him standing near the top of the stairs. Weapons swung in his direction. Safeties clicked off. Just then Loki leaped through the air, catching the lead agent by his left forearm. The man screamed as the animal's powerful jaws bit to the bone, shaking viciously from side to side, tearing cloth and flesh. The other agents struggled to train their weapons on the snarling animal, but the quarters were close, and man and dog thrashed about wildly.

Something snapped in Eugene's brain. He knew what he must do. And he must do it now, right now. Loki was buying him the time he needed. He dashed down the hall to the closet where he kept the shotgun. Throwing open the door, he grabbed the weapon and a handful of shells from the shelf. Frantically, he began to stuff the brass-based, red plastic cylinders into the gun's action, as Will had shown him. He racked the slide, feeding a round into the chamber. He turned back toward the stairway on a dead run. An ear-piercing staccato filled the house as a Russian machine gun opened fire. Eugene heard Loki whimper and knew that his companion was dead.

To his horror, his wife Lucille was standing at the top of the stairs. She had hurried out of their bedroom at the first sound of entry and now stood looking down at the Russians with her hand over her mouth. As he ran toward her, he screamed, "Lucille! Get away!", but it was too late.

Reality seemed to slow to a crawl as he covered the last few yards to where his wife was standing. Slowly she began a terrible, surreal dance, to move about as if she were a marionette on a string. She twitched and twisted, arms flailing at her sides and above her head. Eugene watched as tiny geysers of crimson erupted from the back of her nightgown. Diving through the air, he caught her by the waist and the two of them landed hard on the hallway floor.

Although he had hardly felt it, a round had passed through his left thigh, just below his buttock. For an instant he looked down into his wife's face as the two of them lay there. He was hoping to see her lips move, her eyes blink. But instead he saw only the vacant stare of death.

The Russians surged up the stairway, intent on completing their mission, outraged that they had met with resistance, even if only from a dog. Eugene pulled himself away from the corpse of his wife and, operating on pure adrenalin, swung the muzzle of the Ithaca Model 37 toward the top of the stairs. Just as the first Russian appeared, taking the steps two at a time, Eugene pulled his trigger, unleashing a load of twelve-gauge, double-ought buck that tore through the man's chest and blew his heart out of his back. Bits of spine and ribs struck his companions in the face, causing them to blink and turn away. The soldier fell backward, submachine gun clattering down the steps. His comrades found themselves impeded by his corpse, if only briefly.

The next man in line pushed it aside and stepped over its legs. Eugene got to his knees and shucked a fresh shell into the chamber. When the second man's head appeared, he fired. The blast caught the man full in the face and his head exploded into red mist. Eugene pumped the action again, but not quite quickly enough. The third Russian had reached the top of the stairs and had leveled his weapon. He pulled the trigger, sending a cascade of nine-millimeter slugs stitching across Eugene's body. The kinetic energy of the bullets entering his body threw him across the hall where he slammed into the opposite wall. The impact caused his finger to jerk one last time. The shotgun was pointed in the right direction.

Once again the big Ithaca spoke. The nine pellets of buckshot blew a three-inch hole in the Russian's abdomen churning his internal organs into blood soup. The impact hurled him backward through the air, past the fourth startled Russian.

Eugene sat on the floor, back against the wall, shotgun lying across his lap. He had not the strength to lift it. He knew what was going to happen now. But somehow it didn't matter. A smile crossed his blood-flecked lips. The Russian at the head of the stairs faded in and out of focus. Eugene's head was swimming. As his blood pressure dropped, he experienced something akin to euphoria. Three of those Russian bastards dead, he thought. Not bad for an out-of-shape accountant! The smile was still on his lips as the machine gun chattered away, sending Eugene Beasley into eternity.

CHAPTER THIRTY

Staff Sergeant Ben Briley had been in the Air Force for fourteen years. He had always enjoyed his work, and took a quiet pride in the knowledge that he was helping to defend his country. He had looked forward to retirement after putting in his twenty years. The idea of spending more time with his wife, Mary Ellen, and their two children, was very appealing. He had thought maybe they would travel around the country in their RV, seeing the sights, visiting relatives, just relaxing.

Now all of that was gone. The Conquest had changed everything. The Russians were putting their own people into more and more positions. The top brass all around the country had been replaced months ago. Now, practically the entire officer corps was Russian. He was perhaps the most senior American left on this base. And he knew that at any time now his job too would disappear. Of course, there would be a transition period; he would have to train his replacement in all the intricacies of monitoring the network of defense satellites that had been his responsibility for the past six years.

Ben willed his mind to stop wandering and focused his attention on the massive screen on the wall before him. On it was a representation of the earth's surface and a series of wavelike lines that represented the orbits of every U.S. military satellite in space. He knew that these were not the only satellites up there. The Chinese and the Indians had a few. In addition to these there were civilian communications satellites, and, of course, the Russians had some of their own in orbit. But the Russian devices were second-rate at best. These, the ones plotted on his screen, these U.S. military communications and reconnaissance satellites, were the most sophisticated that could be built. The Russians wanted access to them badly. They could be very useful to an occupying power: not only would they give the Russians state-of-the-art communications ability, but they could be used to monitor virtually every movement on the North American continent. Not a sparrow would fall without the Russians being aware of it. With these, the Russians could monitor every telephone call and radio signal in America.

In fact, for years, certain elements of his own government had been using them for just that: monitoring the movements and communications of U.S. citizens. That had always made him nervous and a bit chagrined. He had been told by his superiors that the various spook organizations like the National Security Agency were necessary, and did good and useful work. He had always been skeptical. It didn't fit his idea of what government was all about; it smacked too much of Big Brother to suit him. But now the spooks had been out-spooked. Some of them had no doubt turned, and were working for the Russians. He shuddered to think of what had happened to the rest of them.

Ben was amazed that he was still allowed to sit here, controlling the fate of these incredibly important machines. Apparently, it was inconceivable to the Russians that an enlisted man would be placed in a position where he could have such power at his fingertips. And, obviously, none of his American superiors had tipped them off. The Russians saw him as some sort of passive observer, a watchman, a living alarm system, nothing more. But he was much more than that. He had it within his power to deny his new masters access to one of his country's most critical national defense assets. He knew that, given the chance, they would turn these satellites against his own countrymen; they would use them to tighten their vice-like grip on his nation by watching everyone all the time.

Ben had heard about the resistance: just whispers among the men, perhaps more wishful-thinking than real. But the Russians were growing increasingly paranoid. Perhaps they had reason. Many men had, in fact, disappeared: deserted their posts and vanished into the night. He was not sure where they had gone, but he had heard rumors: camps being formed in the mountains, resistance cells in the cities. Here, on his own base, there had been isolated cases of what the Russians claimed was sabotage: vehicles mysteriously stopped running, electronic systems were damaged beyond repair.

Ben knew that his time was short. His replacement could arrive at any moment, and then his every move would be under close scrutiny. It would be too late. Still, he hesitated. He thought of all of the years of research, all of the money, that had gone into establishing this satellite network. He had spent years of his life lovingly caring for these devices, treating them as if they were his own. Then he thought of who their beneficiaries would be in the future, and his mind was made up.

This was his chance, perhaps his last. The Russian captain who was now his titular superior had been called away to deal with one of the many emergencies that seemed to be constantly occurring. He was alone. He began to manipulate the controls before him. He watched the board, and noticed that, one after another, the satellites were departing from their assigned paths. Just shutting them off would be insufficient. The Russians would be able to turn them on again. They had to be deflected into useless orbits, away from North America, orbits so acentric that they could never be put into service again.

It took him forty minutes, but at last he was satisfied. The satellites now passed across the poles, over northern Greenland, and over the jungles of Brazil. He was careful to see to it that they had used all of their fuel, so that they could not be repositioned. He spent the next ten minutes destroying the control panel with an axe that he had earlier placed in the closet. This, he knew, was not really necessary. The satellites were now useless. But Ben Briley was a thorough man. He did not want to leave at the Russians' disposal any trace of American technology, of American ingenuity. Once the panel had been reduced to an unrecognizable heap of wreckage, he knew that his job was done. He was satisfied.

Ben took one last look around the room. He felt a flutter in his stomach. One phase of his life was over, and another was beginning. He would take Mary Ellen and the children and drive into the mountains. He didn't know who or what he would find. But perhaps, once again, he could be of service to his country.

CHAPTER THIRTY-ONE

Trace Forester sat in the one luxury he permitted himself in his office: a heavily-padded leather executive swivel chair. Before him, on his desk, was a mixture of blueprints, payroll documents, shipping orders, and all of the other paper paraphernalia that comes with owning a medium-sized factory. Trace was very much a hands-on man: others in his place might have delegated this grunt-work to subordinates. But it was his factory. He had founded it, and he had run it for the past twelve years. Before the Conquest, it had ticked along like a Swiss watch under his guidance. Now things were falling apart. But Trace was determined to make it work for as long as was humanly possible.

Other than the leather chair, the office was Spartan. But its few accouterments suited Trace. The wall to his left held his framed engineering degree. On the wall behind him hung another frame containing the double silver bars of a Marine Corps captain, a Silver Star medal, a Purple Heart medal, and a small, deformed bit of bronze-sheathed lead. It was a bullet that had been removed from his hip by the military surgeons. They had told him he would walk with a limp for the rest of his life, if he walked at all. But as others had done throughout his life, they had underestimated Trace Forester. After undergoing months of excruciating therapy, he had not only walked, but had eventually begun running three miles a day. It had become a habit. Like clockwork, he rose before dawn and put in his three miles. Three times a week he worked out in the room at home which he had converted into a gym. As a result, Trace was lean and moderately well muscled. He was not a fanatic about it. His goal had never been to become Mister America, but he believed that a man should stay in shape. His close call with a crippling infirmity was his constant motivation.

Next to the frame containing the bullet was a wooden plaque on which was mounted a small, single-shot percussion boot-pistol, the kind that was carried so often in the mid-nineteenth century by those who could not afford the new Colt's revolvers. Aesthetically, it was singularly unimpressive: its wooden grips had long ago rotted away, and it was pitted from rust. But it was a piece of American history, and Trace loved it. It had been found under a rock in 1950 by a fisherman looking for bait in the South Fork of the American River, a quarter of a mile upstream from Sutter's Mill. Although no one could prove it, it had almost certainly been dropped by a forty-niner during the early days of the Gold Rush. Sometimes Trace would swivel around and just look at it for a few moments, feeling the decades roll backwards to those lusty years when the Republic was young.

On his desk was a paperweight. But it was not just any paperweight. It was a four-inch section of ore-car rail from one of the old silver mines beneath Tombstone, Arizona. Every time Trace picked it up, he was transported to the year 1881, the OK Corral, Wyatt Earp, Doc Holliday, the Birdcage Theater. It always brought a smile to his lips. He could almost smell the gun smoke in the air; hear the tinkling of a slightly out-of-tune saloon piano. Trace even wore history. His belt-buckle was crudely cast of bronze, and had been found with a metal-detector in Spain. The experts told him it was Roman, two thousand years old. Every time he touched it, he was awed.

On another wall hung a framed print. It was by Norman Rockwell, and it showed a young soldier returning home after World War II. Jubilant parents welcomed him, his dog ran to greet him, and a potential sweetheart peered coyly from the corner of the building. Trace loved Rockwell's work. His home was filled with it. On occasion, while hosting a dinner or cocktail party, he had overheard snide comments by his more effete guests regarding his naive taste in art. To hell with them, he had thought. Let them pay kings' ransoms for their indecipherable impressionist rubbish, their irrational abstract junk, their postmodernist trash! I'll take Rockwell any day!

With the exception of one chair on the opposite side of Trace's desk, a small bookcase completed the office's furnishings. In the bookcase were works of philosophy, history, and political theory. Many might consider these out of place in the office of a manufacturer of industrial transmissions. But in recent years, Trace had become deeply immersed in these subjects. He had spent countless hours studying the Founding Era, the works of Aristotle, Sidney, Locke, of Jefferson and Madison, of Ayn Rand, and others. He felt the need to know what they knew, to climb inside their minds. Over the years, as he felt his country slipping away, he knew something horribly wrong was taking place. But until he understood the works of these people, he couldn't put his finger on it; he couldn't know exactly why it was wrong. Now he knew. The bookcase held one other thing: on its top was a trophy awarded to his son in the state Little League Championship six years earlier.

Trace picked up a sheaf of papers and reached for a paper clip. He pursed his lips in disgust. It was one of the flimsy little ones, an inch long, the ones he'd always hated. He liked the big ones: stronger, more durable, more reliable. Under the circumstances, I guess I'm lucky to have any paper clips at all, he thought. A knock at the door caused Trace to look up. Through the glass, he saw Skip Neely, his plant superintendent. Trace waved him in.

"Hi, Trace," said Neely as he slowly walked into the office, bent slightly at the waist, his face as white as chalk.

"You look like hell, Skip! What's wrong with you?"

"I've been sick as a dog all day. It must have been the jalapenos I had for breakfast. They were a little past their prime. As my old foreman would say, 'I've got fucked-up guts.' I've passed enough gas today to inflate the Hindenburg! Oh, hell, there I go again. Sorry."

In spite of the man's suffering, Trace couldn't help but laugh. "What are you doing eating rotten jalapeno peppers for breakfast?"

Neely collapsed into the chair opposite Trace. "Ah, I was tryin' to finish them off before they went completely to hell. I may never see one again. I guess I pushed my luck a little too far."

"Where'd you get 'em, anyway? I haven't seen a jalapeno pepper in six months!"

"My brother-in-law knows a trucker who smuggled 'em up from Laredo last month."

"Can you finish out the day, or do you want to go home?"

"I can't go home, Trace. If the Russians catch me, they'll arrest me as a 'slacker.'"

The two men reflected on this unfortunate truth. Finally, Trace said, "How's that Bridgeport mill doing? It didn't sound too healthy this morning."

"It's down. I think it's a bearing."

"Terrific! Now I can fill out six different requisition forms–in triplicate–and submit them to the Ministry of Production. If we're lucky, we might get a replacement in three months!"

"There's Kolhaus Bearing over in Michigan City. Last I heard they were still in business. We've got some cold-rolled steel flat-stock we won't be needing for a while. I'm sure they could use it. I could load some onto the truck, drive over there and swap it for some bearings."

"Forget it! If the Russians caught you pulling an under-the-table black market deal like that, you'd end up in a labor camp!"

"What the hell are we going to do, Trace? Half the machinery in this plant needs replacement parts! I thought Drugonov said they wouldn't interfere with production! They've created a bureaucracy with so many twists and turns in it that nobody can do business anymore! We can't get spare parts, the electricity goes on and off, even the phones don't work most of the time!"

"Drugonov's changed his tune. Remember the speech he gave when he burned the Declaration and the Constitution? Apparently he's finally come to the realization that his brand of totalitarianism and productivity don't mix. And he's chosen totalitarianism over productivity. He told us he was going to squeeze us dry, and that's just what he's doing. For this plant to run properly, we need a free market. But Drugonov can't permit that. He can't control a free market. And that man is all about control."

Trace saw the dejected expression on his friend's face. "Look, Skip, I don't want you to get worked up about all this. This is my company, and these problems belong on my shoulders, not on yours."

"I've been with you almost since the beginning, Trace. You sweated blood to build this place! Now these bastards are..."

"Skip, you've been a good friend, and you're the best damned plant superintendent in the country! If there's any way to keep this factory running, you and I will figure it out."

Trace changed the subject, hoping to take his friend's mind off their troubles.

"How's your family doing, Skip? Are Maureen and the kids getting enough to eat? I hope they're not living on rotten jalapeno peppers too!"

Neely chuckled.

"No. Maureen's folks still live on the farm. Even though the Russians are confiscating most of what they produce, we're still able to get an occasional chicken or some vegetables. But you wouldn't believe what we have to go through to get it! You'd think we were smuggling guns or something!

"Two weeks ago, we went down there and they gave us a chicken. Maureen wanted it alive, so it wouldn't spoil on the trip home. I put it in the trunk and covered it with some rags. I had to tie its wings closed and put a rubber band around its beak to keep the thing from making any noise when we came to the checkpoints! A couple of nights ago we finished off the last of the chicken soup–just broth, really–that we made from cracking open the bones."

Trace nodded and gave Neely a forced smile. He twirled a pencil in his fingers. It had become a nervous habit. He stopped as soon as he saw Neely studying his hand. He didn't want him, or any of his employees, to get any sense of the anger and frustration he felt. He wanted to convey a sense of confidence to his people. But that was becoming more and more difficult as his situation deteriorated.

"Trace, you're as wound up as a two-dollar pocket watch, and don't try to hide it! I know you too well! You're taking on the problems of everybody in this plant! How long can you do that without cracking up? And I've seen you slipping silver coins to our people!

"Christ! If the Russians find out about that, they'll put you in front of a firing squad!"

Trace nodded slowly. Neely was right.

"Listen, Trace, why don't we cash it in, just disappear. People all over the country are doing it! Why work for these bastards? Why put yourself through all this so that some Russian seven thousand miles away can eat caviar?"

Trace looked his friend in the eyes. "I'm almost at that point, Skip. It'll just take a little more to put me over the edge."

The two men were silent for a moment.

"What's this, Trace?" Neely asked, picking up a volume from Trace's desk..

"It's a book by John Locke."

"What's it about?"

"It's about what kind of government people should have if they're going to be free."

"It sounds like something we all should've read a long time ago. Is this a recent interest of yours?"

"No. I've been reading this sort of thing for quite some time. I wish I'd taken some courses on it in college."

"Hell, Trace, you probably would've just gotten a bunch of statist claptrap from what passes for professors these days. You're better off studying it on your own."

"Yeah, I guess you're right. That's a shame though." He pushed himself away from the desk. "I need to stretch my legs. I think I'll take a walk onto the floor and see how things are going."

Trace walked slowly from machine to machine, the ones that still had operators that is. When the Russian fiat currency had been introduced, inflation soon reached a point where a man's weekly wages wouldn't even buy groceries. Many left. Trace could do nothing but watch them drift away. As Neely had said, Trace had given his people silver coin from time to time, not only to help them out, but also to keep them from leaving. But he couldn't do it for everyone. Only small businesses could get away with that. And so his work force grew smaller and smaller. Of course, there were laws against quitting one's job. But when a man or woman had a family to feed, even Drugonov's dictates took second place. There were jobs to be had, under the table, at two, even three dollars a day in silver. That kind of money would buy more food that a bushel basket of that Russian garbage. And if official paperwork were required, that too could be arranged–for a price.

Trace turned a corner into the north wing of his plant. There he saw the man he despised most in the world, next to Drugonov himself. Captain Gevork Alikhanov was his "Commissar of Production," assigned to him four months earlier. The man knew nothing about the machine-tool industry, and most of what he said made no sense. But he had made it clear that his orders were final. He spent most of his time goading the machinists to work faster, to increase production. He presented Trace with ridiculous quotas which could not be met under the best of circumstances. Trace had heard his men grumbling, had heard several of them say how much they'd like to punch Alikhanov's lights out. Trace thought that if they'd been single, they probably would have. But they had families to consider. He had often told Neely that he too would love to have ten minutes in a room alone with the man.

With Alikhanov was a group of about fifty Americans. Trace had never seen any of them before. They were ragged, and seemed weary. Some were in their prime, but others were old and appeared ill. One elderly man was wearing nothing but his underpants. An overweight, middle-aged woman wore a flower-print house dress and fuzzy pink slippers. Two Russian soldiers were chaining them with leg irons to the lathes and mills, one person to a machine. Trace felt his blood boil. This couldn't be happening! he thought. Even these sons-of-bitches wouldn't go this far!

"Alikhanov! What the hell is going on here? Who are these people?"

"Forester, this is your new work force. Production has dropped to unacceptable levels. I have been authorized to use conscript labor. These workers will remain chained to their machines at all times. They will sleep on the shop floor. If you choose to give them blankets, you are free to do so at your own expense. They will be fed by the State once a day. We will keep close track of their production, and if they do not meet the State's expectations, they will be liquidated and replaced by others."

Trace's hands balled into fists. It took every ounce of his willpower to stop himself from snapping the man's neck.

"You will not chain people to machines in my factory! I will not permit it!"

Alikhanov's reptilian face broadened slightly, the corners of his thin lips, like earthworms, curling upward.

"Let's not have another debate about who is in charge here, Forester. You will simply lose, as you always do. I have the entire coercive force of the State at my disposal, and you have...what? What is that colorful expression you Americans use? 'Jack-shit.'

"You will get used to it Forester. In time, these people will become like furniture, like the lamp fixtures hanging from the ceiling. Besides, being assigned to conscript labor is mild treatment! You should pay a visit to one of our labor camps if you want to see how difficult life can be!"

"What did these people do to deserve this?" Trace demanded, voice trembling.

"What did they do? Why, nothing. They were just...at hand."

"Have any of them had any training as machinists?"

"How should I know, Forester? I am a Russian army officer, not a biographer."

"How the hell do you expect them to run this machinery?"

"That is your problem, if you value their lives, that is." The ignorant martinet tucked his clipboard under his arm, turned on his heel, and walked away.

It was almost eleven at night. Only the security lights prevented total darkness, casting an eerie glow over the strangely-still steel giants of the factory. The occasional rattle of chains broke the silence, echoing from wall to wall. Trace walked down the aisle between the machines he loved so well. He was carrying a three-foot-long set of bolt cutters. He turned into the north wing, and could now hear low moaning all around him. In less than one day, the leg irons had cut into the flesh of these peoples' ankles, leaving them torn and bleeding. Trace could not imagine how they could manage a month, or six. He came to a woman lying on her side, shivering.

"Help me," he said. "I'm here to set you free. Turn your foot upward. That's right."

He placed the powerful jaws of the cutters over the rivet holding the leg irons together. One squeeze cut through the quarter-inch steel like butter.

"Here, take this."

He handed her a piece of cloth tied at the top into a bag. It contained five dollars in silver.

"God bless you," she said.

Trace patted her on the shoulder and pointed toward the exit.

"You have eight hours to get away from here. Don't go back home. That's the first place they'll look. I recommend going down into the Appalachians. Hide in the forest. It'll be tough, but it's your only chance."

She nodded, rose, and moved away quickly. This scene was repeated forty-nine times in the next two hours. Trace tried to give each person a few words of encouragement, and then the money. He had brought a pair of his own trousers, a shirt, a pair of work shoes, and a warm, heavy coat for the nearly-naked old man. The old fellow took his hand and kissed it.

It was done. They were all gone. Now the real work would begin. Trace went to the welding department and rolled out an oxyacetylene cutting-torch. He went from machine to machine, cutting off spindles, turrets, drive shafts, wrecking gears, motors, bed-ways. Trace knew exactly what to do to permanently disable each machine in the factory. It felt strange to be using his expertise for destruction instead of production. But chaining people to his machines had been the last straw, the act that had pushed him over the edge, as he and Neely had discussed earlier.

He had gone to Neely's office and left him a brief note explaining what had happened, and recommending that he, too, leave as soon as possible, preferably that very morning. Skip always arrived an hour or so before Alikhanov, so he would have a chance to make his getaway. The shit was going to hit the fan, and Trace didn't want his longtime friend to be standing in front of it. Alikhanov would be left holding the bag, with no one to blame, no one to punish. When the word reached his superiors, Alikhanov might find himself in a labor camp. Trace smiled at the thought. By five-thirty he was finished. He slung his pack over his shoulder, took one last look at the place he had built, and sneaked out like a thief in the night.

CHAPTER THIRTY-TWO

You could almost hear the August sun sizzling in the noon sky. Trace Forester smelled the hot, baked dust in this western Kansas town. The heat rose in shimmers from the cracked pavement in the distance as he walked down the nearly deserted street. Tired buildings reached up out of the dirt like the bones of a sun-bleached skeleton. Shop windows dark, empty, dead. To his left, an old man sat in a rusted sheet metal chair on the wooden boardwalk. His eyes followed Trace as he approached.

The old man wore a faded blue cotton shirt with one cuff missing, and a pair of overalls that had been patched so many times they looked like a crazy-quilt. He wore a straw hat, dilapidated almost to the point of nonexistence. He was barefoot. His face was age itself: rock weathered by eons, hard, craggy, crisscrossed with crevices like canyons. But he was clean-shaven, a rarity these days. Most men had taken to growing beards since the razor blades had run out. It had been over a year since the Conquest, and it showed.

As Trace came near, his ancient face broke into a broad smile, canyons changing course, his three remaining teeth, worn and yellowed, like fence posts in a cavern. His old hands grasped the chair's armrests, gnarled and leathery, arthritic knuckles all in rows. Trace supposed that this old farmer had moved mountains with those hands in his long life, performed unimaginable tasks, endless labors, in the scorching heat and the numbing cold, year after year, decade after decade. But now those Sisyphean labors were done. No one knew. No one remembered. No one cared. But it seemed the old man did. Trace could see the pride in his face.

He couldn't help but return the old man's smile.

"Hello, old timer."

"Hello yerself, young man. I don't reckon I seen you hereabouts before. What brings you to town?"

"Just passing through. What's the name of this place?"

"'You don't even know where ya' are? Ya' look a heap smarter than that to me, mister! We call it Juniper Creek. Where ya' from?"

"East of here. Indiana."

"Did your vehicle break down?"

"No, I walked."

"Walked! From Indiana to Juniper Creek? Damn! Times is sure tough, ain't they?"

"They sure are. Do you see many Russians around here?"

"Nah. We might see two or three trucks a month. The only time they really come around in force is at harvest time. They take our crops, make a little speech about what good workers we are, tell us how they'll kill us if we hold anything back. 'Sabotage' they call it. They killed ol' Cooter Huggins a few months back. Shot him dead right here in the street! Said he held back a calf. Which he did, 'a course. Dug a pit in his barn, put the calf in it, and covered it over with plywood and straw. Would 'a got away with it too, 'cept the damned thing started callin' for its mother just as the last Russki inspector was walkin' out the barn door!

"Poor Cooter. Knew him since he was a pup. His daddy too. Used to drink white lightnin' with his grand daddy. Those were the days, boy! By the way, you got anything to drink mister? You know, a sip a' something other than that damned Russki vodka? I'm dryer n' a popcorn fart!"

Trace laughed. "Sorry, but I don't."

Trace couldn't help but notice the old man's belt. Seven or eight notches protruded from the buckle.

"You folks haven't had much to eat lately, have you?"

"It's been slim pickins, I'll say that! Until these damned Russkies come, we had more food than we knew what to do with! This was the breadbasket of America, mister! Beef, pork, chicken, vegetables, fruit, whatever we wanted and all we wanted. Now, once a month the Russkies bring us a truckload 'a frozen soy burgers. Soy! We used to use that for cattle feed! And they don't even give us enough of that! We run out after three weeks, and spend the last week hungry."

"You don't look like you're getting your share, old timer. You're as thin as a reed."

"Oh, hell, it don't make no difference 'bout me. Let the young 'uns have my share. Even if I had enough to eat, I wouldn't be around much longer anyhow. I'm ninety-seven years old, mister! The way I abused this ol' body of mine in my youth, drinkin', smokin', carousin', I figure I been on borrowed time for the last twenty-five years!"

He let out a cackle and rocked back and forth in the chair. Then he became somber.

"Besides, I had enough. I'm ready to go, with the country in the state it's in. I don't want to see no more. Not another day. The Lord 'd be doin' me a favor if he took me right here and now."

"I'm not exactly a kid myself," Trace said. "And I've seen a lot of changes in my time. But what about you? What have you seen?"

The old man leaned back and stared past Trace, into the distance, as if time were rolling backward in his mind. Then he looked Trace square in the eyes.

"Look at me closely, mister, 'cause you're lookin' at livin' history. I met and spoke to Civil War veterans, lawmen, outlaws, cowboys. Through me, you're lookin' back a hundred and fifty years: before the income tax, before the goddamned Federal Reserve, before FDR ruined the country with his New Deal. You may not believe this, but when I was a little boy, I recollect my pa introducin' me to an ol' man–he was over a hundred–who actually met Thomas Jefferson!

"The men in my family always married late. I wasn't born until my pa was sixty-four. He fought under Nathan Bedford Forrest at Shiloh, Murfreesboro and Chickamauga. My pa wasn't born until his pa was fifty-seven. My grandpa fought with Andy Jackson in the War of 1812!

"When I was a boy, the Old West was still a livin' memory. I can remember well an ol' gentleman, his name was John Tillotson, who was a Deputy U.S. Marshal back in the 1870's and '80s. He saw it all, boy! Dodge City and Abilene back in the days of the big cattle drives! He knew Bill Hickok, Wyatt Earp, Bat Masterson! Even met John Wesley Hardin once! He lived a few miles from me in those days. I'm goin' way back to the early twenties now. I used to run errands for him: pick up his groceries, take packages to the post office, stuff like that. Ever' time he asked me into his house, I'd head for the same spot. Over his mantle piece he had hangin' a Winchester rifle, model of 1873 in 44-40 caliber. And not a regular one neither! The deluxe model, with the fancy wood 'n engravin'! Below that was the gun belt he wore durin' his lawman days. It held a Colt's revolver, model of 1873, also in 44-40, nickel plated, engraved, with fancy ivory grips with big American eagles carved in 'em! Man, I loved those guns! He used to let me handle 'em! Even took me out back a few times to give me shootin' lessons!"

The old man looked around, leaned forward and said in a conspiratorial whisper,

"I'll tell ya' a secret. I shouldn't, but I will. When ol' Mr. Tillotson passed on, I think it was in '26, he left me those guns! Put 'em right in his will! They hung over my fireplace for many years. Then the Russkies come. They wanted everybody to turn in their guns, but I fooled 'em!" Another cackle, more rocking. "I greased 'em up good, put 'em in a big piece 'a PVC pipe, glued caps on each end, and buried 'em where the damned Russkies'll never find 'em! I put in a piece 'a paper too, tellin' 'bout their history. Maybe a hundred years from now, or five hundred, this country'll be free again, and some free American'll stumble across 'em. He'll have himself a real treasure!"

He paused, and looked Trace in the eyes.

"I don't know why I told you that, mister. There ain't another livin' soul who knows it. But you got an honest face. You look like a man who can be trusted."

Trace smiled at the old man.

"Thanks. Don't worry. I'll take your secret with me to my grave. And I'm sure that's exactly what a man like John Tillotson would've wanted you to do. It'd be sacrilege to turn his guns over to the Russians."

"You can say that again! If Mr. Tillotson had been alive and the Russkies knocked on his door to take his guns, he would 'a sent a passel of 'em to hell, I can guarantee you that! And the only way they would 'a got 'em would 'a been to climb over a pile of Russki corpses and pry 'em from his dead fingers! That's the problem with this country! We ain't got no more John Tillotson!"

Trace sat on the edge of the boardwalk as a student would before the master.

"Tell me something, old timer. What was it like to live in this country when you were young?"

The old man hesitated for a moment. Then, "Well sir, the grass and the trees seemed greener. The sun seemed brighter. There was a lightness in the air. A lot more people walked with a spring in their step. I don't recall people worryin' 'bout much neither, at least before the Depression. And people were sure of their selves: they knew right from wrong. Not like today!

"People today ain't even sure they got a right to defend their selves! When I was young, anyone who doubted that would 'a been locked up in a lunatic asylum! A man lived his life, and the harder he worked, the better he lived. And he could be sure of the money once he earned it! It was as good as gold, mister! You could take a twenty-dollar bill to the bank, and they'd give you a bright, shiny gold double eagle! If you had a few 'a those in your pocket, you felt as rich as Croesus!

"The big difference between then and now is the government, and not just since the Russkies come. Way before that. When I was young, you'd hardly even know there was a national government, 'cept for the post office. Then government started to grow. The air got heavier.

"When I was a baby, there was Teddy Roosevelt's Square Deal, then Franklin Roosevelt's New Deal. I remember that only too well, that miserable son-of-a bitch! Then Harry Truman's Fair Deal. Damn, mister! Them men was all dealin' from the bottom of the deck! And they dealt us a lousy hand! Then that rascal from Texas gave us his Great Society, which was nothin' more than the New Deal warmed over!

"All durin' these years, it was like people was carryin' a heavier and heavier weight on their shoulders. Taxes went through the roof. It seemed like all the money in the world couldn't satisfy those bastards in Washington! And the money they gave us wasn't worth the paper it was printed on. About right to use in the outhouse, that's all. People started worryin' 'bout all sorts of things. And the government started regulatin' everything in sight! Ya' couldn't take a dump without gettin' a permit from somebody! I'll give ya' an example.

"When FDR was President, I was runnin' the old family farm about ten miles outside of town. My wife 'n I used to grow a little patch of wheat for our own use, not to sell. My wife would grind it into flour and make bread and biscuits and such. Then one of Roosevelt's goons come around and told us we couldn't do it no more. Told me that growin' my own wheat for my own use affected interstate commerce! He said the Supreme Court just handed down a decision that said as much, called 'Wickard versus Filburn'. I'll never forget that name. I recall scratchin' my head and askin' this man how growin' a patch of wheat for my own use had anything to do with interstate commerce. I told this flunky that none of my wheat crossed state lines. This government stooge said that if I didn't grow my own wheat, I'd have to buy it on the open market, and that increased demand would raise the price 'a wheat in this country, which was what Roosevelt wanted! So the fact that I was growin' my own wheat, and not buyin' it from out 'a state, decreased demand and lowered the price 'a wheat in interstate commerce. Therefore, the Court said that my one-acre patch 'a wheat could be regulated by the national government, and so this lackey was orderin' me not to grow it no more! My jaw dropped! It was the craziest thing I'd ever heard! But that's what things had come to.

"That's the kind of thing that put weight on people's shoulders, made 'em feel pressed down. When a man can't grow his own wheat to make his own bread, he don't feel free no more. He feels like he's under somebody's thumb!

"And one more thing. In '34 they started to take our guns away from us. It always seemed to me that the only reason they passed that National Firearms Act was to give the federal agents somethin' to keep 'em busy after prohibition was repealed in '33. 'Course they could 'a just fired those agents and abolished their agency. But that's not what they done. Givin' jobs to some goon squad was more important to 'em than the Second Amendment! Bureau of Alcohol, Tobacco and Firearms my ass! They got no call to regulate any of those things! What the hell business is it 'a government if I want to make a jug 'a moonshine, or grow a patch 'a tobacco, or own a gun? Damn bureaucrats! The country come to be overrun with 'em! And bureaucracies never shrink, mister! Once they're created, they never go away! They just get bigger 'n bigger!

"I watched the federal government for over eighty years, and I can tell 'ya that that's one 'a the golden rules 'a politics! The sons-a-bitchin' bureaucrats breed like rats! Ya' asked me what it was like to live in this country when I was young! I reckon one 'a the biggest differences was that we wasn't overrun with rats!"

Trace liked this old coot; he liked his ginger, and the way he thought. But he knew the man would be dead very soon unless he got something to eat.

"Isn't there a black market here where you can buy some decent food? The word is they're all over the country."

"Yes, there is, if ya' got silver or gold. They won't take federal notes or that damned Russki scrip. And I don't blame 'em! Hah! It reminds me 'a my youth! I seen it come full circle! We're back on a gold standard! But I ain't seen so much as a silver dime in months."

Trace reached into his pocket and withdrew five silver dollars. Then he reached into his knapsack and took out a cloth bag with five more dollars in small silver. He placed the bag and the coins in the old man's skeletal hand.

"Damn! Five honest to God cartwheels! And from the heft of it, this bag feels like it's full 'a silver too!"

He looked up at Trace with concern in his eyes.

"This is a lot 'a money, mister. Are 'ya sure 'ya can spare it?"

"Don't worry, I can spare it. You just get some good meals under your belt." Trace grinned from ear to ear at the old man's excitement.

"I got no words to thank ya', mister. Damn! I'm gonna buy myself a genuine beefsteak! I been dreamin' 'bout eatin' a beefsteak almost ever' night! I ain't seen my choppers in four months, 'cause I ain't had no use for 'em. But I'll dig 'em up and have myself a feast!"

Trace got up, patted the old man on the shoulder, and turned to leave. After a few steps he stopped and turned again.

"One last thing. How do you stay clean-shaven? I haven't seen a razor blade in ten months."

The old man cackled again, rocking back and forth vigorously, as if enjoying his own personal joke.

"Lots 'a folks ask me that! I just wink at 'em. But I'll tell you. I use a straight razor, son! Been usin' one all my life! They never wear out!"

As Trace walked down the street, he saw the only other sign of life in town: a pickup truck parked in front of a café. The truck was at least twenty years old. It was rare to see one much newer on the road these days: the electronic systems in the newer ones made them impossible to repair once their original parts burned out. Only the old ones were simple enough to keep running. At least for them, parts were still available. The junk business was one of the few industries still flourishing in America.

For most people, whose personal transportation had failed them, time was running in reverse. Trace had often thought, as he walked a foot at a time across the vast expanse of America's mid-section, that he had been transported back into the eighteen-forties, when oxen pulled Conestoga wagons across this great land. His people had achieved mastery of distance: they had once crossed the continent almost effortlessly. Now traveling to the next county was a major undertaking.

Trace opened the door of the café and walked in. A small spring-loaded bell tinkled above his head. There were two others there: a woman behind the counter, and a customer. Both looked up. Trace sat down on a stool just as the woman finished pouring a dark liquid into the customer's cup.

"That's not real coffee, is it?" Trace asked, as much cheer in his voice as he could muster.

The middle-aged woman cackled,

"Hell no, mister! I ain't seen none of that in six months! This is somethin' we make up locally, out of burnt nut shells and tree bark. If ya' close your eyes and hold your nose, and drink it real hot, it tastes somethin' like real bad coffee, though."

She placed a cup on the counter and filled it. An acrid, scorched odor entered Trace's nostrils. It didn't bother him. He had gotten used to it as he had crossed the mid-West, passing through town after town, catching rides when he could, walking when the rides weren't there. And then there had been the Russian patrols. He had dodged plenty of them. But on the way, he had been in dozens of cafes like this one; had drunk gallons of local, ersatz coffee. He didn't even bother asking for cream and sugar. Such luxuries had disappeared long ago.

He glanced over at the man sitting two stools down. The man had apparently been staring at him, but when his eyes met Trace's, he looked down into his cup. Trace appraised him quickly, not wanting to stare, but at the same time feeling the need to evaluate this stranger. One got into that habit quickly when running from the Russians, or one did not survive long.

The man's hair was a bit shaggy and badly cut. That was not unusual: most people had given up the added expense of the barber's chair by now. His shirt was of a heavy denim, faded from washing, and torn in places, but carefully repaired by someone who knew what he or she was doing. Around his waist was a two-inch leather belt, again heavy and very durable. His trousers were of canvas, probably Carhart's, well used but in excellent repair. He wore leather, U.S. government-issue combat boots, not perfectly polished, but remarkably so. The man didn't look like a farmer or rancher. He wasn't military either, not exactly. Trace's interest was piqued. He glanced over again and noticed a bulge in the man's right front trouser pocket. It was almost square, but not quite. It didn't look like a wallet. What could it be?

The waitress returned with a plate and put it in front of the man. Trace recognized it instantly. Soy-burger. He had eaten scores of them himself in recent weeks. Actually, they were all right: there was nothing particularly objectionable about them. It just struck Trace as strange and sad that in his own country, one of the greatest beef-producing lands in the world, the inhabitants were reduced to eating make-believe meat. Oh, the feed lots and the ranchers were still producing lots of beef, but as fast as it was processed it was being shipped out of the country, back to "Mother Russia."

"How about it, stranger? Can I get you one of these beauties too?" she asked.

"Sure, why not?" he said.

She hustled off with considerable vigor, as if time still mattered. Trace watched her ample buttocks modulate toward the kitchen. He smiled. She was one of the good ones. She's no doubt been a hard worker all her life and she'll probably drop dead behind this counter, doing her job to the end.

Trace looked over at his companion. It was time to break the ice.

"My name's Trace. Trace Forester."

He extended his hand. After a second's hesitation, the other man reciprocated.

"Bob. Bob Davenport," he said.

"You from around here, Mr. Davenport?"

The man's eyes narrowed.

"Why are you interested in where I come from?"

"I'm not. Not particularly. Just making conversation."

"It's best not to make too much conversation these days. You never know who you're conversin' with."

Trace was sure now. It was a gun: a gun covered with a handkerchief to hide its outline. A medium-frame automatic, perhaps a Walther or a small Glock. If the man had been standing up, it would have been invisible in the trouser's spacious pockets. But sitting down, he could just make it out. He felt invigorated. Perhaps.....just perhaps.

Bob Davenport had finished his burger. Trace felt that time was of the essence. He had to take a chance on this man. He couldn't run much longer, not alone.

"Mr. Davenport, how do you feel about what's been going on in this country?" Trace asked.

Davenport interrupted wiping his mouth with a paper napkin and shot Trace a deadly glance.

"How the hell do you think I feel," he grumbled as he quickly got up to leave.

Trace extended his hand and took Davenport by the arm.

"Wait," he said, glancing toward the kitchen. "I've got to talk to you. I think maybe we can help each other."

Davenport tore his arm from Forester's grasp.

"Help each other how?" he snarled.

"Dammit, Davenport! I'm no Russian spy! I can see you've got a gun in your pocket. That's a death-penalty offense. A man who carries a gun these days can only be one of three things: crazy, a thief, or a freedom-fighter. I'm betting that you're the last. I want in."

Bob Davenport stared into Trace Forester's eyes for a full ten seconds before he said anything.

"Come on out to my truck," he said simply.

Trace stood just as the waitress came out of the kitchen with his soy-burger. He asked her to wrap it up to take out and gave her a silver quarter in payment. As the old man had said, paper money had become virtually worthless. The old U.S. dollar had been demonetized and largely removed from circulation. The Russians had issued their own colonial fiat currency. People used it when they had to: when the Russians were watching. But the economy really ran on pre-1965 silver coin, and an occasional gold piece for large purchases. He had even heard that people were using twenty-two caliber ammunition as money. It was a dangerous practice, but it didn't surprise him. Trace ate his soy-burger as Davenport started the truck.

"We'd better get out of here," Davenport said. "It wouldn't do to be seen sittin' here talkin'. Things have a way of gettin' reported."

He maneuvered the truck into the street and headed west, out of town. Five minutes later, he turned down a farm road and drove a while longer. He came to a stop. Looking around, he appeared to be satisfied. In this flat country, they could see everything for miles. They were truly alone. Davenport draped his arm over the steering wheel and turned toward Forester.

"I'm taking a big chance talking to you like this. I don't know you from Adam's house-cat."

"You don't have anything to fear from me, Davenport. The last thing I want is contact with the Russians. I've been running from them for a month."

"O.K. Let's have it. Tell me your story."

Forester told him the truth: about his factory, about Alkihanov, about the slave-labor. He told Davenport that all he had taken with him was a knapsack with a little food, some clothes and the contents of his home safe: twenty ounces in gold and one hundred fifty dollars face value in U.S. silver coin. He had begun to work his way west, hoping to join a militia group. These units existed all around the country, but he had heard that they were particularly active in the Rocky Mountain states, and that they were eagerly recruiting anyone willing to fight the Russians. He told Davenport about his military experience, and about how he hoped to put his skills to good use. He said he wanted Russian blood, that he could almost taste it.

Bob Davenport listened quietly as Trace told him these things. Then, he asked, "What about family? You got any?"

"Yes, I do. But since I'm wanted as a wrecker, I didn't want them with me; I don't want to expose them to this danger. I sent my wife, Molly and our son, David to our cabin in eastern Tennessee. It's in a very remote area. Their food supply should last about a year. They have a good water source, and weapons to defend themselves if it comes to that. I gave them plenty of gold and silver coin to buy more from the locals when their supplies do run out. I hope to be back with them by then."

For the first time, Davenport smiled: a barely-perceptible curling up of the corners of his mouth.

"All right," he said. "You're in."

The moon was full as the eight pickup trucks waited on the side of the road. Trace was in the third in line. His stomach was tying itself into knots as he thought about what they were going to do. He tried to calm himself, telling himself that his reaction was normal. After all, this was his first real action as a militiaman, his first head-to-head military confrontation with the Russians.

He watched intently the chain-link fence two hundred feet away. He could see men moving on the other side of it, shadows in the pale light. Suddenly, the piercing beam of a flashlight appeared. It flashed on and off three times. The drivers in all eight trucks started their engines and began to move across the crushed rock that formed the outer perimeter of the base.

As they approached, Trace could see that a large hole had been cut in the fence. The first truck in line backed up to that opening, driver and passenger both jumping out as soon as the truck stopped. He was only sixty feet from the fence now, and could see frenzied activity: men loading crates onto the bed of the pickup. When it could hold no more, the driver and passenger re-entered and the truck moved away, quietly but quickly. The next truck in line took its place, and the scene repeated itself.

In a few minutes it was Trace's turn. His truck backed up to the opening and stopped. He and the driver jumped out and ran toward the tailgate. The soldiers had already dropped it and were beginning to load the truck. Someone threw him a crate, and its weight nearly knocked him off his feet. He looked down at it. It was marked "Danger: High Explosives, C4."

Quickly, he turned to the man standing in the truck's bed and passed the box to him. Two men hustled in front of him with another, this one marked "Missiles, Surface to Air, Shoulder-fired". They grunted as they heaved the long box into the truck. Still another was marked, "Rifles, M16." More crates followed until the vehicle could hold no more.

Rick, the driver, hissed at him, "Let's get the hell out of here."

Both men jumped into the cab. Rick put the truck in gear and prepared to move out. Suddenly, Trace's door opened and a large, heavily-muscled man in camouflaged fatigues pushed his way in. Trace's shoulder hit Rick's as he moved to make room.

"Let's go," the man said.

The pickup began to move back toward the road. The three men said nothing as the truck drove along the street fronting the military base. Rick was tempted to drive with his lights off until they got past the base, but decided to turn them on, so as to appear to be just another vehicle. He was very careful not to exceed the speed limit, and to use his turn signals when he changed lanes. The soldier to Trace's right carried an M16 rifle with its butt down against the floorboards. Trace looked at him. He was grim and determined.

At last the fence ended. There was a gate, the western entrance to the base. In front of it was a lighted sign that read, "Welcome to Fort Carson." There was a guardhouse, and Trace knew that there would be someone in it. But the real danger was past: now they were just another pickup truck with some boxes in the back. It would be sheer chance if they were stopped by a Russian patrol. Trace could feel his muscles uncoil.

Fort Carson, Colorado was the home of the 3rd Brigade Headquarters, the 43rd Area Support Group, the 10th Special Forces Group and the 3rd Armored Cavalry Regiment. Eighteen months ago, it had housed more than fifteen thousand active duty personnel. Now that number was less than twelve hundred. Desertion accounted for the rest. Trace had heard that the same situation existed at every former U.S. military base in the country. The top-brass may be corrupt, but the rank-and-file were patriots to the man and to the woman. Those who had not yet left their bases to join the militia were simply biding their time, using their expertise to monkey-wrench everything the Russians might find useful.

Actually, the ones who had not yet deserted were the real heros. As the number of personnel dwindled, the actions of those who remained became more conspicuous. Every day they risked their lives to further impede the occupying power. Tonight was a good example: a dozen soldiers had looted the arsenal right under the noses of the Russians, who had become suspicious and watchful. But they didn't have the people to monitor every inch of a base as large as this one. Those twelve were now with Trace's group, and they would continue their resistance from the vastness of the mountain wilderness.

The eight trucks had split up and were taking different routes out of the area. Trace's was heading west. Eventually, they would begin to work their way north to Wyoming and then to their final goal: their camp in western Idaho. The hole in the fence would not be reported to the Russians until their own people finally discovered it at 3:51 that afternoon. The men had thirteen hours to put distance between themselves and the fort. Ordinarily, they might worry about being picked up by satellite reconnaissance, but it was common knowledge among all militia groups in the country that some unknown hero had risked his life to disable the entire satellite network. No one knew who had done it, but they knew that the Russians were blind. If they could avoid random Russian roadblocks, they would be home-free. If they did encounter one, they would do their best to shoot their way through. Trace was glad that the soldier had joined them.

As they put more and more distance between themselves and the base, the three men began to relax. Trace could see the set on the soldier's jaw begin to soften, and his posture lost its expectant erectness. Rick gripped the wheel more gently, and the color returned to his formerly white knuckles. The soldier turned to Trace and extended his hand.

"Kevin Ceely," he said simply with a smile.

Trace and Rick introduced themselves and shook hands. As they drove, Rick, Kevin and Trace exchanged basic information about themselves. Rick Miller was from back east: from Macedon, New York, a small town near Rochester. He told his two companions about the apples and the grapes and the Finger Lakes in the fall.

Kevin was from Boston. He had been in the Army for three years and had planned to go to college when his current hitch was up. Of course, all of that was history now.

Trace told them about his own military service, his family, his factory, and his long trek across the Midwest.

As dawn approached in the eastern sky, it covered the mountains with a soft blanket of light. Soon they crossed into Wyoming. The hours passed. Near Lander, in Fremont County, they stopped to fill the fuel tank. Trace and Kevin stretched to get the blood circulating again. Then they helped Rick with the four five-gallon jerry-cans of gasoline. As the three men worked, they could not know what events were unfolding twenty miles to their southeast.

CHAPTER THIRTY-THREE

The lone rider tethered his horse to a scrub bush and untied the leather thong that held the gun-case to the back of the saddle. He climbed the rest of the way up the gently-sloping hill until he reached its crest, crawling the last few yards so as not to present a silhouette in the bright morning light. Taking off his ten-X Stetson and placing it carefully beside him, he extracted a pair of compact binoculars from the pocket of his denim jacket and scanned the valley below. Soon he saw it, several miles to the east: a vehicle coming in his direction, kicking up a rooster-tail of dust as it went. He smiled.

General Bukovski sat next to the sergeant as they bumped and lurched down the primitive road.

"Well, Sergeant, how do you like this country? Not exactly the Volga basin, is it?"

"No, General, it is not. It is amazing that anything or anyone can live here," the sergeant answered.

He spoke with a heavy accent, and would have preferred to use Russian. But General Bukovski had forbidden it. All his personnel were to speak English in the general's presence. He wanted them to practice, the better to deal with their new subjects.

"Oh I don't know, Sergeant. It has a sort of majesty about it. In time, I think that I could come to like it. The Americans certainly do. Do you know, Sergeant, that we've lost fifty-eight people in this sector to guerrilla activity in the last month alone? Wresting this land from the Americans is like taking a salmon from a hungry bear!"

The sergeant said nothing. To disagree was unthinkable; to agree might identify him as pessimistic, something the Russian command was trying desperately to deal with: morale in the Russian forces was low, and dropping lower all the time. It had reached the point where not even the local women forced into the camps in the evenings could cheer up the men.

"Slave-whores" they were called, and the soldiers had once taken them eagerly, especially the teenagers. Now they simply went through the motions, furtively, nervously, as if someone were watching. There had even been a case in which a woman had inserted a razor blade into her vagina. When her Russian rapist entered her, he split his penis and bled to death before anything could be done. News of that had spread rapidly throughout the camps, and suddenly these American women didn't seem so attractive.

Another factor that was reducing the libido of the Russian troops was the increasing danger they faced from the growing American resistance. Everyone was thinking about his next patrol, about whether out there, somewhere, was a silent, hidden assailant with a bullet meant just for him. Sleep came only with great difficulty, and only after the point of anxious exhaustion had set in. Men lost their appetites. Brawls among themselves had become common.

The lone rider unzipped his gun-case. Inside was a Savage bolt-action rifle with a fluted, stainless steel barrel. It was not the most expensive rifle in America, but its accuracy was almost unparalleled. It was a weapon to be owned by a man who cared about results, not hoopla. Atop it was mounted a Redfield ten power telescopic sight with mil dot reticle. He had taken many deer and elk with this rifle. Even among his shooting friends, men who had been around fine rifles all their lives, he had a reputation as a crack shot. In fact, he was one of the best long-range shots in all of Wyoming.

He had chosen this weapon from his arsenal for today's task because it was not just a rifle. It was a precision shooting instrument. In the right hands, it was capable of producing what to the uninitiated might seem to be almost supernatural results: placing a bullet in exactly the intended place at ranges that were almost too great for the naked eye to see. And this instrument was definitely in the right hands.

He extended the folding bi-pod from beneath the rifle's fore-end, moved a few pebbles so that the weapon was level, and opened the action. The bolt moved smoothly, exposing the rifle's chamber. From another pocket he took a red bandana, folded over onto itself. He placed it on the ground next to him. Opening it, he uncovered two shiny brass, freshly loaded cartridges. They were in 300 Winchester Magnum, loaded with one-hundred-eighty grain Sierra boat-tailed bullets. Behind each of them were seventy-two grains of IMR 4350 powder, carefully measured on his own hand-loading scale. This load would produce a velocity just in excess of three-thousand feet per second. And the experience of firing thousands of such rounds told him that it was deadly accurate.

He grasped the first round in his fingers and placed it into the weapon's receiver, pushing down on the spring-loaded magazine follower until the cartridge clicked into place. He did the same with the second. Slowly he pushed the bolt-handle forward and then down, locking a round in the rifle's chamber. Lying on his stomach, he lifted the weapon's stock to his shoulder and lowered his head to look through the scope. The crisp, clear image of the valley floor appeared. Swinging the weapon's muzzle to the right, he found the dirt road; further to the right, and yet further, he found the vehicle. He could clearly see the two men in the front seat, bouncing along the washboard surface. Soon they would stop.

General Bukovski unzipped a case, and withdrew a large-scale topographical map of the area. He looked around himself, locating features, getting his bearings. Three minutes later he said, "Stop here Sergeant."

The general stood in the open car, his head several feet above the top of the windshield. He took another look around, referring to the map once again.

"This is it. This is where we'll put the new labor camp. I see that Rodionov was right. This location is first rate: barren country with no place to run, excellent visibility in all directions, and mountains loaded with rock ready to be broken. This will do Sergeant!"

The lone rider could see the general's mouth moving. According to his laser range-finder, the shot was 487 yards: a long way, but certainly not beyond reason. He had hit smaller targets from greater distances in his life. Placing the cross-hairs on the general's forehead, he raised them to achieve the proper elevation. There was a slight breeze from the east, no more than a few miles per hour. He moved the center of the cross-hairs the appropriate distance to the right to compensate for bullet drift. He made these elevation and windage adjustments quickly, almost automatically, making the task seem easy. In fact, it was immensely difficult and required years of practice. His forefinger came to rest gently on Savage's proprietary AccuTrigger, which he knew would break at precisely two pounds. Taking a deep breath, he let half of it out. He concentrated on his sight picture and his trigger-pull. Just a slight pressure now—ever so slight....

Major General Anatoly Bukovski, Commandant of the Fifth Sector, Western Region, was in mid sentence when the big bullet entered just above his left eye. His skull literally exploded, covering everything with blood, hair and bits of brain. His lifeless body cart wheeled out of the vehicle and landed ten feet away, face down in the dust. The horrified sergeant looked at his hands, which were still grasping the steering wheel. A piece of scalp with a few hairs protruding from it was stuck to the knuckle of his right ring finger. His mouth hung open, but no sound came out.

It was almost a second before he heard the crack of the rifle; it didn't even register. He lost control of his bladder, but he was barely conscious of the spreading, hot wetness. Slowly his eyes lifted, to survey the hills around him. It did not even occur to the terrified man to drive away. Where had the shot come from? Who was he? Then he saw him: the far-off shape of a standing man silhouetted against the blue of the Wyoming sky.

Slowly, the sergeant swung his leg out of the vehicle. He tried to stand, but a great weakness overtook him. Like many Russians, he was in awe of the marksmanship abilities of these Americans. He knew that if this rifleman wanted him, he was as good as dead. A horrible sinking feeling overcame him, the feeling of being a hunted animal totally at the mercy of the hunter, surrounded by a cage of mountains, with nowhere to go, nowhere to hide. He fell to his knees beside the vehicle and began to cry. Raising his arms in the direction of the distant stranger, he screamed out, "Noooo! Please!"

The lone rider cycled the bolt, loading the second round into the chamber. He lowered himself into a sitting position, and carefully took aim at the pathetic figure. He saw the Russian grasp his head as if to tear out his hair. Ordinarily, he was a compassionate man, but now his blood ran cold in his veins. The Russian was nothing more than vermin, to be exterminated without a second thought. He pulled the butt of the rifle tight against his shoulder. A touch of the trigger and it was over.

CHAPTER THIRTY-FOUR

The three men moved the carefully-placed brush out of the way to expose the road that led to the camp. It was little more than a two-track trail, really. That was good. With the brush in place, it was virtually invisible. It was unlikely that Russian patrols would pass this way, but if they did, they would be none the wiser.

After they had driven through the narrow opening, they replaced the bushes and branches as they had found them, and painstakingly obliterated their tire tracks leading from the main road. They climbed into the truck and drove in silence through the Idaho wilderness. Three miles later, they were there.

The camp was situated on the southwest side of Spangle Lake, in the Sawtooth Wilderness Area. Trace climbed out of the truck and looked around him. Substantial log buildings rose from the forest floor, interspersed with more temporary sheet-metal ones. Besides the natural cover provided by the trees, all were covered with large pieces of camouflaged netting which were attached to the ground by stakes. Scores of people, men and women, bustled around carrying out ordinary daily chores. They looked lean and fit, hardened by months of strenuous physical work, basic diet, and wilderness living. Many had not been that way a year ago; they had been soft and flabby from all the comforts of civilization. If he had seen them then, he would have thought them unlikely guerillas. Now they seemed to fit this scene perfectly.

Five of the other trucks from the raid on the Colorado arsenal had arrived before them. Trace hoped that the rest had not run into any trouble. A man approached. He was about fifty, hair still as black as coal, with a tall powerful body that looked as if it had been forged from spring steel. He was immaculately dressed in camo clothing, and his boots shined in the sunlight. He looked like a leader.

"Glad to see you men made it," he said as he strode toward the bed of the pickup. "Stingers!" he said as he examined its contents. "Fantastic! We were almost out of them."

"Hello, Major McCabe," Rick said. "We've got two new recruits."

He introduced Trace and Kevin, and the men shook hands all around.

Kevin said, "Should I be saluting you, sir?"

McCabe laughed.

"No, nothing that formal around here. But if it makes you feel more comfortable, you can call me major. If not, then just Richard, or, better yet, Dick. We do have a system of rank in this camp, but we're not sticklers about it. Everyone here knows that we're all in this together. When the shooting starts, though, pay attention to what your boss says. Pull the truck up over there."

He pointed to what appeared to be the entrance to a tunnel.

"Let's get these munitions into the bunker. Then I want you new men to report to my office. It's in that log building over there."

He indicated the largest of the buildings, in the center of the compound. Purposefully, he strode away to attend to the next bit of business.

Trace and Kevin entered the major's office.

"Come in! Sit down, both of you," McCabe said. After they had done so, he continued. "Sergeant Ceely, your military background if obvious. I see by your shoulder flash that you were attached to the Tenth Special Forces Group."

"That's right, sir," Ceely answered.

"Well, don't be surprised if you're field commissioned soon. We need officers with your kind of experience. Trace, what's your background?"

Trace told him about his military history, omitting any mention of his Silver Star. He was careful not to mention his Purple Heart either. He didn't want any questions about his wound, anything that would cause his new commander to question his physical capability. He wanted to start with a clean slate: no baggage, no expectations. The major listened intently as Trace told him about his factory in Indiana and how he had come to leave it.

"A Marine Corps Captain, huh? You're probably as qualified for my job as I am! We need officers desperately, especially those who have seen actual combat. You'll move up fast. As soon as you've proven yourself in a real fight, you'll probably be assigned a unit of your own, like this one. Your engineering and mechanical background should come in handy too. We need people who understand equipment and how to keep it running.

"Now let me explain our situation. We are currently in the guerilla warfare stage of our resistance. Our standing armed forces have been rendered ineffective through the surrender of our leadership. The Russians formally control large areas of the country, and our military activity is limited to hit and run tactics. I fully expect that, as time goes on, we will take back control of more and more of the countryside.

"When that happens, we will switch to partisan warfare, sometimes referred to as 'irregular' warfare. Then we will engage major units of the Russian military head-on. But a lot of work has to take place between now and then. In the meantime, don't underrate guerilla warfare! Remember your history. Our own First Revolution is an excellent example. Washington used guerilla tactics against the British, and, as he became stronger, switched to partisan warfare just as we will. If the South had used such tactics, I doubt the North would have won the War Between the States, or as some like to call it, the War of Northern Aggression. There were those in the Confederacy at the time who made just that argument.

"In our own time, the Vietnamese at first used obsolete bolt-action rifles to fight us, and we threw every thing at them but the kitchen sink, or at least what Johnson and McNamara let us throw at them. The Soviets met the same fate in Afghanistan. Do you remember? The Afghans were making crude copies of Lee-Enfield rifles with little more than files and chisels, and they beat the Soviets flat! I know, a million Afghans died in the process, and, toward the end, the Soviets were hurt by a crumbling economy. But the fact remains that the Union of Soviet Socialist Republics–a superpower at least in a military sense--fought a guerilla war on her own doorstep for ten years, and could not prevail. We're in a much better position than were the Afghans. The Russians have to travel thousands of miles to reach us. That's a long way to go for logistical support!

"The Brits were never able to pacify Northern Ireland. The Israelis could never really control the Palestinians. The Nazis had a terrible time dealing with resistance movements in Europe. As a matter of fact, I can't think of a single case in which an entire occupied people united in resistance has been permanently defeated."

"What about nuclear weapons, sir," Kevin asked. "As we regain control of the country, and the Russians see they are losing, what are the chances that they will use another nuke, like they did in Los Angeles?"

"It' a chance we'll have to take," McCabe answered. "I'm betting that Drugonov wants a productive colony, not a radioactive wasteland. And history is on our side. Look at other conflicts around the world, and I think you'll see what I mean. The Brits never used nukes in Northern Ireland, Israel never used them against the Palestinians, the Soviets didn't use them in Afghanistan or Chechnya, and we didn't use them in Korea or Vietnam. Of course, I could be wrong. In my opinion, Drugonov's crazier than a shit-house rat. There's no telling what he'll do. Like the Afghans, we too may lose a significant portion of our population. But we'll have to risk it, since our only other option is slavery, not only for us, but for our children and their children. I don't know about you, but I'd rather go up in a nuclear fireball than spend the rest of my life under somebody's boot."

"Is there any sort of national leadership for our resistance?" Trace asked.

"No," McCabe answered. "And that's a problem. Our resistance is limited to individual organizations operating essentially alone. The only thing I'm sure of at this point is that units such as ours exist all over the country. I know this because, even though our communications amongst ourselves is poor, word has a way of spreading. Even though it's difficult, people still travel, like you Trace, all the way from Indiana. Although as of now we are operating as individual, discrete units, as time goes on we will become better organized, and will be able to act more in concert with each other. Some sort of leadership structure will gel eventually. In the meantime, our task is to recruit as many additional people as we can, accumulate the most powerful, sophisticated arsenal possible, and to hit the Russians whenever and wherever we see the opportunity.

"I'm afraid you men aren't going to have much time to settle in before the actions starts. We're planning an ambush for tomorrow. I'll be briefing the appropriate personnel within the hour. I want both of you to be there. Report to Lieutenant Juarez as soon as you leave here, he will issue you weapons and the rest of your gear. You'll both bunk in barracks three. As you walk out the door, it's two buildings to your left. Chow's going to be served in a few minutes. Get something to eat, and I'll see you at the briefing."

Trace picked up the enameled iron dish from the stack on the table. Large coffee cans held the silverware. When his turn came, he passed in front of a man doling out boiled potatoes from a large steel pot. These had been grown in the camp. When they ran out, in the winter, sufficient rice was in storage to provide carbohydrates until another crop came in.

The next man behind the tables used a large fork to spear a piece of meat from the heaping platter in front of him. Trace held out his plate. It was venison steak. Not bad, Trace thought as the rich aroma of the roasted wild meat entered his nostrils. He was hungry, not having eaten since the previous afternoon. Finally, he was given a serving of some kind of greens. He wasn't sure what they were, but their dark, verdant color promised plenty of vitamins and minerals.

He walked over to the clearing where many of the others had gathered. Sitting down on the grass, he removed his canteen from his belt and opened it. The others had done the same. There was nothing to drink in the camp except water, but it was some of the best Trace had ever tasted. It came from an artesian spring a hundred yards from camp. He lifted the canteen to his lips: it was cool and sweet. Trace looked around himself, at his comrades in arms. He said nothing at first. He just listened.

"...And then I told Bobby that he'd better get his ass in gear or he'd get left behind!" said the big man to his left. Those who had been listening chuckled. Trace had not heard the whole story, but he smiled none the less. It felt good to be among friends. He had been out in the cold, running for his life, for so long that he now experienced a great sense of relief.

"Yeah, my brother's like that. You practically have to set off a stick of dynamite under him to get him going," said the lanky man sitting cross-legged in front of him.

There was a momentary silence as everyone concentrated on his food. Then another man asked, "John, was your truck a half ton or three-quarter? I remember one time...."

And the conversation continued. No one said anything important: just mundane stuff. Trace found it fascinating. Some of these people might be dead within twelve hours, but none seemed to be affected by that knowledge. As his eyes traveled from face to face, he was conscious of the fact that these people were the backbone of America; they always had been. They had been betrayed by their leaders, by their intellectuals, by the press they counted on to tell them the truth. But they were striking back. They were ordinary people, the kind one would see on any small-town street corner. They were unsophisticated people, unaware of the nuances of political philosophy. But they knew what it meant to be free.

Trace was proud to be among them.

Trace was issued a brand-new M16 rifle and five magazines of ammunition. He was given a change of clothes: government-issue woodland camouflage, and a pair of new boots. He felt a sense of deja vu as he put these on, almost as if he had traveled back twenty years to the time of his military service. Trace sat on his bunk, field-stripping and reassembling his weapon. It had been a long time, but it was coming back to him. The odor of gun oil and solvent brought back memories, some pleasant, some distinctly not. He had been ordered to keep a loaded magazine in the rifle at all times, with the bolt closed on an empty chamber. Everyone in the camp was on high alert, should the Russians ever stumble upon them. No one was ever more than ten feet from his weapon.

Kevin opened the door of the barracks and stuck his head in.

"Briefing in five minutes, Trace."

"O.K. Thanks," Trace answered.

He slung his rifle over his shoulder, left the building, and walked toward a group of people gathered outside the major's office. There was a three-legged easel on which a map of this section of Idaho had been stapled to a piece of plywood. Trace joined the group and sat down.

He couldn't help but notice their weapons. It was an eclectic lot. About half were armed with M16s, as he was. Others had the 7.62 x 39 millimeter SKSs that had become so ubiquitous in the years before the conquest. Still others had variations of the Kalashnikov, many with the silly thumb-hole stocks that had been required by law. He had been told that, where possible, armorers within the camp had converted these to selective-fire. A few had the more sophisticated Heckler and Koch rifles. There were several of what looked to be FN-LAR's. He also saw a couple of Ruger Mini-14's.

Trace wondered where they would be now if the government had succeeded in taking these away, as they had threatened to do so many times. Just then the major came out and approached the map. He had everyone's attention.

"As most of you know, a battalion of Russian infantry is headquartered in Boise. Our intelligence regarding their activities is quite good. We have dealt with them before, with considerable success. Our actions have so far been limited to sniping and the laying of traps and mines. We are now going to step up our activities to a new level. Tomorrow at 0600 hours, a platoon from this battalion will engage in a search and destroy mission. Those they wish to search for and to destroy are, you guessed it, us."

The major smiled, and these twenty-four guerillas, twenty men and four women, one-seventh of his total command, smiled back, if a bit nervously. The major referred to the map, using a stick as a pointer.

"Our information is that they will proceed by truck east on route twenty-one until they reach Idaho City, at which point they will turn south and follow the dirt road to the North Fork of the Boise River. At this point they will be on foot. It is in this area that they hope to find us. And they will.

"Your platoon will be there before them. You will position yourselves along both sides of that dirt road and catch the Russians in a crossfire. Lieutenant Truman and I have agreed upon the exact spot. It affords you maximum cover, and exposes the enemy completely. I want you to hit them as hard as you can. If possible, I don't want one of them left alive. I want to put the Russians on notice that this section of Idaho belongs to us, not to them. After this, I want them to fear for their lives every time they set foot outside Boise city limits. And, eventually, even cowering in the city won't help them. We'll fight them there, and we'll win. Tomorrow's action will be a major step in that direction.

"Today we received seventeen new recruits. Most of them have had military experience. We are getting stronger by the day, and the Russians are getting weaker. As each day passes, we are in an increasingly better position to confront them openly. My information is that the same conditions pertain to other militia units throughout the Northwest. I hope the same can be said for the rest of the country. At any rate, we will do our part.

"But the ultimate outcome is by no means certain. Make no mistake about that. We face a tough, increasingly well entrenched enemy who will force us to fight for every foot of ground. They are in formal control of this country, and we have been relegated to the status of outsiders in our own land. We face a hard fight, and God knows how long it will go on. But we will persevere. We will fight them wherever they are, and whenever the opportunity presents itself. Tomorrow's struggle will be a step, though perhaps a small one, in the re-conquest of our own country. Some of you may not come back from this mission. A human life is a high price to pay, but you realize the stakes as well as I do. Otherwise, you would not be here. Some things are worth dying for, and if liberty isn't at the top of the list, I don't know what is.

"As difficult as it is for me to order some of you to your deaths, I realize that your task is far more difficult. Tomorrow it will be you facing the lead and the steel. Each of you will have to reach deep within yourself to find the courage and determination you will need. I want you to know right now that, as far as I am concerned, you are all heroes. One day, when this is over, the entire country will . recognize you as such. But for now we fight in obscurity, and we die obscure deaths on nameless battlefields. Don't think for a moment that those deaths are in vain. I don't mean to sound maudlin here, but I want you to know that you are the saviors of your country. You are a collection of factory and office workers, mechanics, farmers, even housewives. But when the time came, you declared your willingness to put your lives on the line. That means a lot.

"You are the Unorganized Militia of the United States of America. It was you the Founders had in mind when they wrote the Second Amendment: ordinary men–armed men–who would rise up in defense of their country, when all else had failed, as an insuperable barrier against tyranny. They were confident that such a militia could never be defeated. I share that conviction. And I want you to share it as well. Someday, you will be looked upon with the same reverence with which we look upon the men who suffered and died at Bunker Hill, Saratoga and Valley Forge. Well, I guess I've said my piece.

"Good luck to you all, and give 'em hell!"

The major turned the briefing over to Lieutenant Truman, who dealt with the particulars for the next thirty minutes. He had a hand-drawn diagram of the precise section of the dirt road on which they would ambush the Russians. Each person was assigned a position. Two thirty-caliber machine guns would be used that would be able to rake the road for a distance of at least a hundred yards. If the entire Russian platoon could be caught along that one straight stretch of road, it could be annihilated. It seemed to Trace that the machine guns alone should be able to do it. The presence of the rest of his platoon seemed almost superfluous. But he didn't care about that now. He told himself that all he wanted was to get a piece of the Russians before the machine guns chopped them to confetti. That's what he told himself. That's what he wanted to feel. But a twisting in his stomach said differently.

Trace was assigned to the northwest corner of the area of operations, toward the very beginning of the lethal one-hundred-yard fire-zone, to the Russians' right as they moved south. He was a bit disappointed. The enemy platoon might be completely past him by the time the action started. He was beginning to resign himself to the temporary role of noncombatant when the briefing broke up.

For an instant, he felt relief; the thought of being shot–not killed, but wounded once again–was frightening. He had been through such an incredible ordeal the first time. He felt embarrassed. "Christ, Forester!" he thought. You're a soldier again! Getting shot comes with the territory! If it happens, it happens! Just concentrate on doing your duty!

He found his mixed emotions unsettling, rare in his experience. He had always considered himself a decisive man, and a brave one too, living his life according to Davy Crockett's motto: make sure you're right, then go ahead. This war was right. Still, he felt that sickening twinge in the pit of his stomach. Cowardice? The fact that such a thought had crossed his mind nauseated him. You're no damned coward Forester! Anyone who's been shot would be afraid of being shot again! It's normal!

He swallowed hard and clenched his fists, as if a physical effort would drive such thoughts from his mind. You've faced death before! Your mettle's been tested! Fuck this anxiety! These are just pre-combat jitters! They're nothing new for you! You know damned well that as soon as the shooting starts, they'll disappear like a bad dream! Just worry about getting the job done!

Trace looked up from his own internal skirmish and saw that he was the only one left sitting on the ground. He felt exposed, as if everyone must know what he had been thinking. Quickly he got up and walked back to his barracks to prepare to meet his demons.

The forest was eerily silent. The only sound was the occasional chirping of a bird somewhere in the trees overhead. Trace could hear the blood pounding in his ears. For the second time he checked the chamber of his rifle to be sure a round was present. The adrenalin surged through his veins. Never had he felt so intensely alive. His perceptions were hypersensitive; he was alert to the slightest change in his environment.

Earlier, in the predawn darkness in which his platoon had approached this site, the demons had returned. He had sweated, though the air was cool. At one point, he had looked at his hand, and, as he had feared, it was trembling. But as the moment of actual combat approached, he was relieved to feel only anticipation, an eagerness to get on with it. The demons were indeed dissipating like a mist after the dawn.

The platoon had dispersed itself on both sides of the dirt road. Everything was just as Lieutenant Truman had said it would be. There were no surprises. Twelve militia members were on each side, about ten feet apart. The two machine guns were located at the south end of their position. Trace would be one of the first to see them coming. He reminded himself once again to hold his fire until the entire Russian platoon had entered the Kill Zone. This was critical. If he, or anyone else opened fire too soon, the enemy would disperse into the forest, and then their job would be much more difficult: it would be hand to hand among the trees.

The sun crawled across the sky. Then, as he lay there in the brush, he began to think that his mind was playing tricks on him. He imagined that he heard something: a very slight scuffing sound from the north. Perhaps boots on gravel? As the instants ticked by, it became louder. Then he heard something else: the faint rhythmic clinking of metal against metal. It was time.

He looked across the road and to his right. Almost invisible amongst the vegetation was the face of another freedom-fighter. Their eyes met. Trace nodded ever so slightly, and the other man did the same. The sounds grew louder. Now he could hear the occasional hoarse whisper. His fingers grasped the rifle in a virtual death grip. He would not see them until they were almost on him; the road bent to the left just ahead of him. He stared at the apex of that bend with all his might. Waiting. Waiting.

Then Trace saw him, a lone man, on point, weapon at the ready. He walked confidently and quickly, scanning the brush and the road ahead. The Russian glanced in his direction. Unconsciously, Trace tried to pull his head into his body like a turtle. Although he had taken great pains to conceal his position, he suddenly felt terribly exposed. But the man's eyes passed over him with no response. Then there were more. Two abreast they came, one pair after another.

Trace found himself seeking out their eyes, as if he wanted to see into the souls of the men who were about to be killed. Some of them were just boys. Trace thought of his own son, David, and felt a pang of regret. But it was fleeting. These were the enemy, the men who had enslaved his people.

The young ones were visibly frightened as if they were men immersed in shark-infested waters and were waiting for the unseen attack. There had been a few such missions before, and there had been no trouble. Still, they seemed afraid. Everyone knew that the Americans were out there. It was only a matter of time. They knew they were guilty. They felt like invaders. They expected retribution. After all, how would they react if someone occupied their land, enslaved their people?

The last pair passed Trace's position. Something was wrong. There were only twelve Russians. Where was the rest of the platoon? The squad marched on. Everyone held his fire, waiting for the rest to appear. They did not. Seconds passed like hours. The enemy began to approach the end of the Kill Zone; soon the machine guns would have to open up, or allow the Russians to pass unscathed. Trace looked to his left. Where the hell were they?

Suddenly, the air exploded with the sound of automatic weapons fire. It was the machine guns. Lieutenant Truman had made the decision to take what he could get. Trace could not see it from his cover, but the Russians were falling like tenpins. Other militiamen opened fire. The remaining enemy were enveloped in a virtual cloud of lead. A few tried for the edge of the road, seeking cover in the trees. But they ran right into the Kalashnikovs and SKSs and were cut down in short order.

Trace decided he had to do something. He dashed out of the brush and onto the road, running north toward its apex. As he passed it, he ran head on into the second squad, who, in turn, were running flat out to the south, running to the sound of the guns, running to assist their comrades. In an instant, Trace was among them.

The startled Russians skidded to a stop. They hesitated to react for a fraction of a second. Trace used the time to squeeze the trigger. His M16 was one of the newer ones, and fired three-shot bursts. These he unleashed at the men all around him as quickly as he could. He was totally exposed.

Within a second's time Russian bullets began to zip around him. One of them tore his sleeve, barely nicking the skin. Another creased his scalp above his left ear, sending an unnoticed trickle of blood down the side of his head. He was no longer thinking about his own life; he assumed that it was forfeit. He was intent on taking out as many of these men as he could before he met his end.

He could not let them reach his own platoon, whose position was now obvious. If he didn't stop them here, the Russians could move into the forest and attack his people from behind on both sides of the road, catching them in a crossfire, destroying them. Trace couldn't let that happen. He was in a position to save lives here, to further the cause.

His magazine was empty. Nine dead Russians lay at his feet, a few killed by their own comrades in the melee. The other three had fled into the forest and were being hunted down by other members of the militia. They would not get far. Already, shots were ringing out from the trees, Russians screaming as their lives left them. Trace just stood there, numbed. His rage subsided and a feeling of wonder overcame him. He was still alive. It was over. His muscles uncoiled as if he had been given a shot of morphine. Then he began to tremble.

Quickly he examined himself, looking at his legs and torso, running his hands across his chest and as much of his back as he could reach. He looked at his arms and hands, ran his fingers across his face, scalp and neck checking for blood. He noticed the crease over his ear and probed it with his fingertip, finding it trivial. Just a ruined haircut! he thought, as he laughed out loud. He laughed in part because he was virtually unscathed, but mostly because he had not let himself down, nor the other members of his platoon. When the moment of truth arrived, he had performed well. And he had been right: once the shooting started, he had not experienced the slightest trace of fear. The demons were banished forever. A hand touched his shoulder. Turning, he saw Lieutenant Truman. The lieutenant was smiling from ear to ear.

"That was one hell of a show, Forester!" he said. "I've never seen anything like it! You took on the whole damn squad single-handed! You bought us the time we needed to finish off the first squad, and prevented us from being attacked in the rear by the second! The major's going to hear about this!"

Several other militia members began to strip the Russian corpses of anything useful: weapons, ammunition, bayonets, canteens, compasses, even the buttons from their shirts. Trace watched them in silence. He had killed these men: he, Trace Forester. Part of him felt exhilarated, almost giddy at the relief and the sense of triumph. The rest of him felt repulsed. The dead eyes of one young man, no more that eighteen or nineteen, stared up at him accusingly.

For the briefest of instants he felt regret. But it was at that moment that he steeled himself and became resolved to accept no guilt for his actions. He stood erect and looked down at the corpse, right into its eyes, not with guilt, but with determination. I was not the aggressor here, he thought. You were.

CHAPTER THIRTY-FIVE

"Benedict, what are you holding back? Don't think you're above being put in front of firing squad! I'd as quickly kill you as I would any other American!"

"I'm holding back nothing, Maximum Leader! I swear to you! I've given you all the information we have on the militia movement in this country!" pleaded the former president.

"I don't believe you! No modern state would allow armed hooligans to organize right under its nose! What were you thinking of? How could you permit such a thing?" Drugonov demanded, arms waving in front of the face of the seated American.

"You have to remember, Maximum Leader, that before you liberated us, we were not yet a totalitarian country; we were simply moving in that direction. Our plans were not yet complete. My party, to the extent that it controlled government, was moving steadily in the direction of greater governmental domination. We were even successfully dragging the opposition with us! We had reached the point where, if anyone seriously questioned the premise that the individual should be subservient to the State, they were considered to be dangerous radicals, outdated reactionaries.

"Our press saw to it that they were either ignored or laughed at. The mere mention of shrinking the government, of reducing the size and scope of the State, was no longer considered acceptable political discourse. Even our worst ideological enemies didn't dare whisper such ideas in public! They had been punished at the polls for simply suggesting a reduction in the rate of growth in government, much less for actually making it smaller!

"How did we achieve that victory? The key to it was that we had successfully made a great many of the people dependent on a massive, redistributive State. Millions looked to us to take care of them. We used every election to put them deeper and deeper into our pockets; we offered them more and more. To many, it was irresistible. We convinced them that they needed us, that they were helpless without us. Once we had accomplished that, the rest was bound to fall into place.

"It's true, there were still those who clung to obsolete notions of individual liberty, but I always believed that they were in a distinct minority. We were all sure that we had bred that out of them! Our intellectuals had seen to that. We had raised an entire generation with no knowledge of liberty, with no conception of what it means to be free. We took great pains to avoid such things in our schools. For years we had told our children that ideas like liberty, limited government and the importance of the individual should be ignored. We told them that they were just the ancient rants of 'dead white men', and were not to be taken seriously. Maximum

Leader, we were in the process of accomplishing the greatest philosophical debouchment in the history of the world!"

"Then why am I meeting with such resistance!" Drugonov howled, fists shaking at the ceiling.

"We tried to take the guns away, but it was a very delicate process politically. We had to move slowly, incrementally. Every time there was a shooting, especially if it involved children, we used the opportunity to push for more gun-control. We hammered away at the idea that guns equaled crime, even when the data became overwhelming that it did not. We even tried to redefine the Second Amendment, to convince the people that it did not refer to an individual right to keep and bear arms at all, but only to a collective one, that it applied just to state National Guard units.

"It was tough going, but I am convinced that in the end, we would have accomplished our goal. In fact, I was about to fabricate a series of events that would have justified total confiscation when your people arrived. If you had just held off a few more months, the American people would have been disarmed. They would have been defenseless. We would not be having these problems."

"Are you blaming me for your own ineptitude, for your own weakness?" Drugonov shouted. "You should have had the strength to crush these radicals! No modern government places its control of the populace in such jeopardy!"

"It has to do with our history, Maximum Leader, with our culture," Benedict offered meekly. "Culture is not changed overnight. Not even in a generation. The values of individualism, of self-defense, and of the right to overthrow a tyrannical government still exist in this country, despite all our efforts. You would not understand, but these things are deeply embedded in our Anglo-Saxon traditions.

"Since this issue has taken on such political importance, I have been forced to become something of an expert on it. If I may be so bold, I'll give you a short history lesson on the subject. Perhaps then you'll see why we have had such a difficult time rooting out and disarming these dangerous radicals."

Benedict produced several sheets of paper from his jacket pocket.

"I've written some notes with quotations you might find interesting. They'll give you an idea of how firmly entrenched the poisonous concept of an armed citizenry is in this country, and exactly what we're up against."

He reached into another pocket, withdrew a pair of reading glasses, and put them on.

"The legal recognition of the right of self-defense has been traced back in the ancient British records to at least the seventh century, and no doubt goes back long before that. Unlike in the rest of Europe, in Britain the individual possession of arms was not seen as a danger to the political status quo, but as its greatest defense. Keeping and bearing arms among the general populace was seen not as a threat, but as a right. In 1181, the Assize of Arms of Henry the Second required all British citizens between the ages of fifteen and forty to purchase and keep arms. In 1369 Edward the Third required all able-bodied men to practice with bow and arrow in their leisure time.

"The term 'militia' was first used during the reign of Elizabeth the First: a universally-armed people ready to come to the defense of their country. John Locke, who, more than any other man, transmitted the philosophy upon which this country was founded, wrote, 'Whosoever uses force without right puts himself into a state of War with those, against whom he so uses it, and in that state all former Ties are canceled, all other Rights cease, and every one has a right to defend himself, and to resist the aggressor.'

"The English Declaration of Rights of 1689 guaranteed the rights of virtually all Englishmen to possess arms. The tradition was carried on in this country. In 1623, Virginia required all men traveling in the countryside to be armed. They even ordered everyone to bring their weapons to church! Our Revolution started because the British attempted to disarm the men of the Massachusetts Militia at Concord. Here are some quotes from the Founders on the subject. Patrick Henry said, 'Resolved, that a well-regulated militia, composed of gentlemen and freemen, is the natural strength and only security of a free government.' Noah Webster wrote, 'Before a standing army can rule, the people must be disarmed, as they are in almost every kingdom in Europe. The supreme power in America cannot enforce unjust laws by the sword; because the whole body of the people are armed and constitute a force superior to any band of regular troops that can be, on any pretense, raised in the United States.' Samuel Adams, discussing the proposed Constitution, declared, 'that the said Constitution shall never be construed....to prevent the people of the United States who are peaceable citizens from keeping their own arms.' Richard Henry Lee argued that, '...to preserve liberty, it is essential that the whole body of people always possess arms, and be taught alike, especially when young, how to use them...'

"Patrick Henry also said this, 'The great object is that every man be armed,' and that, 'Everyone who is able may have a gun.' Thomas Jefferson wrote, 'The strongest reason for the people to retain the right to keep and bear arms is, as a last resort, to protect against tyranny in government.'

"Congress authorized the creation of a citizen Militia with the Militia Act of 1792. It required that all able-bodied white men between the ages of fifteen and forty-five be enrolled in the Militia, and that they provide themselves with a suitable weapon, ammunition and equipment. That law stayed on the books until 1903. So you see, Maximum Leader, the problem we are currently facing has deep roots."

"By God, Benedict! If I didn't know better, I'd say you sympathized with these people!"

"Maximum Leader, just because I am familiar with these ideas doesn't mean that I condone them. I condemn them! I've always condemned them, and so have all enlightened people in this country! In an age of statism, in an age when individual rights can no longer be tolerated, but must be sacrificed for the well-being of the collective, civilian possession of arms is an outdated and dangerous idea.

"People who believe in it have been the bane of my professional existence. I have done my best to thwart them, to harm them; all the elite, the truly progressive, in America did. An armed citizenry has always been the last, the ultimate, defense against statism in this country, and, as such, they have been the enemies of all right-thinking people. They are stubborn bastards, these so-called 'patriots.' I will help you to destroy them in any way I can.

"One more thing: before our liberation, we did manage to infiltrate their various units across the country with our own BATF and FBI agents. Many of them are still in place. Now, of course, those agencies are under the command of your KGB. Communications are poor at the moment, but as they improve, I expect more and more of their reports to come in. This may give us the tool we need to put an end to end this annoying resistance."

"You'd better be right, Benedict! I'm holding you personally responsible for crushing these fanatics! If you don't, there will be hell to pay, not only for you personally, but for millions of these dependent cattle you've been cultivating all these years! We will see if these patriots value freedom enough to stand by and watch as millions of their countrymen are annihilated! We will see how dedicated they are to an abstract principle when faced with the reality of a mountain of corpses! We will see how much blood it takes to drown the flame of individual liberty in this colony!"

CHAPTER THIRTY-SIX

Major Trace Forester looked across the table at his officers. They studied the map before them, planning for the unit's next action. To his left sat Captain George Luttrell, second in command, but at the moment, for lack of lieutenants, in charge of a platoon. Luttrell had been with the organization since its inception, years earlier, since long before the Conquest. Trace was depending on him for advice.

To George Lutrell's left sat his brother, Edward. Ed had also been in the unit since before the occupation. He was a lieutenant, and a very capable one. The other three platoon leaders rounded out the group. Five platoons didn't make for much of a battalion for a major to command. But such was the present nature of the American Militia. Losses had been heavy in recent months. Many units around the country were under manned.

"Is everybody clear on this?" Trace asked. "I want the first and third platoons to engage the Russians here."

He pointed to a little-used secondary road where, he had been informed, a Russian unit would be on routine patrol the following day.

George spoke up. "Are we sure they haven't been tipped off? Remember the last time? They seemed to know we were coming. They were waiting for us. We lost seven people that day."

"I know, George. If I didn't know better, I'd say we had a leak somewhere," Trace answered.

Things had not been going well recently for the militia, anywhere in the country. Their early successful momentum had slowed, or stopped altogether. In some parts of the country they had suffered serious reversals. American attacks had been anticipated; base-camps had been raided. All told, thousands of militia members had been killed. Dozens of units had been put out of commission completely.

The Russians weren't bothering to put the Americans they captured in prison. They were not being treated as prisoners of war, but instead as terrorists. Torture was standard procedure. But because of the fragmented nature of the independently-operating militia units, captured Americans could not reveal much. After they were wrung dry, what was left of them was dispatched with a bullet to the back of the head. The militia movement was in trouble. The question was, why?

Trace had been field-commissioned shortly after his first action. In the intervening months, he had distinguished himself again and again. He had proven himself to be an extraordinary leader: fearless, innovative, daring. Two months previously he had been given his own command: a new camp that had been formed near Missoula, Montana. His unit was tough and aggressive. But it had had little success. The Russians had countered his every move. Twice he had relocated the base-camp just in time: both times the Russians had attacked their previous location, only hours after they had abandoned it.

"Brief your people. We'll meet here again at 20:00 hours. The operation goes off at 05:00. I'll see you then," Trace said.

The officers pushed back their folding canvas chairs from the two card tables that they had been using and filed out of the tent. The American militia no longer had the luxury of wooden buildings. Russian raids had become too frequent. Even these tents would have to be abandoned in an emergency.

Most men slept in fox holes or slit trenches, and when they slept at all, it was with one eye open. Sentry duty had become as important as life itself. In the event of an attack, Trace wanted his people to have as much advance warning as possible. He had inaugurated a sort of distant early warning system, placing sentries a mile or more away, using civilian two-way radios and a few precious night vision scopes.

Dogs were being used extensively, and had proven themselves invaluable on a number of occasions. Everyone was on edge. If the Russians had experienced paranoia early in this conflict, it now seemed that it was the Americans' turn to feel it. No one could figure it out. It was as if the enemy had developed a sixth sense, allowing them to locate the American camps no matter how well they were hidden.

Trace folded his arms in front of himself and stared glumly at the map. He felt as if he were not in control; as if the Russians had the upper hand. It was inconceivable; things had started out so well. Now, he spent ninety percent of his time avoiding capture, and only ten percent on offensive actions. All around the country, other militia commanders felt the same way.

"Major Forester," someone called through the tent flap.

"Come in," Trace said.

A corporal entered. Beside him was a stranger, someone Trace had never seen before.

"A new recruit?" Trace asked.

"No sir," answered the corporal. "He's a messenger from regional headquarters."

The man introduced himself. "I'm Lieutenant Rohn, Major. Bruce Rohn."

"Have a seat, Lieutenant. What can I do for you?"

"I think there is something I can do for you, sir," the Lieutenant said, handing Trace a manila envelope sealed with a metal clasp.

Trace opened it and read. His eyes narrowed with concentration, and his fingers gripped the sheaf of papers more tightly. At last, his eyes rose and met the Lieutenant's. The men looked at each other solemnly.

At precisely 20:00 hours, the platoon leaders re-entered the tent. Trace was seated at the head of the two joined card tables. Usually, he tried to smile at his subordinates, to put them at ease. Now he found that impossible. He felt a mixture of anger and sadness, and he could not stop it from showing.

Before each man at the table was a file folder. Trace told them, "Do not open these folders until I tell you to. Right now I want you to tell me about your preparations for tomorrow. Frank, how are your people?"

Lieutenant Frank Campbell, seated to Trace's right, informed him that all was go. His people had prepared their gear and were getting ready to turn in. He had told them to be prepared to move out at 04:00. Trace nodded his approval. Two other lieutenants said much the same thing regarding their platoons.

Edward Lutrell said, "My people are raring to go, Trace. As always."

Trace nodded. He pushed back his chair and stood.

"Ed, after our first meeting today, you disappeared from camp for a while. Where did you go?"

"I just went for a walk, Trace. I wanted to clear my head, that's all."

Trace paced slowly around the table until he stood behind Lieutenant Lutrell.

"How long have you been with the Militia, Ed?" Trace asked.

"Almost since it started, I guess. A long time. What's this all about, Trace?"

"It couldn't be that you went into the woods to find this, could it?"

Trace reached into his pocket and withdrew an object slightly larger that a pack of cigarettes. He placed it on the table in front of Lutrell.

"It was buried two hundred yards from camp. You were seen digging it up, Ed."

Edward Lutrell looked at the incriminating object and stammered out a denial.

"I—I've never seen that before in my life, Trace. Honestly! There's been a mistake!"

The transmitter was standard Russian issue. Everyone around the table recognized it. George, seated next to his brother, stared at him in disbelief. At last he said, "Is this true, Ed? This can't be true! Trace, I can't believe that my own brother....."

"I'm not a traitor, George, I swear it! Christ, I'm your brother!"

Suddenly Trace reached into his pocket and pulled something out. None of the men noticed. He took the two handles in his fists and formed the wire into a loop. In a flash, he dropped the loop over Edward Lutrell's neck and pulled it snug. He placed his knee between the shoulder blades of the startled man and applied enough pressure to make his point.

"Now," he said, "I want everyone to open the files before them. I received this information today by messenger from headquarters. It is a copy of a personnel file: a personnel file from the Bureau of Alcohol, Tobacco and Firearms. You will see that it belongs to one Edward Lutrell. That's your photo, isn't it Ed?"

Lutrell, who could barely breathe, glanced down at his picture.

"It says that you've been with them for more than three years, Ed," Trace continued.

George had finished reading. He looked into his brother's face. Concern had turned to contempt.

"All this time, Ed. What did they pay you? What's the price for turning against your own country? Against your own brother? All those people dead. Our people, Ed."

To the extent that the piano-wire garrote would permit, Ed looked imploringly into his brother's eyes. He found nothing there but coldness.

"George, it's your call," Trace said.

In a dead, emotionless voice, George Lutrell said, "Finish it, Trace."

Trace grunted as he jerked the two handles of the garotte. The thin, tough wire cut through skin, muscle, the carotid artery and the esophagus. Ed Lutrell jerked spasmodically, blood squirting across the table. He fell backwards onto the floor, writhing silently. In a moment it was over.

Across the country similar scenes were taking place. One more unsung hero, working in the very midst of the enemy in Washington, D.C., had risked her life to smuggle out diskettes of personnel files of BATF and FBI undercover agents who had turned against their own countrymen. No one would ever know her name or her fate. But because of her, hundreds of traitors around the country would die, and thousands of patriot's lives would be saved. Because of her, the movement to defend her country's liberty would gain new life. The paranoia would end. The Unorganized Militia of the United States could go back on the offensive.

CHAPTER THIRTY-SEVEN

David Forester parked his motorcycle in front of the convenience store, got off, and did a few deep-knee bends to get the blood circulating again in his legs. He had been riding for a long time. This western Montana town had more signs of life than most he had seen. Many stores and shops were open, and people seemed to be going about their business almost normally. He saw little Russian presence here. That was just as well, since he did not have a travel permit.

He had been very lucky on his trip from Tennessee, not being stopped once by a Russian patrol or checkpoint. But then, he had been careful to use nothing but back roads. Even so, several times he had had to quickly pull his bike into the brush as a truckload of the occupiers passed him. He suspected that the rank-and-file among them realized they could not monitor every road in America. A lot of people were traveling without permits; the Russians simply were not able to enforce their own regulations.

He walked into the store and looked around. There were a few loaves of bread, probably stale, on the shelves. Some cans without labels were lined up neatly next to the bread. Below them was a paper sign that said simply, "Meat." David wondered whether it was horse or dog.

The cooler next to the wall held nothing but artificially-sweetened licorice soda, the ubiquitous "Happy Worker" brand that everyone in the country had grown to hate. He longed for some of the sweet, ice-cold water from the spring back in Tennessee.

"Is this all you have to drink?" he asked the girl behind the counter.

She was pretty, this girl, with delicate features and long, blonde hair. David noticed that she was about his own age. He also noticed that she had a strange, lonely air about her, as if she were looking for something, or someone.

"We've got vodka," she answered, pointing to a row of bottles on a shelf.

Everyone had vodka. And it was cheap, subsidized by the State. The Russians were well aware of the political benefits of keeping a subservient population intoxicated. They had been doing it in their own country for generations. David took a can of the hated "Happy Worker" and walked toward the counter. At least it was cold.

As he approached the cash register, he saw something that he had seen many times before on his trip: a cardboard display covered with small cellophane packets filled with white powder. It was heroin, sold under the brand name "From Russia With Love." It sold for twenty-five New Cents per packet, a paltry sum that even a child could afford in the inflated occupation currency. David had never heard of

Leonid Uglanov, nor had most Americans. But this was Uglanov's doing. To him, America was an enormous market for the product of the poppy fields of central and southern Asia. There was much money to be made, and as the head of the Russian Mafia, now an organ of the state, Uglanov was not about to pass it by. But his mission was not simply to make money. As a member of Drugonov's government, everything he did must now also serve the state. That is why he had reluctantly priced his product so low.

The object was to addict all of the "weakies," as Drugonov called them: to clean out the gene pool. The goal was to kill off, hopefully through an overdose, all those without the strength to resist the temptation of a pleasant but potentially lethal substance that was universally available at a ridiculously low price. After this had been accomplished, Drugonov and his minions supposed, only the strong would be left, only the productive.

Next to the display of heroin was a jar filled with reusable glass syringes. This was also part of the plan. Addicts would reuse these needles, and pass them around to their friends. Disease would be spread, and again, the weakies would die. Disposable syringes had been outlawed, except in the hospitals that served Russian nationals. Heroin addiction was roaring through the inner cities, where drug use had always been rather common. Each day in those cities trucks drove slowly along the streets, calling for people to bring out their dead. No one had seen anything like it since the Black Death. The suburbs and even the rural areas were not immune.

David placed his can of "Happy Worker" on the counter.

"What kind of money do you take?" he asked.

"Silver, if you've got it," she answered, looking into his eyes a bit too long to be coincidence.

David felt a stirring within himself. He took out a silver dime and placed it on the counter. The girl quickly scooped it up and put it in her pocket. The cash register was reserved for transactions in the worthless paper fiat-currency, just in case the Russians checked. The girl was still looking at him, as if she hoped he would say something to her, and not simply walk through the door and out of her life.

"My name's David," he said, smiling at her for the first time.

He could see her visibly relax, and a shy smile crossed her lips.

"I'm Karen," she answered.

Her eagerness did not surprise him. He had noticed that, since the Conquest, many people seemed to feel the need to open up to each other, to draw closer in this difficult time. Americans seemed to feel bound together in a way that had not existed for a great many years. Something like it had existed after the World Trade Center and Pentagon disasters, and the events that followed. But now the feeling was so strong as to be almost tangible. The personal barriers that people had erected around themselves in the beforetime had disintegrated. It appeared that many needed the comfort of a smile or a simple touch, even if from a stranger.

"Why are you here?" she asked.

"To meet my father. That's all I can say."

"That's all right. I understand," she answered in a soothing voice, as if she wanted to calm him, to offer him whatever reassurance she could. She said it in a tone of absolution, as if to forgive him for whatever he might have done, or might do. Times were difficult for everyone. Under these circumstances, all could be forgiven.

"I have to leave now," he said. "There's somewhere I have to be before dark. But if I can come back into town, could we meet? I mean, I'd like to get to know you."

She smiled warmly.

"Sure. I get off at nine."

David had had to identify himself to two guards on his way into the militia camp. It had been touch and go for a while, but at last he had convinced them that he was indeed Trace Forester's son. Now he walked toward the tent where he had been told he would find his father. There were men standing outside talking. It took him a moment to recognize Trace. He had lost weight, and was in uniform. When he saw him, David stopped.

"Dad?" he called out.

Trace stopped his conversation in mid-sentence, recognizing the voice which seemed to come from another life. He turned and looked at his son, fifty feet away.

"David? David!" he answered, breaking into a wide grin.

David ran to him and the two embraced. It had been sixteen months since they had seen each other.

"What are you doing here?" Trace asked. "How is your mother? How did you get here?"

David laughed.

"Whoa! One question at a time, Dad!"

Now the reality of what had happened began to sink in. Trace realized that his son was in great danger, as they all were. He had left a safe place, where he was supposed to be taking care of his mother, and was now in the middle of a partisan war. Trace felt anger well up inside him.

He held David at arms length, and asked him harshly, "What the hell ARE you doing here? Do you realize what you've gotten yourself into? And you've left your mother all alone in the middle of nowhere! What the hell were you thinking?"

"Dad, I had to come," David answered defensively. "I'm nineteen now. I'm plenty old enough to fight! I felt awful back there in that cabin, safe while other people were fighting my battles! I felt like a coward, Dad! I'm an American too! This is my war as much as it is yours! And Mom will be fine.

"I cut enough firewood and laid in enough supplies to last at least a year. And there are people back there, Dad. Good people. Neighbors. People she can count on to help her out if anything happens. Mr. Staley, he lives about eight miles away on the other side of the mountain, said that he'd check up on her once a week. Don't worry, Dad! She's going to be fine!"

Trace studied his son's face. He could see that he was sincere. And Trace trusted his judgment: the boy had always had a good head on his shoulders. And he had to admit, there were many Freedom Fighters right here in his own camp who were younger than his son. David was right, as much as Trace hated to admit it.

After lunch, Trace showed his son around the camp. He arranged for David to be issued a uniform, a weapon and all of the other accouterments of a guerilla fighter. Trace then brought David into his tent.

"This is our area of operations, Dave," he said, circling an area with his finger on the map lying on the card tables.

"The Russians know we're here, and they're beating the bushes pretty heavily looking for us. For the last month or so, I've been concentrating on just staying out of their way, avoiding them for the most part. We've had some security problems, like a lot of other units around the country, but I think we've finally cleared those up. Now we can go back on the offensive. The day after tomorrow, I'm planning to hit them....here."

He pointed to a crossroads about fifteen miles from camp.

"They patrol there regularly, and they've gotten a bit sloppy. They seem to think that they own that area. I'm going to show them that they don't. If you'd like, I can arrange for you to be in on that operation. What do you say?"

"Terrific!" David exclaimed. "I promise I'll make you proud of me, Dad."

"Don't try to be a hero. I want you to come back here in one piece. Just keep your head down until you learn the ropes. Pay attention to what your superiors tell you. They've had lots of experience. I mean it, David! Those are real bullets they're shooting out there!"

"Don't worry, Dad. I'll be careful. In the meantime, Dad, do you mind if I go into town? I met someone there and..."

"Absolutely not! You're not to leave this camp, David! That's an order! And I'm not just your father now! I'm your commanding officer! No one leaves this camp except on my explicit orders! You were lucky getting all the way out here without any problems. Don't push that luck too far.

"The Russians move in and out of that town, and all it would take is one incident, one slip, and they'd have you. Now you know where this camp is located. They would do anything to extract that information from you. And believe me, you would talk! Everybody does."

"All right, Dad," David answered sheepishly.

The sun was sinking fast in the west. David paced back and forth among the trees, thinking. He didn't want to disobey his father, especially in his new role as David's commander. But he wanted to see Karen. He wanted to see her badly. He had the feeling that she needed him, that she was alone and needed his help. There had been something in her eyes, something that pleaded with him. He couldn't stand it anymore. He'd have to take his chances with his father's wrath.

He pushed his motorcycle down the trail toward the road. He didn't want anyone to hear him starting it. When he was a few hundred feet away, he fired up his machine. As he rode, further and further from camp with each turn of his wheels, he felt as if his father's eyes were on him. He felt guilty, torn. By the time he was half way to town, he had convinced himself that he was doing the right thing. If his father had only seen Karen, he would understand. Still, there was a twisted feeling in his stomach. Something within him disagreed.

It was a quarter to nine. David didn't want to be seen loitering on the streets, so he went into a bar to pass the time. He hated the taste of beer, and he despised liquor even more, so he had no choice but to drink "Happy Worker." The cloying artificial sweetness of the liquid made him grimace.

Next to the bar was a television. David had not seen television in months, and had not missed it. He recognized the man who filled the screen: it was Charles Frost, the famous network news anchor who had been broadcasting since before David was born. His perfect teeth and perfect hair seemed obscenely out of place in the current circumstances. David listened.

"The traitorous terrorists who refer to themselves as the militia, continued to take a pounding around the country today. Heroic government forces successfully crushed them in their camps near Akron, Ohio, Jacksonville, Florida and Springfield, Massachusetts. We are assured that these gangsters will continue to receive punishment until their entire rotten insurrection is destroyed. Once again this network appeals to any of you who may be thinking of joining these criminals to put such thoughts aside.

"You will be caught, and you will be destroyed. Remember, your duty is not to some dead accident of history, but instead to the future! Your duty is to the collective! It is patriotic to sacrifice yourself! Don't be fooled into thinking that these people are fighting for your freedom. Nothing could be further from the truth.

"They are attempting to resurrect a corrupt, outdated capitalist empire: a bloodthirsty empire that for decades sucked the life from the poorer countries of the world! Now that vicious country has been replaced with an altruistic colony, a peaceful, orderly colony dedicated to sacrificing itself for the well-being of others. What higher goal could we hope to achieve?

"Once again I will remind you that concealing the identity of one of these criminals is a capital offense. If you know anyone in a so-called militia organization, it is required that you inform the authorities immediately. And you children, if you see a gun in your house, or if you hear Mommy or Daddy saying bad things about the government, tell the nearest soldier. It is your responsibility as a good citizen of the collective."

It occurred to David that the militias must still be effective. They must still be a thorn in the side of the Russians. Why else would the networks be placing such an emphasis on them? But it frightened him that the Russians had been so successful in destroying militia camps around the country. He had heard that the traitorous BATF and FBI had infiltrated many units. He had also heard that someone had smuggled some diskettes out of their headquarters containing all of the personnel files of those treasonous bastards. As his father had told him, things should be looking up from now on.

It was five minutes to nine. David left the bar and walked toward the convenience store. He got there just as Karen was taking off her apron.

"David!" she said, surprised. "I didn't expect to see you so soon."

"I just couldn't stay away," he said, smiling. "I thought we could do something tonight. Maybe go to a movie or something."

"That's a great idea. There's a movie in town that I have to see before it closes at the end of the week. The Russians are requiring everybody to see it."

"OK. Let's go," he said jauntily.

As the two walked to the theater, neither spoke. By her silence, it seemed to David that she was waiting for him to open the conversation, to tell her about himself. He wanted to tell her everything: about his trip across the country, about his father's role as militia commander, and about his own job as a Freedom Fighter. But he hesitated. There was plenty of time for that. Besides, the less she knew about him the better it would be–for her. Knowledge had become a dangerous thing.

There were two movie theaters in town, but they were both showing the same film: "My Life is to Serve." Everyone in the country was required by decree to see it. Ordinarily, David would have deeply resented being forced to sit through such propagandistic trash. But tonight he was with Karen, and that made it all right.

The two stood in line for their tickets. There was a good turnout: many people in the town had been putting off seeing the film, but now the deadline was drawing near. No one wanted to experience the wrath of their conquerors over something as meaningless as a movie.

"These Hollywood bastards!" the man ahead of them whispered to his wife. "It's too bad the bomb didn't get all of them!"

"Howard, shhhh! Do you want the Russians to hear?"

"They can't hear me. They're too busy doing other things. Really! I wish all of these movie people had been sleeping in their beds when the bomb went off. The damned traitors! They're happy as hell working with the Russians! They'll do anything to keep their mansions and their Mercedes! Even if it means turning against their own people!"

Most of the motion picture industry had been destroyed when Los Angeles was obliterated. But a substantial number of key people had been out of town at the time. Some of these had bravely refused to collaborate with the Russians entirely, and had paid the ultimate price. Others had set up another motion picture center near Miami, and were cranking out propaganda potboilers at the behest of their new masters. But the man in line was right: many were willing participants. The destruction of what they had always seen as an immoral system, capitalist America, and its replacement by a coercive state premised on the value of altruism, was just what some had longed for.

The vast majority of them had never thought the issues through. They were incapable of anything so intellectually rigorous. They were philosophical ignoramuses who just "felt" that self-sacrifice was the right thing to do. They "felt" that the United States was evil, and should be taken down a peg or two, made subservient to someone or something, anyone or anything: the United Nations, a

Global Government, Vladimir Drugonov, it didn't much matter. Prior to the Conquest, many had spent years, decades, posing as experts on this subject or that, using their high profiles to preach their vacuous hatred and opposition to anything American. Now, they "felt" comfortable, at least ideologically.

Their cocaine-induced political hallucination had become reality. They expected to do well under the new regime. After all, were they not precisely the kind of "useful idiots" for whom Lenin had jokingly given thanks? Surely they would be rewarded by this new totalitarian! The Russians' perpetual need for propaganda would assure them a continuation of the elite lifestyle they had come to take for granted. Altruism, self-sacrifice, was all well and good, as long as they were not the ones who were expected to sacrifice themselves. Heaven forbid they should be expected to reduce their consumption of Beluga and Bordeaux! The thickness of this hypocrisy had not escaped the American people. Collaborationist film makers and actors rarely ventured out in public. Several had been assassinated. They could indeed keep their mansions and their Mercedes. But their mansions had become prisons, and their Mercedes stayed in the garage.

After Karen and David had bought their tickets, they were confronted by a Russian corporal with a clipboard.

"Names!" he demanded in heavily-accented English.

Karen gave him hers, but David was not sure what to do. He experienced a wave of anxiety as he realized the danger in which he had placed himself. But it was too late now. He could not run away. The only thing he could think of was to give a false name. The first one that popped into his head was that of his second grade teacher.

"Douglas," he said. "Douglas....Randolph."

The Russian wrote it down and motioned with his head to the entrance. David relaxed a bit. Maybe he had overreacted. Maybe there was nothing to worry about after all. Few in the theater that night were aware of it, but the film they were watching closely resembled the creations of the Stalinist era: it was full of happy, singing industrial and farm workers, including children. One scene showed an American female farm worker giving a basket of vegetables to a Russian officer, and then happily kissing his hand.

The movie's plot involved a man who, at first, does his work grudgingly. He is very unhappy. He yells at his children and threatens his wife. Then, his wife convinces him to see a film in which he discovers how wonderful the Russian people are, how worthy they are of his sacrifices. He experiences an epiphany. Now, he finds joy in his work. The closing scene shows the man and his family purposefully striding into the gates of a factory, singing the movie's theme song, "My Life is to Serve."

"My life is to serve!"

"There is no I!"

"There is only you!"

"You, the great people of Russia!"

A chorus joins them as a rising sun bathes the factory entrance in golden light. There is no applause, no reaction at all as the theater's patrons watch the credits rolling, as they are required to do. When the house lights finally come up, everyone at last feels free to get out of their seats. David smiles at Karen and they both roll their eyes at each other. It is all they can do to keep from laughing.

The night air is refreshing as the two leave the theater, arm in arm. David hardly takes notice of the two Russian soldiers flanking the exit. In a second's time they have him, one on each side, hammer-locking his arms behind his back. He looks into each of the two expressionless faces as a sick-anxious feeling sweeps over him. An officer approaches. "So, Mr. Randolph! I wonder why it is that your name does not appear on our records for the inhabitants of this town? Who could you be?"

He moved so that his face almost touched David's. The Lieutenant smiles, David can smell his cologne.

"I can assure you, we will soon know the answer to that question!"

Trace Forester trained his binoculars onto the main square of the town from his vantage point on the nearby ridge. George Luttrell, his second in command, was at his right elbow. He too was peering through glasses into the town. The place was crawling with Russians; an entire company had moved in during the night. Two platoons from Trace's short-handed battalion were strung out along the ridge line, awaiting orders.

Trace had been awakened during the night with the news that his son had been apprehended in town. Naturally, his first thought was to rescue him. But how to do it without jeopardizing his command? The Russians knew the militia was in the area, but had so far had no luck in pinpointing them. If David had talked, if he had told them who his father was, this could be a trap: his son was being used as bait to draw him out. Or David could have told the Russians the camp's location, in which case they might already be on their way here; the camp could be hit at any minute. He had to move his people immediately. It took until well past dawn to gather together their supplies and munitions and transport everything across the valley. This was their sixth move in four months, so everyone knew exactly what to do. The operation went smoothly. Now he had the luxury of worrying about his son.

Trace was eleven hundred yards from the square. The figures moving about were like insects to the unaided eye. It was easy to feel detached from them and their fate. They seemed no more important than ants crawling on an anthill. Russians. Americans. They all looked the same from here. Only through the lenses of a glass did they assume human form. Only then did they become real.

Trace had to blink his eyes, to arouse himself to the realities of the moment. He had to remind himself that this was not all some kind of surreal dream. One of those seemingly-irrelevant specks was his son: his flesh and blood.

"There he is, Trace!" Captain Luttrell said. "They're leading him out into the square now."

George was right. Through the glass, Trace recognized David. He moved slowly, haltingly, dragging his right leg. His left arm hung down at an odd angle, as if it were broken. Trace could not see the welts on his face, shoulders and back, where the rubber truncheons had cracked into his flesh. Trace also could not see the blood on the front of David's pants. The Russians had inserted a glass rod into David's penis, and, when he would still not give them the information they sought, they had broken that rod with a rubber hammer, slowly, so slowly, one blow at a time.

"Get in line! All of you!" the Russian captain shouted.

The Americans, most of them uninjured but very frightened, hastened to obey. There were twenty-six of them. The mayor was there, as was the police chief. Several members of the town council were also there. The rest were made up of the town's most prosperous merchants. They were the pillars of the community. And then there was David.

"I will give you one last chance to tell me the truth! Where is the militia?! I know that you are concealing their location! I know that they are within twenty miles of this very spot! Tell me now, or you will all die!"

The Mayor burst out crying. Alice Hubbard, who ran the Clean-Spot Laundromat, looked at him disgustedly and poked him in the ribs with her elbow. Others, men and women, were trembling visibly. The Russian decided to change his tactics.

"There is no need for this," he said in a conciliatory tone. "Do you think I want this? But I am under orders. Please understand. I have no choice in the matter. If one of you, just one of you, will tell me where the militia camp is located, you can all go free! You see, how easy it is? No one must die!"

He looked hopefully down the row of faces.

"Please, do yourselves a favor! Just a few sentences, and you will all live long and happy lives!"

Ed Cox, the owner of the hardware store, said in a voice breaking with terror, "Don't you think we'd tell you if we knew? All we know is that they're out there somewhere! They move around! There's no way to tell!"

Scores of townspeople had formed a crowd well behind the Russians. They watched this spectacle quietly, in an almost detached manner. Many were intensely angry, but they did not let it show. Some felt ashamed. The able-bodied among them had had many opportunities to join the resistance. Some had, of course, but not very many. Of all the problems faced by the American militia, this was one of the most serious: the free-rider problem.

If one quarter of the men and women who were able actually participated in the militia, the Russians would be finished in a month. All Americans wanted their liberty back, but many were looking to others to accomplish it for them. No one doubted their patriotism, or even their bravery. It was just that they had not been sufficiently motivated. Why should they participate, why should they risk their lives, give up their property, when they could benefit from the actions of others?

Trace, and a hundred other militia commanders around the country, dealt with this problem on a daily basis. Each asked himself over and over what he could do to attract, to goad, to coerce his fellows to join them. This town was a perfect example. There were three hundred men in town who would have made valuable additions to the militia. But their lives were still reasonably comfortable; the invasion had seemed too distant to be real. They were small-town people who had lived here all their lives. And their town hadn't changed too much, not really. Life was going on more or less normally. Why should they risk their lives? Why should they upset the rhythm of their existence that they all loved so much? Let the others fight, if they so chose. Maybe if things got a lot worse, then they'd join. But for now, there were chores to do, fences to mend, work to be done. They had yet to feel the hot breath of tyranny in their faces; they had never dealt with the inescapable reality of a cold, steel bayonet. Until now.

Russian soldiers began to form in a rank ten yards in front of the Americans. They prepared their rifles. It was obvious what was going to happen.

"Trace! Let's go! We can save them! Order an attack! There's still time! They outnumber us, but at least we can make them head for cover! We can stop the execution!" George urged.

Trace held up his hand, as if to silence the captain.

"No," he said in an icy voice. "It's time this town learned a lesson."

"But Trace, that's your own son down there!"

His voice like death itself, Trace said, "I know."

Both platoons watched as the ant-like Russians raised their tiny rifles to their minuscule shoulders. For a moment, nothing happened. Then the insect-men were seen to recoil slightly. The other insects standing in front of them crumpled into motionless specks in the middle of the street. In a few seconds a muted staccato crackling reached the ears of the Americans on the ridge.

George didn't even want to look at his friend and commander. What had just happened seemed inconceivable. But he could not help himself. What he saw, he would never forget. For the rest of his life, when strength was demanded of him that seemed beyond his ability to provide, he would remember the face of Trace Forester on this day.

The Russians had gone. Trace, George Luttrell and five members of the First Platoon entered the town and approached the square. It was crowded with people; virtually everyone who lived in the area was there. Many were crying, some were cursing, and others just stared at the twenty-six corpses in the street. Trace walked down the line of bodies until he came to David's.

"George, bring David out with us when we leave. I want to bury him in the forest. By God George, the boy never talked." Luttrell just nodded.

Trace looked around himself. They were just average Americans. They wore American clothes and American hats. But if one looked closely, one could see a very un-American look in their eyes: the look of hunted animals. As he moved from face to face, Trace was reminded of old black and white war photos of European refugees: timid, fearful, wanting nothing more than to climb into a hole in the ground, away from prying eyes, away from the bombs and the bullets, wanting nothing more than to be left alone, to be safe. Here was the shock that had been missing. This was the frame of mind he had been waiting for. He climbed over the rear bumper of a pickup truck and stood in its bed, looking down at the whimpering crowd before him.

"Listen to me, all of you! My name is Major Trace Forester. I am the commander of the militia camp in this area."

He had never been in the town before, and was totally unknown to its inhabitants.

A man not far away shouted, "You! It was you they wanted! All of these people died because of you!"

"No," Trace answered. "All of these people died because of you, all of you! They died because you failed to resist! They died because you chose to acquiesce in your own enslavement! They died because you preferred to live your lives as you have always known them, instead of facing the rigors of the struggle to be free! These people paid the price of all those who, at the critical moment, failed to stand up and shout, 'I will not be a slave! I am a free man!'

"History is full of examples of those who were too timid to proclaim their own status as free people! How much better off they would have been to have died on their feet, defending their liberty, rather than spending a lifetime on their knees! History is full of examples of those who have chosen the safe, comfortable path when faced with tyranny instead of risking their lives in the name of freedom. Those people have always lived to regret their decision! When the iron boot of their oppressor grinds them into the dust, their last thought is that they should have fought when they had the chance!

"In the years before the Conquest, we were all guilty of standing by while our liberty slipped away. We let it be taken from us bit by bit, in the name of 'fairness', 'social order', or simply because we didn't want to be called 'mean spirited'. Those of us who complained among ourselves were waiting for some great turning-point, some event that we could point to as the definitive moment at which we should stand and fight. But that moment never came. They never do. Liberty drains away slowly, like water from a leaking bucket, one drop at a time. To paraphrase the poet, our liberty disappeared not with a bang, but with a whimper. The Conquest was simply the logical culmination of our own lack of resolve. We reaped what we had sown.

"Yes," he continued. "It was we they wanted. And if you could have, would you have given us to them? Would you have revealed our position, ended our resistance, to save the lives of these people?"

He looked around, waiting for a response. There was only the occasional scuffing of boots on concrete. There were, however, some accusing eyes. Trace took notice.

"What kind of people are you? What kind of people let their homes be invaded, their town taken over; their fellow-citizens murdered, and then blame the men and women who are fighting for their freedom? Do you realize what's at stake here? Do you realize what you're becoming? Your country has been conquered! You are not ranchers, you are not farmers, you are not merchants! You are slaves! Slaves of the Russian Empire!

"You seem to think that you can carry on with business as usual! There is no business as usual! You seem to think that this unpleasantness will go away by itself! Nothing will go away by itself! You must end it, with your sweat and, if need be, with your blood! Nothing matters but your liberty, the liberty of your children, and of their children after them! For months we have been recruiting in this area, and not one in ten of you has volunteered! Don't bother telling me your excuses! Tell it to them!"

He pointed to the row of bodies, his finger shaking with emotion.

"Explain to them why you don't think that your, and their, liberty is worth fighting for! Explain to them why you were not willing to defend their lives when they needed it most! And which of you will it be next? How many more of you will the Russians kill because you just can't be bothered to fight for your own freedom?

"I offer you today a chance of redemption. Come with us! Join us! Fight for your liberty as your ancestors before you have done! You have seen the result of doing nothing, here, today, in this square! Stand up like free men and women! Defend your homes! Defend your country! How many of you are with me?"

Scores of hands shot up. People babbled excitedly among themselves.

"We're with you, Major!" shouted one man.

Others shook their heads in agreement.

"Thank you," said Trace, nodding to the chagrined but rejuvenated crowd. He raised his hands for silence.

"There is one last thing I have to say. To those of you who are still undecided, I will quote Samuel Adams, one of the founders of this country. He once said, exhorting his countrymen to resistance in seventeen seventy-six, '*If ye love wealth better than liberty, the tranquility of servitude better than the animating contest of freedom, go home from us in peace. We ask not your councils or arms. Crouch down and lick the hands which feed you. May your chains set lightly upon you, and may posterity forget that ye were our countrymen.*'"

CHAPTER THIRTY-EIGHT

He checked his hair in the small pocket mirror he always carried. It had been sprayed firmly into place before he left the studio. But there was always the possibility that a strand or two had fallen out of place. He grinned in an exaggerated manner into the glass, moving his head from side to side, looking at his teeth. White, straight, and perfect, as always. At last satisfied, he sat straight up in the chair and felt for the knot in his tie, to make sure it was centered properly. He made a few minute adjustments.

How dare they keep him waiting! He, Charles Frost, America's top-rated television anchorman, winner of numerous prestigious awards, the man to whom millions looked for their nightly news, one of the most trusted men in America, according to the polls! He was not one to be kept waiting in some anteroom like any lackey! Didn't they know how much money he made? Didn't they know how influential he was? Why, he could walk into any restaurant in New York and get the best table in the house with a simple snap of his fingers! This was intolerable! He would have to have a few words with Mr. Drugonov, that was all there was to it!

Drugonov had the political power, that was true, but so what? He, Charles Frost, had dealt with kings, presidents and emperors for decades! He was on a first name basis with the most powerful people in the world! Drugonov may have political power, but he, Charles Frost, had an even greater power: persuasion. He could make or break politicians; he had done it a hundred times! Who persuaded the American people to vote for that clown Benedict? He had! He could convince the American people that up was down, black was white, and that the sun rose in the west. He had been doing it for years! He could lead those sheep off a cliff if he wanted! Drugonov had better not forget that!

The door to the inner office opened, and a Russian colonel walked out.

"Mr. Frost. The Maximum Leader will see you now."

How kind of him, Charles Frost thought as he rose and walked toward the open door. Drugonov was seated behind his desk. He did not even look up from his paperwork as Frost entered. He said simply, "Sit."

Charles Frost raised his chin in indignation, and clasped his hands behind his back. The impudence of this man! Now was the time to put him in his place! Quite literally looking down his nose at Drugonov, he said, "I would prefer to stand. I'm sure this won't take long. I have work to do. At the studio."

He pronounced that last word slowly and with emphasis, as if it were intended to awe the person who was fortunate enough to hear it from such distinguished lips. Drugonov smiled, still without looking up, and placed his pen carefully onto the papers he had been reading. Then he lifted his head, just slightly, and looked at the man standing before him. He raised his eyebrows at Frost, and gave him the kind of wicked little grin that a small boy might give to someone who was about to be the recipient of a practical joke.

"Charles Frost!" he said, standing and then slowly walking around the end of the desk. He continued to smile. "America's conscience! The most influential man in the country! No, on the continent! No, perhaps in the world!"

He raised his left index finger in emphasis. Charles Frost turned slightly to face him. A smile came across his face. This Drugonov might understand his true importance after all. Charles Frost replied in the oleaginous, dulcet tones that had thrilled millions from coast to coast for twenty-six years.

"Yes, Drugonov. And I must say that I don't appreciate being kept waiting..."

Drugonov's right fist shot outward into Frost's solar plexus. He threw the punch with the skill and power of a well-trained boxer, pushing off with the ball of his right foot and putting his entire weight into the effort. Frost crumpled to the floor like a discarded tissue. He lay there in a fetal position, legs twitching spasmodically, mouth wide open, gasping for breath like a dying fish. Drugonov looked down at the man, eyebrows raised once again, the sly, boyish grin returning to his face. He kneeled down and grasped Frost's cheeks in his left hand, squeezing them hard until his mouth formed no more than a vertical slit, turning the man's head so that he could look into his eyes. They were wild with panic.

"I may have just killed you, Charles Frost. Some men do not recover from such a blow. If you do not begin breathing within the next several minutes, your brain will begin to die. Imagine that! Such a quick, glib, investigative brain! Slowly dying, cell by cell, losing its power, losing its functions one by one, until you are nothing more than a piece of meat, with no more brains than...than....a hamburger!"

He burst into laughter. "I made a joke, Charles Frost! Ah, but you are not laughing."

Drugonov sat on the floor beside Frost, clasping his knees with his arms. He patted him gently on the shoulder.

"There, there, my friend. It is all right to die. We all must, you know. But how ignominious it would be for a man of your stature to die on the office floor of a barbarian such as me!"

Drugonov sniffed the air, and wrinkled his nose. "My goodness, Charles Frost! Have you soiled yourself? How ignoble of you! Well, I suppose that when one must go, one must go!"

At last Frost inhaled loudly. He breathed in and out rapidly and deeply, replenishing the oxygen in his blood.

"There you are! You see? You're none the worse for wear!" Drugonov said cheerfully.

He stood, and waited for Frost to do the same. Eventually, the man came to his knees, and then shakily to his feet. Still panting, he stared at Drugonov, abject fear in his eyes. Drugonov resumed his seat behind the desk.

"Now tell me something, Charles Frost. Have you been doing all you can to smooth the way for my administration? You have a great deal of power at your fingertips, a great deal of influence. But I have gotten the impression that you are not one hundred percent behind the Occupation. Convince me that I am wrong."

Frost replied unevenly, haltingly, his breath coming to him in short gasps.

"I can assure you, Dru–, Maximum Leader...that I have done everything.. that I know...to persuade the American...people...of the righteousness...of your cause!"

Frost bent over, hands on knees, feeling he may vomit. He trembled, so weak it took all of his effort to stand. The room before him was dark: tunnel vision, lack of oxygen to the brain. He tried to continue.

"Of our cause.... Because....it is our cause.... you know. Like you....I have always hated....this country! I have always hated....what it stood for! I became a journalist....to bring it down.... to change the world....for the better!"

Frost's legs buckled, but he was able to recover before he fell to the floor.

"Maximum Leader.....may I sit down now?"

"I'm afraid not, Charles Frost. Your opportunity for that has passed. You chose to stand, and stand you will. In fact, I find such a request at this point disappointing. I respect strength above all else, strength of all kinds. How can a man who does not have the strength and determination to stand before me after only one blow have the strength to be my principal mouthpiece in the destruction of his own country? How can I trust such a man to be truly committed, to obey orders no matter how difficult they may be? Your physical weakness reveals an intellectual weakness, a weakness in character, a lack of toughness in body and mind. It tells me that you have never been truly tested, tempered in life's fires. You have never been forced to overcome adversity. You have led a soft life. Perhaps I expect too much from you, Charles Frost. Perhaps you should be replaced by someone with more...fortitude."

Drugonov's reference to him as a 'mouthpiece' stung what was left of Frost's pride. But what he was hearing terrified him. Replaced? Thoughts of losing his penthouse apartment, his Ferrari, his privileged access to the best food and medical care raced through his mind. He saw himself on the street, cold, hungry, like the millions of other nameless, faceless riffraff in this city.

He had never given any of these human dregs a second glance, and now he was facing the prospect of becoming one of them! It was unthinkable! He had to salvage himself, quickly and convincingly. He forced himself into an erect posture, almost at attention. He wiped the grimace of pain from his face, and concentrated on breathing–and speaking–evenly.

"Maximum Leader, I assure you that you can place your trust in me. You will never find anyone better suited to your purposes. I have always been one of the anointed, of the elite, one of those with a true, clear vision of where this country should go, of what it should do. You are now the arbiter of this country's direction, and I swear I will be as effective in achieving your goals as I have always been in achieving the goals of my fellow elite. In the end, we are all collectivists. We all espouse altruism. Only the details have changed.

"For years I have used my talents to convince the American people that the old concern for the rights of the individual is bankrupt! I have taught them the value of sacrifice: to sacrifice themselves, and to expect sacrifice from others! Never has that goal left my mind! Most of my colleagues feel the same! Every time a champion of individualism has risen in this country, we have derided him, ridiculed him, belittled him, if not actively, then by omission! I have contributed–in no small way, I can assure you–to the making or breaking of scores of politicians, who either agreed with my vision or did not. Believe me, Maximum Leader, I can be trusted!"

"All right, Charles Frost. I am in a good mood today. You will not, at least for now, be forced to join the plebeian horde." Drugonov smiled. "That is what terrifies you, isn't it Charles Frost? That is the sword I will hold over your head. You fear it more than a bullet! Imagine, the great Charles Frost, rummaging through a garbage can looking for scraps of dog meat; or chasing a rat down an alley with a stick, hoping to kill it and eat it raw before someone stronger comes along and takes it from you! That is the stuff of nightmares, is it not, Charles Frost? It can all be avoided–if you do your job. I will give you one last chance to prove your loyalty to me. Convince the people to turn against the militia! Be relentless! Hammer away at them! I want the militia destroyed within a month, and, if you do not do your part to help me achieve that, there will be hell to pay."

Drugonov smiled his wicked, mischievous little smile and stared into Frost's eyes, the boyish twinkle returning. "I wonder if it is possible to make a thermidor with rat instead of lobster? What do you think, Charles Frost?"

Frost was breaking down. As much as he tried to retain his composure, he trembled visibly.

"Trust me, Maximum Leader. I will convince them! I have always convinced them! I will not fail you!"

He began to back away toward the door. Several large stools fell from the cuffs of his trousers onto the carpet. Both men looked down at them.

"Don't forget to take those with you," Drugonov said pleasantly.

"You don't mean that I should..."

"Yes, yes! Pick them up! Take them with you!"

Charles Frost hesitated for an instant, then knelt down, and with both hands grasped the feces. He stood, a bewildered, lost look on his face. He held his hands in front of himself, and looked at his own waste with wide eyes.

"That's it!" Drugonov said. "The colonel will see you out. That is all."

CHAPTER THIRTY-NINE

Rose and Anthony D'Lucca had been living in the same house in Paramus, New Jersey for thirty-nine years. The house was nothing special, but Rose had always loved it. It was where they had raised their children, where they had invested most of their lives. It was their place. She stood at the kitchen sink, finishing the dishes. It would never have occurred to Rose that she should have a dishwashing machine; she was a plain, hardworking woman who complained about very little. To her mind, she had everything any woman could want. Rarely did thoughts of her family leave her mind.

She glanced out the window above the sink, and smiled as she watched her Tony puttering around his tank-truck, checking hydraulic lines and tires. Tony had been a truck driver all these years. He had always provided a good living for his family; he had always put plenty of good food on the table. He had always been a kind and gentle man, and a loving father. To Rose, he walked on water.

The last dish was rinsed and carefully placed into the wire rack next to the sink. Rose dried her hands on the towel. She turned and examined the rest of the kitchen. With a practiced eye, she looked for anything that might be out of place, for any dust in the corners or smudges on the table. There were none. She was very fussy about cleanliness, and it showed. The entire house was immaculate. Tony liked it that way.

On the wall was a large photograph of the entire family. As always, she smiled as she looked at it. There was Tony Jr., a big, strapping man who lived only a few blocks away with his own family. There were his wife, Teresa, and their two children, Bruce and Carol. Her heart swelled as she looked at her grandchildren. She was so proud of them. Her daughter Amanda was there with her husband and three children.

Then there was her other daughter, Christina. She was not married yet, and that fact had worried Rose. But three months ago she had become engaged to a very nice boy from Englewood Cliffs, and that made Rose feel better. Her family was doing well, as well as any mother could hope for. Rose just wished that the old times would come back; everybody was suffering so under this occupation. She and Tony had not been able to invite them over for dinner in more than a month. There was so little to eat. She knew what her children were going through to provide for their own families, and it made her sad.

The door opened, and her husband entered. The sadness left her as she looked at him. He was past his prime now: he had lost most of his once-magnificent hair, and had a bit of a pot belly. But in his day he had been a very handsome man.

Many times Rose had felt pangs of anger and jealousy as she noticed other women casting glances in his direction. When that happened, she had always taken Tony's hand and gripped it tightly, or put her arm around his waist, as if to hold him to her. But that had never been necessary. Tony had always been completely faithful.

He smiled at her. It was the same smile that she had seen on their first date, so many years ago. He walked to the sink, picked up a bar of pumice soap, and washed the dirt and oil from his hands. Turning to her, still smiling, he put his hands around her ample waist. Pulling her to him, he kissed her on the cheek and buried his face in her neck.

"Well, what's this all about!" she said, almost giggling.

He said nothing for a second. Then, "I just want you to know how much I love you."

She stroked the back of his head.

"My Tony. Don't you think I know that after forty-one years? I love you too, darling."

He pulled away slowly, walked out of the kitchen and into the living room. Rose followed.

"Tony, don't you have to make a delivery today?" she asked.

He answered in an almost absent-minded fashion, "Yes. I have one more run to make."

Tony sat down in his favorite chair: a big, red, overstuffed thing that Rose would like to have gotten rid of years ago. But Tony loved it. He had watched lots of football games from it over the years, had spent uncounted hours in it laughing with friends and family. Some of her fondest memories were of him sitting right there tickling his grandchildren as they sat on his lap, squealing with delight.

"Rose, would you mind getting me a drink?"

She looked at him out of the corners of her eyes. It was only ten o'clock in the morning. He never, absolutely never, drank during the day.

"Sure Tony," she answered. "Would you like a glass of wine? We still have a little of that nice Chianti that you like so much."

"No. No, I think I'll have a whisky."

Now she was worried.

"Tony, what's wrong? This isn't like you."

"It's nothing, honey. My nerves are just a little on edge, that's all. You know how it is."

Slowly she went to the sideboard and poured him a shot of bourbon. She handed it to him, and sat in the other chair across from her man.

"Is there something bothering you, something that you'd like to talk about? You know you can tell me anything."

He smiled at her again, a slightly sad expression on his face.

"Rose, I wish we had more. I wish I'd been a better provider."

"What are you talking about? You've been a great provider! We've never wanted for anything in our lives!"

"I know. But look at what we've really got. Our savings are gone; the money is worthless. My life insurance isn't worth the paper it's printed on. We've got this house, and the car, and that's about it. I wish I had more to leave to you and the kids."

"The kids are doing fine! And don't worry about me. As long as I've got a roof over my head, I'll be all right. Why are you talking like this, Tony? You're not sick, are you? My God, you're sick, and you haven't told me! What is it Tony? What's wrong with you?"

He chuckled a bit.

"No. I'm not sick. I was just thinking, you know, with the way things are and all, nothing's for sure any more."

She was not used to hearing Tony talk like this. It unnerved her. She got up, crossed the floor that separated them, and knelt down in front of him, placing her hands on his knees. Their eyes met.

"Don't worry about a thing, Tony. We'll be fine. Something will happen soon. It has to. Things are bound to change for the better. We've gone through rough times before. Remember, when we were first married, we lived in that tiny cold-water railroad flat? Remember the neighbors downstairs, and the noise they used to make? Compared to that, this isn't so bad. We'll get by, Tony. Don't worry."

Tony looked down at his wife.

"You're a strong woman, Rose. You're a good woman. No man could ever ask for a better wife than you've been. I'm the luckiest man in New Jersey."

That was one of his favorite expressions, and she smiled on hearing it. He patted her hands, and began to stand up.

"I guess I'd better make that run now."

She watched as her man walked down the sidewalk toward the big, shiny tank-truck. Slowly, he climbed into the cab. In a few seconds, she heard a familiar rumbling and saw the first puffs of diesel exhaust erupt from the stacks. She had better get dinner started.

Tomatoes were almost impossible to get, but she had traded an old silver necklace for a bag-full. Also, she had some of the soy that everyone was using instead of meat. She would make Tony's favorite dish: spaghetti and meatballs with her own special sauce. He always said that she made the best sauce in the world. But good sauce took time. She reached under the counter for her big pot. Who was going to get this delivery of gasoline, she wondered? Tony had not said.

Anthony D'Lucca shifted into high gear as he entered the Palisades Parkway. Before the Occupation, it had been illegal to drive commercial vehicles on this highway. But now no one cared about that. He drove at a steady fifty miles per hour toward the George Washington Bridge. He glanced at his watch. Timing was critical. Yes, he decided. He should be right on the button.

Tony had never thought of himself as a hero. Neither had anyone else, with the possible exception of his family members. He had always just wanted to lead a quiet, comfortable life, surrounded by the people he loved. But the Russians had made that impossible. They had ruined everything. They had conquered the country that he loved more than life itself.

He could remember, when he was a little boy, his grandfather would put his arm around him and tell him in his broken English how important it was to live in the United States. His grandfather would tell him stories about the Old Country, about how hard life had been, about the hopelessness that hung over the people like a shroud. Then he would talk about coming here, about the fears of being in a new place, an alien place; about the excitement of passing through Ellis Island, of seeing the majesty of the New York skyline for the first time; about feeling the seething pulse of its life's blood on the streets. His grandfather had told him never to forget how lucky he was to have been born in this country. He never had.

Tony was not a highly educated man. He didn't know much about political philosophy. But he had read the Constitution. He and Rose had visited Mount Vernon and Monticello on vacation a few years ago. They had also been to the Gettysburg Battlefield, and had seen the places where thousands of men, on both sides, had fought and died for what they believed in. And he knew the difference between freedom and slavery. He knew that this country had given him a lot, and now it was time for him to give something back.

The bridge was only a mile ahead. There was a slight haze in the air, and the city of New York ahead of him looked grey and misty. Traffic was nonexistent. In fact, he had not seen a car coming in the opposite direction since he entered the Parkway. That was good. He wouldn't want any innocent bystanders to get hurt.

Captain Mikhail Zhilinski stood on the front of his tank, the first in the column. With a critical eye, he examined the line of machines behind him, an entire company of iron behemoths, massive, unstoppable. He was very proud.

He had been ordered into New Jersey. It seemed that an urban militia in Newark was creating problems. A considerable number of soldiers had been killed, including several officers. No one had been able to find these people. They seemed to melt away like snow in the spring. They fired their weapons from rooftops, from alleys, from passing vehicles. And when the Russians tried to pursue them, they disappeared like ghosts.

It was obvious that the community was harboring them. And for that, they would have to be punished. He would teach them a lesson they would never forget. His company would flatten their homes, destroy their neighborhoods, crush their bodies under its treads. Never again would they dare to rise up against the Russian Empire!

This was to be his first actual combat operation. Since the invasion, he had been assigned to occupation duty, which really amounted to nothing more than making one's presence felt. His tanks had been placed in strategic positions around the city, more to intimidate than anything else. He, too, had lost people. New York was not without its snipers: cowards who killed his men from their million-and-one hiding places in that concrete jungle.

At first his people had reveled in their status as conquerors, looting at will, taking women whenever they liked. Now they kept their heads down; now they stayed safe within their steel cocoons, safe from an enemy they could never see, but who was always there. The captain climbed into his tank, picked up the radio microphone, and ordered his column forward. With a jolting surge the machines began to move out.

There was a break in the median, to allow police and other service vehicles to turn around on the Parkway. Tony used it to move into the northbound lane, although he was driving south. He accelerated through the final turn toward the bridge entrance. As he passed the toll booth, entering the bridge in the wrong lane, the attendant screamed at him and waved his arms, assuming that Tony did not know what he was doing.

Captain Zhilinski stood with his head and shoulders above the tank's hatch. It was a beautiful sight, this New York. And what a magnificent bridge! Ahead of him, the pavement stretched across the Hudson River. He was enjoying himself immensely. Never had he felt so powerful, so fulfilled! As he looked ahead, something caught his eye. There was a vehicle on the bridge, and it was in his lane. But that was impossible. Nothing had entered the bridge westbound ahead of his tanks. He peered at it intently. As he watched, it slowly grew larger. He could see now that it was traveling very quickly. And it was coming right for him.

Anthony D'Lucca shifted through the gears. His truck's big engine howled. He was pushing it to the limit. Ahead of him he could see the first tank. He knew that behind it were many more. Behind him, in the big stainless-steel tank, thousands of gallons of gasoline were about to be put to use.

Zhilinski felt a surge of adrenalin course through his veins. This madman! This damned American! He was threatening his command! Only a few hundred yards separated them now. He ducked his head into the tank.

"All stop! Load the cannon! Quickly! Blow that truck off the bridge! Hurry, man!"

The gun crew scrambled madly to obey his orders. They threw the breech of the big weapon open, and reached for one of the huge brass-cased shells. But Zhilinski knew that it would not be in time. A strange sense of peace came over him as he once again raised himself above the tank's hatch. As the truck grew closer, he could see Tony's face, he could even, for an instant, look into his eyes. He saw a look of hate and determination. But he saw no fear.

When the truck hit the lead tank, it was traveling at more than seventy miles per hour. Tony, not wearing a seatbelt, was thrown through the windshield. Almost instantaneously, the big tank ruptured, sending a wave of the volatile fluid washing over Zhilinski's tank. When it hit the hot exhaust stacks of the machine, it ignited. Now it was a wall of fire. The gasoline wave moved down the line of tanks, engulfing one after another.

Several of them, further down the line, tried to avoid the conflagration. They turned hard right and gunned their engines. They drove through the retaining wall of the bridge and plunged slowly, majestically, into the river below. Perhaps they were the luckiest of all. For the rest, death came hard. Nine tanks were incinerated, the men inside them reduced to charred skeletons. The mission to Newark would never take place, and the New Jersey militia would be left intact, to continue its guerilla war.

The people of the area would never learn Tony's name. Those who happened to be looking in the direction of the bridge would see the ball of fire in its center, but it would be days until they learned what had happened. They would take heart from the event; they would know that one of their own had died to regain their freedom. Tony's death would serve to make hundreds of thousands of men and women stronger, to intensify their will to resist, to give them hope. Tony D'Lucca was a pretty good provider after all.

CHAPTER FORTY

Steven and Katherine met when they were both teaching part-time at El Paso Community College in far-west Texas. There had been an immediate physical attraction, but both were mature, actually middle-aged, almost painfully practical people. They were past the stage at which their hormones dictated their actions. Over time, however, each began to see the other as a practical, stable potential mate. Both had spent their early years pursuing academic goals, and had had neither the time nor the inclination for romantic involvement. But they had reached that portion of their lives when choosing a partner to share what years remained to them seemed, well.... practical.

Katherine had come from a farming family in the upper Midwest, but since moving to El Paso had always chosen to live in a tiny, cheap apartment. Her paltry salary as an adjunct instructor had seemingly left her little choice. Steven, however, had chosen a different route. Unlike Katherine, all his life he had lived in apartments: cramped, noisy, and always belonging to someone else. His father had done the same all of his life, as had his father before him. Steven had seen his father's near-panic as his retirement years approached and the realization finally crashed down upon him that he had nothing to show for forty years of work except a few sticks of furniture. Even his car had always been owned by his company.

Since childhood, Steven had seen his father as short-sighted, indecisive and somewhat cowardly. What kind of man would forever be satisfied with living under someone else's roof, with cravenly conforming to often unbelievably arbitrary rules laid down by a stranger holding the medieval title of "landlord"? What man, possessing a shred of common sense, would willingly throw his money away month after month, year after year, paying off someone else's mortgage and with nothing to show for it himself? In the center of a large city it was understandable. There was no option. But in the suburban, semi-rural areas in which Steven had grown up, there were parcels of land and houses galore. Perhaps more than anything else, young Steven had resented his early apartment-dwelling because he had never been allowed to have a dog.

As an only child, he had wanted the companionship of a dog so badly that he could taste it. Now, as an adult, albeit a poor one, he was determined that he would not share the same unproductive, frustrating, constricted fate his father had inexplicably chosen. It was unavoidable that he should take an apartment upon first arriving in town, but he swore that at his first opportunity, he would purchase a piece of land that would become his own.

One day while driving through the lonely desert east of the city, he saw a billboard offering one acre lots for one-hundred-sixty dollars down and forty-nine dollars a month. Here was something that even someone working at the fringes of academia could afford. The land was desolate and totally unimproved, it was true: nothing more than a tiny patch of desert scrub in the midst of an infinitude of desert scrub. But it was land, an actual piece of the earth: one-hundred ninety-six by two hundred twenty one feet on a side. He could get down on his knees on this land, and take it into his hands, and wonder at his ownership of it. The very thought seemed miraculous. No one in his family in at least three generations had owned so much as a single square inch of land. And now, after a mere one-hundred twenty of those forty-nine dollar payments, he would be the first.

`He could afford only a very small travel trailer in which to live, the kind that fits into the bed of a pickup truck. It was only thirteen feet long, with no indoor plumbing or running water. It was very old, and had been used hard for many years. In the wintertime the frigid west-Texas wind would howl through it almost unimpeded. He lived on his land for the first five and a half years with no electricity. He read and prepared his lectures by the light of a kerosene lamp. He shit in the desert like a coyote, and carried his water in five-gallon plastic containers that he would fill at a sympathetic gas station. And all this time, all these years, he was teaching students: hundreds of them. Occasionally one would refer to him as "Professor." He found that amusing. If only they knew.

Amidst this rather depressing scene, a long-sought after light came into Steven's life. He finally got a dog. One day after class, shortly after purchasing the land, he was struck with an overpowering urge to find some living creature with which to share his life. There were no landlords to deal with now. He drove to the local animal shelter, and walked down the concrete sidewalk surrounded by cages filled with dogs. Some were obviously terrified, and tried to claw through the chain-link fence to reach him.

"Take me home with you!" they cried as clearly as if they had spoken the words in English. His heart almost broke as he looked at them. Then he came to a cage containing only two puppies. They were from the same litter, he was told, and had been brought in just that morning. All had been adopted except these two. One of them leaped about the cage joyfully. The other sat quietly in the middle of the cage. Steven knelt down to study them. There was something about the quiet one, something in its eyes.

He said hello to the young dog, and its head turned inquisitively, as if the animal were trying to understand what had been said to him. Here was an intelligent dog. Here was the dog that Steven had been waiting for all his life. Steven called him Peanut because of his small size. He was to become the greatest dog any man could ask for.

As time went on, Steven found other work to supplement his income: tutoring perhaps, or teaching English as a second language, for which there was a seemingly infinite demand in this border community. He never had enough money to build a real house on his land, although he had had a few false starts. He did, however, install electricity, which was a truly momentous event.

He purchased a two-thousand five-hundred gallon water tank, so that water could be delivered by truck. He fenced in his land, which enhanced his sense of ownership. Then, after nine years of living in the truck camper, he finally found a substantially larger one that he could afford. It was twenty-five feet long, and seemed like the Palace at Versailles.

During this time, there was a one-year period in which Steven made a very respectable amount of money. He knew that the job would not last long, and was determined to do something meaningful with this windfall. A fifteen-acre parcel of land came up for sale not far from his one-acre homestead. The price was twelve thousand dollars. He jumped at the opportunity, and managed to pay it off entirely during this relatively prosperous year. He could have spent the money on a real mobile home, which would have made his life a great deal more comfortable. But he had become accustomed, to the extent that one could become accustomed, to the life of a poor eremite. Also, a mobile home seemed such a transient thing: it could be damaged by the frequent strong winds, or burned in a fire. And it was not really a house, as he had always envisioned one. Most of all, it was not land. Land was forever. It would last for eons, and it would be his for as long as he lived.

Steven and Katherine met occasionally on campus. They chatted, discussing their lives in the superficial, guarded way reserved for those seeking a potential mate. Coffee together in the cafeteria evolved into lunch, and then dinner. Their conversations became more intimate, more revealing. They began to be drawn more closely toward each other, each feeling a growing need for the other's presence.

Katherine visited Steven's property. She was impressed by the fact that he had managed to acquire sixteen acres of land on the pittance he had been paid over the years. It was on one of these visits that they first made love. Each had been celibate for a long time. Their pent-up lust, and the uninhibited way in which they vented it amazed them both. They married three months later, almost a year to the day before the Conquest.

During their courtship, they had often discussed politics. Steven was a political scientist, and was deeply immersed in the subject. He watched the collapse of the Soviet Union and the eventual rise of Drugonov with deep concern. He studied Russian culture, carefully read Drugonov's speeches, and monitored the Russian press. This obscure, second string academic saw the threat long before virtually anyone else. He began to make plans, and eagerly sought Katherine's opinions. She came to share his concerns. Eight months before the Conquest, they put their plans in motion.

They sold the fifteen-acre lot near El Paso, and purchased eight acres of wilderness property twenty miles northwest of Silver City, New Mexico. Together, they cleared an acre of forest, and began to build a log cabin. Neither knew anything about the subject of cabin-building. Their approach to the problem was almost comical: not one move was spontaneous. They employed the scientific method as if they were doing research for a journal article. They ordered books on the subject, and drained the Internet dry of its cabin-building content. They then built a second structure for storage of supplies, and lastly, a smokehouse.

On weekends, they made the four-hour journey from El Paso to their remote new property, bringing with them fifty-pound bags of rice, beans and flour. These they stored in sixty-gallon plastic barrels purchased at flea markets. These barrels had originated at the local soda bottling plant. They spent hours poring over lists of what they would need in the event of an invasion: everything from toilet paper to photovoltaic panels, from soy sauce to a wind-powered electric generator. They brought load after load of supplies to their retreat in Steven's old, but well-maintained pickup truck.

Weeks and months passed. And then it came. Drugonov was in New York and the President of the United States had capitulated. Katherine and Steven were ready.

"That's it. Line up the sights, and squeeze the trigger gently," Steven said.

Kathy applied as much concentration to this task as she had ever done earning her two Master's Degrees. The Smith and Wesson Model 15 thirty-eight special barked. The tin can flew gratifyingly off the log and into the air.

"I like this gun," Kathy said with a smile. "It fits my hand perfectly. I think I could get very good with it."

"First of all, it's a revolver, Kathy. And, secondly, you had better get good with it. You'll need all the skill you can get before this is over."

Steven had been a member of the National Rifle Association for twenty-five years, and had owned and shot weapons all his life. In the corner of their cabin was a press for reloading ammunition along with all of the other accouterments necessary for that task. Sixty pounds of gunpowder for both rifle and pistol resided in the storage shed, along with twenty-five thousand primers and hundreds of pounds of lead wheel-weights and equipment for casting bullets. He had brought a carefully thought-out battery of weapons to the cabin including revolvers and semi-autos in all calibers from .22 to .45 Colt, two twelve-gauge Ithaca pump shotguns, two SKS rifles, one Chinese and the other the much better grade Russian model, two Kalashnikov rifles, one of Hungarian manufacture and the other Bulgarian, the latter pronounced the finest in the world by none other than Mikhail Kalashnikov himself.

He had twenty-five magazines for each of the Kalashnikovs, thirty thousand rounds of ammunition, and a supply of spare parts in case of breakage. All of these were for close-in work. He was prepared for long range needs as well. In a pawn shop in El Paso, he had found a Yugoslav-made Mauser 98 that had been rebarreled by the Israeli military for the 7.62 NATO round. With his twelve power Burris scope, it was superbly accurate.

After long hours of practice with it at ranges out to eight-hundred yards, using loads that he had carefully designed for that particular rifle, he felt capable of hitting the vital zone of a man-sized target at that range with virtually each shot. He had familiarized Kathy with each of these weapons, and she too had become proficient with them.

"If you like that handgun best, we'll consider it your personal sidearm," Steven said. "Keep it near you at all times, carry it with you whenever you leave the cabin, and keep it clean, oiled and ready for action. The ammunition I've loaded for you is pretty hot stuff. It should do the job when the time comes."

"Do you really think it'll come to that?" Kathy asked.

"Who knows? We're way off the beaten path here, about as isolated as you can get in the lower forty-eight. But there's always the possibility of a Russian patrol. And then there are our own people. It's hard to tell what's going on out there, but I suspect that there's a certain amount of lawlessness, banditry. We haven't seen anybody yet, but I think it's only a matter of time."

Kathy was in charge of agriculture, and Steven of construction, maintenance and hunting. Of the two, Kathy's job was the harder. There was a large garden, covering more than half an acre. Kathy grew everything from cucumbers to zucchini. She had planted fruit trees and grape vines. She had to tend a dozen chickens and she had to milk the goat. Steven pitched in whenever he could, but the bulk of the burden fell on Kathy. Everything they grew was to be preserved by canning, a skill that Kathy had fortunately learned during her childhood on the family farm. They planned to share that chore when their first crop came in.

One day, Kathy had just finished milking that marvelously productive goat when he appeared. Peanut saw him first. The dog, which had been lying next to Kathy, at first growled and then jumped to his feet, pointed toward the woods, and began barking. Kathy looked in the direction Peanut was indicating and, after a second or so, saw him: just a face peering out of the forest at the edge of the clearing. She put down the pail of milk and drew the Smith and Wesson from its holster. Peanut ran forward a few feet, and then just stood his ground, ready to defend his family.

"Steven! Come here now!" Kathy yelled.

Steven had never heard that tone in her voice before: a mixture or fear and aggressive determination. He dropped the axe with which he had been chopping wood, picked up the Bulgarian Kalashnikov that was resting three feet away, and ran around the northeast corner of the cabin, racking the bolt on the weapon as he ran.

"Get down, Kathy!" he shouted.

She immediately assumed a prone position, revolver pointed in the direction of their unwelcome visitor. Steven, seeing that same face in the woods, dove to the earth as well, drawing a bead on the man. Seconds passed, but they seemed like hours. Finally, Steven said in a firm, loud voice,

"Come out of the woods with your hands over your head!"

Slowly, tentatively, the man came forward, hands in the air. Behind him walked a boy of about nine and a girl somewhat younger, perhaps seven. They too had their hands above their heads. The man did not appear to be armed. Kathy and Steven did not let down their guard: they kept their weapons pointed at the center of the man's mass. He came to within fifteen feet of them and stopped.

"I don't mean you no harm, ma'am, sir. I ain't armed."

Kathy and Steven rose from the ground.

"Keep your hands right where they are, mister," Steven ordered.

He approached the man and, holding his rifle pointed at the man's chest in one hand, patted him down for weapons with the other. He found only a pocket knife, which he tossed to the ground. Steven took two steps backward and examined his visitor.

The man was about six feet tall, with filthy, matted hair that had not seen a pair of scissors in months. He wore a full beard: only those who had thought ahead still had a stock of razor blades. His canvas jacket was dirty and torn over the left shoulder. The remnants of a denim shirt, badly-worn blue jeans and square-toed boots completed his outfit. But what struck Kathy and Steven most was his degree of emaciation: he didn't appear to have a single ounce of fat on his frame. His pants were obviously several sizes too big, though they may once have fit him, and were held up by a length of rope. In his thin, hollow-cheeked face, his eyes seemed immense. They peered, unblinking, at Kathy and Steven with a look of exhaustion tinged with panic.

The children were in even worse shape. They, too, were pathetically thin, their clothes in shreds. The little girl clung to her father's jacket, almost hiding behind him, and peeked out with tired, almost lifeless eyes. Every few seconds she was convulsed with a wracking cough. The boy was trying to be brave, looking unwaveringly at Steven, but his trembling lower lip revealed his fear.

"Who are you, and how the hell did you find this place?" Steven demanded.

The man slowly lowered his hands to his sides. His son did the same.

"My name's Martin. Keith Martin. We live about five miles north of here..."

"That's a lie!" Kathy said, acid in her voice. "No one lives five miles north of here. We've checked."

"Well, we do now, me and the kids. It ain't much: just a sort of lean-to near a stream. We had to get out of Albuquerque. The Russians, they shot my wife, and we had to get out. We had no place to go, so we just drove until we ran out of gas, and then walked until we couldn't walk no more. And that's where we set. I guess it's as good a place as any. Better than Albuquerque, anyway."

"How did you find this place? How did you know we were here?" Steven asked, still very much on guard.

"We had to get somethin' to eat. We ain't really ate nothin' decent in over a week. And even then it wasn't much. We were goin' to walk into Silver City when we came across a sort of road cut through the woods. It didn't look like anybody had used it in a long time, but I figured it was worth followin', just in case somebody lived at the end of it."

Steven's mind raced. What should he do with this intruder? He and Kathy had worked so hard to remain unseen, and now their security had been breached. Thoughts of killing the man flickered through his mind. But then he would have to kill the children too. That was unthinkable. Damn it, he told himself. This was a time to be tough, ruthless! His and Kathy's survival depended on it! But no, he couldn't kill children.

"If you're looking for a handout, forget it," Steven said.

The man looked at the garden, the vines, the fruit trees, the two goats, and finally at Steven and Kathy themselves.

"Are you sure you couldn't see your way clear to help us out?" he asked. "It's mostly for the kids, you see."

Steven's eyes narrowed.

"This is no time to ask for charity, mister. I hate to be hard on you, but in these times it's every man for himself. You should have prepared better. You should have seen this coming. I did. If you have something of value to trade, then we can make a deal together as equals. But I won't give you something for nothing."

"I ain't asking you to."

The man reached into his pants pocket and withdrew a handful of small objects, which he then held before him.

"I'm looking to trade these for some food."

In the man's hand were four dimes, eight twenty-two-caliber rounds of ammunition, and one thirty-thirty cartridge.

"Are those dimes silver?" Steven asked.

"They sure are. That's all anybody will take these days."

"How are people valuing those things on the outside?" Steven asked.

"Well, in Albuquerque, a silver dime will buy about as much as an Old Dollar used to. Twenty-twos are valued at two to a dime. And center-fire ammunition trades at twenty-five cents silver a round."

Steven began to feel his muscles relax. He ventured a look at Kathy, and saw that she too had softened her gaze on these unwelcome intruders. This was not an enemy, a looter or a thief, but a free man seeking a free exchange, value for value.

"What do you think, Kathy?" he asked.

"I think they're all right," she said. "Let's trade with them."

Steven lowered his rifle.

"All right, mister, ah, Keith. We can use those twenty-twos and the silver. We don't have a rifle chambered for thirty-thirty, but I suppose we can use that round for barter."

"Ammunition is as good as gold, mister. Honest."

"I believe you. Come inside and have a cup of coffee. We have a pot of venison stew on the stove. You're all welcome to a bowl of it as part of the deal."

"Real coffee! I'll be damned! You hear that kids? We're goin' to eat!"

Steven and Kathy charged the Martins half a dime each for the stew: one dime and one twenty-two-cartridge total. All three were given a large glass of fresh goats' milk as part of the bargain. They listened as Keith Martin told them of the conquest of the country, the Russian occupation, the labor camps, the mass liquidations, the cowardice and the treason on the part of their former leaders. There was much he did not know, of course, communications being what they were. But he told them what he knew, and that was bad enough. Kathy's and Steven's only contact with the outside had been by short-wave radio. But the world was being strangely silent about the Conquest of America, no doubt intimidated by Drugonov.

After they had finished eating, Steven took the man out to his smokehouse. Kathy examined the little girl, whose name was Jennifer. She suspected that the child had pneumonia. Kathy prepared an injection of penicillin, which had been one of many medical items she and Steven had purchased over-the-counter in Juarez months before the Conquest. They had brought with them enough antibiotics and other medications to equip a small clinic. As Steven and Keith walked toward the outbuilding, Steven asked him, "Why haven't you shot a deer to feed yourselves, Keith?"

"Don't have no gun," Martin answered.

Steven felt like cursing the man for a fool, but decided that it would accomplish nothing.

"I have a single-shot twelve gauge that I'd be willing to sell. I want twenty dollars for it, but I'd throw in twenty rounds of double-ought buck, or deer slugs if that's your preference. If you're a good hunter, that's twenty deer."

Martin's face lit up.

"Twenty dollars is a hell of a lot of money, Steve. I don't know where I'd come by that much. But I sure would like to have a twelve-gauge! That would keep the three of us alive!"

"How are you at chopping wood?" Steven asked.

Martin smiled. "About as good as the next man, I guess."

"I'll allow you two dollars a cord, but I mean a real cord, not a face cord. Cut ten cords, and the shotgun's yours. I'll throw in food, drink and lodging for you and your children while you're working."

"You've got a deal, Steve," Martin said. The two men shook hands.

In the days and weeks that followed, Steven engaged in some reconnaissance. How many other neighbors did he have? How many others had sought the solitude of this wilderness to escape the horrors of the occupation? As it turned out, quite a few. Several hundred in fact.

Two miles east of the property, there was the conjunction of two old, dirt logging roads. People began to congregate there on Saturday mornings, just a few at first, then more. They brought with them items, mostly of their own manufacture, which they hoped to trade for other items that they needed. There seemed little danger of Russian patrols. No one had seen a Russian in all the months since the occupation began, at least this far north of Silver City.

A primitive division of labor began to emerge. Kathy and Steven started bringing smoked and jerked venison, vegetables and goat's-milk cheese to this incipient marketplace. Soon simple barter was supplemented with the beginnings of a money economy as people brought out their silver coins and ammunition.

An economic historian would have found all of this fascinating: a thousand years of economic development compressed into the space of a few weeks. It always amazed Steven how many people had failed to prepare themselves by stocking up on the most basic items. For months prior to the Conquest, as he saw it approaching, he purchased exactly those things: basics that he thought would be in short supply simply because they would be overlooked by the average person. There were matches, for example. Under these primitive conditions, fire was essential. But few had thought of it. Steven had bought thousands of books of paper matches, and hundreds of boxes of wooden ones. The books of paper matches he sold for ten cents each, and the small wooden ones for fifteen. He also did a thriving business in sewing kits, of all things. Prior to the Conquest, he had found a catalog selling German military surplus sewing kits for ninety-nine Old Cents each. They were really quite ingenious: they were little folded cloth pouches that included everything one would need to do almost any kind of clothing repair imaginable. No one else had them. He sold them easily for a dollar fifty cents, silver.

And then there were razors. It is amazing how dirty many men feel when they have not shaved. Steven sold them disposable plastic razors, which he had bought ten for an Old Dollar before the Occupation, for fifty cents silver, each. He had stockpiled hundreds of these, and he always sold out as many as he brought to the market. The income from these alone allowed him and Katherine to live in what passed for comfort in these troubled times.

Katherine also was doing well. Although she had never had any formal medical training, she had prepared herself in the months before the Conquest to provide the kind of basic medical services she thought would be most in demand in a survival situation. It was she who took charge of purchasing the inventory of antibiotics and other pharmaceuticals in Juarez. She read numerous books on the kind of illnesses and injuries that she might encounter, and trained herself in how to deal with them. She spent hours every Saturday giving injections, stitching wounds, even pulling teeth. She dreaded the day she would be called upon to perform an appendectomy or some other type of surgery, but she supposed that it was inevitable. As much as she dreaded such a situation, when that day came, she felt competent to handle it.

Irene Beemis, who was as tough-looking a woman as any had ever seen, brought sturdy, durable cotton shirts and pants made on an old treadle sewing machine from some bolts of cloth which she had wisely hoarded before the Conquest.

Chuy Pacheco was quite a skilled gunsmith, and, given a week's notice, could make just about any part a person might need for just about any firearm in existence. He set up an old card table at the intersection, and did a brisk repair business.

A.J. McCarty had been a welder-fabricator before the Invasion, and had turned his talents to black-smithing. He made a little of everything useful, but specialized in knives, an item that was always in demand. He made a very strong and functional hunting knife from old high-carbon steel railroad spikes. Many more of his knives were made from old automobile leaf springs. A specialty of his was a massive coffin-handled Bowie knife with a blade nearly twelve inches long and a quarter-inch thick. Its grips were made of elk antler. It was not a particularly practical knife for day to day usage, but every man seemed to want one none the less. A.J. sold all he could make. His wife, Ellen, stitched together the sheathes for all of these creations from deerskin.

Ellis Wilton was married to a feisty but good-natured woman named Lupe. They had lived in Socorro, New Mexico before the Conquest. He manufactured a crude but practical sort of shoe, similar to the old and almost forgotten Mexican "tegua." They were ankle high, the upper made of deer or elk hide, the sole of tire tread. They even had the beginnings of a Goodyear welt, which made them quite durable. They were comfortable and almost impossible to wear out. He sold these for two dollars a pair: a bit steep, but well worth it for those whose pre-Conquest shoes had given out. Lupe made burritos and enchiladas, which she kept hot on an old plow disk that had had re-bar legs welded to it. She sold these two for a dime.

In time there were many others. No handouts were asked for and none given. This marketplace represented capitalism in its purest form, though few of its participants would have recognized it as such. Value was exchanged for value. Sometimes goods were sold for cash: silver coin, and sometimes for other goods as barter. On occasion, goods were traded for labor if the purchaser had nothing else to offer. But nothing was given for nothing.

On one occasion, a man showed up with a gold Double Eagle, a twenty-dollar gold piece, dated 1904. The marketplace practically came to a standstill as everyone examined this rare beast. There was a great deal of discussion as to what it might be worth. It was finally decided that it should trade at its face value: twenty dollars in silver. Numismatic value under these conditions was no longer a consideration. No one at the market had enough silver to make change for a single purchase, so the owner of the coin simply bought what he wanted from a number of merchants, and left it to them to sort out the details among themselves. Silver dimes, quarters and halves flew from hand to hand, along with ammunition of various types, until the exchange was complete to everyone's satisfaction. Chuy ended up with the Double Eagle, which made him feel like a rich man, which in fact he was. He smiled from ear to ear for the rest of the day.

One Saturday a stranger showed up at the market. This, in itself, was no cause for alarm. Newcomers were not uncommon. People were still fleeing the cities, although it had been many months since the Conquest had taken place. But there was something about this one, something that put the regulars on their guard. His clothes were nearly new, and not the sort one would wear under these primitive conditions. He was clearly a city-dweller out of his element, and by the looks of him, he had made no preparations for wilderness living.

The man walked through the tiny market, examining everything with an aloof bearing, as if he were too good to consider purchasing such crude products. He approached Steven and Kathy's table, which was nothing more that a four-by-eight sheet of plywood on four sections of log. The smoked venison smelled wonderful. The man had not eaten in two days. He looked at the goat's milk cheese, and began to salivate.

"What kind of meat is that?" he asked.

"It's venison. Smoked venison," Steven answered. "I also have venison and elk jerky."

The man licked his lips. "How much for a pound of the smoked stuff?" he asked.

"Twenty-five cents. Two dimes and a twenty-two."

The stranger fidgeted. He reached into his pocket and pulled out a piece of paper.

"Here's a New Dollar. I'll take four pounds."

Steven looked down at the piece of fiat currency that was being offered him. He glimpsed the visage of Drugonov, posed heroically his bust surrounded by wreathes of gold oak leaves.

He looked up at the man and chuckled.

"Nobody takes that junk here, mister. It has no intrinsic value. It's not money. It's backed up by nothing. We deal in real money: silver or gold, or anything else of real value."

"But the government says this is real money. It says right here on the front, 'This note is legal tender for all debts public and private.' You have to accept it. The state says so."

"I don't give a damn what the state says. That stuff isn't worth the paper it's printed on. Look, mister, I don't know where you're from or what you've been taught to believe, but in this place, we're all free-market capitalists. We trade with each other value for value. I have food to offer you. That is a real value. It will keep you alive. You're offering me nothing in return. That is not a free-market exchange. I'm not interested."

"This money is no different from the paper money we used before the Russians came! That wasn't backed up by gold or silver either, and everybody accepted that!"

"And that was our mistake. Maybe if we had refused to accept it in those days, and refused to accept a lot of other things the government was doing, we wouldn't be in the mess we're in now. I'm sorry, mister, but that piece of paper won't buy you the time of day in this marketplace."

"Look," the man said, his voice lower and now clearly pleading. "I haven't eaten in a couple of days. I'm afraid I'm beginning to starve, I mean really starve. I need food. Doesn't my need mean anything to you?"

"No, it doesn't."

"But doesn't my need place a moral responsibility on you? Doesn't the fact that I really need something mean that you're obligated to give it to me, even if I have nothing to give to you in exchange? Every enlightened, thinking person feels that way, don't they?"

"I don't."

"But what if I were to die? Wouldn't it be your fault? Wouldn't you be responsible? Doesn't my need give me a right to the product of your labor?"

"Your need places no moral burden on me. I have invested my life in producing this food: my time, my intellect, and my labor. To demand the product of my labor while offering nothing in return is to demand a part of my life. My life is my own. You have no claim on any portion of it."

Steven continued. "You say your need gives you a right to the product of my labor. Two people cannot have first claim, or a right, to the same economic good. Either I, as its producer, have a right to it, or you do. If the product of my labor is yours by right, as you assert, then I, by definition, have no right to it. If I do not, in fact, have first claim, or a right, to the product of my own labor, I am relegated to the status of slave. A slave is a person, who, by definition, does not have first claim to the product of his own labor. I choose not to accept the status of slave. I am a free man, and what I produce is mine by right."

By now, a number of other people had gathered to hear this exchange. The stranger's eyes darted back and forth at the growing crowd.

"Look," he said. "You can't get away with this! My need does give me a right to what you've produced! I can't explain how, it just does! Everybody knows that, or at least they used to!"

Steven and Kathy looked at the man now more out of pity than anger or resentment. Here was a man who was not intellectually suited for life. He was like a man drowning, unable to swim, surrounded by a reality with which he could not deal.

"I'm sorry for you mister," Steven said quietly. "I truly am."

"You haven't heard the end of this!" the man shouted. "Any of you! I'll go to the authorities in Silver City! I can find this place again, and I'll bring them here! You'll be sorry! You'll all be sorry!"

Men's eyes met. They said nothing, but they knew what had to be done. Two of them took the stranger under the arms and began to lead him into the forest.

"Where the hell are you taking me! Let go of me!" he yelled.

The man began to flail his legs, but two more onlookers came forward and grasped them firmly. Soon they had all disappeared into the trees. Everyone there knew what was about to happen. They all stood in place, somberly waiting. The stranger's shouting could be heard by all. Then it happened: a single shot rang out. Slowly, without a word, everyone turned and walked away.

CHAPTER FORTY-ONE

The mountain air was redolent with the scent of ten million trees. Last night's rain had released the rich, spicy odor of the forest, and it filled Molly's nostrils as she pumped the well- handle, bringing up the cold, sweet water from the bowels of the earth. She brought the bucket into the cabin and placed it on the counter next to the porcelain-covered sink. A year and a half ago, she would have thought that living under such primitive conditions would be intolerable. The home she and Trace had shared with their son had had every creature comfort. To be living with hand-drawn well-water and kerosene lanterns would have seemed inconceivable. But the fact was that she loved it. The water seemed all the sweeter for her having drawn it. The lamps had to be filled from time to time, that was true, but their warm glow created an intimacy that could never be matched by incandescent lighting.

In their old home, the heat from the oil furnace had unfailingly kept them warm. But she had never appreciated it as she did the uneven heat from the old cast-iron stove because this stove she stoked herself, one log at a time. Molly had gotten tougher, in both body and spirit. She winced sometimes when she remembered how, in her old life, she would complain about the least little thing: the dishwasher failing to remove a bit of egg from a plate, the housekeeper not folding their clothing just as she wanted it. God, she wished she could apologize to that woman! Now she performed physical labor that she would have thought impossible before. She had just dug a new latrine, with her own hands, with a pick and shovel! Eighteen months ago, she could not have imagined that possible, she, who had grown up with a maid and a gardener to perform every menial task, she, who would never have dreamed of touching something so mundane and demeaning as a shovel. Now, she relished it.

She was proud of every drop of sweat her body produced. The hardest labor, fortunately, had been done for her. David had chopped enough firewood to last for a very long time. And her neighbor, Hansen Staley, came by from time to time to do some of the heavy lifting. He was past seventy, but these mountains had kept him young. She felt as if it would do the same for her. She had lost every ounce of what Trace sometimes referred to as "baby fat." With each task she performed, she could feel her muscles gaining strength. She had never known she could feel so fit.

The war had served to toughen her spirit as well as her body. She resented the Russian Conquest with a depth of emotion she had not known she possessed and yearned for her country to be free again. She had never been a student of American history, but in recent months she had become immersed in it. Trace had always liked it, and the cabin had a shelf with a few dozen books on the subject. At night, in the yellow kerosene light, she pored over those books. She read of the founding era, of the philosophy of the men who had created this country, marveling at the purity of their belief in the value of the individual.

Unfortunately, that belief had not been entirely consistent. For many years it had not included Blacks, nor even women. But she came to realize that the first task of the Founders in 1787 had been to forge a nation: to construct one government that would be acceptable to a country riven by sectional differences. Distasteful, even ridiculous, compromises had to be made, such as counting five Black slaves as three people for purposes of representation. But they accomplished their purpose, and they laid the groundwork for the progress in civil rights and civil liberties that would eventually come. The issue of slavery would be decided by their grandchildren.

Molly came to understand that the destruction of American liberty had been a gradual process; it had taken many years, years during which the government: the President, the Congress and the Courts had twisted and distorted the Constitution to their own ends. The Conquest was the final push into the abyss, the logical culmination of a process by which a free people had committed philosophical suicide. It was the corpse tumbling into its grave.

But it was not quite over yet. The American people, faced with the stark reality of their own moral abdication, were at last fighting back. Like a candle flame that had almost flickered out, but had then found a new source of fuel, they were sputtering back to life. Her own husband, she had heard, was a key figure in that battle. Mr. Staley had told her that in town they were talking about Trace Forester as a great hero, one who could lead them out of this ignominy. He had told her that her Trace was the Commander of the Northwestern region; in charge of all militia activity from Montana to the Pacific.

Every time Mr. Staley came to visit, she plied him for more information, but there was not a great deal to be had. She had been told of a battle here, a triumph there, and of losses as well. Still, she took heart from the knowledge that her people were fighting on. She wished she could join them. Many women were in the militia; she knew that. She felt perfectly capable of contributing to the effort. But where would she find Trace? She had no idea where he was. He had told her to stay here, in this cabin. Still, she would not hesitate to join him, if only she could. But she was afraid of exposing herself, not for her own well-being, but for Trace's and David's.

If she left here, and were captured, she might prove a valuable weapon to the Russians against the man she loved so much. They might use her for blackmail, forcing Trace to curtail his activities. That she could not stand. She would rather be dead.

David had left many months earlier, and she had had no word of his fate. Many nights she lay awake in her bed worrying about him. But she felt sure he was with his father, and that he would be safe. She had to believe that.

Molly turned to the bowl of carrots she had pulled from the ground that morning. She had some onions and some potatoes as well. Yesterday, Mr. Staley had given her a piece of venison wrapped in newspaper. She would make a stew.

She wished that Trace and David were here to share it with her.

Lieutenant Zakhar Vorotyntsev crouched in the brush as he watched the cabin. The woman had been inside for twenty minutes now. His orders were to take her alive. There were many questions his superiors were eager to ask her. Her husband, this Forester, had become a major obstacle in the process of pacification. Enormous forces had been arrayed against him. But each time it seemed he would be caught, he slipped away.

There was great frustration at Headquarters. Perhaps this woman could give them some clue as to his habits, his thought processes, his behavior. Perhaps she could be used as leverage to force his surrender. His men had searched for this cabin for two months. It was her neighbor who finally talked, the old man who lived across the mountain. It had taken them twelve hours to extract the information, and what was left of him in the end was not a pretty sight. But he had talked. They almost always did.

The lieutenant had seen no sign of a weapon. Perhaps this would be easier than he had expected. With a slight movement of his hand, he signaled to his men to approach the cabin. The first fifty feet would not present difficulties: it was heavily-wooded, and his men could move from tree to tree. However, the last fifty would be in the open: the trees and brush had all been cleared away. Slowly, silently, the soldiers began to move.

Molly stood at the sink, humming a tune that had been popular before the Conquest. She couldn't remember its name, nor even any of the words. But that didn't matter. The song reminded her of happier times, and she smiled. She looked down into the sink at the carrots as she peeled them. For no particular reason, she lifted her head and glanced out the window. She saw them: a dozen men, no, more, coming out of the tree-line, crouching down, weapons leveled.

Her breath caught in her throat. The panic felt as if a jolt of a thousand volts were running through her body. She dropped the knife, and was for a second paralyzed, galvanized with fear. Then a thought forced its way into her consciousness: the gun. Get the gun. She ran as best she could to the corner of the room, her legs barely functioning. There, leaning against the wall, was a MAC-90, a semiautomatic version of the Kalashnikov in 7.62 by 39 caliber. It was one of the ridiculous thumb-hole stock versions that had been mandated by law some years earlier. A loaded, thirty-round magazine protruded from the bottom of the receiver.

Molly picked up the rifle and racked the bolt, as Trace had shown her, sending a round into the chamber. She tried to remember everything she had been taught about the weapon. The safety, check the safety. It was off. Good. It should be ready to fire, one round with each pull of the trigger. The thought flashed across her mind that it would be wonderful if this rifle were fully-automatic, if she could unleash a hail of lead at her attackers with one pull of the trigger. But the law had not permitted such a thing.

Her body was almost frozen with fear. Her legs stopped working, and she slid down into the corner until she was crouching on the floor, rifle pointed at the door. They were being very quiet, these men. There was utter silence. The seconds ticked by. Suddenly the door burst open, and the men began to rush in: two, three, four of them. They did not see her on the floor in the corner, and that gave Molly a precious advantage. She held the rifle in the direction of the nearest man and pulled the trigger. An insanely-loud boom filled the small room, and Molly recoiled from the noise. But she kept pulling the trigger, over and over again. The bullets drilled through her opponents, sending them sprawling across the floor. She began to scream at the top of her lungs, screaming in rage, screaming at the madness of it, all the time pulling the trigger. Three more men entered the room, and she shot them as well. She could see more of them outside the door, and she trained the weapon in their direction, sending round after round in the direction of the startled soldiers.

Lieutenant Vorotyntsev had to force himself to remember his orders: this woman was to be taken alive. She had already killed half his command. It would be so easy to simply toss in a grenade and be done with it. But he could not do that. Silently, he pointed to three more men who were spread across the log wall on the opposite side of the doorway. He indicated that they were to enter the cabin. They were good soldiers. They did as they were ordered.

Molly used these seconds to assess her situation. Shell casings littered the floor, a lot of them. That meant she had only a few rounds at best left in the rifle. There were four other loaded magazines in the cabin, but she had packed them away in a cabinet. They were beyond her reach. And she couldn't make her legs move. She was frozen in the corner of the cabin, as if cemented there. And then they came. The three Russian soldiers stormed through the doorway. Molly's rifle blasted two rounds into the first of them, and he tumbled to the floor. She pulled the trigger again. Click. Nothing. The other two Russians were momentarily impeded by the corpse of their comrade. Molly had a split second to think.

"Trace. David. They will make me talk. No. I will not let that happen."

She remembered something Trace had told her years earlier, about how North Korean spies were instructed to kill themselves if apprehended when no other means were at their disposal. She extended her tongue as far as it would go and bit down on it lightly. She closed her eyes. Then, with the heel of her right hand, she struck the bottom of her chin with all her might. Her tongue flew forward and landed on the floor. Molly opened her mouth, and blood gushed out in a torrent. The two Russian privates stared at this horror with wide eyes. It was a sight that would never leave them.

Molly looked at their expressions and smiled, a smile punctuated by a river of blood. She had beaten them. As the seconds passed, the two men standing before her began to blur. Molly slowly slumped over into a growing pool of her own blood. Still, she smiled. Her last conscious thought was that Trace would have been very proud of her. She had indeed played her part in the War. She had fought her own single-handed battle against the invaders of her country, and she had won.

CHAPTER FORTY-TWO

Webster C. Haines had been a Federal District Judge for seventeen years prior to the Conquest. His walls were covered with photographs of himself with governors and presidents, with celebrities of every stripe. His tables were cluttered with all the awards and mementoes of a distinguished legal career. He had been considered for positions on Courts of Appeals, and, several years ago, there was even talk about his eventually reaching the Supreme Court. As a judge, he had been politically correct. He had always been a good judicial activist: using his authority, not to uphold the Constitution, but to make a better society, a more fair society. That was what really counted, he had always thought. He agreed with Justice Ginsburg: the Constitution was irrelevant. He had not shed a tear when the Maximum Leader burned it.

Now everything was different. He had made it clear to the powers-that-be that he would play ball with his new masters. After all, he had never really believed in all of that hogwash about liberty. This country meant nothing to him. The only thing he cared about was Webster C. Haines. He had always gone in whichever direction the wind had blown. In past years, it had been in the direction of liberal activism. Now it mandated subservience to the Russians. He had been rewarded for his cooperation by being made Commissar of Sector Three. As such, he was now much more than a judge, he was a god. He had always known that he was a member of the elite, of the chosen ones. He had always felt that he was better than the rest, that he deserved more. Now he had it. These poor unwashed cretins, these vermin, were under his control. Things were as they should be, as they always should have been.

Webster C. Haines was naked. He never wore clothing in his home, all the better to indulge in his life's great passion, and, now, his principal past-time: the enjoyment of little boys. All his life he had been forced to hide this desire. He had even gotten married, because that was what a judge was expected to do. Now that harridan was gone: he had seen to it that she was sentenced to twenty years at hard labor. What was the charge? He didn't remember. It didn't matter. What counted was that no one survived such an ordeal. Good riddance, he thought every day of his life.

Oh, the woman had been innocuous enough; she had even tried to please him during their twelve years together. But every time they had made love, he had tried to imagine himself with a small boy. His imagination was not that vivid, and as time passed he had become increasingly frustrated. He began to see her as the obstacle, the barrier that prevented him from enjoying the objects of his true desire.

Now she was gone, there was a new order in the land, and he was free to be himself.

The boys were all around him; twelve of them, at the moment, chosen by their photographs in class yearbooks from their elementary schools. Of course, nowadays children such as these were working in the fields, but he had the authority to have them brought to him, and that is what he had done. They were pretty boys, with lean bodies and soft, curving buttocks. He had made sure that none was over the age of nine. He had never understood why that particular element of his fantasy existed, the age limitation, but it always had, and so he had indulged himself.

He walked from the hallway into the living room. The twelve boys, all naked as ordered, were scattered about, waiting for his next instructions. Some stood shyly, attempting to cover themselves with their hands. He had strictly forbidden this, and he picked up the riding quirt that was leaning against the wall. The boys looked horrified. Several of them began to tremble visibly. They knew what was about to happen. He lashed out at the nearest boy, hitting him on the arm. The boy screamed, and clapped his hand over the stinging wound.

"There, you see? You see what happens when you disobey me?"

The boy he had struck began to cry, and Judge Haines stroked his hair.

"Don't worry. Judge Haines will make it all better."

He sat in the large reclining chair, still touching the boy's hair. He let his hand run across the boy's shoulders, down the small of his back, and then over the twin mounds of his buttocks. As always on such occasions, he had developed a huge erection. The boy was only eight, and didn't weigh more than sixty pounds. The judge picked him up by his waist, and began to carefully lower the boy onto his lap. He wanted the penetration to be swift and smooth. It would be his fifth of the morning.

He heard footsteps in the hall. So did the boys, and they looked in the direction of the doorway expectantly. They knew that no one had ever dared to intrude on the judge before, but they desperately hoped that someone was coming to rescue them. One boy had already committed suicide, and others were thinking about it. Then he appeared, standing tall, in camouflaged clothing, carrying an SKS rifle.

"Put the boy down, Haines! It's over! You're coming with us!"

The judge did indeed put the boy down, and sprang to his feet. He looked absurd, standing there indignantly, naked, erection preceding him. "How dare you?! Who the hell are you, to come barging in like this! I'll have you shot!"

"I think you're a little confused, Judge. It may be the other way around," said the tall militia man.

By now four more members of the militia had appeared. The boys cheered wildly, jumping up and down, tears running down the cheeks of some. They ran to the men and hugged them, hugged them desperately, seeking reassurance, seeking their strength. The men responded, getting down on their knees, enveloping the children in their arms, telling then that their ordeal was over.

"Put your arms behind you, Haines. Now!"

The judge did as he was told. Handcuffs were applied, but no attempt was made to dress the man. To the almost hysterical laughing of a dozen greatly-relieved children, Judge Webster C. Haines was led out his front door and into the back of a waiting van. There were three other militiamen in the van, and they looked at Haines with hatred in their eyes.

"Listen! We can make a deal," the judge suggested surreptitiously. "Do you want boys? I can get them for you!"

His panic-stricken eyes moved desperately from face to face.

"Little girls? I can get those too!"

"Why you goddamn, filthy son of a bitch!"

The soldier opposite him smashed the butt of his M1 Garand into the judge's cheek, the bone breaking with an audible crack. Haines' head slammed into the wall of the van and he fell sideways, dazed.

An hour later, the van arrived at its destination: a logging road in a remote area of forest far from the nearest living soul. By now the judge had regained consciousness and was fully aware of the fact that something very bad was about to happen. He was dragged out of the vehicle and across the forest floor. In a clearing, more men waited. There were women too. A fire had been built, and pieces of iron, reinforcing rod and fireplace pokers, had been placed in it, where they glowed with a white heat.

Webster C. Haines was staked to the ground on his back, arms and legs spread, still naked. He looked up at these people through bleary eyes. Though the side of his face was badly swollen, he managed to say,

"Who are you people?"

They looked down at him solemnly. At last one of them said,

"We're the boys' parents, Judge."

For three days and three nights the screams echoed through the trees. The birds heard them, and abandoned their perches; the deer heard them, and moved off to quieter areas. As time passed, the agonized sounds became more and more faint, until they could barely be heard at all. At last there was nothing but the faint rustle of a breeze passing through the leaves.

CHAPTER FORTY-THREE

El Paso, Texas

Ralph Sellers had been owner of Armadillo Motorcycles for many years. He was a man who had forgotten more about Harleys-Davidsons and custom bikes than most experts would ever know. He had a reputation as an honest man who did very high quality work at a fair price and therefore had a loyal following in the El Paso Harley Community. He was the kind of guy who, especially after you got to know him, would bend over backwards to fix whatever problem you had and keep your ride in tip-top shape.

He was also a patriot, to put it mildly. The Russian occupation ate away at him like a cancer. Sometimes at night he would wake up in a cold sweat, muscles tense, teeth gritted, ready to go out and kill the first Russian he could find. But he had more important work, and he knew it. Keeping Harley-Davidson motorcycles running and on the road was more important than any role he could play as an ordinary soldier in the Militia, as tempted as he was from time to time to join it.

Harley-Davidson motorcycles played an integral, and incredibly effective, role in the Resistance. They, and the people who owned and rode them, had been a thorn in Drugonov's side since the beginning of the Occupation, and, as time went on, that thorn worked itself deeper and deeper into the dictator's flesh. What started as occasional confrontations between Harley-Davidson riders and Russian soldiers and security personnel had gradually become more and more organized, larger and larger in size and scope. Individual riders had become squads, then platoons, then companies which had become more daring as time went on, first attacking individual Russian personnel, then, as their confidence and combat skills improved, entire military units. And what particularly frightened Drugonov was the method of their attack. They would hit and run, come out of nowhere with great speed and no warning, in the most unlikely places, attacking fortified locations where his men had every reason to feel secure. Then they would ruthlessly massacre his people indiscriminately, from privates to generals, even the American female collaborators whom the Russians hired to "entertain" their men. Some of his personnel had been beaten to death with brass knuckles.

One of his general officers had been tortured for two days by a heavily-tattooed southern gentleman using nothing more than a pair of pliers. The general had talked, as they always did, revealing troop movements, convoys, everything. They even took body parts, heads in particular, as trophies, Drugonov supposed. These were men and women who made the Russian mafia seem like choirboys.

Their hatred of him and his occupation seemed to know no bounds, and he was confounded as to how to deal with them. Remembering his Russian history, they reminded him of Genghis Khan and his hoard of Mongols: a light cavalry which swept through an entire region, leaving behind nothing but death and devastation. But these horses had pistons and cylinders.

They call Harley-Davidsons *"The Great American Freedom Machine"*. Once in a while, before the Conquest, you could see a Harley rider wearing a belt buckle, a patch on his jacket, or a t-shirt to that effect. Those had been outlawed by Drugonov long ago as "reactionary" and "anti-social". Wearing one had become a death-penalty offense. But the riders of those motorcycles had never abandoned the sentiment behind that expression.

Harley-Davidson riders were perhaps the most overtly patriotic, Hell-for-Leather and Damn-the-Consequences bunch of people in the United States. They were not criminal in any way--quite the contrary. Harley clubs regularly participated in charity events throughout the country before the Conquest. They were thoughtful, caring people. But as Drugonov had learned, don't try to arbitrarily tell them what to do. They seemed to share a disdain for authority matched by no other segment of the population. They had no quarrel with living by the rules, as long as the rules made sense and did not infringe on their liberties in any way. That's where the Russian occupiers encountered their problem with them. It was a natural conflict, inevitable under the circumstances: a totalitarian dictator attempting to dominate a group of indomitable individualists. Drugonov was used to dealing with sheep, not wolves. He was used to dealing with people who were willing to trade their liberty for a free set of false teeth, not individuals who felt that they had nothing more important to lose than their freedom, and were more than willing, even eager, to kill and die in the process of defending it.

Every day, Drugonov got reports of confrontations between his people and Harley-Davidson owners which convinced him that these wild Americans would just as soon kill a Russian as look at him. He had liquidated hundreds of them in the process of trying to subjugate these anti-social "barbarians", but still they came, apparently fearless and totally defiant, not giving a damn about his fiats, pronouncements and orders. His statistics indicated that for every one of them whom he killed, he lost two point seven of his own people—clearly a losing battle. At this rate, before he eliminated all of these determined individualists, his entire occupation force would be wiped out. It was a situation analogous to that of Europe in World War II: if every Jew had killed the Gestapo agent who came to take him to the camps, Hitler would have run out of Gestapo agents long before he ran out of Jews. That was theoretical. These fanatics were actually doing it.

There's something almost mystical about owning and riding a Harley-Davidson. Perhaps the man is attracted to the machine because of his own, inner personality characteristics. Or perhaps the machine changes the man: makes him someone different, someone special, someone not to be toyed with. A collection of nuts and bolts, pistons and cylinders, properly designed and assembled, with over a century of pure American tradition behind it, takes on a special aura. That aura surrounds a man—or a woman—and permeates him or her when he or she mounts the Beast and pulses, throbs down a highway, sensing the immense power at his or her disposal. There is nothing else like it. You can feel the aura by just standing next to a Harley-Davidson. Mount one and the aura intensifies. Start the machine, and the aura becomes electric: floods of adrenalin course through the veins; the nervous system transmits mega-voltage. Kick it into gear, let out the clutch, and surge down the road and one feels more than human—superhuman: ruler of the highway, ruler of the world.

Owners of rice-burners may have quicker, more agile machines, but they are just that—machines. The Japanese spent immense amounts of time and money trying to create that aura for their own products, but they failed. Some look like Harleys, sort of. Some sound like Harleys, sort of. But only Harleys have the aura. Anyone who rides both knows it in an instant. "Rolling Thunder" is an expression often used to describe the Harley experience, and perhaps nothing comes closer to capturing the essence of it all. Thunder is wild and free, powerful and unpredictable. It is an irresistible, somewhat frightening, force of nature. Riding a Harley-Davidson allows a person to capture all of that wildness, that freedom, between his legs and amplify it to the threshold of his tolerance with the twist of a throttle.

The government of President Judas Benedict had often discussed outlawing motorcycles in the United States, supposedly in the name of "safety". The real reason was because Benedict and his administration realized that, among all of the population segments in the country, two would most resist their authoritarian plans for America's future: gun owners, and Harley-Davidson owners. These people, often one and the same, were least likely to be cowed by swaggering petty-tyrants carrying badges whose official governmental policy was to turn them into sheep in the self-sacrificial, altruistic society that Benedict and his kind envisioned. And so, just as their intention was to eventually, and incrementally, outlaw private gun ownership, they also wanted desperately to outlaw motorcycles--especially Harley-Davidsons.

But Judas Benedict realized that, in Harley-Davidson owners, just as in gun owners, he was up against an irresistible force and an immovable object. They would not cave in to his directives, passively turn in their beloved machines at government collection centers. Even a so-called "Buy-Back" program failed miserably, as if the state had sold the Harleys in the first place. It became clear to President Benedict and his sycophants that these people would resist, and resist fiercely. They just weren't like most Americans. Whenever the subject came up in the Oval Office, not only did President Benedict break out into a cold sweat, but his advisors became visibly agitated. Chief of Staff Lysander Elfman, in particular, would tremble, and once related to the president how he felt a terrible fear in the pit of his stomach whenever a Harley, or, worse yet, a group of Harleys, would pass him on the highway. What he did not reveal was how small and impotent such an experience made him feel, in spite of the great power and influence he wielded in government. The idea of dealing with a real man had always terrified Elfman, as it did most tyrants. That included President Judas Benedict.

So Harley-Davidsons had not been outlawed before the Conquest. After Drugonov's accession to power, he too soon came to realize that here he was dealing with a breed of people who would fight him to the death—perhaps even his own. And that scared him. He considered ordering the machine-gunning of any motorcycle seen on any road or highway in America. But one day he received a package at his New York headquarters that made him think twice about such a policy. In the box was the head of a Russian major general wearing a Harley bandana and with his severed penis protruding from his mouth. Also in the box was a note that read "We can get to anybody. Even you." He knew it was true.

Every political leader knows that one determined man, willing to give his life in the process, can assassinate anyone of his choosing—even a man with the layered, airtight security of Maximum Leader Drugonov. This was beyond his experience. No one had ever dared to challenge him so openly, so daringly. He was used to being the intimidator, not the intimidated. Drugonov didn't mind the thought of millions dying at his command, but the prospect of his own death terrified him. He dreamed of that head in the box. He dreamed of the ragged, jagged cut across the throat, as if the head had been severed with something very dull, very slowly and very painfully. He dreamed of the eyes. My God, the eyes: open, glaring, frozen in horror. He doubled his security detail.

And so in the first months after the Conquest, he instituted a half-measure. Rather than outlaw the possession of motorcycles, he instructed his occupying military forces to stop all motorcycles on the highway under any convenient pretext—speeding, riding too slowly, having an improperly functioning tail light or failure to use a turn signal when changing lanes--and confiscate the machines. If the rider resisted, he or she was to be liquidated on the spot as an enemy of the State. This policy was put into effect—for about two weeks. Eleven thousand five hundred fifty-three Russian soldiers were killed in the process of its execution. Only ninety-four Harley-Davidsons were successfully confiscated during this period. Drugonov received a report of one of his officers being decapitated with one swipe of an eighteen-inch kukri knife being carried by a heavy-set, bearded Harley rider who took exception to having his bike taken from him because he was supposedly riding at fifty-one miles per hour in a fifty mile per hour zone. The man reputedly simply rode away into the night, never to be seen or heard from again.

Shooting was the most common method by which his agents were dispatched. The fact that possession of a firearm under the Drugonov regime was a death-penalty offense didn't seem to deter these "anti-social, reactionary maniacs", as he was fond of describing them, at least in the safety of his private offices. In public, he didn't refer to them at all. He could not admit to the rest of the American colonists that a segment of their population had not been conquered with the rest of them, that they still roamed the land at will, defying him and all of the great might of his totalitarian regime.

His revised strategy was more draconian. It was slower, involving more subterfuge, but might produce better results in the long run. It would avoid most direct confrontations with these "maniacs", would save the lives of thousands of his soldiers, and just might result in the ultimate eradication of this impediment to his total, absolute control of his new American colony.

First, the Harley-Davidson factory was converted to the production of washing machines. The supply of new motorcycles would be terminated. Once word of this impending seizure reached Harley-Davidson, management and employees sabotaged every piece of equipment in the plant: cutting production machinery in half with oxy-acetylene torches, demolishing precision equipment with sledgehammers. The plant would produce no washing machines, nor anything else while under Russian control. Secondly, all repair shops were closed, their owners threatened with prison-camp internment should they be apprehended working on even one motorcycle. There was nothing Drugonov could do about shade-tree mechanics, but he did prohibit the delivery of any parts currently in the postal pipeline. The existing supply of spare parts in every motorcycle shop in America was confiscated. It was Drugonov's hope that as the Harleys slowly wore out, the problem of recalcitrant Harley riders would solve itself. But he did not reckon with men like Ralph Sellers, and many others like him around the former United States of America.

It was three-forty A.M. Ralph was performing a "Hillbilly tune-up" on a Heritage Classic. This involved some intricate modifications to the stock carburetor to achieve more horsepower and better throttle response, without the need to replace the carb with a more high-performance model, none of which were available now anyway. The bike's owner had almost been caught the night before while hosing down a Russian squad with an M16 at a roadblock. The surviving Russians had given chase, and, though the rider got away without a problem, he thought it had been a little too close for comfort. Hence Ralph's intervention. Once he was done with the bike, it would never be close again.

Ralph worked by the subdued light of a twenty-watt bulb, with the doors of his shop blacked out with plastic sheeting. No one passing down Rushing Street should be able to know anyone was at work. He typically worked three or four hours after midnight, when the Russian patrols were at their slackest and there was the least chance of being caught.

The carburetor was back in place. The job was done. Ralph didn't dare start the bike to test its function, as he would normally do, because the thundering sound of the high-performance, free-flow exhausts might attract attention. But he knew it had been done right. He had done so many Hillbilly tune-ups that he could almost do them in his sleep. He was lowering the bike to the floor when it happened. The sheet of black plastic covering the entrance to his shop was torn down and a man in a Russian Internal Security uniform burst in, sub-machine gun at the ready.

"So, what have we here? An illegal repair shop fixing these damned machines!"

He looked at the computerized transceiver which he had removed from his belt. "Our records show that an Armadillo Motorcycle shop located at 5246 Rushing Street ceased operations months ago. This location is now registered as a vacuum cleaner repair shop. But this is not a vacuum cleaner, is it? You are repairing a Harley-Davidson motorcycle. How unfortunate for you. You will pay a very heavy price."

Ralph took two steps backward as the security officer approached the Heritage.

"They are quite beautiful, I must admit: all of this chrome and lovely paint. And such powerful machines, as our forces have discovered all over this damnable country of yours. We have nothing in our military inventory which can catch them. Our standard-issue five-hundred c.c. Podkorov motorcycles are pathetic by comparison. By the time one of these shifts into third gear, our riders cannot even see their tail lights."

He looked over and smiled at Ralph.

"All the more reason to crush such a machine into scrap metal! And you, my friend, will spend the next ten years breaking rocks for your porridge."

The man's curiosity got the best of him. He had felt the aura.

"Do you know, I have never actually sat on one of these? What is it like, I wonder? You, my condemned friend, stand in front of me where I can see you, and keep your hands behind your back!"

When Ralph had assumed that position, the Russian seemed to relax, but always with his eyes on his opponent. To properly mount the motorcycle, he discovered that his machine pistol was in his way. He hesitated for a moment, then decided to suspend the weapon from his wrist by its sling as he grasped the right handlebar grip. He swung his left leg over the bike's seat. Placing his other hand on the grip, he smiled at Ralph.

"So this is how it feels! No wonder you Americans love these so! I feel as if my—how do you Americans say it—my dick—has grown six centimeters just by sitting on this machine!"

"Yeah, that's how it feels, you Russki cocksucker!"

What the Russian had not noticed was that Ralph had been carrying an eight-inch screwdriver in his back pocket. This he now held in his left hand, being left-handed. He sidestepped the front wheel of the Harley and lunged at the still-smiling Russian, driving the tool into the man's left eye with all of his strength. Before the Russian officer could even react, Ralph was twirling the screwdriver in a circular, stirring motion, mixing the man's brain into mush. This consumed less that a second. The now-dead officer slumped forward onto the gas tank, blood pouring from his eye socket. Before the blood could ruin the paint job, Ralph stepped back and, with his left foot, kicked the corpse off the bike and onto the floor. *Stupid bastard!* he thought. *Shoulda shot me while he had the chance.* Ralph had killed four other Russian agents in the preceding months, but none had been quite this simple. *If this is the best the Russkis can do, they're in for a real hard time!*

He replaced the plastic sheeting, doused the light, and walked out the side entrance of his shop. Rather than use his cell phone, which could be traced, he went down the street to the corner of Rushing and Dyer, where there was a pay phone. The Russians were notoriously inept at tracing pay phone calls, since the equipment to do so had been destroyed by the telephone company employees prior to abandoning their jobs. Ralph deposited a few coins, punched in a number, and waited. Three rings later, a low voice answered,

"Yeah."

"I have some trash to take out, and some scrap to git rid of. Let's gitter done."

Then he hung up. The entire conversation lasted less than three seconds. "Gitter done" was Ralph's favorite expression. It had always been his philosophy as the owner of a motorcycle repair shop. Now it referred to something entirely different. But it told the man on the other end of the line who he was dealing with. "Taking out some trash" meant disposing of a Russian corpse, and "getting rid of some scrap" meant making an official Russian vehicle "disappear". Special task forces of volunteer Harley riders had been formed to perform these functions, and they got plenty of practice. The corpse would be buried deep in the desert long before the sun rose, a west-Texas desert so vast that finding it would be essentially impossible. The Russian's patrol vehicle would be driven into one of the many obscure canyons in the area. It would be weeks, even months, before the Russians discovered it. By dawn, it would be as if nothing at all had happened. And Ralph Sellers would go on fixing Harleys—and killing Russians.

Something big was up. Word had come through the grapevine that a large, very critical Russian truck convoy would travel from the former Ft. Sam Houston in San Antonio to the former Ft. Huachuca in Arizona. It would be carrying sensitive, virtually irreplaceable electronic communications intercept equipment—the best the Russians could muster—to replace what had been destroyed at Ft. Huachuca when its patriotic American staff had demolished the place before abandoning their posts to join the Militia. The convoy would consist of at least twenty-five large trucks, and would travel west on Interstate 10, directly through El Paso.

Ralph thought about what the loss of such equipment would mean to the Russian effort to rule their American colony as he stirred the big pot which rested on the propane burner. Ralph had been active in the Resistance since the beginning. He acted in a de facto leadership role, helping to coordinate the efforts of the various Harley clubs in the area. Surreptitious meetings were held at the Armadillo shop: quiet, deadly meetings in the still of the night at which the destruction of this Russian facility or of that platoon of Russian soldiers was discussed. The bikers would roar away, and the deed was shortly done. Ralph knew he was taking a chance, acting as "Biker Central" for all of El Paso, helping to concoct plans for the destruction of his enemy. After all, thirty or forty Harleys parked in front of his "vacuum cleaner repair shop" were bound to attract attention. But he didn't give a shit. He hated the Russians' guts. He kept two Heckler and Koch MP5 submachine guns behind the counter—one for each hand—for his last stand, should it ever come to that.

The Russians suspected Ralph of all sorts of things. He had been raked over the coals many times by the Russian intelligence service. More than once he had been tortured, including having electrodes attached to his genitals. They could never make him talk. They had worked him over so thoroughly that they were sure he knew nothing about the Resistance. No one could endure what they had put him through without talking. Ralph, they had become convinced, was a simple shop owner, as he had always told them. He even fixed a vacuum cleaner now and then.

It was almost dawn. It had been cooking for hours. It should be ready now. Ralph reached down into the pot with a pair of tongs and withdrew the skull. There was a slight chip over the left eye socket where his screwdriver had entered. Extracting the brain and boiling away the hair and flesh was time consuming, but well worth the effort. The gleaming white skull was now ready to join the others on the "Wall of Shame", a series of shelves against one wall of the shop holding the skulls of scores of Russians who had met their end at the hands of the El Paso biker Resistance.

That Russian truck convoy presented an irresistible target. It was time to get busy and do what he did best: organize an attack. Ralph locked up his shop, once again walked to the corner and inserted some coins into the pay phone. He called the head of "Los Lobos", one of the local Harley clubs.

"Hey Pancho! How's it goin' man? Let's all get together tonight for a poker game. No limit. Yeah, that's right. The usual time."

He hung up the phone. "Pancho", Edwardo Felix, would contact the other club leaders and the word would spread like the threads of a spider's web that an important meeting was to be held at the Armadillo. "No limit" meant that the target was critical, that all the stops were to be pulled out, that everyone should be ready to put his life on the line. According to the pipeline, the convoy was scheduled to travel through El Paso at about eleven A.M. the following morning—thirty hours. Ralph, Pancho, and all the rest would be ready.

Ralph glanced at his watch. It was two-seventeen in the afternoon before the attack. He was a little sleep-deprived, not having gotten to bed until almost eight that morning. But he was so psyched about the upcoming attack that he probably wouldn't have slept much longer even if he had had the chance. He had to put in a normal day's work—fixing vacuum cleaners, just in case the Russians decided to check up on him again. He was replacing the drive belt on an old Hoover when the door to his shop opened.

"My name is Isikov. Lieutenant Isikov. I have recently been transferred to this sector, and I have decided to check certain, how shall I put it, certain locations of interest. Your name is prominently mentioned in our files. You have been under suspicion for some time. I understand that our security forces have questioned you repeatedly, using somewhat strenuous means."

"Yeah, that's right. I guess you could call hooking electrodes to a man's balls and turning on the juice strenuous, at least if you're on the receiving end."

"Ha, ha! Mr. Sellers, I'm glad you have a sense of humor. It can be useful in a strained relationship such as ours."

The lieutenant strolled around the shop, looking at vacuum cleaners and parts of vacuum cleaners on the floor and on the counters. He picked up a part from the counter, examined it briefly, and put it back down. He noticed his soiled fingers, and seemed disconcerted. Withdrawing a linen handkerchief from his trouser pocket, he wiped his impeccably-manicured fingers until he seemed satisfied that he no longer suffered the presence of such proletarian filth.

"You know," the lieutenant said in an entirely cavalier voice, "I would have shot you long ago, if the decision had been up to me."

He turned and looked Ralph directly in the eyes.

"You are totally immersed in this damnable Resistance. I can sense it. And as soon as I get the slightest shred of evidence to that effect, I will personally put a bullet behind your ear."

Ralph just smiled.

"It's nice to know I have friends in high places, lieutenant. But as you can see, I run a simple vacuum cleaner repair shop now. If you're looking for the Resistance, you'll have to look somewhere else."

His muscles tensed ready to spring on this primped peacock of a soldier if he made the slightest move in the direction of the shop in the rear of the building. There were four Harleys there, in various stages of repair. One step in that direction, and it would be the lieutenant who would receive a bullet behind the ear. Ralph felt the reassurance of the Makarov pistol in his back pocket. But Isikov did not make that fatal move. Instead he walked toward the "Wall of Shame": fifty-three shiny, white skulls, all with their teeth extracted to prevent identification by dental record, all neatly arranged on shelves against the wall.

"I've been told about this rather grisly display. It's really quite famous among our people here, you know. A bit morbid for a vacuum repair shop, isn't it?"

"Maybe so. But I collected these to make a point. I've seen a lot of my friends die at the hands of your people. I don't want to see any more killed. I knew some of these men, knew them for years. Enough is enough. This is a reminder to everyone who comes in here that resistance is useless. You people are in charge, and that's that."

Ralph tried very hard to sound sincere. His acting was better than he had any reason to expect. Isikov approached the wall and picked up the last skull on the bottom shelf, the one Ralph had just boiled that morning. Sellers felt a pang of tension as he watched the lieutenant turn the skull in his hands, examining it from every angle. Ralph was afraid that the sinus cavities might still contain some water, which, if it spilled out, would give his game away. Then he would have to use the Makarov.

"One of our internal security officers did not report in at the end of his shift this morning. This area was his responsibility."

Still holding the skull, he looked over at Ralph.

"You wouldn't know anything about his disappearance, would you? Did you hear or see anything unusual very early this morning?"

"Sorry, lieutenant. I was dead to the world until about seven."

"Dead to the world. I assume that means you were asleep."

"Yeah. Out like a light."

The lieutenant pursed his lips and shook his head.

"You Americans and your slang. I studied English for five years in Moscow, but every day you continue to surprise me with these ridiculous expressions. So you saw nothing? You heard nothing? I sincerely hope that you are telling the truth, Mr. Sellers. For if I discover that you are not, I will see to it that you will experience such things that electrodes attached to your balls will seem pleasant by comparison."

He hefted the skull of the security officer in his hands one more time before replacing it on the shelf. Ralph didn't know whether to laugh, or shoot this bastard just out of principle. He gritted his teeth at the threat; if there was one thing Ralph Sellers couldn't stand, it was being threatened: especially by an effete popinjay like this.

"You have nothing to fear from me, lieutenant. Here, look."

Ralph pointed at the certificate of appreciation he had received from General Kirilov for his assistance in pacifying the Eighth Military District, which encompassed far west Texas and southern New Mexico. It hung over his cash register, and had provided many a laugh for Ralph and other members of the Resistance.

"Yes, very impressive, Mr. Sellers."

The lieutenant leered at Ralph, sarcasm in his eyes.

"You may have fooled my superiors, but I am not at all convinced. From now on, you will be under my personal magnifying glass. One false move and your skull will join those on this wall."

Ralph examined the lieutenant's head carefully.

"Yes," he said slowly. "There is room for one more, isn't there?"

Ralph Sellers' ambitions for the American Resistance in El Paso far surpassed the simple repair of a few motorcycles. From the beginning of the Conquest, he had thought long-term. When the Russians ordered the closure of two Harley-Davidson dealerships in the region, Ralph had approached the owners of each and presented them with an ultimatum: use 'em or lose 'em. The Russians were going to crush the machines into scrap anyway, so he persuaded each dealer to contribute their Harley's to the Resistance while there was still time. Sure that new Harleys would be essential for the future of the Resistance, Ralph was able to pick up several hundred machines as patriotic contributions. Working with all of the local biker clubs, they were able to hire every piece of excavating equipment in the area, under the table of course, and constructed an enormous underground warehouse in the desert. Here, they stored nearly three hundred Harleys. A crew of men painted them in camouflage colors and maintained them in perfect condition for the time when they would be needed. No one knew precisely when that would be, but Ralph and the others knew that the time would come. Ingeniously, Ralph ordered mounts fabricated and welded to the frames of the bikes that would allow them to be fitted with M-60 machine guns, so that the passengers behind the riders could wield enormous firepower when the bikes were put into use against the Russian occupiers.

Seven miles away, in an equally remote stretch of desert, they built another underground bunker to hold the entire spare parts inventory of both dealerships, which it was clear the Russians would soon confiscate. Tons and tons of parts were there, enough to keep hundreds of Harleys running for decades.

It was nine o'clock in the morning. Hundreds of Harleys, from all of the clubs in the region, were assembled in front of Ralph's shop. They filled the parking lot and spilled over onto Rushing Street, covering it with gleaming machines, road warriors and rat-bikes for two hundred yards in each direction. It would be the staging area for the attack on the convoy. Everyone had brought weapons of their own, usually semi-automatic rifles like Kalashnikovs, H-K 91s, and M-16s which had been converted to full auto. There were as many women present as men. Some would operate the motorcycles themselves, but most would be passengers, riding behind their husbands or boyfriends, and they would constitute a major part of this attacking force's punch. They would wield the rifles, and after their magazines were empty, toss the grenades which would help destroy the oncoming Russians. Ralph had something for the riders to use as well. He had put together hundreds of Molotov cocktails, one and a half liter wine bottles filled with a mixture of gasoline and detergent, with a piece of cloth stuffed into the bottles' mouths: simple, but extremely effective. Three hundred fifty or so of these, combined with the destruction the ladies were going to exact, should be sufficient to turn that twenty-five truck convoy into a smoking ruin.

Such a collection of motorcycles was bound to attract Russian notice. Any patrols approaching Rushing Street from any direction would be reported immediately by radio. Those patrols would be dealt with, no matter what the cost. The destruction of this convoy was simply too critical to be deterred by anything short of a full Russian battalion. The route to the Interstate was being watched carefully, and any threatening Russian presence there would be eliminated as well. As far as the El Paso biker Resistance was concerned, this was for all the marbles. After the mission was accomplished, many of them would have to "disappear", at least for the foreseeable future. But that was a price they were willing to pay.

There was little doubt that this Resistance force had sufficient potency to get the job done. But the logistics of the attack presented problems. I-10 was divided into separated east and west-bound lanes. If the bikes rode in the east-bound lanes, and the Russian trucks were approaching in the right-hand west-bound lane, the distance between them would be too great for an effective attack. So Ralph decided that the bikers would ride east on an access road to the Lee Trevino overpass, turn left under it, and then right, onto the west-bound exit lane. They could then ride east in the west-bound passing lane of the Interstate, and pass within feet of the Russian trucks.

Every rider was given a Molotov cocktail. No one needed instructions in how to use them. Ralph carried a radio transceiver on his belt, which was always on. He passed through the immense gathering of Harleys, shaking hands, slapping shoulders, and offering words of encouragement. Suddenly the radio clicked twice. Someone with a similar set, miles away, had hit the send button twice in quick succession. It was the beginning of the signal. Ralph stopped and pulled the radio from his belt, waiting for what he hoped would be the second, and confirming, part of the message. Then it came: three more rapid clicks. The convoy was at mile marker ninety. It was time to roll. Ralph Sellers climbed onto the back of a flatbed truck. He raised his hands for silence. The din of the motorcycle warriors diminished.

"Alright everybody, the time has come. The convoy is at mile marker ninety, probably traveling at their usual regulation speed, about forty-five miles per hour. Most of you have seen combat before. A few of you have not. But you all know that this operation is absolutely critical. If we can prevent the Russians from setting up this communications surveillance equipment, we will be performing a great service for our country. The Russians will stay in the dark for years to come, the Resistance all across this country will be able to communicate freely, and by then we can drive these bastards back where they came from. And before this is over, I want Drugonov's head as a fender ornament on my road-warrior!"

The crowd cheered, clenched fists shot into the air.

"Not all of you will make it. If you're shot badly, and you don't think you'll be coming back, crank your throttle and ride head-on into the nearest Russian truck. Every bit of damage we can do to them will count.

"I want you to know how proud I am of you, you wonderful patriots, every one of you tattooed, bearded sons-of-bitches! If everyone in this country were made of the same stuff you are, this Conquest never would have happened in the first place! But this is our chance to make it a little shorter, and to free our fellow Americans from this yoke of Russian tyranny! The Russians are terrified of Harley-Davidsons! After today, they'll be having nightmares about them!"

More shouts and raised fists.

"Good luck to you, and let's give 'em hell! Let's show 'em what a bunch of pissed-off west-Texas bikers can do!"

That entire section of El Paso reverberated to the thunderous roar of hundreds of Harleys starting their engines. They began to roll toward the Interstate, Ralph in the lead. His Molotov cocktail dangled from his neck by its paracord thong.

Three hundred seventy-eight Harley-Davidson motorcycles rode the wrong way on the westbound lane of Interstate 10. They did a constant seventy miles per hour. When the convoy came into sight, that speed would increase—to eighty, ninety, perhaps even one hundred miles per hour. They would be on the convoy so quickly that the Russians would not even know what was happening, hopefully not have time to react.

At last, in the distance, on the flat west-Texas desert, a speck was sighted by the lead riders. The speck became a pencil line on the ribbon of highway. Throttles were cracked. Pistons moved more and more quickly. Carburetors sucked in more gas and air. The desert echoed with the unmistakable cacophony of the famous two-cylinder Harley engines. The roar was ear-splitting, but nobody cared. Adrenalin was flowing like cheap wine. The entire attacking force began to accelerate.

Seventy-five. Eighty. Eighty-five. Ninety. The distance was closing quickly. The pencil line had become individual trucks, trundling along at their standard forty-five miles per hour.

There was one armed lead-vehicle, and as the bikes thundered to within two hundred yards of the convoy, its startled—amazed—machine gunner opened fire. But he was so frightened that his fire was erratic, and had little effect. Russian bullets bounced off the pavement and sprayed into the desert. A few riders were hit, including Ralph Sellers, who took a bullet in the left shoulder. But it wasn't even close to being enough to stop him. His blood was fifty percent adrenalin, and the wound went almost unnoticed. With his left hand, he reached for his Kalashnikov, pulled the trigger and sprayed the lead vehicle. The Russian staff sergeant's head exploded in a bloom of red vapor, and the enemy machine gun went silent. Sellers held the trigger down as he screamed past the convoy at almost one hundred miles per hour. As he approached the last trucks in line, he lifted the Molotov cocktail from around his neck, lit it with his cigar, and hurled it at the Russians. He wasn't sure what he would hit, but he sure as hell would hit something. He did indeed. His gasoline bomb crashed through the windshield of the last Russian truck, turning the cab into an inferno occupied by two screaming enemy soldiers, whose flesh was rapidly hardening into a black crust.

Hundreds of Molotov cocktails poured into the convoy, filling the air like a swarm of insane fireflies. Explosions were everywhere. The Harley ladies leveled their weapons, held down their triggers, and raked the trucks with a hellish fusillade of bullets. When their magazines were empty, they went for their grenades, and hundreds upon hundreds of those broke through the canvas sides of the trucks, turning the sensitive equipment inside into junk.

The entire attack consumed twelve seconds. What was left was horrific to see: every single truck was on fire; many had overturned, covering the highway with corpses and demolished electronics. A few had coasted into the desert, their dead drivers roasted to a crisp. The attack had been such a surprise, and had been carried out with such lightning speed, that the Russians had had virtually no time to react. Only three Harley riders were killed, and nine wounded. The wounded included Ralph Sellers. But he was smiling from ear to ear as he led the riders back to El Paso, mission accomplished--in spades. Later that day, when Maximum Leader Drugonov heard the news, he pounded his desk, foamed at the mouth, and ordered the execution of every officer associated with the convoy and its assigned task. Russian heads rolled, but the beer flowed freely at the biker-bars of El Paso that night.

CHAPTER FORTY-FOUR

Directive 1378:

From: American Imperial Headquarters, New York
To: All District Commanders

In light of continued resistance by American militia forces despite our warnings, I consider it imperative that we inflict a lesson on the subjects of this colony. At 1400 hours EST on 3 September, you will collect in a central location one in ten subjects from all urban areas of more than fifty thousand population. These subjects are to be executed by firing squad. You are to tolerate no resistance. Any overt resistance should be dealt with by immediate execution. You are to instruct your personnel accordingly. You are to focus your efforts on populations of Negroes and Hispanics: these subjects are least suited to our needs, being the least skilled and least educated of our colonial subjects. Our needs for manual labor have been fulfilled from other sources.

We can accomplish two goals with this action: first, we will terrorize the American population into submission, and, second, we will liquidate those who are least productive.

You will require all television stations in your respective areas to broadcast these executions live. Further, you will require all subjects to view these executions on pain of death.
Drugonov

Louise Mosley bustled about her small living room, straightening, tidying, looking for dust. Her son Tyrone, who had taken to calling himself Ahmed Mohammed, had left the remnant of a soy-meat sandwich on the coffee table. She picked up the plate and carried it into the kitchen. There, her daughter Lashaunda was busy at the sink washing dishes. In the second bedroom, Louise could hear her two grandchildren playing some sort of noisy game. The third grandchild, too young to play, sat in a stroller and bounced up and down, sucking on a pacifier.

"Tyrone! Get in here!" Louise shouted.

A few seconds later the eighteen-year-old appeared in the doorway.

"Aw, Mama! Come on! You know my name is Ahmed Mohammed!"

"All right, Ahmed Mohammed, finish this sandwich before I whip your skinny behind! I don't work all day and half the night so you can waste food!"

The young man mumbled to himself, "You call this food?"

"I heard that! And yes, until something better comes along, I call that food! Now eat it!"

Louise worked as a health care provider in a retirement home about twenty blocks away. For years, she had been on welfare, but that had ended with the Occupation. So had the rent subsidies on the apartment. So had the food stamps. So had the medicaid. Now it was all on her shoulders. Sometimes, at night, she stared into the darkness and wondered how she was going to deal with it all.

That damned man of hers had disappeared for good; she hadn't seen him since five years before the Conquest. Now she could really use his help. It had been bad enough before the Russians came, with her raising two children alone, and then Lashaunda's children on top of it, but now it was tougher than ever.

And Lashaunda's man was promising to be just as worthless as her own. He stopped by once a week or so, to spend time with the girl. They were alone together for a few hours in the bedroom, and then he disappeared into the night. He never brought over any food, or any money, or anything useful. Louise was wondering if a fourth grandchild was on the way. God forbid, she thought.

Louise was only thirty-six years old, but she felt sixty. She just hoped that the job at the home held out. She had heard that many retirement homes had been closed by the Russians. A story was also circulating about what had happened to those poor old people: they were no longer productive, and so they were done away with: injections, administered by Russian medical personnel right in the homes themselves. At least they said it was painless; the old folks didn't suffer.

It pained her to see Lashaunda following the same path she herself had taken: pregnant at sixteen, drop out of school, and look forward to—nothing. Lashaunda had even outdone her. Here she was, only twenty, with three children already, not to mention the fourth that Louise suspected was in the oven. It made her sad, but she consoled herself in the knowledge that at the end of it all, a better world was waiting.

The television was on, producing white noise to which no one was listening. There really wasn't much to watch: just programs about service to the state and documentaries about Russia. Once in a while, there was a program about the evil things her own country had done over the years. Louise knew a lot of it was not true, but she watched it anyway. Her seemingly impossible schedule exhausted her from time to time. The most comfortable place to sit and recuperate was the sofa. And as long as she was there, she might as well do something. So she watched television.

This was one of those times. Louise almost collapsed onto the sofa, a groan escaping her lips. Before her on the screen was yet another presentation of the evils of the United States. This one seemed to be about racism. There were grainy monochrome images of lynched Blacks, scenes of fire hoses being trained on civil rights demonstrators, Black men being attacked by police dogs, and the motel balcony in Memphis moments after Dr. Martin Luther King had been shot. These were accompanied by a running commentary on the depravity of pre-Conquest America.

The voice on the television made the case to Louise that racism, individualism and the free market were all inseparably intertwined. The United States, it said, had been a country in which some people had been free, that was true: free to enslave and subjugate their fellow man. The market had been free, that was true: free to force Blacks and Hispanics into penury and servitude. The old system of individualism and freedom had been fundamentally corrupt. It had been a sham, designed merely to justify exploitation of minorities.

The system conceived by the Founders in Philadelphia had been morally bankrupt, designed to preserve the perquisites of an economic and racial elite. It had been based on selfishness, and this, the commentator assured her, was the most monstrous evil of all. Throughout American history, one race had selfishly subjugated another, the more able had selfishly taken advantage of the less able, the strong had selfishly subdued the weak. The root of all suffering in this insidious republic had been the desire of some to selfishly enjoy their lives at the expense of others, to steal from them what they produced through the satanic machinations of the free market.

She continued to watch as ancient film clips appeared of Andrew Carnegie, J.P. Morgan, Henry Ford, and John D. Rockefeller. These, she was told, were the archfiends of capitalism, the architects of selfishness in America. The old capitalist system had one saving grace: it had been productive. The policy of the New State would be to retain those productive elements, while rejecting the rest, selfishness and greed. The American people would work. They would produce, but not for their own benefit. A new day had dawned. The Russian people, and the benevolent Russian state, would relieve America of this terrible moral burden, this ethic of selfishness.

Her people would now be free to embrace the philosophy that their leaders, moral, intellectual and political, had espoused for decades: selflessness. They would at last be free to sacrifice themselves for the benefit of others; they would be free to follow the normal dictates of the human soul, unchecked by the grasping claws of selfish capitalism. Their efforts were needed, needed by others. Their Russian brothers and sisters were counting on them, depending on them to produce those things needed to survive and to live a life of comfort and dignity. And was not need a sufficient claim on the product of another's labor? Did we not all know this to be true? Have you not been told this all your lives? Now, at last, you have the opportunity to put this noble belief into practice! The screen was filled with happy, smiling workers producing goods on an assembly line, working in the fields. These people, she was told, had discovered the joy of productive self-sacrifice!

But, the announcer said, not everyone chose to join this new tide in history. There were criminals, malcontents, who resisted the state and its benevolent motives. They refused to subjugate their own welfare to that of the masses, refused to accept the idea that morality consisted in the greatest good for the greatest number.

Louise watched images of men being hauled off the ground with ropes around their necks, twitching, kicking in the air as their lives slowly left them. The scene changed to an antiseptic-looking white-tiled room, a meat locker, with trees of meat-hooks hanging from rails in the ceiling. Screaming men, eyes wild with horror, their hands and legs bound and with nooses of wire around their necks were lifted onto these hooks and allowed to hang from them. Louise could hear wet, gurgling sounds as the men thrashed to their deaths, blood spraying in all directions as the wire cut its way through their flesh. This, she was told, was the fate of those who insisted on thinking of themselves first, who refused to accede to the state, who felt they were too good to sacrifice themselves for the well-being of their Russian brethren.

The camera zoomed in on the face of a man on a hook. A rivulet of blood poured from his open but silent mouth. His eyes bulged monstrously as his body shook gently in its death-throes. The camera panned back, revealing to Louise hundreds of men, naked, hanging six to a tree of hooks, still at last in the cold whiteness of the meat locker, like carcasses waiting for the butcher.

The program continued. The new system, under Russian rule, would be different. The old Bill of Rights, written by white men for white men, has rightly disappeared, to be superseded by true liberty at long last. Under the new system, each person's rights would be respected, each person's "true" rights: specifically, the right to dedicate one's life to the benefit of others, the right to engage in the most highly moral cause imaginable: the sacrifice of one's own interests for those of humanity, even to the extent of survival itself.

In exchange for such selfless behavior, the Russian state would see to it that the necessities of life would be provided. Each person would have the right to claim the product of the labor of every other person. Mutual self-sacrifice would be the order of the day, each thinking less of himself than of his neighbor. With the Russian anthem low in the background, the announcer drew the viewer's attention to groups of shabbily-dressed Americans, many of color, filing onto busses in some unspecified city.

"Look," he said, "These were common street people, who were about to experience the magnanimity of the Russian state. They were being bussed to their new homes, homes provided to them free of charge. They would be given food, clothing, medical care and jobs. Now there is true liberty, he emphasized: freedom from want, freedom from fear!"

A man in one of these lines of derelicts caught Louise's eye: he was wearing a bright red navy watch cap, and was staring into the camera, a quizzical look on his face. The scene dissolved into the dual image of America's two greatest proponents of self-sacrifice, one old and familiar, the other new and dynamic. Sergei Drugonov's smiling face appeared on the left and Franklin Roosevelt's on the right.

Louise was still shaking from the terrible images she had just seen, but at the same time she felt a stirring deep within her. The announcer was right, wasn't he? He had only repeated things she had been told all her life. She had been intellectually prepared to hear them through decades of indoctrination. Self-sacrifice was good–wasn't it? Those selfish people deserved to die, didn't they? She did have a right to a place to live, food, clothing, medical care and a job—didn't she?

She had always been told so, by the brightest minds, the most important leaders in America. All those years during which she had been on welfare, she had been told that it was hers by right, hadn't she? What did they call it? An 'entitlement', that was it! The self-anointed leaders of the Black community had said so, the politicians had said so, the social workers had said so. Why was the current situation any different? Why should she feel so uneasy?

Then it came to her: now it was she who was working, she who was asked to engage in self-sacrifice, she who had something to lose. She was proud of the fact that she was pulling her own weight, and the idea that she should sacrifice herself and her family unsettled her. She was very confused: torn between her lifelong belief in the virtue of sacrifice, and her concern for herself and her family. She experienced a pang of guilt, so intense that it made her grimace. Yes, she was being asked to sacrifice herself and her family. What of it?

Didn't every person have a right to every other person's life? Everybody said so! Who was she to be selfish, now that the shoe was on the other foot? Still, there was something unnatural about it. She was their mother and grandmother! She had to put them first. Louise had never thought about such things before, but she now wished that she had. She felt curiously unarmed, intellectually unequipped to defend herself and her family. She felt as if she were being asked to unravel some great mystery, or to repair some complex machine, without the requisite knowledge.

A face appeared on the screen. It was a smiling, familiar face, one that Louise had come to trust. He was a nationally-recognized leader of the Black race, a man of the church, although he had always seemed to Louise to be more of a politician than a preacher. She had always listened to him, respected his opinion. He said to her,

"Brothers and sisters. All of my adult life, I have struggled against the powers that be in this country, against the rotten system that first enslaved us and then betrayed us. And so have you. We have struggled together. We have suffered the tribulation, and we have survived it! Our new Russian leaders will show us the way to Paradise! Listen to them! Obey them! Don't resist!

"Now I say to you, 'We are alive, our time has arrived!' Say it with me! 'WE ARE ALIVE, OUR TIME HAS ARRIVED!' Together, we can...."

For an instant, the screen went blank. Then it was filled by the figure of a local news personality holding a microphone, doing a remote broadcast from the street.

"Are we on Bob?" he asked someone camera right. Then, "Ladies and gentlemen. We have been asked to bring you coverage of what we have been told will be an important event here in the city of Houston. At this point, we don't know any more about what is going to happen than you do. We have simply been instructed to be at this location at this time."

A Russian officer moved into the picture from the reporter's right, apparently oblivious to the fact that he was now on camera. He listened carefully to every word the reporter said. The newsman cast him a sidelong glance and appeared to lose some of his locally-famous suavity. His next words were choppy and broken.

"As you can see behind me, people are being asked to leave their homes and to come out onto the street."

The absurdity of his choice of verbs was emphasized by the scream of an elderly man seen being prodded forward at the point of a bayonet. Virtually every American on the street was Black, with a smattering of Hispanics. Russian soldiers were attempting to bring some order to the chaotic scene, pushing and prodding people with their rifles into columns of three, each column standing shoulder to shoulder with the columns on either side of it, all along the sidewalk.

One strapping young black man obviously resented the rough handling. The viewers could see him slam his hands into the chest of the Russian before him, causing the soldier to take several steps backward. No one at home could hear what he was saying because of the ambient noise of the crowd, but it was obvious that he was shouting at the Russian, gesturing at him, seemingly challenging him.

The soldier raised his rifle, and the first shot of the day rang out. The back of the young man's head came off, spraying those behind him with a grisly mist. His corpse collapsed like a rag doll, arms and legs akimbo. People began to scream. More soldiers leveled their weapons, and something like order was restored.

"My God, what's happening here?" the reporter wailed.

"That is enough!" the Russian officer shouted, tearing the microphone from the other man's hand and pushing him aside.

"I am the military commander of the Houston area," he began. "What you are seeing is being repeated in every city in the United States. It is the price you must pay for your continued resistance. One in ten of you will die! Here, in Houston, that will involve over two hundred thousand persons. The continued operation of your militias will not be tolerated! Let this be a warning to those of you who survive. If you know someone in the militia, or have knowledge of militia activities, report to the appropriate military authorities at once! If resistance continues, another one in ten of you will be liquidated!"

The Russian colonel nodded to the major behind him, who, in turn, blew a whistle. Each column of three had before it a soldier, who now pointed his weapon at the first in line. None of the Americans on the street had heard what the colonel had said into the microphone, and so did not know that their lives were about to be snuffed out. They had been horrified by the death of the young man, but only a few suspected the nature of what was about to happen. Most still thought that they were simply to be counted, or perhaps even issued rations. Louise could see a woman with her young son standing in front of her, the woman's eyes darting from side to side with the furtive look of a hunted animal. In another column, there was a man in late middle age, bald head fringed by a ring of grey, holding a can of beer.

Louise imagined that the Russians might have interrupted his televised football game. She saw an elderly woman, body bent with the weight of years, apparently being told by the Russians to stand erect. One of them put the butt of his rifle under her chin and pushed upward, as if that would straighten her decayed spine.

Louise knew these people, not literally, not as individuals, but they were her people, people she had grown up with, people with whom she had spent her life. This may be happening on the block next to hers, she thought. What she was watching was not a movie, she reminded herself. These were not fictional characters experiencing some remote horror in some distant land. They were real. She was one of them.

The reality, the immediacy, of what she was seeing crashed down upon her in wave after wave of crushing realization. Louise began to feel ill; dreading what she knew she was about to witness. And yet she could not tear her eyes away. Here was a lesson, a part of her said. There was something here that she must learn. Something vitally important. A horror this intense must have an equally profound meaning. If she learned that lesson now, perhaps there would still be time for her to put together the pieces of the puzzle that so confused her.

As the soldiers raised their rifles, as the last seconds of these living human beings drew to a close, Louise felt as if she might lose her mind piece by piece, as if she were tumbling down a flight of stairs, uncontrolled, falling into a black abyss. As if on cue, the young soldiers pulled their triggers. The high-velocity bullets tore through each set of three bodies, and, with their remaining energy, pinged against the concrete and brick behind. Three dead with one bullet. Not bad, the colonel thought. His superiors would surely praise his frugality.

Two hundred fifty nine people were dead on this particular city block. Eleven remained alive. For the most part, they were children, so small that the first volley had gone over their heads as they were sandwiched between two adults. Some were unscathed. Some of the older children, the taller ones, had suffered horrible wounds. Louise saw one young girl, perhaps twelve, writhing in agony on the sidewalk, surrounded by the still corpses of her neighbors. The right side of her skull had been shot away, and the pink-white of her brain was clearly visible to the viewers. As the rest of her body thrashed about helplessly, her right arm and leg twitched in a spastic dance of death.

The camera caught a Russian soldier approach the girl, look down at her, and then up at his comrades. With a broad smile on his face he said something to them in Russian. It must have been a joke, because laughter could be heard from those off camera. With the tip of his bayonet, he probed the girl's exposed brain, as if testing its texture and resilience. The laughter continued. His curiosity satisfied, the soldier then proceeded to carry out his orders. Slowly, as if savoring some sort of sensual experience, he pushed his blade into the girl's brain. As the bayonet cut its way into her temporal lobe, inch by inch, and then, ever so slowly, into her cerebral cortex, one could see her bodily processes being disrupted, her functioning being destroyed bit by bit.

The spasms on her right side stopped. She lay still. Then her back arched and her mouth opened. She emitted a sound like a dog barking, sharp, staccato. Then the heaving of her chest stopped; she could no longer breath. But she was not yet dead. Her eyes said that. At last the soldier grew impatient, his lust for gore sated, at least with this victim. He began to move his rifle in a stirring motion, scrambling the girl's brain as biology students will do to a frog before dissecting it. His pace quickened, as if he sought to liquefy her brain, to homogenize it into soup. Now she was well and truly dead.

Some yards away, a little boy stood crying. He had not been touched by the fusillade. He clutched a toy in his arms, the same sort of action figure that Louise had bought for her grandson. He wore a bright red T-shirt emblazoned with the face of a smiling cartoon character. His mother and grandfather lay dead at his feet. A soldier approached him, patted him on the head, then on the shoulder and gently took the toy from his hands. The boy looked up at him imploringly, as an adult who might take care of him, protect him from the horror. The soldier bent down, and the little boy reached up to put his arms around the Russian's neck, seeking comfort, seeking refuge.

With a thrusting motion that was almost too quick to follow, the soldier drove the blade of his combat knife into the boy's stomach just above his pelvis. With a rapid upward movement that lifted the child off his feet, he opened the boy's torso as if with a zipper. For an instant, Louise saw a look of shock and betrayal on the boy's face, as a torrent of blood gushed out onto the sidewalk. The boy's intestines spilled out, hanging down around his knees. He fell backward onto a pile of corpses and let out a bloodcurdling scream, still very much alive. The soldier stood and watched; wondering how long it would take for the child to die.

An officer approached, holding his hands to his ears. He found the screaming unpleasant and distracting. He gave an order to the soldier in a few brusk words of Russian. The man nodded sharply and proceeded to bend over the small body. He lifted up the child's chin, almost gently, and, with the same knife, quickly slit the boy's throat. But the cut was not deep enough. The boy still breathed, with a strangling, gurgling sound. Again the man applied his knife, this time with more deliberation. Bearing down on the blade, he slowly drew it across the boy's throat. The camera's microphone could pick up a sharp, snapping sound of cartilage and gristle being torn. This time it was sufficient, cutting through the windpipe and the carotid artery all the way to the spine. The little corpse at last lay still.

A few feet away, an infant cried softly, still held in its mother's dead arms. Another soldier, with a cigarette dangling from his lips, took the baby's ankles in his hand and lifted it off the pavement until it hung upside down. He took a step back, off the curb, and stood on the side of the street. With his free hand, he removed the cigarette from his mouth, and flicked away the ash. He called to someone at a distance, someone who was not on the screen. He lifted the screaming baby up and pointed to it, a broad smile crossing his face. Apparently he had gained the attention he sought, because he then proceeded with the task at hand.

He swung the baby forward and then back several times, gaining momentum with each swing. Then, with a grunt of effort, he brought the child full circle, over his head. At the same time he squatted down to be closer to the surface of the pavement. With all his strength, he slammed the baby's head into the curb before him. The child's skull exploded like a blood-filled balloon. The soldier tossed the little corpse onto the heap. He took another drag from his cigarette, looked down at himself, and swore. On his freshly-pressed trousers were blood and bits of brain.

The other children were dispatched in similar fashion. None of them was shot. Cold steel is cheaper than gunpowder. At last the task was finished; all was quiet. Two hundred sixty two black persons and eight Hispanics lay on the sidewalk and spilled out onto the street. The entire episode had consumed twelve minutes, sixteen seconds of air-time.

Tyrone and Lashaunda had joined Louise in the living room, and the three of them gazed fixedly at the atrocity that unfolded on the screen before them. The Russian officer reappeared and once again warned the viewers against supporting the militia, but Louise could hear none of it. There was a roaring in her ears, as if from a great wind. She felt light-headed, as if she were dreaming. Her son was saying something, hatred in his face, but she could not hear him. She watched, incredulous, as her grandchildren played gaily on the floor before her, innocent, unaware.

Behind her something seemed to explode. Lashaunda and Tyrone reacted instantly, but to Louise everything seemed to be happening in slow motion. Someone was shouting: a strange, unfamiliar voice. She turned to see who it was: a man with an ugly face, a uniform, and a rifle. His mouth moved, forming words. He seemed angry: his features were contorted. He looked at Louise and motioned with his rifle. She was trying to understand him, but the roaring in her ears was too loud. All she could make out was the word "nigger, nigger, nigger," being repeated over and over again in a strange accent.

"Nigger! Out!" Corporal Koliev shouted again and again, motioning viciously toward the broken-down door with his bayonet. These, along with "whore" and "whiskey" were the only words he knew in English. Tyrone was not large, only five feet nine inches tall, and the Russian outweighed him by fifty pounds. Still, he was ready to fight. He bounced up and down on the balls of his feet, fists clenched, lips compressed into a snarl. Louise simply sat on the sofa, a vacant look in her eyes. Lashaunda decided to take the initiative.

"Come on, Mama," she said gently, placing her hands under Louise's arm, lifting her to her feet. As the two women moved toward the doorway, a second Russian entered. Koliev jerked his thumb in the direction of the three children, now no longer playing, but watching this scene with intense curiosity. The soldier hustled toward them, slung his rifle over his shoulder, and began to push the two toddlers toward the door. Almost as an afterthought, he reached back and grabbed the smallest child by the back of his shirt and lifted him out of his stroller.

The Mosley family was hustled at gunpoint into the dimly-lit hallway of the apartment building. All but the children, and a detached Louise, knew what was about to happen to them. As they approached the stairs, Tyrone yelled, "You son of a bitch! You're not going to shoot me down like a dog!"

He threw himself at the corporal, oblivious to the man's bayonet. Koliev had not expected resistance, and did not react well. Tyrone grabbed the rifle's barrel and pushed it aside. With his other hand he punched the corporal in the face. Blood gushed from a broken nose. The two men fell to the floor, struggling. Koliev's rifle was useless to him now. Tyrone's fingers dug into the man's throat, tearing at his esophagus. The young man screamed out his rage as he thrust his entire weight onto the tips of his thumbs buried in the Russian's neck.

A shot rang out. Tyrone's body was flung to one side by the impact of the nine-millimeter bullet as it tore through his right temple. He lay on his back in the hallway, dead eyes staring directly at Louise, who stood stock still, mouth forming a perfect circle, the horror of her only son's death crashing down upon her and pushing her further beyond the edge of sanity.

The second soldier stood in the hall, pistol in one hand, the youngest Mosley in the other. Koliev slowly sat up, gasping for breath. At last he said to the others, practically in a whisper, "Nigger! Out!"

Louise was the first in her row, with Lashaunda standing directly behind her. All of her friends and neighbors formed similar rows, just as she had seen on television. Louise was not sure what was real and what was not. She seemed to float over the sidewalk. The Russian standing before her might not really be there, she thought. Perhaps she was watching all of this on television. Yes, there is a camera now, and it's pointed straight at me.

She smiled and straightened her house dress, wanting to look presentable to all the people at home. Deep within her mind, her last remaining shred of sanity awakened, and the smile left her lips. An electric jolt ran through her body as the adrenalin surged within her veins. This is really happening!–a part of her mind told her.

She looked down at her three grandchildren, and, concentrating intently, realized that they were going to die. But why? What had they done? Oh yes, she remembered. Self-sacrifice. Self-sacrifice is the new order of the day. The people– the people have a right to my life. Who am I to say otherwise?

She looked into the eyes of the soldier standing in front of her, and saw only hatred. That puzzled her. She was acting as a good subject, wasn't she? Louise had time for only the beginning of a thought, as the bullet entered her forehead:

"Who am I...."

CHAPTER FORTY-FIVE

The forests of the Great Smoky Mountains of western North Carolina can seem almost primeval. One can walk through them and swear that he is the first person to tread that soil. Eons of fallen leaves silence the human step as one passes through the shafts of light filtered by the canopy of branches above. The land and its wild symphony of vegetation have formed a conspiracy to confuse the human mind; all but masked from sight is an almost infinite profusion of mountains and valleys, ridges and glens in which, it seems, one could become lost for all eternity. It was in this place that Leonard Tiffin made his home, and it was in this place that he was about to make his stand.

Leonard Tiffin was fifty one years old. Forty-seven of those years had been spent in these mountains, learning every tree, every rock, every animal's den, every trickle of water for thirty miles in all directions. Leonard Tiffin was a mountain man. The other four years had been spent in the United States Marine Corps. Being a young man of modest experience, Leonard at first didn't know exactly what to expect from the Corps. He looked at the various areas of specialization that they offered, and considered them carefully and earnestly. It soon became clear to him that the Corps placed great value on marksmanship. And shooting was what Leonard Tiffin did best.

As a child, he had started with a bolt-action twenty-two caliber Winchester with which he routinely broke wooden match sticks at fifty feet. His father had taken great delight in tossing shotgun shells into the air and watching his son hit them with uncanny regularity. At the age of ten his dad gave him a surplus 1903 Springfield 30-06 and some Lake City ammunition. Soon he was shooting squirrels out of the trees at impossible ranges.

For his next birthday, his father bought him an El Paso-made Weaver K6 scope, one of the ones made when Bill Weaver still ran the company. They bent the bolt down on the old warhorse of a rifle, mounted the Weaver, and Leonard became a true holy terror. He was hitting targets that other men couldn't even see. Leonard Tiffin had become a rifleman.

As the years passed, Leonard became better and better. In his eighteenth year, he used some of the money that he had made from hunting pelts and bought a Remington Model 700 action. This he sent off to Hart for a heavy-contour barrel in .300 Winchester Magnum. On this rifle he had mounted the best variable-power scope that Leupold made. With this weapon he truly discovered his love for long-range shooting.

He became obsessed with the idea of being able to kill a man at an even thousand yards. It was not that he intended to kill anyone. Leonard was well known as a peaceable and law-abiding young man. Everyone said that there was not a finer young man anywhere to be found. But it was the challenge of the thing. Leonard knew that there were evil people in the world, and he had been raised to defend himself and what was his against such people. He just wanted to be ready.

In those mountains it's difficult to find a spot in which a man can shoot at a true thousand yards. The land just isn't level enough. But Leonard found such a place: there was a clearing near the top of one ridge near his home, and he calculated that the distance to the top of an adjacent ridge was just about one thousand yards.

He had Bud Atkins cut him a piece of half-inch steel plate that was ten by fourteen inches: about the size of the vital area on a man. This he suspended from an inverted c-shaped piece of reinforcing rod the ends of which he had embedded in the ground in concrete. His goal became to hit this plate regularly from the prone, sitting and standing position. He figured that if he could do that, he could out-shoot ninety-nine point nine nine percent of everyone on the planet.

He quickly became engrossed in all the arcane aspects of long-range shooting: weighing and neck-turning shell-casings, experimenting with various powders, concerning himself with the ballistic coefficients and cross-sectional densities of various bullets, becoming intimately familiar with elevation and windage, and even with the effects of humidity on the flight of a bullet. It soon became clear to him that, to be a truly versatile shooter, he would have to practice at ranges other than one thousand yards.

Evil people can be encountered close-up as well as far away. He practiced at one-hundred yard increments from one hundred yards to a thousand. He carefully compiled notebooks full of data on all of his different loads, at every different range, under every conceivable condition. Though Leonard never received the training for it, he would have made an excellent scientist: he was careful, thorough and methodical.

His first time at the Marine Corps' firing range was an eye-opener for both Leonard and his superiors. From the beginning, he was shooting five-shot groups from one hundred yards that could be covered with a nickel; from two hundred, with a quarter. And that was with an off-the-shelf M16. He was startled by the attention he received. What he was doing seemed ridiculously simple to him. Everyone could do it. Couldn't they?

As soon as it was organizationally possible, Leonard was sent to sniper school. He soon found out that there was more to sniping than just shooting. But he took it all in easily. The mathematics of trajectory and windage that so challenged the others was second nature to him; he had mastered it years earlier. He became proficient at concealment and at stalking, and in all of the other skills of the master sniper. He became a very dangerous man.

At the end of his hitch, the Corps made it clear to him that if he chose to stay in, there was a bright future for him. But he felt that he had absorbed all that he could. And he longed for his mountains. He went back to North Carolina and lived his life as a quiet, solitary man. Then came the Conquest.

As a patriot, Leonard was horrified by what was happening to his country. But he, in his mountain fastness, was relatively untouched by it. He was virtually self-sufficient, hunting his meat and raising his vegetables. He had clothing enough to last for decades. There was a small patch of tobacco. He even had a still for making some of the finest whisky in the region. He had a truly impressive supply of reloading components, and, perhaps most important, several safes full of rifles and handguns.

He would sometimes go for months without seeing a living soul. That was the way he liked it. And that was the way he hoped it would stay. But hundreds of miles to the east, in Washington, D.C., a Russian clerk had done a computer check to see who had not turned in their guns when ordered to do so. There were literally millions of such people. Many of then had joined the militia, thereby disappearing as far as the Russians were concerned. A few had resisted the confiscation, and had been shot for their trouble. But on this day, the Russian clerk had instructed the computer to sort through the former BATF files, those hated yellow forms, and identify everyone who possessed more than a dozen registered firearms, and who had not turned them in. This narrowed the search somewhat.

Still, by the end of the day, the clerk had reams of printouts with many thousands of names. He brought them to his lieutenant, who would pass them up the chain of command. Eventually, they would be distributed to teams of New BATF agents, BATF agents under the old guard who had decided to stay on and work for their new KGB masters. More than ninety-six percent of old-BATF agents had decided to do so. It was some of these who would be paying Leonard a visit.

It was the morning of a fine, crisp early autumn day. It had rained the night before, a gentle rain that had brought out the rich, verdant odor of the forest and its billions of living things. On the porch of his cabin, Leonard sat in the rocking chair that had been handmade of the finest hickory by Old Man Peterson years before. He was cleaning an old Mosin-Nagant rifle, a Finnish Model 28/30 with a Sako barrel, perhaps the most accurate of the entire Mosin-Nagant series.

Though it wasn't much to look at, he valued that rifle for its elegant simplicity, its history and its beautiful functionalism. From time to time, Leonard would look up from his task to see the wooded hills that he loved wreathed in mist at this early hour, the eerie quiet broken only by the occasional soft, slapping sound of a water droplet falling from a leaf onto the forest floor. At his feet was his best friend: a Labrador Retriever named Bubba.

Bubba had chased many rabbits and squirrels through these mountains in his day. He and Leonard had been on many a hunt together. But now he was getting on in years, and spent most of his time lying on the porch of the cabin soaking up the sun. Leonard reached down and scratched the dog behind his ear, and was rewarded with a few wags of the animal's tail. And then they both heard something. Distant. Low-pitched. Bouncing. Wheels in ruts. A car or truck, coming his way.

He reached over for a box of ammunition and loaded the old Mosin, putting about ten extra rounds in his shirt pocket. Stepping off the porch, he walked into the trees next to his cabin. At fifty yards distant, he crouched down and waited. Four minutes later, he saw it: the familiar old Ford pickup of one of his nearest neighbors, Orville Pettis, who lived only six miles away. Leonard had not seen him in over a month. Orv' seemed to be in a hurry. The old truck bounced violently over the potholes in the road, and skidded to a stop in front of the cabin. Orville threw open the door and jumped out. A few seconds later, Leonard came out of the tree line, a broad smile on his face.

"Orv! What the hell's up? I haven't seen you move so fast since you tripped over that log full of bees! You look busier 'n a one-armed paperhanger!"

"Leonard! You got trouble, boy! They's people lookin' for ya. Gov'mint people. They smell like BATF. They's askin' 'bout where you live. Came to see me 'bout an hour ago. Didn't tell 'um nothin', a' course. But they's bound to get it outta somebody 'for too long."

Leonard looked down at the ground and pondered. He had expected this to come sooner or later. He had too much of a paper trail for the Russians and their American lackeys to ignore. Over the years since the Gun Control Act of 1968 he had purchased scores of weapons on the books. He had also purchased scores of them off the books, but those mattered little now. Many of the registered guns he still had; some he had sold or traded away over the years. But for every one of them, a damnable piece of yellow paper existed in some government file. The filthy, lying politicians had always promised that registration would never be a first step toward confiscation. No one who owned a gun had ever believed them.

"How many were there, Orv?"

"Six. Five men and a woman. In two black Chevy SUV's. Listen, we cin round up some of the boys 'n give 'um a real warm welcome, if 'ya like."

"No, Orv. I don't want to cause my friends no trouble. I can handle this by m'self. You go on now. Git home. This ain't none of your affair. I'll be all right. Don't worry 'bout me. The goddam, traitorous BATF agent's never been born who can take me in my own mountains."

Lanisha Jackson puffed nervously on her cigarette. It was her sixth that hour. Her heavy smoking, plus the fact that she was forty pounds overweight had caused her to take some ribbing from the other BATF agents. They usually asked her how many fleeing suspects she had run down that day. But she tried to brush them off, usually responding with the one-word reply, "Succa!"

Actually, she thought that the smoking added to her effectiveness rather than detracted from it. Her voice was deep and gravelly. She counted on it to intimidate people, to bully them. She had discovered in her twelve-year career with the agency that the vast majority of people were so frightened, so cowed, by the thought of having the full weight of the government come down upon them, that a sharp command from her was usually enough. This was even more true now that the Russians were in charge.

As a BATF agent under the old United States government, she had never been overly concerned with anyone's rights. But now she didn't even have to pay them lip-service. She could threaten people, beat them (when they were in restraints, of course), even kill them, with complete impunity. She enjoyed working for the Russians. Totalitarianism struck a chord deep within her.

Next to Lanisha, at the wheel, was Howard Marquart, a sixteen-year veteran of the agency. For thirteen of those years he had pushed paper, and lifted nothing heavier than a pencil. When the Russians took over, they put their own people in all the cushy jobs, and Howard had accepted a field assignment. He hated it. It was not the storm-trooper tactics that he minded. They actually added spice to the work. He had killed eight people in the past two years, and he found that especially stimulating. But he hated the physical discomfort of it. The hours, the noise, the people.

Howard had always been a sedentary man, a homebody. He enjoyed long, hot baths, manicured nails, and the comfort of his own bed. Now he found himself working under the most appalling conditions, like right now: bouncing along a dirt road in the middle of nowhere on his way to deal with some inbred hillbilly gun-nut. Howard was in a bad mood. He felt put-upon, resentful. He wanted to put this poor, ignorant fool out of his misery, confiscate the guns, and go back to the motel.

In the back seat sat Roger Broomfield. He leaned forward, forearms on the back of the front seat, peering intently through the windshield. Lanisha thought he was getting a little too close.

"Get off me, boy! Yo' on me like white on rice! Get back, o' I'll cold cock you so hard you won' know whether to shit o' wind yo' watch!"

Broomfield leaped backward and folded his hands in his lap, as a child would do after being scolded. It was not the first time she had said bad things to him, hurtful things. He stared impassively through dead, expressionless eyes at the back of Lanisha's head. He didn't like her. He really didn't. Someday he would make her pay, like all the others who had wronged him. Every one of them would pay. People like Lanisha, people at the hospital, all of them. He reached over and picked up the Heckler & Koch MP-5 submachine gun from the seat next to him. Placing it in his lap, he stroked its smooth receiver, fondled it, made love to it with his fingertips.

Roger had not taken his medication that morning. Sometimes he forgot. Whenever he forgot, he began to feel strange. Wild thoughts flashed through his mind, crazy thoughts. He knew they were crazy, but there was nothing he could do about them. During the interview process for the BATF, they had purposely kept his medication from him for several days, to see what he would do. They had kept him in a room, with a cot and a bucket. On the third day, someone brought in a cage full of rabbits, and placed it on the floor of the room. After Roger had twisted off all the heads, three men had come in. They were smiling. Roger had the job.

In the second car were three other agents. Tony Procelli was the driver. He was from New York. He liked to tell everyone that he was "connected." He hoped it would frighten them enough so that they wouldn't hurt him. Whenever he was sure it was safe, he killed people, usually by shooting them in the back after they were handcuffed. In his office, he had hung on the wall an oversized, painted plywood cutout of a Colt Peacemaker. Every time he killed someone, he would invite his co-workers into his office for the "ceremony." Using an absurdly oversized Pakistani Bowie knife, he would cut a notch in the grip of the wooden revolver. There were now fourteen. Then he would treat them all to cake and ice cream. It worked. People stayed away from Tony.

Next to Tony sat Max VanEck. Max was a thoroughly unremarkable man who intensely disliked what he was doing for a living. He hated shooting people, especially the frightened, unarmed ones with whom he usually dealt. He often dreamed about it at night. He would quit, but there was his mother to think of. He had lived with her all his life. She depended on him. And now she was old and in poor health. If he stopped bringing home a paycheck, what would become of them? Besides, if he quit working for the Russians, they would immediately suspect him of disloyalty. Nobody quit working for the Russians. And he had to admit to himself that things were better now than they had been under the old Republic. Society was more orderly, more controlled. He had always agreed with Lenin, that liberty was so valuable it had to be rationed. As much as he hated his job, the thought of bringing order out of chaos gave him a certain satisfaction.

In the back seat of the second car sat Paul Tully. He was only twenty-three, and on one of his first missions for the agency. He had been a junior in college when the Russians came and ended most higher education in the country. But during his attendance there, he had become deeply enamored with Political Science. He had thought, before the conquest, that he might continue in that field all the way to the PhD.

There was little call for political scientists now. That had not shaken Paul's commitment. He read voraciously. He was particularly fascinated with the politics of coercion: how to use political systems to make people do things that they would not do of their own free will. Of particular interest to him was the use of blackmail, threats and torture to achieve political aims. Paul had made an in-depth study of the use of electricity and of the dozens of mechanical devices that had been used over the centuries to break the body and the will. His professors at the university had introduced him, in a roundabout way, to the concept of force, and in the process instilled in young Paul a love of Marxism.

He had studied the masters in the field of coercion: the KGB and its predecessors, the East German Stasi, the Gestapo, Saddam Hussein, and all the rest. Those same professors had also, inconsistently he now recognized, tried to convince him to hate fascism. Many times, in his conversations with them, whenever they sought to revile someone in the harshest terms, they referred to him as a fascist. It seemed that anyone who disagreed with their own particular brand of Marxism was automatically a fascist.

But in his own reading, he had discovered that the two systems, communism and fascism, were virtually identical: they differed only in who had de jure ownership of the means of production, a trifling distinction. The only criteria that mattered, Paul realized, were that both systems were collectivist and totalitarian. He was attracted to them both. Statism was the common denominator; that is what he loved. He admired Hitler and Stalin with equal passion. In them, and in a hundred lesser despots, he saw men who knew how to use power. They had not been afraid to do whatever was necessary to strengthen the state, and themselves. Human life had meant nothing to them, and it had come to mean nothing to Paul.

People were insects, sometimes useful for the continued existence of the State, and sometimes harmful. Then they must be squashed. Paul wanted to be like those two great men. He wanted to work his way up in the Great Machine of the State until he, too, enjoyed absolute power over men. He was careful to ingratiate himself with his Russian superiors, hoping that they would sense his eagerness to do their bidding. He was more than ready to place all of his knowledge at their disposal.

Paul realized that his position was totally amoral. But morality was for fools. Power was what counted. As a BATF agent, he was getting his first taste of it. He had killed once already, and he liked the taste of blood. He had felt a surge of adrenalin, the kind of wild, primal blood-lust that he suspected Hitler and Stalin must have felt after their successes. He reveled in his ability to snuff out a human life, in the sheer power of it. Paul hoped that this day would offer another such opportunity.

Leonard Tiffin lay in the blind he had built on the side of the ridge five hundred yards from his cabin. From there he had a clear view of his home and the surrounding area, and of the road leading to it for a distance of about a quarter of a mile. He could have moved back further. His shooting ability certainly would have permitted it. But he was confident that run-of-the-mill BATF agents, with their nine-millimeter weapons, would literally not be able to hit the broad side of a barn at this range.

Leonard was essentially invisible. Even without the blind, the ghillie suit that he wore would have made him virtually impossible to see. It was made of strips of cotton cloth dyed green and brown to match the surrounding vegetation, and sown to a loose shirt and pants made of netting. The hat he wore was also covered with such strips. His face was expertly painted in camouflage. His rifle, too, was camouflaged, wrapped in green and brown tape with more strips of cloth to break up its lines. It was his trusty Remington Model 700, now on its fifth Hart barrel. He scanned the entire area with his Carl Zeiss-Jena binoculars. He waited. All was silence.

The old feeling had come back to him. He had wondered if it would. It was a sensation of supreme competence, of masterly control over a dangerous situation. It was the product of his Marine Corps training. He had never killed anyone before, and he had been concerned that under such pressure, the feeling would desert him. It had not. He was ready. At this moment, he was the ultimate predator.

The big, black Chevy lurched along the dirt road, veering into ruts and bouncing over potholes. Howard looked into his rear view mirror and saw that the second vehicle, with Tony at the wheel, was doing the same. Howard had really come to hate this assignment. He winced when he thought about how sore he was going to be in the morning. He just wanted to kill this son-of-a- bitch, get out of these woods, and take a hot bath. Next to him, Lanisha was trying to find her mouth with the filter of her cigarette, bouncing up and down on the seat like a beach ball. A long ash fell onto her lap, and she yelled, "Sheeeit!" as she brushed it away.

In the back seat, Roger was singing a song that he was making up spontaneously, something about turtles in the moonlight, and tapping out the beat with the palms of his hands on the vehicle's head liner. Suddenly, Howard slammed on the brakes and yelled, "Shut up, both of you! There's the cabin."

They were about three hundred yards from it. There was a slight rise between it and the vehicles, but almost all of the small dwelling was visible. Seeing no place to pull over, Howard just switched off the ignition. Tony did the same in the second car. Everyone sat quietly and looked for signs of life. They saw nothing.

"Everybody put on your vests," Howard said.

Because of his seniority, he was in command of this operation. The three in the front vehicle began to don their bulletproof garments. These would protect them from anything up to and including a .357 Magnum revolver round. They were useless against a .300 Winchester Magnum. The three men in the second vehicle saw what they were doing, and began to follow their example.

Howard took out his Russian-made binoculars, an excellent copy of the wartime German Zeiss model, and intently studied the cabin and the surrounding area. There was no movement. Howard slung the binoculars around his neck, opened his door very quietly, and signaled for the others to do the same. The six BATF agents squatted behind the lead Chevy for a brief conference.

"All right. Let's do it exactly as we planned. This guy has no reason to suspect that we're coming, so we should have the element of surprise on our side. Spread out into the trees, not so far that you lose contact with each other, and string out into a line. That way we all can see what's happening to the people ahead of us.

"When we get up to the cabin, Tony, Max and Paul will cover the rear and the sides. Lanisha, Roger and I will storm the front of the cabin, kick in the door, kill this bastard, and get the hell out of here. Are you all ready?"

Everyone nodded in the affirmative. Howard headed out first. The six agents moved horizontally, to find cover in the trees, and began moving toward the cabin, each in a crouch. They were all armed with H&K nine millimeter submachine guns, and Glock nine millimeter pistols. The rain had softened the underbrush, and they moved with remarkable silence. They were confident of success.

The superb optics of the Zeiss binoculars gave Leonard a razor sharp image as the agents exited their vehicles, and crouched down behind the first, for a conference he supposed. Then they rose and began to move through the woods, slowly, carefully. Leonard smiled. The lead agent stayed on the shoulder of the road. Leonard could not know that this was because Howard did not want to soil the cuffs of his trousers in the woods.

An overweight Black woman moved along clumsily through the brush. Suddenly, she tripped over something and landed on all fours, the H&K in the leaves three feet in front of her. Leonard saw her head shake, but he could not hear the obscenity she emitted.

Another one, on the other side of the road, put on a comical display of darting from tree to tree. He would peer stealthily around the tree, and then spring for another further ahead, with an affectation of spy-craft. Leonard thought that this would be the way Curly the Stooge would approach this particular task. He had to keep himself from laughing out loud.

The agents were on both sides of the road, moving slowly toward his cabin. Leonard wondered how many times they had done this before, how many other Americans these people had subjected to this kind of treatment. Was it the Russians, or had they always been this way? He thought for a moment. No, it was not the Russians. This had always been standard procedure for these people. Under their new Russian masters, they may have at last felt free to unleash all of their hidden aggression, aggression that they had masked, however slightly, under the old regime. But these were the same people, Leonard decided, that they had always been.

An anger began to well up inside him. What was it about America in its last decades that could spawn such monsters? What does it take for a man to turn against his countrymen, to seek to strip them of their liberty? What kind of a poisonous worm must live in the mind of a man who actively pursues courses of action that would turn his fellow citizens into helpless, unarmed serfs? Whatever doubts, whatever hesitation Leonard may have had about this day's work disappeared. He concentrated on the job ahead of him.

The lead agent was within fifty yards of the cabin, the latter-most at about eighty. Leonard raised the butt of his weapon to his right shoulder. The forend rested in an adjustable bipod. He pulled the rifle into his body and peered through its optics. He had sighted in the weapon for a five hundred yard zero. That is, the two hundred grain Federal boat-tail bullet from the big .300 Winchester Magnum would strike at point of aim at that distance. The Leopold Ultra M3 tactical scope was at ten power. This scope was equipped with a mil dot reticle; that is, instead of having traditional cross hairs for sighting, that feat was accomplished using a series of tiny dots along both the horizontal and vertical axes of the scope's objective. Center to center, these dots were exactly one mil apart, or one sixty-four hundredth of a circle. That works out to one yard at one thousand yards. At five hundred yards, each mil, center to center, represents eighteen inches. The mil dot system was superb for calculating range, trajectory and windage. Today it didn't appear that windage would be a problem. The air at his location was dead calm. But there might be wind at the target. He checked through his scope. There was none. The leaves on the trees were motionless.

Leonard moved the butt of the rifle slightly until the last man in line was in his sights. It was Paul Tully. Paul had just taken a position behind a tree about seventy-five yards from the cabin, pointing his H&K in its direction, praying that someone would step out, so that he could get credit for killing him. Leonard estimated that Paul was five hundred fifty yards away, and compensated for the extra range by raising his sights about ten inches, roughly half a mil. He gave one last glance for a freshening breeze, and began to take his shot. His fingertip touched the trigger.

It was a Shilen trigger, set to break at one and a half pounds. Slowly he applied pressure, and the ounces accumulated. He concentrated on his breathing. Calm. Regular. Take in a breath, and let out half of it. Then finish the trigger pull. Many rifle shooters say that as you squeeze the trigger, the shot should come as a surprise. Leonard had never believed that. He had trained himself to know precisely when the trigger would break. When his finger pressure reached exactly twenty-four ounces, the trigger broke like a glass rod, sending the bullet down range at two thousand eight hundred thirty feet per second. Leonard had not tried for a head shot. At this range, that would be a dicey proposition, although it could be done. He had concentrated on hitting a vital area, just as he had practiced years ago on that old steel plate.

Max VanEck, eight yards ahead of Paul, heard a slapping sound, and then a groan as if someone had been kicked in the chest. He began to turn to see what had happened when the crack of the shot reached him. Max instinctively ducked and looked around himself. He could see nothing unusual. He could not even be sure from where the shot had come, because of the way it echoed and re-echoed from the sides of the narrow valley. Max glanced behind him and saw Paul's legs protruding from behind the tree. He decided to take a look. Reaching Paul, he crouched over the body and felt for a pulse.

Leonard watched carefully as the other agent foolishly exposed himself. He had a clear view of the man's entire back. Quickly cycling the bolt action, he took aim. It was almost the same shot, just a few feet lower. Again he squeezed the trigger. Again the rifle roared. Max VanEck never knew what hit him. The bullet entered exactly in the center of his spine, and blew his heart out his chest. He was dead before he hit the ground.

Tony Procelli was fifteen yards ahead. He had heard two gunshots, but they had been very far away. He was not aware of what had happened to his two comrades. It never occurred to him to turn around and look. He was watching the people ahead of him. He had no idea where the shooter was, because of the echoes. Cringing, he lay on the ground, frantically looking around for a way out. He didn't give a damn about the mission any more. All he wanted was out. No one had ever shot at him before, and he found the experience terrifying.

Tony presented a near-perfect target for Leonard, whose elevation above his targets allowed him to look down on them somewhat. Tony was lying with his head toward Leonard. The rifleman aimed at the agent's shoulders, compensating for the extra forty yards range by raising his sights a fraction of a mil. Leonard was slightly off. The bullet hit Tony directly in the top of his head. It shattered his skull, exploding it like a melon, passed down through his neck and into his torso. It exited six inches below his navel, churning his insides into a sort of Tony-gut-soup.

Roger Broomfield either didn't know or didn't care what was happening. The poor soul whom the Russians had hired because of his pathological disregard for the lives of others, apparently also had none for his own. He walked out from behind a tree and began screaming. Raising his H&K, he fired the entire magazine into the forest in a wide arc, at one point nearly hitting Howard and Lanisha ahead of him.

The nine millimeter is a pistol round of very limited power, and none of Roger's bullets came within three hundred yards of Leonard. He felt a momentary pang of regret as he watched this obviously deranged man through his scope. Then his resolve returned. This man was no more deserving of pity than any of the others. He sent off a round which mercifully ended Roger's existence.

Howard, now having heard four shots, had correctly determined the direction from which they were coming. He lay on the ground behind some bushes, scanning the hillside with his glasses. Even if it had occurred to Howard to look five hundred yards away, instead of the two hundred as he was doing, he would never have seen Leonard. Leonard was a part of the forest.

"Where the hell is that son-of-a-bitch?" Howard yelled, just as a fifth round struck him in the forehead.

By this time, Lanisha Jackson was absolutely panic-stricken. She knew that everyone else was dead. She had never been left alone before. She didn't know what to do. She, too, had concluded that the rounds were coming from the hillside to the north. Fumbling with the controls, she pointed her weapon in that direction and pulled the trigger. The rounds sprayed into the brush, left and right, high and low. Not one of them came within five hundred feet of Leonard. Now there was nothing left to do but run. She tossed aside her weapon. Waving her arms over her head and screaming at the top of her lungs, she lurched down the road toward the vehicles. She had never been good at running, and the forty extra pounds didn't help.

Now this is a challenge, Leonard thought. The overweight woman presented a large target, but she was moving so erratically that he didn't know if he could hit her or not. Then he remembered shooting those aerial shotgun shells with his dad so many years before. The average man runs at six miles per hour, and the lead at five hundred yards would be seventy-four inches, or four mils. Leonard estimated that Lanisha was running at about four miles per hour. He led her by about fifty inches, two and three quarter mils, and squeezed off a shot. Lanisha felt her left knee explode. At that instant, it didn't hurt very much. It just wouldn't work any more. She collapsed onto the road in a heap. Then it began to hurt.

Leonard looked through his scope and saw his last target lying still in the dirt. He thought that his job was done. He stood, folded the bipod onto the rifle's for-end, and began to walk down the hillside. As he approached Lanisha, it became all too evident that she was not dead. Leonard had not heard such a string of obscenity since leaving the Corps.

He stood over the woman and looked down at her. She looked up at him, and the grimace of pain on her face turned to horror. With the ghillie suit and the face paint, he did have an unearthly, bigfoot-like appearance.

"Please Mister! Don' kill me! I din' do nothin' to you!" she pleaded. Just then she reached for the Glock at her side. Leonard kicked it away. It spun off harmlessly into the dirt.

"You were about to kill me, weren't you? To execute me, for ownin' guns?"

"No, no!" Lanisha screamed. "All we wanted was to check some serial numbers, thass all!"

"Lyin' bitch! You lyin' whore bitch!"

"Listen, mister! I was just doin' my job! I just take orders! You can't blame me for what the BATF does!"

"Sorry. The Nuremberg Defense won't work here. It you agree to work on their terms, you're as guilty as they are."

There was no point in wasting a round on this one. She wasn't worth the powder. Leonard drew his combat knife and knelt beside the woman.

"What you goin' t' do wid dat?" she asked, terror in her voice.

"What you think I'm goin' to do with it, BATF whore bitch?"

Lanisha opened her mouth wide and let out a bloodcurdling scream. This presented Leonard with an opportunity, a novel way to exact vengeance against this woman and all she stood for, to pay her back for all of the treason, for all of the treachery she and her kind had committed against the American people. With his right hand, he placed the knife into her mouth and against the back of her throat.

Lanisha knew something horrible was happening and tried to reach for the knife, but by then it was too late. Leonard had struck the pommel of the knife with the heel of his left hand with all of his considerable strength. The razor-sharp blade severed Lanisha's spinal column and caused extensive bleeding, though it had missed all of the major arteries. Its tip protruded from the back of her neck.

Leonard withdrew his blade with a jerk and wiped the blood off on Lanisha's blue BATF windbreaker. He stood and looked down at her. She was not dead. Her eyes were impossibly wide, staring into the sky, and her body twitched involuntarily though she was paralyzed from the neck down. He saw that she was chocking on her own blood, drowning in it. That would be too fast, he thought.

He turned the woman over on her side, and the blood began to pour out onto the ground. It was not a river of blood, but it was sufficient. Leonard was no doctor, but he was pretty sure that it would be a few hours before she was dead. He walked over to the porch and took off his ghillie suit. He sat in the rocker that Old Man Peterson had made of the finest hickory many years before. Bubba raised his head and looked up at his master. Leonard reached down and scratched him behind the ear again. Picking up the old Mosin-Nagant, Leonard soaked a cleaning patch in Hoppe's Number 9 solvent. He smiled at the aroma. It was wonderful. It reminded him of so many good times over the years. He chuckled to himself. "It wasn't even a contest, Bubba," he said. The dog put his head back down on the wooden porch and fell asleep.

CHAPTER FORTY-SIX

The air was crisp and clean on this early September day. The deep blue of the little lake glittered like a jewel in the morning sunlight, its sapphire waters resting in the soft folds of the surrounding hills. On the lake's shore was a clearing, and it was across this that Trace Forester strode, moving toward the cabin at its edge. He did not have the luxury of appreciating the surrounding beauty. His mind was elsewhere. There was work to be done, critical issues to discuss. The meeting that was about to take place in this Arkansas wilderness would determine the future of the resistance, and in all likelihood the future of the United States itself.

The two militiamen flanking the cabin's door snapped to attention as they saw the Northwestern Regional Commander approach. It had been some three years since the Conquest and in that time he had grown lean and tough, much stronger than he had ever been in his life. His leathery skin, wind-burned and tanned, supported a plain military uniform, undistinguished except for the two silver stars that he wore on each shoulder.

His eyes burned with an intensity that made most men uncomfortable; they seemed to pierce directly into the soul, and had been responsible for the uncovering of more than one traitor. Back in the days when he had owned the factory in Indiana, he had considered himself a good judge of character. However, the events of the past three years had sharpened his perceptiveness to an uncanny degree: the lives of a great many men had depended on his judgment in this regard, and he had become nearly infallible.

Physically, he had been luckier than many. He had received several flesh-wounds, but they had healed quickly and had not affected his performance. The only outwardly-visible sign of the wounds he had sustained was a long, ragged scar running down the left side of his face. The man who had wielded that Russian bayonet had not lived to tell the tale.

Trace had risen through the ranks by a combination of ability and default: when decisions had to be made, when action had to be taken, Trace had always been there. When other men vacillated, Trace had displayed decisiveness. When others urged excessive caution, he had demanded bold action. He had discovered a natural ability to lead within himself, as well as a soundness of judgment possessed by few men.

Throughout his rise, his commanders had deferred to him, seeking within him the qualities they themselves lacked. From his first command of the camp in

Montana, he had moved to head the militia of the entire state. He had met with great success, recruiting thousands, and eventually pushing the Russians out of the cities and then out of the entire state. When the militia commander of Washington state had been killed in action, and the commander in Oregon captured, Trace filled the vacuum.

He had accepted enormous new responsibilities, but had handled them brilliantly: harassing the Russians, dodging and weaving, bleeding them little by little. Eventually, the United States Northwest Regional Militia came to control ninety percent of the land area of the region, having pushed the Russians into a handful of small strongholds from which they hardly dared venture.

Today's meeting was unique. It would be the first time since the Conquest that the entire national command structure would come together in one place. Prior to today, none of these men had even met, though they had communicated by various means as circumstances had permitted. Such a meeting was exceptionally dangerous: one leak and the Russian occupiers could decapitate the entire militia movement. But it had been determined that this meeting was necessary. The war to reconquer the United States, the War of the Re-conquest, as it had come to be called, was at a critical turning point. For the first time, the militia leadership seemed to be in disagreement, and success hung in the balance.

Trace entered the cabin and saw that it consisted of one large room. Whatever furniture it had once contained had been discarded, and replaced with one large table and chairs. At this table sat three men, with a fourth standing, arms folded, several feet away. Their conversation stopped as they saw Trace, and they looked up at him as at a stranger. Two hours earlier, none of these men had ever seen each other, and this was the first time any of them had seen Trace Forester. The four men stood and smiled. One of them extended his hand. It was strong, and as hard as if it had been carved of oak.

"You must be Trace Forester," he said.

"That's right," Trace answered, smiling in turn at his comrades in arms.

He took the man's hand and held it in a prolonged firm grasp, as if grateful for a meeting of friends long delayed. With a practiced eye, Trace took the measure of these four men. He was not disappointed. Each gave the impression of having been tested again and again under the most trying conditions, forged like tempered steel in the flames of battle. They were dressed in the same unostentatious uniform that he himself wore, with only their two stars as insignia of rank. Their hair, all graying, was cropped close in an efficient, businesslike manner. Their bodies, too, were lean and hard, every ounce of fat long since consumed by their prodigious efforts to restore liberty to their country. Trace noticed something else: they had a faint look of exhaustion about them, as if their long, continuous conflict were wearing them down, strong men being pushed to their limits, and slowly being ground down as the strongest granite will do after eons of sandstorms. He wondered if it showed on his face as well: the interminable hours, the endless concentration, the gut-wrenching feeling of sending men to their deaths, however just the cause.

"Have a seat, Trace," said Carl Pettigrew, Southeast Regional Commander.

Pettigrew had achieved a certain notoriety, even among the top militia command. Three months earlier, his forces had surrounded Birmingham, Alabama and had obliterated an entire Russian regiment. That action had marked a turning point in the war: the United States militia was moving out of the phase of guerilla warfare and beginning to engage in partisan warfare.

Rather than just hitting and running, acting as a thorn, however painful, in the enemy's side, Pettigrew had met the enemy on his own terms, had engaged him on a level battlefield, and had won. This had been made possible by dramatically upgrading the capability of the militia: turning it from a rag-tag group of patriots into a disciplined, organized force, improving communications and transportation, logistics, and, perhaps most important, improving the militia's weaponry. As had the militia as a whole, Pettigrew had taken every opportunity to strip the enemy of its most potent weapons, slowly accumulating everything from machine guns to armor.

As had happened throughout the country, the melange of small arms with which the militia movement had started its struggle, ancient Springfields and Mosin-Nagants, lever-action Winchesters, Chinese and Russian SKSs, and whatever else the government had seen fit to leave to the American people at the time of the conquest, had been replaced by the latest in Russian weaponry. This had greatly simplified the supply of spare parts and ammunition. But Pettigrew had gone beyond this. He had even managed to acquire several helicopter gun-ships, and had used these to great effect against the startled Russians at Birmingham. Trace was anxious to find out just how he had managed to pull that off. The victory had been stunning, although the Americans had not been able to hold the city in the face of massive Russian reinforcements. Everyone in the room suspected that it was this humiliating Russian defeat that had shocked Drugonov into making his latest pronouncement.

Albert Rauda, the Northeastern Regional Commander, sat across from Trace. He too had racked up a string of impressive victories, although he had his nose badly bloodied at the battle of Syracuse. Pennsylvania, outside the city of Philadelphia, was almost entirely under his control, as were large areas of upstate New York, western Massachusetts, and most of the states of Vermont, New Hampshire and Maine. Trace noted with a smile that Rauda wore on the sleeve of his uniform a patch containing New Hampshire's motto: Live Free or Die. He recalled the stories that had circulated widely throughout the country, of the New Hampshire Militia at the Battle of Concord, charging into the Russian machine guns, dropping in wave after gory wave, but finally capturing their objective. It was said that there had not been one Russian survivor. As Trace looked into Rauda's steely eyes, he believed it.

Patrick Scanlon sat to Rauda's left. He was a scrapper who had grown up on the streets of Chicago. Before the Occupation, he had tried his hand at boxing. Trace noticed the gnarled hands on the table before the man: several knuckles had been broken, and the bones had not knit well. Also, those hands were covered with scars. Trace knew that these were not all from the ring. It was well known that Scanlon had beaten several Russians to death with his bare hands, ostensibly to gain information. It was also said that he had continued to beat them long after they had given him the information he sought.

It was no secret that Scanlon considered Russians to be the lowest form of life. He killed joyously, with passion. He had risen through the ranks because he was a master at the ambush, a skill that he had developed during his street-fighting days. Early in his militia career, he had ambushed and destroyed squads, then platoons. His subordinates had learned from his example, and now Scanlon's forces were luring entire companies into their destructive webs throughout the entire Midwest. He had a reputation for being a hard drinker, but no one could point to an instance in which liquor had impaired his performance. It was said that Pat Scanlon never took prisoners.

Cayetano Melendez, commander of the Southwest Region, sat at the head of the table to Trace's right. His dark, smoldering eyes revealed an anger that had become a permanent part of his makeup. He had never much cared for Anglos, but had come to hate Russians even more. His parents, four uncles, three aunts, five brothers and three sisters had all been incinerated when Los Angeles had gone up. All of his neighbors and all of the friends with whom he had grown up had been reduced to glowing ash and scattered to the wind.

Cayetano had been in Albuquerque when they met their end. He found himself at times overwhelmed by an irrational guilt that he had not died with them. Sometimes, at night, when he was alone, he would slip into a profound depression accompanied by a baseless panic, an almost overpowering anxiety. It terrified him; at such times he was sure that he was losing his mind, that he would forever be a quivering living corpse, divorced from reality, relegated to a hell that no one else could know.

Cayetano Melendez had discovered his own personal monster which would, at times, grab him by his hair and shake him to his roots. In those moments, the thought of ending his life seduced him as no beautiful woman could; a voice within him cried out for relief, for an end to the pain. More than once, on those dark, horrible nights, he had taken his pistol in his hand. But one thought kept him alive, one great desire; one ambition that raged like an inferno within him: revenge. He would kill Russians; he would wade through an ocean of their blood until it quenched that fire and drowned that monster. And so, with the sunrise, he always found the strength to muzzle the beast, to once more chain it to the floor of his soul, at least for a time.

During the course of the last three years, other events had pushed him even closer to the edge of insanity. As an ordinary soldier, early in the Occupation, he had seen an entire family in Naco, Arizona, seven people, crucified in their front yard as collaborators. Click: another notch toward madness. A whole town in southern Utah had been annihilated, every single man, woman and child. By the time Cayetano and his unit had arrived, their bodies had bloated in the sun, and the carrion birds had done their work. Click: one more notch. The Russians treated everyone badly, but they considered Hispanics to be nothing more than vermin. He had seen his people poisoned, starved, worked to death, raped, tortured. With every event, Cayetano's sanity slipped away bit by bit. Click, click, click.

Trace looked at the man, but could see none of his inner torment. But there was, he decided, something in the eyes, something terrible, something dangerous. And everyone knew that Cayetano Melendez was indeed a dangerous man. No one in the militia movement had thought of more ingenious and horrific ways to kill Russians. His methods were so gruesome that he would not have been tolerated as a commander had he not displayed such brilliance in the field. He was known among the Russians as "the Ghost": he would appear out of nowhere, viciously strike his enemy, and disappear like smoke. Melendez had resurrected a form of obsolete combat that the West had not seen in a very long time: light cavalry.

Melendez was not purely Hispanic. Some of his ancestors had been Apache. He recalled tales from his childhood about how his aboriginal forebears had tormented the U.S. military, striking unexpectedly and retreating into the trackless wilderness, only to attack again at the time and place of their choosing. He saw this strategy as perfectly suited to the current conflict. His men knew the mountains and deserts of the Southwest like the backs of their hands, and, on horseback, slipped easily across territory that was impassible to Russian vehicles. The enemy had given up trying to catch him on the ground, and had long ago resorted to helicopter gunships in their attempts to neutralize his forces.

But Melendez had seen to it that his men had a good supply of shoulder-fired surface-to-air missiles, at first American stingers, and later their Russian equivalents. They had shot down one hundred sixteen aircraft so far. This was a price that the Russians were increasingly unwilling to pay and they had ceded large swaths of territory to Melendez' forces. As long as they stayed in their mountain redoubts, they were invincible.

Melendez had not done so well in the cities, at least so far, and these were where the Russians were holed up. But he was constantly adjusting his tactics, probing for weaknesses, infiltrating the cities to sabotage facilities and assassinate high-ranking Russians. In general, the war was going well for Cayetano Melendez, and the other men around the table respected him greatly for his talents.

"Trace, we hear that things are going well in your area. But I'm sure you're having the same kinds of problems that the rest of us are having."

It was Pettigrew, leaning forward on his elbows at the table and giving his full attention to Trace's response.

"We've had our share of success, Carl," Trace answered. "We've denied the Russians most of our territory. We've pushed them into enclaves in the cities. But I don't think we've hurt them as badly as it seems. We have yet to meet them in a pitched battle and win. They still have a tremendous advantage in heavy weapons: armor, artillery and air assets. But we're taking more and more of those away from them all the time. Still, to this point, I don't think that we've done much to destroy their war-fighting capability. At least not yet: controlling territory is one thing, destroying the enemy is another."

Albert Rauda spoke up. "I know what you mean, Trace. I'm as frustrated as you are. But I keep telling myself that these things take time. In the last month, we've managed to capture eleven heavy tanks and thirty-nine pieces of artillery.

Everything intact. We've been shooting down helicopters like there's no tomorrow. I plan to engage the Russians in a major confrontation very soon. If we're successful, I think it'll turn the tide in the Northeast. But I'm beginning to wonder if the game is worth the candle, considering what Drugonov has up his sleeve."

"I think we've done a hell of a good job so far, considering where we started," Pat Scanlon said. "My people are preparing now for an all-out assault on Omaha and St. Louis within the month. I've practically cut off Chicago from the outside world. To me, it seems that the whole tenor of this war is about to change. If we can get some more heavy weapons, challenge the Russians on the ground, we can really hurt them. But I agree with Al: maybe we should rethink this whole thing if Drugonov really means what he says."

"That's exactly why we're here, General Scanlon."

No one had seen him enter. Houston Trainor walked to the table as the four other men stood at attention.

"At ease. Please, as you were," he said with a smile. The tall man from Texas shook hands all around and then stood at the head of the table, assuming leadership of the group easily, naturally, as a man would who had spent many years in command of other men. The three stars on his shoulders, indicating the highest rank in the United States militia, glittered as he sat down. The others followed.

None of the men at the table knew much about General Trainor. It was said that he came from one of the three hundred families that had constituted the original Anglo settlement of Texas. One of his ancestors had fought with Sam Houston at the Battle of San Jacinto, and he had been named in honor of that occasion. Before the Conquest, he had made a career in the Army, rising to the rank of Brigadier General.

When the Russians arrived, he, like all high-ranking officers, had been offered a reward for his "cooperation." Everyone in the militia knew what happened next: when his superior called Trainor into his office and offered him a position with the occupation forces, Houston Trainor had drawn his pistol and shot the Major General between the eyes. The rest was history.

"First," he began, "I want to congratulate all of you on a job well done. Better than that: on an almost miraculous job. You men have taken a rag-tag bunch of pot-bellied civilians and turned them into the finest guerilla fighting force in the world. In three short years, you've driven the Russians out of our countryside; you've turned them into paranoids, desperately clinging to every square inch of territory they still manage to hold. Each of you has increased the strength of his forces to the point where we are nearly ready to meet the enemy head on, in open battle. But, of course, we couldn't expect Drugonov to take this lying down.

"As you know, he has threatened to destroy one U.S. city every month unless we surrender. We have no idea which cities he has in mind, so countermeasures are impossible. He's had plenty of time to plant nuclear devices in every city in the country, if that was his intention. I think we have to take him seriously; that son of a bitch is ruthless enough to carry out his threats. And so we have to decide, here and now, what we are going to do. Should we keep fighting, and perhaps lose tens of millions of our countrymen? Or should we call it quits, submit to Drugonov, and save all those lives?"

There was a stillness in the room, as each officer contemplated his response. Then, Scanlon spoke up. "Jesus. I can't imagine Chicago or St. Louis or any of my cities just—gone."

"Atlanta, Miami, Richmond—vanished?" Pettigrew said. "The thought of it makes my blood run cold. I want this country to be free as much as any man alive. But can we ask our people to pay that kind of price?"

"Take it from me, my friends," Melendez added. "To lose an entire city that one loves, to see it turned to ashes, with all of its people, is an unspeakable horror. We must think about this very carefully."

Trainor watched his subordinates closely, trying to read their faces, see into their minds. He decided to probe a bit.

"Am I to take it that you would recommend putting an end to the resistance? Consider your responses well, gentlemen. We've seen one of our great cities vaporized. Can the country withstand more of that?"

Albert Rauda had been staring out the window. Without diverting his gaze he said, "How much can our people sacrifice for their liberty? If we could ask them, what would they say? It may be months before we're ready to strike at the heart of Russian power in this country, before we can achieve any kind of real victory. By that time, several more of our cities could be gone, millions more dead. I hate like hell to say it, but perhaps life without liberty is preferable to no life at all."

"Trace, what do you have to say?" General Trainor asked in a low, calm voice.

Trace Forester, who had been staring at his fists clenched before him on the table, raised his eyes to Trainor's and said in a voice that shook with emotion,

"Is life so dear, or peace so sweet, as to be purchased at the price of chains and slavery?"

"Patrick Henry," Pettigrew said, almost under his breath.

Trace pushed back his chair and rose slowly. One by one, his eyes met those of the other four men around the table. He turned and walked to the opposite wall, stood there for a moment, as if contemplating, and then faced his fellow officers once again. In a quiet, measured voice, he began.

"General Trainor, you say that the question before us is whether to keep fighting, at great cost, or to surrender. Let us think carefully about the full import of those two options. What is ultimately at stake here? For what do we fight? For our liberty, of course. It's been suggested in this room that life under Russian dominion— without liberty-- is superior to death. But would that really be life? Is life possible without liberty?

"Let's define our terms. What is life? Of course, on the most basic level, it is self-sustaining biological activity, perhaps a series of chemical reactions. That alone would be sufficient to describe the life of a bacterium or a plant. And it is only that kind of purely biological existence that the American people would experience under Drugonov and his successors.

"But life to a man is a great deal more than simply a chain of chemical reactions. It is as much intellectual as biological. To be truly alive, a human being must realize his potential; he must work to accomplish a set of goals; the loftier those goals, the better. Each man must push himself to be the best that he can be, to reach his absolute limit in productivity and accomplishment. Anything less is subhuman. Anyone who settles for less sacrifices his self-esteem, his mental health, and perhaps his very survival as a living organism.

"But human survival, fulfillment, and happiness are not guaranteed in this universe. Unlike other animals, the means for our survival do not occur in nature. We must modify nature in order to survive. We must discover ways to build our homes, grow our crops, and fashion our clothes. And how do we gain the knowledge necessary to achieve these goals? It does not come to us through instinct, but through our faculty of reason: our ability to integrate sensory percepts into concepts, and those concepts into ever larger and more useful ones. To achieve those things necessary for survival and happiness, each man must use his rational faculty, his ability to reason—which is uniquely his as a human—to choose from among an infinite number of possible courses of action. Some of those courses of action will be efficacious, and will lead to survival and happiness. Others lead to destruction. There is no mechanism that will guarantee that man will choose to pursue the correct courses of action: he is neither omniscient nor infallible. But reason is his only tool for doing so. Some men go though life using their faculty of reason rarely, if at all, because man is a creature of volitional consciousness: he can choose to be conscious, that is, to use his faculty of reason, or not to use it, and live an unconscious, irrational life.

"The ability to pursue those courses of action which our reason tells us are necessary for our survival and happiness is called rights. The freedom to exercise our rights in a social context is called liberty. Plants and animals have no rights. They do not choose from among various possible courses of action; those which they pursue are, so far as we know, dictated by biology or by instinct. And that is sufficient for their survival. Not so for man. We possess no instincts that will allow us to survive. We alone require the ability to decide, through the use of reason, which courses of action we will pursue in order to survive and fulfill ourselves as human beings. That is simply another way of saying that we must be free to exercise our rights, and to live in a condition of liberty if we are to survive physically and psychologically. If this sounds strange to you, it is because Americans have forgotten what rights are. Not one in ten thousand could define them as I have just done.

"This confusion has had profound implications for our society, to the detriment of the American people. One good example involves property rights: the right to own, use and dispose of the property which we have produced or earned through our own efforts, following courses of action which we have chosen using our faculty of reason. I choose property rights because they are so critical to human survival; unlike the other animals, we must own property: food, clothing, shelter, if we are to survive. Without property rights, no other rights matter.

"Decades ago, our national ignorance concerning the true nature of rights, including property rights, allowed a perversion to enter our political life. We were told that we each had a right to the property of others. Our self-serving politicians---nothing more than welfare pimps, really---discovered long ago that they could gain votes, and personal power, by pandering to those who had been convinced that they had a right to what others produced, that they could commandeer the wealth of its producers through the use of coercive government."

The men around the table looked intently at Trace. They were hearing something they had never heard before. It was as if a mist were lifting before their eyes. He decided to give them more detail. He felt it was urgent that these men understand fully.

"Common thieves make such a claim to the property of others through the use of brute force. They point a gun at your head and say, 'Give me your wallet or I'll kill you.' We, as a country, chose a less direct, a less overt, method. Coercive government, voted into office by those who seek what they have not earned, acted as the intermediary: it would hold the gun to the head of the producer under cover of law, and distribute the stolen booty to its faithful, dependent constituents. It was armed robbery by proxy.

"Now we are faced with armed robbery on an unprecedented scale. Drugonov demands not some of the product of our labor, but virtually all of it. Our rights to pursue courses of action of our own choosing, to produce for our own consumption and for that of our families, our ability to live like free men and women, not just in the economic realm, but in every sphere of human activity, all of these have been shattered by the crack of the Russian whip. The condition of liberty which is necessary for the free exercise of our rights, which in turn is necessary for our survival, no longer exists.

"If liberty is the ability to exercise our rights, and rights are the ability to pursue courses of action of our own choosing in our lives, and if we must pursue efficacious courses of action in order to survive as human beings, then liberty is a requirement for human life. Without that liberty, we may be able to survive as biological organisms, at least for a time, but we will no longer be human. We will be little more than bacteria. Liberty is a necessary condition of human survival. We can no more survive without it---as true, fully-functional human beings--- than a plant can survive without sunlight. As it says on your shoulder patch, Albert, we really must 'Live Free or Die'.

"And you, Albert, mentioned sacrifice; you asked whether or not our people should be asked to sacrifice their lives for their liberty. I say to you that such an exchange would be no sacrifice. When we give up something we value more for something we value less, that is a sacrifice. We can value nothing more than our liberty; without it we have no life as true human beings. Death is preferable to life as a slave. Life, as a slave, as a purely biological organism, is not the ultimate value; liberty is. If we give up our lives in a struggle to regain our liberty, we are making a good trade. It is no sacrifice. No other rational option is open to us."

CHAPTER FORTY-SEVEN

The grizzled old wino staggered out of the alley. He stuffed the filthy, damp handkerchief into the pocket of the tattered double-breasted suit-coat that he wore over his strappie undershirt. His head swam. All morning he had been drinking "Pink Ladies": the juice of canned Sterno strained through a piece of cloth. If only he could raise thirty-five New-Cents, he could score a half liter of the cheap vodka that the Russians made available in abundant quantities to all of their American subjects.

He kicked the week-old sheet of newspaper out of his way–the only thing that moved on the street beside himself and proceeded deeper into the center of the city, occasionally leaning on the walls of buildings for support. He passed one of the street signs that could be seen all over every city, town and village in the country. It said, in bright red letters, "Don't do it! It is forbidden!"

The old man, who had haunted the back streets and alleys of Boston for many years, found himself in a familiar place: on the sidewalk in front of Faneuil Hall, one of the most historic of Boston's many landmarks, known as the "Cradle of Liberty" because of its use by Revolutionary patriots as a meeting place. He looked around himself, weaving slightly as he turned. Most of the windows in the lower stories of the surrounding buildings had been broken. This had happened all over the city, and, in fact, in every city in America. Window glass had become impossible to get, and the street hooligans realized that they could throw rocks with impunity, causing near-permanent damage. The Russians didn't care.

His bleary eyes attempted to focus on the sidewalks. Yes, they were still here, he thought, at least some of them. A handful of pedestrians could be seen walking slowly along the street, heads bowed as if in submission. One of them carried a dead cat in a plastic bag. The wino noticed that others eyed the man with envy. A few of the younger ones moved threateningly in his direction. The man was dressed in what had obviously been an extremely expensive cashmere jacket and wore the finest of leather shoes made in Dublin.

He had clearly made an attempt to keep up his appearance, but the occupation had taken its toll. His clothes were stained and shiny with wear, and the sole of one of his Irish shoes flapped with each step. The man noticed the attention his cat-corpse was drawing, and clutched it tightly to his chest. Though it was three days dead, he still did not want it to be stolen. He had a family to feed. People in Boston had died for less.

Everyone was sick to death of eating soy: soy burgers, soy soup, soy chowder, fried soy, grilled soy, boiled soy. Many people literally dreamed of eating real meat. It had become a citywide, indeed a nationwide, mania. But there was not much of it left to be had in any American city, including the city of Boston. Everyone had eaten their pets long ago.

Occasionally one could still find a stray, and a substantial industry had been built up hunting them. Hundreds of people, mostly young men, prowled the alleys and parks of the city, searching for any dogs or cats that still lived, usually shooting them with crude crossbows made from two-by-fours and automobile leaf springs.

One Boston entrepreneur was doing a thriving business selling homemade rat traps. Those more intrepid souls ventured into the sewers of Boston, setting lines of such traps, exactly as the beaver trappers had done in the Rocky Mountains when the country was young. Millions of rats had been caught and voraciously devoured by the population of the city.

A cookbook had even been produced on an underground press instructing Bostonians on the "One Hundred and One Ways to Prepare Rat." Even the pelts had not gone to waste. Tailors throughout the city did a thriving business fashioning them into coats and jackets which were eagerly purchased by Bostonians anticipating the frigid winter to come. Never in history had a city put its vermin to such good use. But now even the rats were running out.

If one were fortunate enough to possess dog meat, and for some reason did not need it for one's own consumption, it could be traded for ten liters of vodka per pound. This vodka could, in turn, be traded for sugar, soap, or, if one had enough of it, even a black-market injection of penicillin. Cats brought slightly less. To make cat meat palatable, one had to cook it into a stew with lots of onions and cayenne pepper or some other equally strong spice. But onions and spices were in short supply. Few could stomach straight cat meat. If one could find a litter of kittens, however, they traded at par with dog. Kitten meat was less pungent than adult cat.

There was even a market for entrails. Dog entrails brought five liters of vodka per pound, and cat entrails brought four. Some people made them into a kind of soup, similar to the Mexican menudo. If one had the proper spices, it was considered quite desirable. The entire traffic in meat, of course, was done without benefit of refrigeration. That had disappeared two years earlier. Much of the dog, cat and rat meat that was consumed had passed through a number of hands, over a period of days. By that time it had decomposed somewhat, making the addition of potent spices all the more important. For a time, pigeons had provided much needed animal protein. While they lasted, they supported numerous entrepreneurial hunters armed with blowguns made from PVC pipe using bamboo darts. But now they had become almost extinct. Whenever one came on the market, Bostonians were quick to snap it up at a premium price. They were referred to as 'Occupation Squab.'

The wino smiled. Ever since he had taken to the bottle at twenty-three, he had been one of Boston's dregs. He had caught on early to what the Russians were doing to street-people, and had managed to avoid the patrols. He had many hiding places throughout the city. If nothing else, he was a survivor.

"They don't look so high and mighty now, do they?" he asked himself in a slurred voice, as he watched the disheveled citizens of Boston trudge by.

He remembered times when people in fine clothes had actually spit on him, on their way to a theater or a restaurant. He remembered people stepping around him on the sidewalk as if he were a pile of feces. Now it was their turn, he thought with pleasure. An idea struck him. He laughed out loud through his toothless mouth at the very thought of it: it was something he had always wanted to do.

Standing directly in front of the Hall, he unzipped his trousers and began to urinate into the street. A long powerful stream of liquid arched through the air, glistening in the midday sun. It splashed onto the street with a sound that seemed to resonate, to echo, from the silent buildings.

"Hey!" he yelled. "Look at me!"

A few of the bedraggled pedestrians lifted their heads to take in the sight.

"What are ya' gonna do about it, huh? Why don't ya' call the coppers, huh? Ha! Ha! Ha! Ya' sons-a-bitches! Ya' whores! Look who's on top now! At least my belly's full! It's full of liquor and dog meat! That's more than you can say! Hey buddy, come over here and I'll piss on your shoes! Ha! Ha! Ha!"

That day in Boston was unusually warm for the beginning of October. But the people of the city had long ago become accustomed to being hot. The air conditioning had gone out the summer before last, as it had throughout virtually all of the country. Across the city, those few who still had business to conduct shuffled down the sidewalks listlessly, almost furtively.

Under different circumstances, they would have been embarrassed by their appearance. Now, it didn't seem to matter. Freshly-laundered shirts had become an incredible luxury, a pressed suit unknown. The women had lost their chic, cosmopolitan look. They wore whatever was left to them, soiled and torn. Many were barefoot. Everyone dreaded what winter would bring.

Most of the shops were closed, the goods they had once sold to luxury-conscious Bostonians shipped off for Russian consumption. There was a State department store, of sorts, called the "Workers' Paradise" where a meager selection of goods could be bought if one had the proper credentials: a rough cloth resembling burlap in dark blue, needles, buttons, imitation leather for making shoes, assuming one had the tools and the skills. There was little else. Many sardonic jokes circulated about the joys of wearing burlap underwear. Few subjected themselves to such torture.

Every ten blocks or so there was a Workers' Clinic, where the people lined up for hours to be treated for everything from brain tumors to dysentery and cholera. The technicians manning these clinics had virtually no formal medical training, and could offer little more than a sympathetic ear and an aspirin tablet. For the truly privileged, Russian nationals and high-ranking American collaborators, there were hospitals, with real doctors and real medicines. But for virtually all Bostonians, indeed, for virtually all Americans, such luxury had become only a dream.

Sometimes, as one walked across the city, one could hear the screams of those who sought medical treatment on the black market, always as a last resort. Its practitioners, for the most part, had no qualifications, no degrees. But they did have strong stomachs. Perhaps it was a man being held down by three others in the bed of a pickup truck as his broken leg was set. Or someone in an alley being slit open with a pocket knife to remove a bloated appendix. Such treatment was essentially the equivalent of a death sentence. But those in desperation resorted to it none the less.

The city was just getting over an epidemic of cholera. Even now, with the disease almost having run its course, several hundred people a day were dying. The number had been in the thousands a few months earlier. Boston had resembled a medieval charnel house. Dump trucks had cruised slowly up and down the streets, gathering the corpses that people had disposed of during the night.

The sewage treatment plants had stopped running, and raw sewage had backed up into the water supply. The hottest items in town were clear plastic jugs. Everyone wanted them. There was a rumor that someone had traded a Rolex watch for a dozen of them. There was no disinfectant to be had, but someone at Harvard had recommended that tainted water be exposed to sunlight in order to kill the deadly microbes. It had worked. The porches, stoops, and windowsills of Boston had blossomed with the jugs, all jealously guarded as if they were filled with gold.

The bum sat on the steps of Faneuil Hall, forearms on his knees. He called out to the people as they passed.

"Hey, ya' prick! Give me thirty-five cents! Hey, whore! Can ya' spare a quarter?"

Just as he was about to say something to a tall man in a crushed fedora, something strange happened. In the tiniest fraction of an instant, everything turned a blazing white. The wino threw his forearm up to cover his eyes. But it was too late. He was already blind.

On Otis Street in Somerville, Mary Hurley swept the piazza of her old frame house as she had done every day for sixty-three years. She was known in the neighborhood as a wonderful old woman, who had always had a special affection for children. Many residents in their forties and fifties remembered Mrs. Hurley fondly from their childhoods. Once a sprightly, vivacious Irish lady with a brogue you could cut with a knife, now she was bent with age and spoke mostly to herself. Her bony fingers grasped the broomstick, skin like translucent parchment, veins blue and protruding.

Her husband had died a lifetime ago, it seemed. Her children had moved on, even the memory of them fading from the old woman's clouded mind. Decade after decade, life had gone on around her, here on Otis Street. Families had come and gone. Children had been born, grown up, and died. It had been a good life. Mary would not have changed much of it. Physically, little in the neighborhood had changed. The same old buildings were there that had been there fifty years before. Bricks poked up through the thinning asphalt of the street, remnants of an age even before Mary's arrival.

Her thin cotton dress, the one with the faded pink flowers, hung from her withered body, damp from the midday heat. She would have been uncomfortable, if she had still been capable of noticing such things. Two young boys ran by, bouncing a rubber ball, heading for the schoolyard at the end of the street. There they would play a boy's game, bouncing the ball against the tall brick walls of the school building. They shouted boy expressions to each other, filling the air with a kind of exuberance rarely heard these days. Mary looked up from her sweeping.

"You boys! Quiet! You'll wake up Mr. Chase!"

Walter Chase, a longshoreman, had been her next door neighbor for more than fifty years, but he had died long ago. As she looked through age-dimmed eyes at the boys running off, the air instantly became intensely bright, like nothing Mary had ever seen before. Even through her cataracts Mary was blinded by it: sizzling, dazzling white-hot light. It was as if the sun itself had come down out of the sky to touch the old rooftops of Somerville.

At twelve-seventeen eastern time it happened. The ten megaton hydrogen bomb had been in a crate marked "machine parts" in a warehouse in South Boston, not far from the old Naval Shipyard. It had been detonated by remote control, on Drugonov's direct order. All Russian officials had quietly left the area the night before.

Its first effect had been to bathe the city in an intense white light. Everyone in the streets, and most people in their homes were blinded instantly. Even those in darkened basements were affected. This was followed by a shock wave of enormous proportions. Within a few seconds, it had reached Logan International Airport, to the north. Aircraft were blown away like children's toys in a tornado. Terminal buildings were demolished so quickly as to be almost instantaneous.

More than eleven hundred people were killed in that place instantly, their bodies torn apart, pieces scattered in the ferocious wind. A fraction of a second later, the Old North Church met its end; the site from which Paul Revere had been given his historic signal was reduced to splinters. Twelve one-hundredths of a second later, the shock wave reached the Bunker Hill Monument. The grand old obelisk stood its ground defiantly for a fraction of a second, weaving perilously, but then gave up the ghost and toppled down the hill into Bunker Hill Street, demolishing a row of houses in the process.

The Massachusetts Institute of Technology and Northeastern University were turned to dust almost simultaneously, Boston University a few milliseconds later. Then came Harvard University and, shortly after that, Boston College. Every tall building in downtown Boston was blown away, sending a blizzard of broken glass, aluminum and concrete all over the city. The blind old wino was blown two hundred feet through the air, and splattered against the side of a stone building like a bug against a windshield.

The shock wave continued to radiate outward in all directions, like the ripples in a pond after a pebble has been dropped into it. Revere, Everett, Brookline, Roxbury and Somerville ceased to exist at about the same time. Mary Hurley was blown through the air, her head splashing against the heavy wooden corner post of her piazza, killing her instantly. Her corpse flew down Otis Street at six hundred miles per hour, what was left of her head and her left leg coming off in the process.

The rest of Mary Hurley embedded itself in the wall of a frame house half a block down the street, a millisecond before that house itself was reduced to matchsticks.

The shockwave was followed almost instantaneously by the heat of the fireball itself. This spread outward at incredible speed, thousands of degrees Fahrenheit. South Boston, virtually at ground-zero, melted into glass, its residents literally vaporized. The U.S.S. Constitution, dismasted and capsized onto her port side by the shock wave, burst into flame. The waters of the Charles River and of the harbor itself began to boil. Great plumes of superheated steam erupted from them as millions of tons of water turned to gas.

As the shock wave had done, the fireball spread outward, engulfing more and more of the City of Boston and its metropolitan area with each passing second. The entire region, from Braintree in the south, to Lynn and Wakefield in the north, and almost to Framingham to the west, was incinerated by the very fires of Hell.

The flash could be seen from Portland, Maine to Bridgeport, Connecticut. Windows throughout New England rattled; people stopped whatever they were doing and looked toward the massive glowing cinder that had, a few moments before, been the city of Boston. No one knows how many millions died in the initial blast. Hundreds of thousands more would die in the months ahead from burns and radiation sickness. Such was the outcome of Drugonov's threat. Such was the price cf liberty.

CHAPTER FORTY-EIGHT

"...if you have a smoothly functioning and formidable army, make your opponent think you are incompetent.

You may be right at your opponent's doorstep, but let him think you are far away.

Bait your opponent, and if he takes the bait, trap him and destroy him."
Sun Tzu

Corporal Ramon Sandoval threw the HMMWV around yet another corner on the dirt road near Petaluma, California, north of San Francisco. The big diesel engine screamed as Sandoval tore down the road, a rooster-tail of dust following him. Next to Sandoval sat Private Skip Corwin, who turned from time to time to see the status of their pursuers. The Russians, in their own HMMWVs, were three hundred yards behind. They had gotten no closer than that since the two Americans had encountered them and lured them into the chase ten minutes earlier. Sandoval's machine went around a blind corner. Corwin yelled, "Now Ray!"

Sandoval slammed on the brakes and guided his vehicle toward the left side of the narrow track. It was imperative that the HMMWV flip over. Quickly the machine slowed to twenty miles per hour as Corporal Sandoval drove off the left shoulder. At this point, Corwin bailed out. Sandoval cramped the wheel all the way to the right, and the machine slowly began to go over. He jumped out just in time. Both men, unhurt, ran for the trees and safety. They had accomplished their mission.

Lieutenant Petr Vilenskaia scanned the tree line and decided that it was no use pursuing the Americans. They were like rabbits, he thought: impossible to catch. As he walked around the overturned machine, he noticed something protruding from under the passenger's seat. It was the corner of a valise. Leaning into the vehicle, he grasped it and pulled it out. Inside was a sheaf of papers.

Vilenskaia's English was only mediocre, but he understood at once that they were of military significance. He would take them back to his colonel. Hopefully the retrieval of these documents would cause the colonel to overlook the fact that the Americans had escaped. Perhaps, if they were truly valuable, he would be rewarded for his trouble. Very satisfied with himself, the lieutenant ordered his men back into their vehicles for the return trip to the base.

Trace Forester could see the steely resolve in the eyes of the soldier before him. It had been that way all afternoon, as he had moved from unit to unit inspecting the troops. Every one of them, man and woman, showed Trace that he or she was ready for whatever may come. Now it was night, time for whatever fitful rest the soldiers could find, time for one last meal, one last equipment check before the apocalyptic events of the morning.

For months the Russians had been concentrating their forces that had previously been scattered throughout the West. As the Militia had become more effective with time, better organized and better equipped, its actions had become increasingly bold. The Americans largely owned the countryside. A great many Russians had been killed. The invaders had gradually assumed a bunker mentality, forming themselves into enclaves along the coast: Seattle, Portland, San Francisco. The latter was by far the largest.

San Francisco was the center for Russian activity west of the Rocky Mountains. In the metropolitan area were concentrated no less than three full infantry divisions, a formidable force. But the Russians had made some mistakes. In underestimating the American Militia, they had neglected two things: air cover and armor. After the conquest, the Russians had found that the vast majority of aircraft, armor and artillery that they had hoped to capture from the U.S. military and to use in the occupation had either disappeared or been sabotaged beyond repair by departing U.S. forces. Their only other option, importing such things from the Motherland, was both time consuming and expensive.

Besides, the Russian military had degraded so severely between the collapse of the Soviet Union and the rise of Drugonov that they simply didn't exist in sufficient quantity. They possessed some of these assets in their American colony, of course, but not as much as they would have liked. In a stupendous act of hubris and self-deception, the Russian military leaders in San Francisco had convinced themselves that such weapons were not necessary to defeat their disorganized opponents. Other Russian leaders around the country had discovered differently in recent months, but the message had not sunk in with their Californian comrades. General Trace Forester would now try to make them pay for their shortcomings, in blood.

Time was of the essence. In a little more than twenty-four hours, Trace had moved seven brigades to within striking distance of San Francisco. These consisted of twenty-eight thousand infantry, two-hundred fourteen Abrams tanks, two-hundred ninety-one Bradley Fighting Vehicles, and four battalions of artillery, each consisting of twenty-four one-hundred fifty-five-millimeter howitzers. He even had at his disposal nineteen Apache helicopter gun ships, complete with a full complement of missiles.

Most of this armor and artillery, as well as the helicopter gun ships, had been spirited out of U.S. military installations all across the country at the very outset of the Conquest, before Drugonov had had time to install his own forces at those bases. The soldiers, marines and airmen who had accomplished this were some of the greatest heroes of the American resistance. As soon as they had become aware of Benedict's capitulation, they had exercised initiative, as individuals or small units, to deny Drugonov the use of their most valuable and irreplaceable combat assets.

The tanks, artillery and helicopters had been hidden in a thousand and one places: deep within forests, marvelously camouflaged in mountain canyons, and sometimes buried under the earth itself, all in preparation for just such a moment as this. The Russians had gone to great lengths to discover these weapons, and they had been successful on occasion. But the United States is a big place, big enough to hide almost anything.

This somewhat unorthodox collection of military assets would have been roughly the equivalent of a division in the old U.S. Army. Each brigade followed the "All Arms" theory of war-fighting, in that each was largely self-contained: it consisted of infantry, tanks, artillery and carried with it its own fuel, ammunition, food and spare parts. Every brigade was independently maneuverable, capable of striking the enemy from unexpected directions, of taking advantage of any enemy weaknesses. The accumulation of such force in one place, under one commander, and virtually under the noses of the Russians, was an astonishing feat. But it was necessary if the U.S. resistance was ever to move from guerilla warfare to conventional warfare, and defeat the Russians in open battle.

Similar actions were being carried out in other parts of the country. The resistance was rapidly gaining momentum. It had assumed an almost frantic character. There was not much time. One U.S. city per month was facing the threat of destruction. Chances were being taken, operations mounted, that might otherwise have been delayed pending further preparation.

Such confrontations were fraught with danger. Defeat in open battle would mean the loss of equipment and materiel that had taken years to accumulate. Many brave Americans had given their lives in its acquisition. Defeat would mean setting back the re-conquest by years. It might doom it entirely. This was the kind of gamble, as opposed to a mere risk, that Irwin Rommel had warned against: defeat would be utter and unrecoverable. But even the Desert Fox had admitted that such gambles were occasionally necessary. Such was now the case.

What had hastily been designated the First Brigade was encamped south of Lake Berryessa, north of Vacaville. The Second Brigade was east of Elk Grove, along the Cosumnes River. The Third was east of Stockton, north of the Tullock Reservoir. The Fourth was west of Modesto, at the juncture of the Stanislaus and the San Joaquin Rivers. The Fifth was southwest of Turlock, where the Merced joins the San Joaquin. The Sixth was due east of San Jose, in the Diablo Range. The Seventh Brigade, the bait in the trap, had at twenty-hundred hours that evening, moved into position east of Walnut Creek, the closest to San Francisco itself.

Russian radio traffic out of San Francisco indicated that these movements had been accomplished without detection. American militia communications personnel monitored every word. If the element of surprise were lost, the coming engagement could turn into an American debacle.

Lieutenant-General Michel Chernyshevsky studied the documents that his adjutant had just brought him. From time to time he looked at the map mounted on the wall next to his desk. As the full import of what he saw became clear to him, a thin smile crossed his face. He stabbed a button on the intercom.

"Have Generals Khudiakov, Panteleev and Sviatikov report to my office immediately!"

Forty minutes later the meeting began.

"These documents were captured early this afternoon," Chernyshevsky began. "They present us with an unparalleled opportunity to end the resistance in this region once and for all."

He passed around copies for his three division commanders to examine. All of them were fluent in English.

"As you can see, the American militia has moved an entire brigade just east of Walnut Creek. From these documents it is clear that this represents the cream of the militia forces in the West. They possess tanks, armored personnel carriers and artillery. They must have drawn these resources from all along the Pacific coast. Their hope is to convince us that they are a regiment, and not a brigade, draw a few regiments of our infantry out of San Francisco to meet them, and annihilate us."

Major General Sviatikov spoke up. "How do we know that this brigade is all that exists? Perhaps this is a trap. Perhaps they have an entire division. We have been very lax in our reconnaissance of this area. Perhaps too lax. It is possible that we have been too self-confident."

Major General Panteleev joined in. "Yes. I don't like this. We have been holed up in this city for so long that we don't really know what's out there. We send out patrols from time to time, to make ourselves feel secure. But so many of them have been destroyed that the men now fear the very thought of leaving our enclave. Our patrols are now very cursory. The men stay on the safest routes, in the safest areas. They are easily evaded. Our air reconnaissance has been nonexistent due to the shortage of spare parts. The Americans could have anything out there. They melt into the fields and forests like phantoms. I agree with Sviatikov. There may be more to this than meets the eye."

"Are you suggesting that I have been lax in my command responsibilities?" Chernyshevsky growled. He looked from face to face for a response. "If our reconnaissance has been lacking, that has been through no fault of mine! How can I make aircraft fly without parts? How can I operate armored personnel carriers when they are constantly being sabotaged by spies? How can I force men to do what they will not do? Can I go on every patrol myself? Can I manage everything at once?"

Major General Khudiakov broke the uncomfortable silence.

"Of course not, sir. But you must admit, these forests and mountains could hide a great deal. How do we know that this is not a trap?"

Chernyshevsky relaxed.

"For two reasons, gentlemen. First, I do not believe that the Americans are capable of fielding a division-sized force. They are amateurs, citizen-soldiers. They do not possess the expertise to handle such a thing. They do not have the materiel, the weapons-systems to make such a force possible. Yes, they have small arms, as we have all found out to our displeasure. And apparently they have managed to put together enough armor and artillery to equip a brigade. But all of our intelligence tells us that they have these things in very small quantities.

"From these documents, it is clear that this one brigade represents a maximum effort on their part. Once we destroy it, they will be rendered virtually impotent with the exception of scattered guerrilla operations.

"Secondly, these captured papers make it clear that they have dispersed what forces they have. As you can see on page six, they plan simultaneous operations against Seattle and Portland as well as here in San Francisco. They simply cannot have divisions in each of those places. It is impossible. I would be surprised if their forces outside Seattle and Portland had any armor or artillery at all. I suspect they have concentrated all that they have of those resources here, against us.

"If I am correct in this, and I am very rarely wrong, it is all the more reason to destroy this brigade. We will be destroying the backbone of the American resistance in the West. We cannot miss this chance."

General Khudiakov spoke up. "What is your plan, sir?"

"I will use all three divisions. It will be a wonderful opportunity to crush this brigade, to obliterate it! We will show these Americans what overwhelming military power can do! It will set an example that will echo across the entire colony! We could defeat them with much less than three divisions of course, but this will give our people a chance to stretch their legs. They have been cooped up in their barracks for too long.

"Turn them loose! As Churchill said, this will give me an opportunity to blood my hounds! Yes, a taste of American blood is just what they need! It will be the best thing for them!"

Chernyshevsky did not mention that Drugonov admired success. The destruction of an American brigade, the end of the resistance in the West, might be an opportunity for him to pick up another star.

Trace strode into the tent. The commander of the Third Brigade and its regimental commanders stood at attention. It was twenty-two hundred hours: less than eight more to go until the operation commenced.

"At ease, gentlemen. I'm sure our plan of action is clear to all of you. In the last weeks, we've analyzed and re-analyzed it. The last thing I want to do now is make any significant changes. But I want to take this opportunity to touch bases with you to see if there are any last minute problems. I think it would be prudent to run through the scenario once again while we still have the chance.

"As you know, I have spent last night and today meeting with other senior commanders in as many of the brigades as I could reach. I think we're as ready as we can be. Do you see any problems that we can correct?"

The faces around the table looked confident in the harsh light of the gasoline lantern. These were men spoiling for a fight. They were the cream of the crop. Some had been officers at the company or battalion level in the old U.S. Army. Others had risen from the ranks of the militia. Each was as tough as a steel I-beam. At Trace's question, they all shook their heads. No. There were no problems.

"Very well. Let's take a look at this one more time."

A large map of central California had been spread out on the table. On it were marked the positions of the seven U.S. brigades with arrows drawn indicating preferred directions of movement. But these were not cut in stone. All American commanders had been schooled in the principal of initiative: if the enemy acted in an unexpected manner, they were ready to act similarly. Therein lay one of the great strengths of the U.S. battle plan. Trace used a pen as a pointer.

"Chernyshevsky has three divisions here in San Francisco. They are predominantly infantry, very light in armor and air assets. Our radio intercepts indicate that he's taken the bait: he plans to move all three of his divisions out to meet our Seventh Brigade at first light. That means that the Russians will have to cover about forty miles of terrain. As soon as they make contact, Seventh Brigade will retreat eastward toward Stockton. Chernyshevsky will follow, we hope, moving another twenty or so miles east. At that point, First Brigade will already have moved south along highway eighty, and Sixth Brigade will have moved north along highway eight-eighty, cutting off any Russian retreat.

"Second Brigade will have moved southwest along route five, Third Brigade will have moved due west toward Stockton, and the Fourth and Fifth Brigades will have moved north along highways five and ninety-nine. We will form a sack, and, if all goes well, Chernyshevsky will fall right into it: a classic envelopment.

"We will attack both close and deep. Our artillery will reach far into the Russian forces, disrupting them, causing chaos. We have only nineteen Apaches, but we'll use them to their best advantage: destroying whatever armor the enemy has with their missiles. Our own tanks will breach the Russian lines, engaging any remaining armor as well as infantry. After the heavy slugging is over, our own infantry will join the battle.

"They'll have one hell of a job to do. We estimate that the enemy has around sixty thousand infantry to our twenty-eight thousand. But we have one great advantage: we are a brotherhood, and the Russians are not. Our people know that they are all fighting together for a great cause; the Russians are demoralized. Most of them just want to go home. Given that, two to one odds look pretty good.

"This will be an extremely compact battlefield. A lot will be happening in a very small area. I am hoping that Chernyshevsky uses standard Russian tactics: waves of attacking echelons hoping to defeat us by attrition at the point of attack. Those tactics will fail. Our attack will be fluid, dynamic.

"Each of our brigades will operate independently, capitalizing on any enemy weaknesses. The Russians' rigidity will be their downfall. They discourage initiative among their commanders; we require it. That is a strong element in our favor: perhaps a decisive one. I will remain with this brigade. My command post will be as close to the action as possible. I will tell you what I have told the other senior commanders: once the fighting starts, I want as much information as I can get as quickly as I can get it.

"Keep your communications people on their toes. I need the big picture. Other than that, I place few restrictions on your actions. You are all experienced men, and I expect you to use your best judgment. As you know all too well, our force does not have a lot of 'legs'. Each of our brigades has enough fuel and ammunition for two days' operations maximum. Just rounding up enough tank trucks to supply our armor with fuel was a hell of a job. We have left ourselves no resources for retreat. There will be none. This will be a fight to the death.

"We have to hit the enemy hard and defeat him in a hurry. Keep in mind that our objective is to hammer the enemy from all directions with everything we've got. Go for the jugular! Be merciless! Obliterate the enemy! Remember Los Angeles, Boston, and New Orleans! Thank you, gentlemen. Give 'em hell!"

Trace stood outside his tent and looked at the millions of stars in the clear California sky. He had done everything that any commander could do. Now success or failure rested in the hands of his subordinate commanders and in the hands of the soldiers themselves. It was twenty-three hundred hours. The operation kicked off at 0400. Russian radio traffic indicated that they expected to contact the Seventh Brigade at nautical twilight, or 0640.

He needed sleep, but he doubted that he would get any. There was too much anticipation, and its accompanying adrenalin. Radio intercepts still indicated that the Russians were preparing to move with all three of their divisions; there had been no change of plan on their part. There was tremendous chatter as these thousands of men, in their scores of units, prepared themselves for battle. In five hours, six of his brigades would begin to move. The timing had to be perfect. Too early, and it would tip his hand. Too late and the Seventh Brigade near Walnut Creek would be left to fight it out alone.

He let his mind drift back twenty-two hundred years, to 216 B.C., to the battle of Cannae. In his attempt to conquer Italy, Hannibal's army of forty thousand met a superior Roman force of fifty thousand. Just as Trace was about to do, Hannibal met the concentrated Roman army in the center, lured them forward in a feigned retreat, and encircled them with his cavalry. The Romans found themselves in a sack, exactly as would the Russians. Further, only those soldiers on the periphery of the tightly-packed Roman formations could fight. Those in the interior were essentially useless. The massed Russian forces would face the same dilemma. Hannibal lost six thousand men, but the entire Roman army was annihilated. Trace had read his history. He was hoping that Chernyshevsky had not.

Soldiers strolled by, as if seeking to relax before the action began. Trace wondered if they were finding sleep as elusive as he was. Probably. In the starlight, he saw a woman approaching. Even in the dimness, and in spite of the less-than-flattering battle dress uniform that she wore, her femininity was obvious.

Trace felt a stirring within him. It had been such a long time. Molly had been dead for nearly two years. He had not touched a woman since the last time he had been with her. At times, he had thought that such feelings had burned themselves away in the fires of all the battles he had fought. He had come to think of himself as a machine, a fighting machine, devoid of human feeling. Now he was discovering otherwise. It was a discovery that was not entirely unpleasant. In a strange way, it made him feel like a whole man again. He felt relief at that. The woman came closer.

"General Forester! I could hardly see you in this light. I'm Lieutenant Cummins. Like the diesel."

She chuckled gaily.

"My first name is Lisa."

"I know who you are, Lieutenant. You command the First Platoon of Company C. I remember you well."

He could smell soap and musk and a trace of cologne. God knew where she had gotten it. He could smell her hair. His muscles tensed. She was beautiful he thought, truly beautiful. He began to experience a bit of dizziness. Perhaps it was just his powerful need, or perhaps it was the upcoming battle. Or perhaps he was just allowing himself to be reborn as a human being. He felt as if the floodgates were about to burst.

There was a silence. Then, Lisa said, "Maybe I'd better leave you alone. You must have a lot to do. I don't want to waste your time."

She turned to go.

"No!" Trace said, taking her by the arm, which he had not intended to do. He let her arm go immediately, embarrassed.

"Please don't go. I'd like to talk for a while. Would you stay with me?"

He had not meant to put it that way. It had just come out.

She smiled up at him.

"Of course I will, sir."

She seemed to sense something. Could she know?

"Let's go into my tent," he said.

Again she smiled and nodded. She brushed by him, her shoulder touching his chest. The gasoline lantern had been set on low. In the pale white light, Trace took her all in. She reminded him vaguely of Molly. She had the same auburn hair, the same green eyes. The corners of her mouth curled up in a delightful elfin way. At that moment, Trace knew that she knew. Somehow, she knew.

His hands trembled as he touched her waist. The smile was still on her lips, inviting, telling him that she understood, and that it was all right. It told him that she wanted this as badly as he did. Behavior that would have been unthinkable in ordinary times somehow seemed to make perfect sense seven hours before a monumental battle.

He lowered his face to hers. She responded by putting her arms around his neck. Very gently, hesitantly, their lips touched. This was the point of no return for Trace. His long-pent up passion raged within him. He kissed her again, with more intensity. His arms engulfed her body. She responded by thrusting her fingers into his hair and pulling him into her.

"Oh, God!" she said as his lips ravaged her neck. "God help me, but I need this!"

In moments they were naked, writhing on the cot like two animals, entwining themselves together. It was the lovemaking of two people who knew that they may not live to see another starry evening. They might never again touch the flesh of another human being, never again experience the joy of sexual release, never again feel truly complete. They were purging themselves of their great need, each using the other, and, at the same time, giving to the other of themselves. Each sought to bring the other to new heights, to unknown raptures. Through this each would derive a selfish pleasure. It went on and on. Ninety minutes later, it was done. They lay together on the cot, exhausted. Their naked bodies glistened with sweat in the cool night air. All of their tension had left them. Their muscles were relaxed, flaccid. Each drifted off to sleep.

Trace woke abruptly at 0206 hours. He was alone. For an instant, in the fog of his sleepy mind, he forgot where he was, what was about to happen. But only for an instant; lucidity returned like an electric shock. Though he had slept only a few hours, he felt refreshed. He dressed quickly and left the tent. Outside, people were moving with a purpose. The minutes were ticking by.

Trace sat in the HMMWV and watched the obscurity of night slowly give way to the first hint of sunrise. A slight brightening in the eastern sky was followed by knives of light stabbing the darkness. The birds were singing loudly in the trees, welcoming the new day. It would be difficult to imagine a more peaceful scene. It all seemed strangely nightmarish: a paradise soon to be defiled by wholesale death. Any minute now.

Several radios were mounted in the vehicle. All were on, but they were quiet: radio silence was being maintained. These radios were themselves quite a story. Like so many other tools of the U.S. Militia, they were the product of improvisation and considerable ingenuity: citizen-band radios that had been souped-up to increase their range and modified with specially-made crystals to achieve a unique frequency. To minimize the chances of detection, they were used as infrequently and as briefly as possible. It appeared that so far the Russians had not caught on. In a few moments, such secrecy would no longer matter. And then they heard it: big guns in the distance. They were probably Russian, since the Seventh Brigade had no such weapons. The radio came alive.

"Bravo three, this is bravo seven. Contact. I repeat, contact. Enemy armor advancing across a broad front. Initiating Plan Alpha."

Plan Alpha called for the Seventh Brigade to meet the enemy, retreat rapidly luring the Russians along, and then hold its ground, fixing the Russians in place while the other six brigades enveloped and destroyed them. Trace saw in his mind's eye what must be happening. At this very moment, his people were dying, but not without effect.

Radio silence no longer mattered. The outlying brigades had begun moving at 0400, and by now were approaching the positions in which they could support the embattled Seventh. Trace grasped a microphone and began to broadcast.

"Brigades report your positions!"

"First Brigade! Approaching Vallejo on Route 80."

"Second Brigade! Fifteen miles southwest of Lodi."

"Fourth Brigade! North of Tracy, lead elements approaching Byron!"

"Fifth Brigade! East of Livermore! Moving north by northwest!"

"Sixth Brigade! Moving north of Pleasanton!"

"Seventh Brigade! Heavy fighting with Russian armor, but there's less of it than we thought! They're moving their infantry into position ahead of the tanks! We're beginning our retreat eastward!"

Trace's own Third Brigade was west of Stockton, and he expected contact with elements of the Seventh at any time. When the two brigades were united, they would make their stand. They would hold their positions and slug it out with the Russians, fixing them in place until the other American units arrived.

Private Amos Purcell was a member of the First Platoon, Company C of the Seventh Brigade, Lisa Cummins' command. His platoon had been assigned the task of holding a hill several miles east of Brentwood. It was his unit, and others like it, that would fix the Russians in place, unwavering, allowing the other American brigades to close in. Facing him and the men and women around him was a seeming juggernaut: massed Russian infantry, and, in the distance, a number of armored personnel carriers. Amos Purcell was at the apex of the battle, in the very vortex of hell.

The First Platoon had two mortars, which they had been firing constantly for the last ten minutes. These weapons were a bit primitive, but they were very effective. They had been surreptitiously manufactured by a machine shop in Washington State. Similar shops had contributed to the war effort, in great secrecy, all over the country.

The mortars were wreaking havoc on the Russian infantry, but they were brave and continued their advance. As the Russians moved forward, the mortar-men walked the rounds closer and closer to their own position. An armored personnel carrier turned its attention to the hill, and began to fire in its direction. An American to Purcell's left leveled a very unusual device at the dangerous machine: an antitank weapon patterned after the old World War Two German "Panzer Faust." Its bulbous projectile sat on the end of a tube like the head of a giant match. These too were made in underground factories across the country.

The APC was no more than eighty yards away now. Its high-velocity cannon rounds either sizzled through the air over the heads of the First Platoon, or erupted in geysers of earth just in front of their position. One round caught a corporal from Baton Rouge full in the chest, and he came apart like an exploding manikin, blood, entrails and bits of bone spraying his comrades.

The Panzer Faust erupted, its projectile clearly visible as it rocketed toward the oncoming machine. It hit the APC dead on, causing its front end to literally lift off the ground. The machine exploded in a ball of fire, and almost instantly rounds inside it began to cook off, causing a loud staccato.

All around Amos Purcell men and women were dropping. But they were not dying for nothing. They were exacting a terrible toll among the oncoming Russians. There was no cover for the attackers, and the remaining Americans lay prone atop the hill, firing their weapons down upon the Russians in semi-auto mode: one round, one kill.

Inexorably, by sheer weight of numbers, the Russians began to overwhelm their adversaries. Russian and American corpses littered the ground, sometimes piled two or three deep. The side of the hill was a charnel house, attacking Russian infantry running over the bodies of their fallen comrades, slipping and falling in the spilled gore of the dead.

There were eight Americans left, then six, then four. Still they maintained their discipline, placing one deadly round after another into their foes. At no point had anyone considered retreat; they had been ordered to hold that hill, and they would do so or die in the attempt. The Russians wavered from time to time under this withering fire, but the Americans never did.

The seconds ticked by, but here they meant nothing. Time seemed to stand still, frozen by the ferocity of this horrendous slaughter. The human mind simply cannot deal with such a sight. Amos and Lieutenant Cummins were the only two remaining alive. In front of the Lieutenant was a score of Russian dead. Amos glanced over at her just as she thrust her bayonet into the gut of an enemy. Blood poured down her left side, from her shoulder, and from a head wound. Still, she fought on. His last sight of her was as she was overcome by four of the enemy, stabbing her, shooting her. Then, Amos was alone.

He did not know it, but he had killed eighty-three Russians with his carefully-placed fire that day. He continued to squeeze his trigger, now down to his last magazine of ammunition. His enemies were only twenty yards away. To his own surprise, he discovered that the prospect of death did not frighten him. In fact, in these last seconds he began to feel a strange calm wash over him. Dyin's not hard, he thought. It's livin' that's the tough part. His mind began to drift, to drift off to another world, another time.

Amos had always been big for his age. Thoughts of his childhood flashed through his mind. He had never done well in school, and sometimes the other children made fun of him. But they were always careful not to push him too far; he was not prone to violence, but his classmates feared his potential wrath.

In his rural Mississippi home he had experienced racism, some overt, some covert. The old unreconstructed crackers were the worst. They gave him a taste of what his parents and grandparents had had to endure. He had tried not to let it bother him. These people were dinosaurs, he knew. They would soon pass from the scene, and things would be better.

He had excelled in football, making Allstate in his senior year as right guard. But that was the end of his halcyon years. His academic record was so poor that even his gridiron achievements could not earn him a place in college. He went to work as a maintenance man in the very school from which he had graduated.

There were many snide remarks from the older students about the football star turned toilet cleaner.

That was sixteen years ago. It took an act of supreme will to prevent himself from feeling like a failure. Amos had never married; had never even courted a girl. He considered himself too awkward and too ugly to even try. He developed a little drinking problem: nothing serious enough to disrupt his life. There was just a need to escape from reality from time to time, even if only for a few hours. But always, deep down, Amos knew that he was a good man, that he had value, that he was good at something, and that someday he would find that something. Today was that day.

All of these thoughts came back to him, here, in the ultimate moment of truth. He fired the last round from the last magazine from his rifle. Thirty Russians rushed toward him. He rose to his feet, drew his pistol, and, very rapidly, but with great deliberation, killed twelve more. Still, they came. Amos picked up his empty rifle, bayonet attached, and spread his legs slightly, ready to engage the enemy hand to hand.

A round tore through his shoulder, and another through his thigh. Still, he stood his ground. Another round entered his torso, and a fourth grazed the right side of his head, tearing off his ear. Amos stood his ground. Then they were upon him. Again and again he slashed and thrust with his bayonet, tearing the enemy apart with his great strength. A bayonet entered his side, embedding itself to the hilt. Amos stood his ground. He butt-stroked a Russian with his M16, and its plastic stock broke. He was reduced to punching his enemies with his massive fists, and three Russians died of these crashing blows.

A soldier leaped at Amos, knife in hand. Amos caught him by the neck and by his belt, and lifted the man over his head. Just then a gust of wind caught the American flag, which had been placed at the top of the hill. It fluttered in Amos's direction and draped itself over his shoulder. For an instant he stood there, like a rock, enemy held overhead, bayonet protruding from his side, nearly naked to the waist, blood streaming from half a dozen wounds, and his country's flag embracing him, gracing him, granting him an immortality reserved only for heroes.

"Come in! Come in, damn it!"

Major General Sergei Khudiakov shouted into the radio's microphone, attempting to establish contact with the First Division, under Panteleev. All around him, artillery shells exploded, from howitzers in the distance and from Abrams tanks on all sides of him. What little armor he had had at his disposal had been destroyed at the outset of the battle. Khudiakov and the division immediately to his south, under Sviatikov, appeared to be completely surrounded. Both divisions were taking a horrendous pounding. An Apache helicopter passed overhead, raking his exposed infantry with torrents of lead from its chain gun.

"Damn these Americans!" Khudiakov yelled at no one in particular. "Where the hell did they get helicopters?"

He ducked beside his command vehicle to avoid the airborne onslaught. He saw dozens, scores of his men dropping everywhere he looked. One hundred twenty-millimeter rounds from the surrounding Abrams tanks were exploding everywhere, tossing his men, and pieces of his men, into the air like rag dolls.

Both Khudiakov and Sviatikov had met unexpected resistance when they slammed into the American Seventh Brigade. They thought their enemy would evaporate like the mist before the force of three full divisions. But that had not been the case. The Americans had stood their ground, taking incredible casualties, but accomplishing their mission: fixing the Russians in place and allowing their comrades to envelop them.

Now that envelopment was almost complete. Panteleev was their only hope. He must break through to the west so that the other Russian divisions could retreat back to the safety of their enclave in San Francisco. But Khudiakov had lost contact with him thirty minutes ago. The General could not know that the American First and Sixth brigades had moved into position west of Panteleev, and were blocking any retreat. They had closed off the neck of the sock. The Russians were trapped.

The Russian divisions contained virtually no artillery, and so could not answer the strategically-placed American howitzers, whose one-hundred-fifty-five millimeter rounds were raining death upon the enemy. His armored personnel carriers, the heaviest armor at his disposal, had engaged the American Abrams and Bradleys, but had lost badly. The American vehicles now roamed the battlefield almost at will, obliterating whole units of Russian infantry, slashing through the enemy like hungry lions through a flock of sheep.

For the first time in his twenty-six years of military service, Sergei Khudiakov had the acid taste of defeat in his mouth. His mind raced. What should he do? Where can he go? He did not know. The enemy was presenting him with more problems than he could solve; they had run him out of options.

Discipline was beginning to break down. Artillery fire came down as if in sheets, and many Russian soldiers had broken under the strain. They were abandoning their units and rushing pell-mell across the battlefield, looking for anything to hide behind or under. Some were frantically digging with their entrenching tools, trying desperately to create some cover for themselves. But it was in vain. The white-hot splinters of shrapnel sizzled through the air cutting men to ribbons by the thousands.

"Panteleev! God damn it! Where the hell are you!"

Khudiakov screamed into the microphone. But General Panteleev was beyond answering: he had been killed eleven minutes earlier when a round from an Abrams exploded less than three feet from him and a group of his senior officers.

"Sviatikov! Come in!"

General Sviatikov too was dead, killed by a round from one of those makeshift mortars with which the Americans were so skilled. More than half of his command, twelve thousand six hundred men had already died, and the maelstrom of carnage continued.

Khudiakov knew none of this. All he knew was what he could see before him: shells exploding everywhere, bodies tossed into the air, pieces of men littering the blood-soaked ground. What had been an entire Russian infantry division had been reduced to nothing more than fish roiling about in a barrel, to be destroyed at the enemy's pleasure. Khudiakov wondered how many of his men were left. Ten thousand perhaps? Six?

He began to think of surrender. Would the Americans offer such an option? They had not done so as yet, at least not to his knowledge. Would they really obliterate his entire division, to a man, without offering surrender? Could they be so cruel? Then he remembered Los Angeles, Boston and New Orleans. He cringed at the thought. Hope disintegrated, and he wished that the next shell would find him. At least, as their commander, he owed it to his men to die by their sides. His wish would come true within moments.

Trace Forester stood upon the battlefield. He took in the incredible slaughter that his forces had wreaked upon their adversaries. The ground was covered with corpses and pieces of corpses so completely that one had difficulty walking without stepping on them. The artillery bombardment had lifted three hours earlier. Then the American infantry was turned loose. They swept down upon the field of battle like the wrath of God, shooting and bayoneting any remaining living Russians. Trace had known that it had to end like this; he could have done nothing to stop them even if he had wanted to. Their blood-lust was too strong; they had seen too much and had endured too much to show mercy. A few of the enemy had no doubt escaped, but only a very few. Three Russian divisions had simply ceased to exist on this day.

California, the west coast, and the entire country west of the Rockies was once again in American hands. There would be more battles to fight, more of the enemy to kill. But this part of America was America again.

CHAPTER FORTY-NINE

Sergei Drugonov leaned over the table while studying the map of New Jersey and the surrounding area in his office in the Empire State Building. Beside him stood Marshal Sokolnikov, Commander of all Russian forces. Sokolnikov was more interested in Drugonov than in the map. He had never forgotten his treatment at the hands of the Maximum Leader. He had never forgotten the threat against his daughter. Events in the intervening several years had reinforced his belief in Drugonov's madness.

Many times he had thought of killing the man. But Drugonov was not stupid. From time to time, he reminded Sokolnikov of his daughter's vulnerability. The Marshal studied Drugonov as one would study a mad, dangerous animal in a cage.

"Here, Sokolnikov! This is where we must stop them! We must hold them at the Delaware River, at Trenton! If we can stop them from crossing there, we can reorganize our forces and turn all of New Jersey into a bastion! We can prevent them from threatening New York!"

You mean protect your own rear end, Sokolnikov thought. Drugonov was becoming less rational by the day. The Marshal watched as he ranted and raved, shaking his head back and forth, saliva flying in all directions. Drugonov stabbed the pencil into the map at Trenton with such force that it broke.

"They cannot possibly defeat us! We have two full corps, four divisions, blocking their advance! What do you think, Sokolnikov? What is your, shall we say, professional opinion?"

Drugonov pronounced the word 'professional' in an exaggerated, mocking tone, as if daring the Marshal to lose control, to explode. Sokolnikov knew that such a reaction–overt insubordination-- would be the excuse Drugonov needed to liquidate him and his family. Drugonov had always seemed to sense that Sokolnikov's commitment to the entire concept of American colonization was weak. In fact, the Marshal had thought it a bad idea from the outset, and, as much as he tried, he could not always conceal his dissent. As a result, Drugonov never missed an opportunity to express his displeasure: snide comments, veiled criticisms, implications regarding Sokolnikov's competence. But he needed the man. Sokolnikov knew that that was the only thing keeping him, and his family, alive. He was the best, most experienced officer at Drugonov's command. And so the Marshal tolerated these barbs, but only barely. Long ago he had promised himself that his fingers would someday encircle the throat of Sergei Drugonov and crush the life out of him.

A knock at the door.

"Enter," called Drugonov.

An orderly opened it and in rushed a soldier in a tattered and dirty uniform. His epaulettes indicated the rank of General. He stood at attention in front of Drugonov.

"General Prokopovich!" said Drugonov, strain in his voice. "I sincerely hope that you are here to report total victory."

General Andrei Prokopovich said nothing for a moment, as if mustering his courage.

"We did all that we could, Maximum Leader! No one could expect men to fight harder than did ours! They died as heroes of the Rodina!"

"Tell me, you fool! What has happened?" Drugonov demanded, his fist pounding the table.

Prokopovich cleared his throat.

"The Americans had much more armor and artillery than we expected. I don't know where they could have gotten it. They knew exactly where we were. They pounded our positions for hours! We tried to prevent them from crossing the river, but the artillery fire totally disrupted our front lines. They first landed at a place called Washington Crossing, and before we knew it they were coming across the river everywhere we looked. Whenever we blocked them at one point, they would move to another. It was like trying to stop water pouring through a sieve."

"Didn't you annihilate them as they landed? You incompetent jackass! I'll have your head sent back to Moscow in a bottle!"

"Maximum Leader, we tried! But we found ourselves on the defensive almost immediately! The Maryland and Delaware Militias attacked us on our left flank, the New York and Pennsylvania Militias on our right, and the New Jersey Militia attacked us from the rear! We were encircled before we knew it! We killed them by the thousands, but still they fought! Wave after wave of them! I barely escaped with my life!"

"Your life, you swine! Your life isn't worth the bullet to end it! Get out of my sight!"

Prokopovich hustled out of the room, thankful that he had not been shot on the spot.

"Four divisions! Incredible! Now what are we to do, grand Marshal of all the armed forces of Russia? It is time you earned your pay! Give me a solution to this disaster!"

Sokolnikov said in a calm voice,

"I suggest first that you remove your headquarters to a more secure location. If Prokopovich got here, the Americans cannot be far behind. Then we can evaluate our position, and see what can be salvaged."

"Good! Good, Marshal! We will move immediately to our emergency redoubt!"

He pushed a button on his intercom.

"Have my car ready to leave in five minutes! Order the entire staff to burn all the files, destroy all computer hard drives, and prepare to evacuate this building! And order our sappers to demolish all bridges and tunnels into Manhattan!"

He took his finger off the button.

"That should give us some time! Let this Trace Forester swim the Hudson and we'll see how much fight he has left in him!"

General Trace Forester, Commander-in-Chief of the Militia of the United States, emerged from the Manhattan side of the Holland Tunnel and onto Spring Street. Behind him was an entire army, though some might have called it a mob, from the looks of it: exhausted men and women, some in uniform, some in rags, armed with every imaginable weapon. But this mob of Patriots had defeated the best their enemy could throw at them. They came in trucks and on foot, on Harleys and on bicycles.

The tunnels and bridges had not been blown. Militia units operating within the interior of the city had known about the planted charges for months, and had watched carefully for any attempt to utilize them. When the Russian units arrived to detonate these explosives, the militia fell upon them, emerging almost miraculously from side streets and alleys. Drugonov had tried mightily to destroy these people ever since the occupation began, but it was one of the wonders of the war that they had continued to operate virtually under his very nose. It was a brilliant operation, and one that these American heroes would brag about for the rest of their lives.

This reoccupation of New York was being repeated at the Lincoln Tunnel and at the George Washington Bridge. Trace's convoy turned left onto Broadway and headed uptown. Hundreds of thousands of New Yorkers thronged the sidewalks, spilling out into the street. New York had not been obliterated as had Los Angeles, Boston and New Orleans. But it had surely been decimated. Two hundred forty thousand had died of starvation.

Nearly four hundred fifty thousand had died of preventable diseases such as cholera, diphtheria, tuberculosis and pneumonia: the diseases of filth and deprivation. Fifty-five thousand had frozen to death in the three winters since the Conquest. Eleven thousand had died of carbon monoxide poisoning from makeshift heaters that had consumed virtually every stick of wood in the five boroughs. Even the furniture collection of the Metropolitan Museum of Art had been reduced to ash in the smoke-filled, airless hovels of Manhattan.

Nearly three hundred thousand had been liquidated for crimes against the state, ranging from outright violent resistance to refusal to accept Drugonov's fiat currency. Two hundred eighty thousand more had simply disappeared: dragged from their beds in the night or from the streets during the day, taken away to the new gulag archipelago to be worked, starved, beaten or frozen to death.

Many of those who had survived lined Broadway as Trace's convoy proceeded north: wraiths waving their emaciated arms and shouting with what little strength remained to them, toothless mouths open, taut, flesh-less skin stretched into unfamiliar smiles. Tears poured down the desiccated faces of those who had sworn they would never be able to cry again. They wept with a depth of emotion they thought had been burned out of them by their cruel occupation. For some, this glorious event was simply too much, and they fell to their knees, giving thanks.

Russians were surrendering en mass. Platoons and companies all around Manhattan were laying down their arms, abandoning their equipment, raising their hands and placing themselves at the mercy of their captors. There was not much mercy left in New York that day. Hardware stores were emptied of their supplies of rope, and Russian officers were hung from lamp posts all over the city. Many were beaten to death with anything that was at hand: sticks, bricks, garbage can lids.

The people of New York, and not just Manhattan, but the other boroughs as well, were venting their wrath on the men who had tormented them so hideously. Even if there had been a civil authority in the city, it is unlikely that any of this could have been stopped. It was a spontaneous eruption of hatred by five million tortured survivors.

Trace's first objective was to seize the means of communications, to tell the entire country of this great victory, and to tell them that their long struggle against tyranny was almost over. There were still pockets of Russian resistance around the country, but with the capture of New York and of Drugonov himself, these were not expected to survive for long. It was clear that the will of the Russians had been broken; that they recognized that further resistance was futile. Trace entered the midtown headquarters of a major television network with two platoons of infantry.

"Search the building. If you find any Russians bring them to me," he ordered.

Corporal Ed Santos was on the fourteenth floor. He checked it office by office. So far he had found no one. It was odd, eerie in a way. This should be one of the busiest places anywhere, but it was as quiet as a tomb. What did they have to be afraid of? Santos thought about the type of television coverage he had been watching since the Conquest, and it all became clear to him. These people have had their heads so far up Drugonov's ass, he thought, that they haven't seen daylight in three years: telling the American people not to resist, to obey orders, to be good subjects of the Russian Empire. For that, they got to keep their penthouses and their Porsches. No wonder they all headed for the tall grass!

He was about to leave the last office on the floor, a corner office with a view of the city that Santos couldn't help but admire, when he heard a noise. It was coming from the closet, a sort of muffled whimpering. Carefully, he approached the door and, standing to one side, threw it open. Inside was a man, impeccably dressed, with each hair in place, crouching on the floor with his arms wrapped around his knees. He stared up at Santos as if he were seeing the devil himself.

"Please don't shoot me!" he cried. "I was only doing what I was ordered to do! I had no choice!"

Santos recognized him immediately. He was Charles Frost, the Voice of the United States, the man whom millions watched every night to learn the truth. But Charles Frost had not been giving them the truth for a very long time, since long before the Conquest. In fact, he had been a major player in preparing the country for that Conquest: slanting the news, omitting the facts, attacking anyone who stood for freedom in a hundred ways, overt and covert. His subservience to Drugonov was the logical culmination of his life's work.

"Get up!" Santos ordered.

Instead, Frost crawled out of the closet on his knees, hands before his face, as if praying.

"Please, please, please don't shoot me! Look, I have money, lots of money! I'll give it to you! Just let me go!"

He reached into his pocket.

"Here! Here are the keys to my Ferrari. It's in the parking garage downstairs! It's yours! All you have to do is turn your back and let me out of here!"

Santos remembered all of the times he had listened to this man vomiting his lies at the American people, doing his best to convince them that slavery was a desirable state of affairs, that their own lives were of no concern; that their only duty was to the collective: the Russian collective.

"Stand up, you piece of shit!" Santos ordered.

Still, Frost cringed on the floor like a whipped dog. Santos knew that he should turn the man over to his superiors. But General Forester had specified that only Russians were to be turned over, hadn't he? He had said nothing about American traitors.

"Have it your way, pig!" Santos hissed as he withdrew his combat knife. Frost's eyes fixed with horror on the shining eight-inch blade.

"What are you going to do?" he begged. "You can't do this! What about due process? I'm an American! I have rights!"

"It's a little late for you to remember that you're an American. As to your rights, as far as I'm concerned, the only right you have is to die slathered in your own blood, like any traitor!"

He grasped Frost by his beloved hair, and lifted his chin into the air.

"Oh my God, no!" Frost cried.

Santos placed the tip of the razor-sharp blade under Frost's right ear, and, with a vicious slash, virtually decapitated the man. Charles Frost's head fell backward as if on a hinge, and he slumped to the floor. His limbs twitched as his life's blood gushed onto the plush cream-colored carpet. Santos looked him right in the eyes. They were still alive. Frost's lips moved, forming unknowable words. Seconds passed, and those same eyes took on a fixed, glazed appearance. Charles Frost was dead.

With a smile, Ed Santos wiped the blade of his knife on Frost's Italian silk suit, and replaced it in its sheath. He couldn't remember when he had enjoyed anything so much.

General Trace Forester looked directly at the camera's lens as he sat at the desk usually reserved for the evening newscaster. In a matter of seconds, he would be speaking to some one hundred million Americans. He had no script and no notes. The words he was about to speak had been burned into his mind and into his heart by three years of warfare. The technician signaled to him that there were five seconds until air time: four, three, two, one. The red light came on, and Trace, whose name was on everyone's lips, was seen by his countrymen for the first time.

"Men and women of America. I bring you wonderful news. This is a great day in our history. Victory is ours. We have our country back at last. I am speaking to you from New York, and as I speak the last elements of the Russian occupation forces that held this city as recently as this morning are surrendering. All across this land, Russian soldiers are laying down their arms, coming to the inevitable conclusion that their attempt to enslave us has failed.

"Soon we will be faced with the task of reconstituting our government. Drugonov may have burned our Constitution, but he did not destroy it. I suggest to you that this time we truly pay attention to what it says, and especially to what its authors intended it to mean. Over the years, the majority of our citizenry and their elected representatives have ignored or forgotten those original intentions, so essential to the preservation of freedom. We should call a Constitutional Convention to clarify its true meaning, so that there can never again be any doubt that it is a document of pure individual liberty.

"It should be clear to each of us after the experience of the past three years that the best way to insure individual liberty is through limiting the size and scope of government. I believe that that was the intention of most of the men at the original Constitutional Convention. They created a government with limited, enumerated powers, and then reminded us in the Tenth Amendment that that government should remain limited. But over the years, parts of the Constitution were twisted, distorted, so as to make a mockery of the limited government envisaged by the Framers.

"The Interstate Commerce clause was originally written to eliminate tariffs placed by states upon goods being shipped to them from other states. This shortcoming in the old Articles of Confederation served to choke off commerce and manufacturing in the original thirteen states. When the Constitution was written, the power to control interstate commerce was rightly given to Congress. But the Supreme Court interpreted it in such an elastic fashion that the result was to give national government virtually limitless regulatory authority. This was not the intention of the Framers. It should be corrected in convention.

"The Necessary and Proper Clause should once again be restricted to apply only to the seventeen powers enumerated in Article One, Section Eight. It should not be interpreted in such a way as to give any group of politicians who happen to be in power the ability to do whatever they consider necessary and proper. This, too, was not the intention of the Framers.

"The Second Amendment should be clarified in Convention, so that there will never again be any doubt that it refers to an individual right, and not a so-called collective one, to possess and bear any weapons currently in use by the military. This would include fully-automatic rifles and machine guns. Fortunately for us, our pre-Conquest government had not succeeded in totally disarming the American people. If it had, the victory we enjoy today would not have been possible, and we would have been under the boot of tyranny indefinitely. The right to keep and bear arms is the ultimate safeguard against statism.

"Also critically important, our entire system of federalism should be resurrected. Federalism is the division of governmental authority between a central government and a series of state governments. It was built into the Constitution, through limits on the national government in Article One, Section Eight and in the Tenth Amendment, as a great bulwark against tyranny. The idea was that no one government should be allowed to possess all of the power. But the National Supremacy Clause in Article Six reduced the states to impotent vassals, allowing the central government to accumulate virtually all the power that mattered. Federalism needs to be restored to our system of government. The courts have consistently refused to do this, perhaps because they, too, benefit from omnipotent national government. What increases the power of one branch, increases the power of the other two as well. This is one example of the way in which our system of so-called checks and balances has failed. In Convention it may be decided to do what Jefferson, Madison and Calhoun demanded: give the states a veto over actions of the national government, allow them to nullify within their own borders national laws with which they disagree.

"Certainly such a system would not be perfect. Many of our southern states, I am sure, would have nullified the civil rights legislation of the nineteen-sixties had they been given the opportunity. But such a state of affairs would have been short-lived. Such nullifications would have been overturned, I am sure, as times changed, as our people became more enlightened. I, for one, trust the American people to ultimately do what is right, even if temporarily they follow the wrong path. As painful and as ugly as nullification may at times be, the alternative is vastly worse: a central government with no meaningful checks at all, free to grow indefinitely until we are once again engulfed in tyranny. Nullification would produce some chaos, but such is the price of liberty.

"And as a further, absolutely essential defense against statism, against coercive, paternalistic government, I suggest that we change the franchise. No one should be permitted to vote who receives any benefits from the State. When we do reconstitute our government, and the first popular vote for elected officials takes place, no one should be permitted to vote who received benefits of any kind from government for the twelve months prior to the Conquest. I would exempt from this requirement only disabled veterans. There is no such thing as the right to the product of someone else's labor. No one should have the ability to vote himself access to someone else's pocketbook. This would shut down once and for all our 'Parliament of Whores' in Washington, putting the welfare-pimp politicians out of business.

"These changes will be called by some reactionary, regressive and undemocratic. Those people will be correct. Such changes would be reactionary: they would constitute a reaction to the failed ideas that led to our conquest. They would also be regressive: a regression to an earlier era, when people, children of the Age of Reason, understood the requirements of true individual liberty. And they would be undemocratic, if we define democracy as an electoral quest for the unearned, as we have for so many years.

"But it is my hope that such people will be in a distinct minority. Their time has passed. We have experienced in the last three years the fruits of their philosophy of government. If it is possible for people to learn from their failures, we certainly should have done so. A new America will arise from the ashes, like an iron phoenix, strong and determined that nothing like this will ever again happen to us, to our children, or to their children, for all time to come."

Trace left the studio and walked out onto the sidewalk surrounded by militiamen. Almost immediately a truck pulled to the curb. Four soldiers jumped from its bed, dragging with them a man whose wrists were bound. It was Judas Benedict.

"We found him in his hotel suite, locked in the bathroom," one of the captors said.

Benedict was sweating profusely, and trembling as if in the grip of some great fever. Trace approached him, though the idea of being in the proximity of this piece of human refuse was revolting.

"General Forester," Benedict began. "I can explain everything! I had no choice! Drugonov had placed nuclear devices in every city in the country! What else could I do but surrender? Just think of the position I was in! I did it for the American people! What would you have done in my place?"

"First of all, Drugonov did not place nuclear weapons in all of our cities. And you knew it. Yes, the truth came out long ago. You could have prevented the destruction of Los Angeles, but you chose not to do so for your own warped, monstrous reasons. The blood of the people of that city, as well as of Boston and New Orleans is on your hands.

"What would I have done in your place? I would have stood up on my hind legs like a man. I would have resisted with every means at my disposal. I would not have ordered the unilateral surrender of our entire armed forces. If Americans had to die in the process, I would have considered that the cost of freedom. I would have personally killed Drugonov on our first meeting. And I most certainly would not have accepted a leadership position in Drugonov's occupation government.

"How many times have you appeared on television, telling your people to accept their fate as slaves of the Russian Empire? How many times have you encouraged them not to resist, not to defend their liberties, to inform on anyone who had the courage to fight? And all the while, you were living in the lap of luxury, your wife murdered at your orders, debauching yourself with an endless train of young boys and girls. You are scum, Benedict. I should shoot you right here and now. But I will let the American people decide your fate. You will have a trial, of sorts, the only kind that we can arrange under the circumstances. And justice will be swift. That I can assure you."

"Wait, General! I have valuable information that I can give you! I can put Drugonov in your grasp! Surely that's worth my life!"

"Where is Drugonov?" Trace asked, acid in his voice.

"Will you let me go if I tell you? Just pretend you never found me! I'll disappear forever! No one will ever know!"

Trace drew his pistol, and raised it to Benedict's forehead.

"I will not let you go, but if you tell me where Drugonov is, I promise that I will not shoot you right here and now."

Benedict's knees buckled beneath him, and it was only because of the two soldiers holding him by the arms that he did not fall to the pavement.

"All right. Don't shoot. Drugonov has constructed a bunker in the vault of the Federal Reserve Bank. Supposedly it's impregnable. He's been working on it for months. That's where you'll find him."

Like Hitler, Drugonov had chosen to go down with his regime. Even if he had tried to flee, it would have been impossible. All of the airports in the New York area were occupied by American forces, and no departures were being permitted.

Trace re-holstered his weapon. Turning to the soldiers, he said, "Put him back in the truck. We're going to Times Square."

Times Square was still packed with celebrants, reveling in their newfound liberty. Cases of 'Duty' brand beer and 'Glory of Sacrifice' vodka had appeared on the street, and the people were imbibing even this swill freely. There was an occasional bottle of genuine pre-Conquest whiskey, worth its weight in silver. These coveted liquors too were being shared by their owners on this jubilant occasion. The two and a half ton truck in which Trace, the soldiers, and Benedict were riding drove slowly into the center of the Square. Trace stood at the back of its bed and raised his arms for silence. This was no mean feat, since there were probably twenty thousand revelers present. But most recognized Trace, and after a few moments, the din died down. Trace raised a bullhorn to his lips.

"I have come here for a serious purpose! I have with me your former president, Judas Benedict."

Two soldiers grasped Benedict by his manacled arms and brought him to the back of the truck, next to Trace, where the crowd could see him. At first there was a shocked silence, as the people of New York looked upon this hated quisling. Then, as if on cue, their anger welled up within them. They began to shout and to shake their fists. It was impossible to discern what they were saying, though the word 'hang' stood out. Trace raised his left arm into the air, calling for silence.

"You will determine the fate of this man, right here and right now. You will be his jury. You will decide guilt or innocence. I will be the prosecution. From his own lips will come his defense. The charge is treason. I say to you that no man in the history of this country has committed such heinous acts of cowardice and treason as has the man you see before you. He willingly participated in a series of acts that had the effect of turning his own people into sacrificial animals. Millions of us have died because of what he has done. Those who did not die were relegated to the status of slave under the whip of foreign masters. These are the charges."

Trace handed the bullhorn to Benedict who, though handcuffed, was able to manipulate the device. Slowly, hesitantly, the former president raised it to his lips. For a moment it seemed that the master of the glib and evasive response, the man who had risen to the top of the political heap through the use of a silver tongue, had nothing to say. Sweat poured down his face, and he trembled visibly. At last, the slightest hint of resolve crossed his face. A shred of the old Benedict, the master deceiver, seemed to rise to the surface. The crowd was dead silent, aware of the gravity of this event, and, much to their credit, willing to give this man a chance to defend himself.

"My friends, my fellow Americans, please listen to me," he began. "I understand that you see me as a traitor and as a coward. I can't say that I blame you. But everything I have done, I assure you, I did for the benefit of humanity. That includes you. I am, if nothing else, a humanitarian. You have made many sacrifices over the past three years. But if you examine your souls, truly look within yourselves, can you not see that those sacrifices were justified? People in other parts of the world were in great need. We had the means to satisfy that need, through our resources, our labor. We were too selfish, too self-centered. All those years we grew rich while others were destitute.

"As to my personal participation, I can assure you it was minimal. I had no relations with that man, that Drugonov. I was as much a victim of his madness as you were! If I had known what kind of man he was, I can assure you he never would have set foot on our soil! I would have defended this country like a junkyard dog! But I believed that we did owe a debt to Russia, and to all of the underprivileged countries of the world. We, who had won life's lottery, could not in good conscience stand by and watch others starve! Give me another chance, give me a chance to redeem myself in your eyes! I can once again lead this country into the future!"

The crowd erupted in outrage, almost obliterating Benedict's final words. Fists shook in the air. Mouths were open wide, spewing venom at this man. Benedict lowered the bullhorn. A look of confusion was on his face. Something was very wrong. The old formula had not worked. These people were not responding to his rationale of self-immolation. They seemed to hate him all the more because of it, as if he had said something offensive, something insulting. But it must work, he thought. It had always worked. An appeal for altruism had always been his ace-in-the-hole. He had always been able to make people feel guilty, greedy, self-indulgent. Certainly these people had suffered, many had died, but was that enough to change their whole world-view? For a century the virtues of altruism had been hammered into their heads. Thousands of politicians had built careers upon it. These people had been thoroughly indoctrinated for three generations. How could any experience undo such powerful conditioning?

Trace took back the bullhorn.

"Listen to me! All of you!"

The crowd quieted.

"You have heard the prosecution, and you have heard the defense! All of you who believe this man to be innocent, raise your hands!"

Moments passed, the crowd subdued. Trace looked for one hand, one vote for acquittal. But it was in vain. Of the twenty thousand present, not one raised hand was to be seen.

"Now, all of you who believe this man to be guilty, raise your hands!"

Instantly a solid mass of hands shot skyward. One voice, well back in the crowd, began to chant, "Death! Death! Death!"

The chant spread, picked up by the multitude in the square. Within seconds, the vote had apparently become unanimous. Twenty thousand of his countrymen and women passed judgment on their former president. Benedict's face showed the horror within him. He looked at Trace, pleading in his eyes. Benedict saw in return only a steely resolve.

The two militiamen lowered the condemned man to the pavement. He was immediately swept away by the incensed New Yorkers. As he passed through the crowd, he was beaten with fists and empty liquor bottles. Someone had a rope, and it was thrown over the projecting arm of a street lamp. Benedict, bloody and terrified, was dragged kicking and screaming in its direction. The hastily-tied noose was placed over his head and around his neck. Irate men began to pull on the other end of the line, and it became taut. Trace could see Benedict's bloody mouth forming sounds, screams of anguish, of terror. But he could hear nothing except the howls of the crowd.

This would be no quick death, as a proper hanging usually is. Benedict would not be dropped through a trap door, to have his neck quickly and mercifully broken. He was hauled up slowly, ever so slowly. When he was six feet off the pavement, Trace could see his legs flailing, could see his face turning purple. His body twitched and convulsed. It reminded Trace of a fish on the end of a line. The rope was tied off to the lamp post. A silence came over the crowd. Every eye was on Benedict the Traitor, Benedict the Liar, Benedict the Murderer.

The former president's tongue protruded from his mouth, impossibly large. An eyeball popped from its socket, and then the other. They hung by their optic nerves onto his cheekbones. Far from shying away from such a gruesome sight, the people seemed to drink it in as if it were a fine wine, to be savored, enjoyed to its fullest. Seconds turned to minutes, and still Benedict was not dead. Nine minutes passed before the convulsions ceased. It was over. Quietly, solemnly, the people began to disperse. They had exorcized a demon this day, and now it was time to go home.

Drugonov strode into the enormous vault of the Federal Reserve Bank. He ordered a lieutenant to close and lock the gigantic door as soon as Marshal Sokolnikov arrived. The Marshal was outside the bank, on Nassau Street attempting to oversee the surrender of his troops in this section of Manhattan.

Drugonov had had installed in the vault a very sophisticated communications system. With it, he could contact all Russian forces throughout his colony. He sat down in front of this apparatus and put on the headpiece that placed a rice-grain microphone before his lips. The frequencies of the headquarters of all of his commanders had been programmed into the device, and he had only to push buttons to switch from one to another. He pushed the first button on the left, for his divisions in New England. They were headquartered just east of Springfield, Massachusetts.

"Komorov!" he growled, referring to General Vladimir Komorov, commander of the Third Corps. No response. "Komorov, you son of a bitch! Answer!"

He received nothing but the low hum of static. He could not have known that just three hours earlier Vladimir Komorov had been killed in action along with twenty-six thousand of his men. The Massachusetts, Connecticut, Rhode Island, New Hampshire, Vermont and Maine Militias had coordinated their efforts in a brilliant assault, virtually obliterating Komorov's Third Corps. They themselves had sustained twenty-two thousand casualties, but they had been victorious. From this day forward, tales would be told from father to son of militiamen charging Russian machine-gun nests armed only with single-shot shotguns.

"Bah!" Drugonov shouted, as he pushed the next button. This call went out to the Eighth Corps, in Montgomery, Alabama. Its mission had been to pacify Georgia, Alabama and Mississippi. But the gentlemen of those states had done a little pacifying of their own, and the Russian commander, Alexander Bakunin, was rapidly assuming room temperature along with almost twenty thousand of his men. Those who survived would come to wish they had not. The Militias of the deep South had no acquaintance with the Geneva Conventions.

Drugonov pushed button after button, spitting out names and curses. He received no response at all. It was over. Even Sergei Drugonov should have understood that. But in his twisted mind there was one last alternative.

"Cowards! Traitors! I am surrounded by them! Very well, then. Let them, let everyone, experience my wrath! I will bring down upon this land Armageddon itself!"

He moved to a second control panel. On it were fifty toggle switches, each of which would set off a ten-megaton detonation in one of the fifty largest population centers remaining in the United States. Above those was a large red button. This would set off all fifty explosions simultaneously. Should it be pushed, one hundred forty-million people would die. The country would cease to exist as a viable political-economic entity.

New York would be vaporized, and Drugonov along with it. But the mad look in his eyes told everyone in the room that he was beyond caring about his own life. He wanted death: death for himself and for every living thing within his reach. If he could not achieve his goal of mastery over a global empire, he did not care to survive, and he would kill every man, woman and child in the world if it were within his power to do so.

He stood quietly before the console. Then his hand began to move forward, toward the red button. Every man in the room was holding his breath. Then he hesitated. Perhaps there was some shred of humanity left within this beast; perhaps deep down the simple Russian peasant feared the fires of an eternal hell, as if he had not already earned them. He took several steps back, and looked around the room.

"Colonel! I command you! Push the button!"

The Colonel stood at attention.

"Maximum Leader! I have followed you with the utmost loyalty these three years. But this I cannot do. It is not war. It is murder: murder on a horrific scale."

"You refuse my direct command?"

"Yes, Maximum Leader."

Drugonov withdrew a Makarov pistol from its holster, leveled it at the Colonel, and pulled the trigger. The man fell to the floor in a heap.

"You! Captain! Come here and push this button! That is a direct order!"

A much younger man stepped forward and snapped to attention.

"Maximum Leader, I too must refuse that order. Such destruction of human life would serve no purpose. Our war is over. It is time to go home, if that is still possible."

Drugonov's eyes narrowed.

"Another traitor!" he spat.

"I am not a traitor, Maximum Leader. I am simply a Russian who is sick of all this..."

The sharp report of the Makarov cut off the captain's response. He fell to the floor next to his colonel. At that instant, Sokolnikov and Forester entered the vault. The Russian lieutenant had not locked the vault door as ordered. He realized that the war was over. He himself did not have the intestinal fortitude to shoot Drugonov, but he hoped that someone else would enter who did. Sokolnikov and Forester had met on the street outside and had made arrangements to discuss an orderly Russian surrender. Sokolnikov had given his service automatic to one of Trace's men, as a sign of surrender and good will. Both men realized that before any formal surrender could be considered, there would be Drugonov to contend with.

Sokolnikov had not considered even Drugonov to be sufficiently mad to push the button, to destroy all of those innocent lives. But when he saw the bodies of his comrades on the floor, he accurately imagined what had happened.

"Forester! We must stop him!" the Marshal shouted.

Drugonov was in the center of the vault, ten feet from the console. Both Trace and Sokolnikov broke into a dead run. Each had thirty feet to cover to reach Drugonov. The Maximum Leader knew that the game would soon be up unless he could neutralize these last two impediments to his plan of destruction. Trace drew his pistol, but before he could fire, Drugonov snapped off a shot from the hip. The bullet hit the left side of Trace's head, and he fell to the floor. Drugonov pointed his weapon at Sokolnikov and pulled the trigger. But, unnoticed by the erstwhile Maximum Leader, the slide had locked back exposing an empty chamber. He was out of ammunition. He made a break for the console.

Sokolnikov was flying now, and he tackled Drugonov six feet from his destination. The two men grappled on the floor of the vault. Slowly, Drugonov dragged Sokolnikov along, pummeling the Marshal with fists and elbows. Sokolnikov released his grip on Drugonov's chest and went for his throat. They were three feet from the console now.

Drugonov gagged as Sokolnikov's powerful fingers dug into his esophagus. Still, with a powerful lunge, Drugonov raised both himself and the Marshal to their feet. Desperately, his right arm lashed out, its fingers seeking the button. He fell short by six inches. He fought with the strength that is sometimes present in the insane. Four inches, then two.

Sokolnikov took a gamble and let go of Drugonov's throat to reposition his hands. One inch. He put one hand behind Drugonov's head and the other beside his chin. Drugonov's finger actually touched the button, but not its top, only its side. One more fraction of an inch. With all the strength he could muster, Sokolnikov pulled to the right with one hand and to the left with the other. Drugonov's quivering finger was poised above the button now. One downward movement and it would be done.

"Crack!"

The sound filled the vault. Drugonov's neck was broken. His hand fell harmlessly off the console. Sokolnikov, exhausted, fell to the floor atop Drugonov's corpse. He was never to be sure how much time passed. But eventually, he felt a hand on his shoulder. He twisted his torso, and looked up. There, standing above him, was Trace Forester, a broad smile across his face. Blood covered the left side of his head and the collar of his uniform, but he appeared to be none the worse for wear. Drugonov's bullet had only grazed him, and the scalp wound looked much worse than it was.

He took Sokolnikov's hand and pulled the Field Marshal to his feet. Then Trace placed both hands on the man's shoulders and said, "I don't know if I mentioned it before, but it is indeed a pleasure to make your acquaintance, Vasili. You're a good man in a pinch. Let's get the hell out of here. I'll buy you a drink."

The End

Printed in the United States
32554LVS00005B/43-102

9 780975 492338